ALL
TRESSED
UP ~ 2

A Sequel

KAREN PRICE © 2017

The dedication:

For Ange, thank you again for all your help, my cougar in arms. It's been great once more

For Keith, my hubby, who puts up with my writing and my obsession with a certain Irish actor and never complains, thank you.

For Millie, the world's biggest Irish Wolfhound, our Princess Diva dog, with the teddy bear face.

And for our new edition Murphy, the Greyhound/Collie cross. Rescue dogs bring such joy.

And in loving memory of Charlie (aka Charlesworth, the best dog ever) in doggy heaven 30.11.17, will never forget my little man. Thank you for the best 8 years ever.

One

'It's orange!' Carling exclaimed, taking a step back from the customer as if she was radioactive.

I glared at her, talk about stating the blooming obvious, I could see that it was orange, in fact the whole of the salon could see it was orange.

She pursed her lips. 'Did you want it that colour?'

'No,' my lady wailed, fresh tears in her eyes. I would kill our junior, I had only just stopped her crying.

'Don't worry, we'll sort something out,' I soothed picking up a handful of her hair, not only was it the colour of a Jaffa but it was also the consistency of shredded wheat.

Bev came to stand by us shaking her head. 'Have you ever thought about having a pixie cut?'

My lady began to sob again, big fat snotty tears. 'Okay,' I declared. 'You two,' I pointed at Bev and Carling. 'Are not being helpful, go away.'

They did, going back to what they should be doing.

'Shay said you'd be able to fix it for me, that you are the best hairdresser he knows, she looked at me in a pleading way.

I smiled tightly, thanks for that Shay. 'Two ticks,' I held my smile disappearing into the back room.

My names Tash, Natasha Turner and I work at *All Tressed Up*, a hairdressing salon in the middle of a large private housing estate owned by friend Beverley Kidman, we've worked together for the last fifteen years.

You may or may not know what had gone on these last few months. I always thought my life was pretty sorted, I was divorced five years ago, Sam my ex, had three affairs. Well he may have had more but three is the number I know about and the only total that he will admit too.

Something good came from my marriage though, two teenagers. Lexi, nineteen, and studying Psychology at Birmingham University, I am so proud of her I could burst. She came out to me as gay about five months ago and is nicely settled in a relationship with Belle, her friend from school and who is also at University.

Jamie, my son is a different matter. He is sixteen and full of hormones and attitude, he lives with his dad which breaks my heart but what can you do?

So, where was I? Oh yeah, anyway five months ago Dale, my brother, who used to be a womanising tosser but now seems to have had personality transplant came into the salon with his new friend Shay. Thirty-two years old, Irish, dark and brooding, absolute clit-throbber. Anyway sensible, boring me embarked on a mad clandestine affair with him. Me! He was ten years younger but the sex was out of this world. I lived in fear of anyone finding out, especially our Dale, who had always been overly possessive of his sister.

It all came to a head when Jamie got arrested for trying to break into cars on Ashmore Park and at the police station I cried and Shay instinctively comforted me and that was when everyone found out about us.

I told Shay to go, choosing my brother over him and then I found out that our Dale had been sleeping with Bev (yes, the salon owner – keep up please) for the last fourteen years and I hated the pair of them.

Luckily Shay stalked me and now we're back together and had the most wonderful Christmas and New Year and to put it simply, we love each other.

I am still a little unsure about the age-gap and he is absolutely gorgeous so I'm a little apprehensive about other women but he is always telling me I shouldn't worry and that he loves me, bless him.

My customer today, Lauren, is a woman that I wonder if Shay has had a dalliance with. I know Dale has, he told me her blow jobs are second to none, she's known as Deep Throat. Shay denies anything but I'm so full of insecurities that I'm not hundred percent sure that she hasn't given him a blow job at the very least.

Anyway, back to business, what the hell was I going to so with Lauren's hair?

'I hope people don't think we did that disaster,' Bev joined me, flicking the kettle on.

'She said her sister did it,' I looked at Bev for inspiration. 'What can I do?'

'She's going to have to go dark, if you put anymore bleach on that it will fall out.' She rinsed out the mugs.

'I could do a dark brown base colour, a few lighter foils and a lot of intensive treatment to try and put some moisture back in her hair,' I brightened a little.

'You have a plan,' she checked her watch. 'It's going to take ages.'

'I'll stay over,' it was well after two o'clock and the salon shut at four.

'Crack on then,' she said cheekily making me a coffee along with her own.

I went back into the salon where Lauren was slumped in my chair sniffing loudly. 'I've got a date tonight, a really hot date,' she squeaked.

'Right,' we had no time to bugger about. 'Do you want to go on your really hot date with orange hair?'

She shook her head mutely.

'The only thing I can do, the only thing,' I repeated. 'Is to cut at least six inches off.'

'No,' she interrupted wailing.

'Listen,' I sounded firm. 'I'll cut it into a chunky longish bob, I'll put a dark brown base colour on with caramel highlights, you will look smoking hot.'

'Smoking hot?' Carling gave me a weird look and I shushed her, it was the first thing that came into my head.

Lauren looked at me doubtfully, stroking her used to be blonde hair that reached down her back.

'It'll look lovely and your fella will love it,' I tried to sell her the idea.

'Really? She asked unsurely.

'Really,' I confirmed.

'Do I have any choice? Can't I just go blonder?' She asked timidly.

'If I try and lighten your hair your fella will think he's dating a skinhead,' I informed her gravely.

She went ashen. 'Fine do what you have to do.'

I nodded. 'Carling get Lauren a cup of something hot,' I instructed, picking up my scissors and cutting six inches straight off the bottom of her hair, Lauren watched me in the mirror trying not to cry.

Carling made her a coffee as I mixed the colours. A deep brown for the base and caramels for the highlights. I slavered on the base colour, popping a plastic bag on her hair and sitting her on the leather settee with a magazine.

'If this looks good when it's done I'll eat my hat,' I whispered to Bev.

'If it looks good I'll give you a bonus,' she mumbled.

'I'll hold you to that,' I grinned. Bev and my brother were still seeing each other and though I was doubtful at first but they seemed to be getting on famously, in fact I think it was her steadying influence that was making him a changed man.

When she and Carling left at four I was waiting to wash the colours from Lauren's hair. I pressed the button bringing the electronic shutters down.

I'm keeping you late, aren't I?' she fretted.

'It's not a problem,' I took her to the basin and sat her down. Shay and I had sex on that chair once, wonderful, satisfying sex and I smiled slightly.

'Shay always says how lovely you are,' she was watching me.

'Does he?' I asked pleased.

'Yes, have you been together long?' If she was surprised at how much older than him I was she didn't let on.

I thought for a moment. 'Five months,' I replied piling on the conditioner.

'He took you to our place at Lytham St Anne's,' she chatted away.

'Yes, it was lovely at Hedgehog Cottage,' I was surprised he had told her, we had gone in November for a couple of days when no one knew about us, well only Lexi and Belle.

'You'll both have to go again,' she offered.

'I'd really like that,' and I would, we'd had a lovely mini-break.

'Get Shay to arrange it,' she smiled.

'I will,' I sat her up, rubbing her hair gently. This was the test, I kept everything crossed.

'It looks so dark,' Lauren had gone pale again.

I didn't answer, picking up my scissors and beginning to cut.

Lauren kept her eyes shut as I worked and I felt for her. If you chose to have long blonde hair why would you want shorter dark hair?

I took my time, cutting into it so the end result was a fantastic textured bob. I wasn't good at everything but I was a damn good hairdresser.

Spraying her hair liberally with heat defence spray I began to blow-dry it hoping that it wouldn't go wrong. It was after five when I finally finished and I had to admit it looked the business.

'You can open your eyes now Lauren,' I told her.

She did slowly, a gasp escaping her lips. 'I look so different.'

'You do,' I agreed. 'I know it's not how you want your hair to look.'

'I love it,' she interrupted me. 'I look sexy and hot.'

I bristled pleased. 'Sure?'

'Yes,' she squealed in delight. 'Shay is right, you are wonderful.' She never even passed out when I told her how much it would be. 'Thank you,' she pressed a ten-pound note in my hand.

'I can't take that, you've spent enough already.' I protested.

'Please take it you saved my life,' she was a little over dramatic.

'Thank you,' I shoved it in my tunic pocket.

Quickly I tidied everything up and then took Lauren out the back way to where our cars were parked, I was ready for home now.

'Thank you again Tash,' she trilled. 'I am going to recommend you to all my friends.'

'Make sure you do,' I smiled climbing in my car and driving the short journey home. Welcoming light spilled from the kitchen window and I paused outside for a moment. The blinds weren't drawn and I could see Shay in the kitchen feeding Millie.

He turned and my breath caught in my throat, he was so beautiful, his lush dark curly hair curtained the back of his neck, dark come to bed eyes and a face that always showed stubble, he was tall, six feet easily and I hoped he would always be mine.

'Hey sweet,' he smiled when I went in the house, his soft Irish accent sublime. 'Have you had a good day?'

'Busy,' I replied taking off my coat and fussing Millie, she came to the salon with me in the week but always stopped at home on a Saturday.

'Did you sort Lauren out?' he passed me a glass of wine.

I took it with a thank you. 'Yes, she was pleased with the end result, tipped me a tenner.

'Excellent,' he checked the pot on the stove.

'Are you cooking?' I asked suspiciously.

'Bev gave me her chilli recipe so I'm giving it a whirl.'

'Can you actually cook?'

He looked a little vague. 'Kind of.'

I doubted it, Moira, his mom, did all the cooking as far as I could tell. 'Scrummy,' I beamed.

'Is that a bit of sarcasm I detect?' he raised an eyebrow.

'No,' I smirked thinking if it was that bad I could always order a take out.

He looked a little hurt as he drank his bottle of lager and I sat at the kitchen table my smile fading a little. 'Why did Lauren phone you about her hair?' It had bothered me.

'What?' he gave the chilli a stir.

'She said that you said I'd be able to put to right, so why did she phone you?' Just what was their relationship?

His face broke into a big grin and he began to laugh loudly. 'Well we were having sex and I said to her did you know your hair is orange and she said never mind that just keep banging away at me.'

'You are so *not* funny,' I scowled.

'But you are dahling,' he put down his lager still smiling. 'She walked past the garage this morning with a hat on and I waved at her and went "Hi Lauren, how ya doing," and she started crying. I was like "hey what's wrong?" and she's like "look at my hair," and she takes her hat off and I'm like "It's orange" and she says "I know," so I say "go and see Tash at All Tressed Up and she'll sort you out," and she's like "thanks Shay, I will".'

I listened to him, trying not to smile, he always ended up making me laugh and ignored my stupid lack of self-confidence.

'I'm going for a shower then, as I've got nothing to worry about,' I left my wine on the table.

'Twenty minutes and everything will be done' he warned.

I nodded scooting upstairs and throwing off my work clothes. Standing under it I let it wash the day off me. I should trust Shay more, he never did anything to give me cause not to, it was just after Sam cheating on me three times that I knew of anyway, I was wary.

By the time I went back into the kitchen, he had dished up the rice, chilli and tear 'n' share bread and had put a couple of lighted candles in the centre of the table. 'Feel better?' he asked.

'Yeah,' I smiled, Shay always took Millie a walk before I got home on a Saturday so I had put my pyjama's on.

We didn't live together but he had his own key so he came and went as he pleased and he spent the majority of the time at mine. Lexi kept on at me to ask him to move in permanently, she was really taken with him but I wanted to give us a little more time, sensible, cautious me. Although it would probably happen of its own accord anyway, some of his clothes were hanging in my wardrobe and his grooming products were in the bathroom.

I watched as he ate his meal, he had told me New Year's Eve that he had fallen in love with me the first time he had seen me which was lovely but today I realised something, I knew very little about his past. No, that's not strictly true, I knew very little about his past relationships would be more accurate.

'You're watching me Natasha,' he cast a glance at me.

'Sorry,' I laughed softly.

He kept his eyes on me, the stare intense. Shay had a way of looking serious even when he wasn't but when he smiled, oh it lit up his whole face. We held each other's gaze and I felt a flutter in my stomach, I only have to look at him to want him.

'How's the chilli?' he asked.

'Good,' I nodded. Good wasn't really the word I would honestly use to describe it but he had gone to so much effort, I would have to try and eat most of it.

'You're lying,' he still held my gaze.

'I'm not,' I ate another mouthful. 'Mmm yummy.'

He raised an eyebrow. 'Natasha!'

'It's edible,' I swallowed quickly. His face fell a little. 'It's your first attempt,' I added quickly. 'It just needs to have a little tweaking.'

'I wanted to cook you something nice,' he felt annoyed with himself.

'It's okay, honestly, I tell you what on a Saturday we'll cook together and I'll teach you.'

'You're so good at cooking though,' Shay had a competitive streak, which was just starting to emerge.

'I've had to do it for years, since I was ten in fact, so I should be. Go on, it will be fun.

'Okay,' he shrugged. 'We'll do recipes on a Saturday.

'Excellent,' I carried on eating, hoping it didn't give me indigestion.

'Fancy a film tonight?' he tore a chink of tear 'n' share.

'Yes, I fancy a good horror.' You couldn't beat a good scare.

'Okay, we'll sort all this out and then settle down,' he put down his fork.

Sounds good,' I followed suit, we had crisps and nibbles in the cupboard if we got hungry later.

Two

'Your tits look bigger.'

I stopped what I was doing, a coat hanger in each hand. 'What?' I looked at Shay, who was lying in bed, a blush creeping up my cheeks.

'I said your tits look bigger,' he repeated slowly.

'I don't know what you mean,' I looked down, I was standing in just my bra and pants trying to decide which top to wear.

'They look larger,' he declared smirking. 'It must be all that hand rearing I'm doing.'

I shook my head smiling. 'I think I've put a bit of weight on,' I admitted.

'Its contentment,' he yawned finishing his coffee.

'Are you getting up?' I fussed. 'We're due at the pub at one.'

He looked at the clock. 'It's only early.'

'But I've got to walk Millie, I've got to feed Millie, have a shower, and wash my hair.' I ticked off my list.

'I'll walk Millie when I get up,' he yawned again. 'You can do your hair.'

'Thank you,' I held the two tops aloft. 'Which one?'

He thought for a moment. 'The tunic with your skinny jeans.'

'Do you think?' I pulled a face. We were all going out for Sunday lunch with Shay's mom, Moira, and her fella Alan plus the whole of his family. He had five daughters so it was going to be quite full on.

'It's just Sunday lunch,' he rubbed his head.

'It's important to Moira,' I reminded him. 'I want to look nice.'

'You always look beautiful,' he assured me. 'Anyway it's casual, just a getting to know each other kind of thing.'

'I'm nervous,' I admitted.

'You haven't got to be nervous' he threw back the covers. 'They will all love you.'

Or they'll think I'm your aunty, I thought. Don't get me wrong my confidence was so much better since Shay and I had got together but part of me would always be self-doubting.

'I hope so,' I took his advice and put the other top back in my wardrobe. I desperately needed some new clothes now I was socialising more.

'I'll take Millie for her walk,' he pulled on a pair of jeans and a jumper.

'Thanks hun,' I was a little distracted, trying to decide what boots to wear.

He watched me for a moment before heading downstairs, a couple of minutes later I heard the front door shut and I looked out of the window watching as he walked down the road with the World's Largest (or so she seemed) Irish Wolfhound, who Dale had asked me to look after for a couple of days last October and who I had gotten lumbered with ever since. He had her from a bloke in the pub, don't ask.

Humming softly I got in the shower and washed my dark blonde hair (out of a bottle) that fell just past my shoulders, before putting it in large rollers. I looked divine, not. My mobile ringing had me diving for it on the bedside table. Sam, my ex, what did he want? 'Hello,' I said a little breathlessly.

'Hi Tash, it's Sam, alright?' his tone was bright.

I wanted to say I know it's you, you prat but instead I said. 'Yes thanks, are you?' I stood in front of the mirror in bra and knickers, I did look like I had put a little weight on, too much good food and booze.

'I'm thinking of taking Jamie away with us on holiday, what do you think about that?'

'You never usually ask me,' I frowned. 'You just tell me. Are you going somewhere nice?'

'Thailand,' he replied and I stopped preening in the mirror.

'How long for?' Why did Sam always have exotic holidays when I struggled to make ends meet? To be fair though he only could do what he did now because he worked with Meera's family in their software business, that's how he had met her, and after their wedding he had gotten promoted to Head of Commonwealth or some shit like that. Talk about it being handed on a silver platter.

'Two weeks.'

'When?' I tried to quell the feelings of jealously. I was happy with my lot, more than happy but still, two weeks in Thailand.

'August, after his exams,' he cut in quickly.

'How much will it cost me?' If it was too much than I would have to say no and Jamie would hate me even more.

'It won't cost you anything,' his voice was jovial. 'I can pay for our son's holiday.'

Oh, okay,' I floundered a little. 'It's fine by me.' Sam was so crafty, he knew Jamie was giving me grief at the moment, so he was spoiling him and rewarding his bad behaviour.

'Great, so what are you up to today?'

I frowned, why was he being all chatty? 'I'm off out for lunch.'

'You not cook on a Sunday, bloody hell Tash are you feeling okay?'

'We've been invited out,' I informed him shortly.

'We?' he drew out the word. 'Still with Paddy then?'

'Still with Shay,' I confirmed. 'And don't call him Paddy. Listen Sam will you have a word with Jamie for me please? He won't come if Shay's here and I don't know why, I just want them to get on.'

'You can't make them get on,' he replied his tone still bright. 'Anyway *Shay* isn't there that often is he?'

I knew he was fishing. 'He is actually,' I blushed but I didn't know why.

'I thought that would be fizzling out by now,' he sounded disappointed.

'Why would it be?' I asked sharply.

'No reason,' his answer was hasty.

I bristled a little. 'If that's everything then I have to go. Shay and I were just about to make wild, abandoned sex when you called and I've left him tied up naked on the bed.'

'Tash,' he tutted annoyed.

'Send me the details of Thailand so I can have a look,' I ended the call.

I was convinced that Sam was behind Jamie making things awkward, some of the things he said were straight out of his dad's mouth but I couldn't prove it. Jamie had liked Shay initially, thought he was cool, so someone had poisoned his mind.

I threw on my dressing gown, going into the kitchen and putting the kettle on. Shay arrived back with Millie and I could see him hold his hand up to Joe next door. I got fresh water for the dog and made us both coffee. Millie took a big drink before flopping down onto the tiled floor.

Shay and I sat at the kitchen table next to each other, coffee mugs on coasters. 'Thanks for taking Millie.'

'Not a problem,' his eyes kept going back to my hair.

'What?' I smiled.

'You have rollers in,' he stared at them.

'Sexy aren't they?' I chuckled.

'Beyond words,' he agreed.

'Sam called while you were out.'

'Did he?' Shay was convinced that my ex-husband was up to no good where I was concerned and I was glad I wasn't the only one who got jealous.

'They want to take Jamie to Thailand in August for two weeks.'

'Thailand?' his voice rose a little. 'Do you think he'll adopt me?'

'He certainly thinks you're young enough,' I tried to keep the resentment out of my voice. It annoyed me though how Sam was always making cracks about Shay's age when his own wife was twelve years younger than him.

Shay ignored it. 'Did you say he could go?'

I shrugged. 'What else can I do? He hates me enough as it is at the moment.'

'Because of me,' he stated flatly. It was the only blotch on the horizon, how my son was being.

'Jamie's just being a shit like he was before I met you,' I replied. 'It's any excuse with him. I wish he was here though, I don't like him living with Sam and having everything he wants.'

'He would be here if I wasn't,' Shay's voice was low. He had tried so hard to build some sort of relationship with Jamie only to have it thrown back in his face.

'You are not going anywhere,' I said forcibly. 'I spent years caving in with Dale, I'm not about to do it with Jamie.'

He smiled softly pulling me from my seat so I was sitting on his lap. Reaching, he kissed me gently, hand sneaking inside my dressing gown. 'You are definitely getting bigger,' he looked at me, one hand clasped on my boob.

'It's all the attention they are getting now,' I grinned. 'I might ask Bev if she wants to go to Zumba.'

'Zumba? Why not come to the gym with me if you want to exercise? Not that you need too,' he added quickly.

'I can think of nothing worse than going to the gym and having to exercise next to all those Lycra clad gym bunnies.' I shuddered.

'You've said that to me before,' he smiled. 'Do you remember, you said when I got engaged to my Lycra clad gym bunny you wouldn't do my buffet?'

I blushed, that was the time Dale got engaged to the bitch from hell Fallon, who had tricked him into believing the baby she was carrying was his, we soon sorted her out though.

It was when I thought Shay and I had no future and I was worried about falling in love with him and stressing about my brother. I had seen them on Bentley Bridge coming out of the gym and talking to two young bints and got all jealous. When he had come round to see if I wanted any help doing the buffet for the party I had said it to him then.

'I'm still not doing it,' I said slyly.

He held me tighter. 'I'll have to get the caterers in then,' he teased.

I chose to ignore him. 'As I was saying I think I'll ask Bev to go to Zumba. We went last year and it's much more fun than the gym.'

'Why did you stop going?' he ran his hand along my leg.

'Bev kept letting me down, looking back she was probably meeting our Dale, and then the winter came and we just couldn't be arsed,' I admitted.

'It'd be good if we got fit together.'

'Horizontal jogging?' I kissed him.

'Yeah,' his hand went higher and he moved his mouth to nibble my ear, succeeding in poking himself in the eye with one of my rollers. 'Shit!' He cursed spilling me off his lap.

'Are you okay?' I tried to look at his eye but he had his hand over it.

'They are fecking dangerous!' he cussed.

'Let me see,' I pulled his hand away. 'It looks fine, just a little teary.'

'It hurts,' he covered it with his hand again.

'You're a bigger baby than the kids,' I scolded, sitting back down to finish my coffee.

'I'm not,' he sulked and I smiled.

'Come on stud, drink your coffee and we'll get ready.'

He nodded reluctantly still playing with his eye, the big girl's blouse.

Three

We arrived at the Spread Eagle about twelve-forty-five, I'd offered to drive, I was worried if I had too much to drink I would make a fool of myself.

A large group was already by the bar and my stomach lurched, I hoped they'd like me. Shay, as if sensing my unease, took my hand. His eye was fine now and my hair had gone perfect, I did feel nice. Mom and dad, had not given me anything in my life except good genes, Dale was the same. The Wilkins were a very good-looking family, it was just a shame that some of the members that were a bit iffy.

'Here they are,' Alan declared on seeing us. He was lovely, Moira's partner, a distinguished looking man, he had a kindness about him.

'Hi,' I trilled, my nerves increasing as everyone looked at us.

He hugged me tightly, shaking Shay's hand as an assortment of adults and children milled around us, there must have been about sixteen of us in total.

'Tash.' Moira welcomed giving me a cuddle. 'You look gorgeous.'

'Thank you,' I took a step back. 'You look lovely too.'

She patted her hair with a grin, giving her son a big hug.

'Now I know you won't remember all of the names but here goes,' Alan took a deep breath. 'Emma my oldest married to Troy and their kids Noah and Mya.'

'Hi,' I held up my hand, they were the most beautiful half caste children I had ever seen.

'Next Sara and her kiddies Lyla and Elise. Jenny and husband Aidan and their lad Jakob, Jemma hasn't turned up yet and there's Lisa married to Nev, no kids yet,' he let out his breath.

Blimey I thought he's right, I'd never remember all of them. He smiled at me. 'And this is Tash, Shay's girlfriend.' I could feel my cheeks redden a little as they all smiled at me, it was alright for Shay he had already met them.

'Tash what are you drinking?' Troy asked.

'Um, cola please, I'm driving,' I itched to touch his skin, it looked like brown silk, I bet he moisturised a lot, especially his bald head.

'Lager Shay?' he flashed beautiful white teeth.

'Cheers,' Shay replied, not looking at all intimidated by such a big family.

It was times like this when I thought people stared at us because of the age-gap but no one seemed to be, maybe I was being a little paranoid.

'Oh my God!' a voice said behind me and although it was thirteen years since I had last heard it, it was one I would never forget. 'Natasha Turner, I don't believe it. What are you doing here?'

I turned slowly, feeling surreal, please don't let it be what I thought it was going to be. 'Oh my God!' she squealed again, flapping her hands, like we were long lost friends.

'How do you know Tash, Jem?' her dad asked possibly thinking I did her hair for her.

She beamed at him. 'I slept with her husband.'

The whole group fell silent and I wanted the floor to open up and swallow me as Shay looked at me in alarm.

'And then, we all ended up at the same party and I realised I'd slept with her brother as well,' she laughed loudly.

'Jemma, Tash is Shay's girlfriend,' her dad informed her quietly.

She laughed again. 'Come on Shay, I'll sleep with you and make it a hat trick.'

I felt myself pale that was just not funny. 'Excuse me I just need the ladies,' I hurried to the loo feeling a little nauseous. Why could I never get away from Sam or Dale's indiscretions, why was I always made to look an idiot? I couldn't go and eat with them now, it was too embarrassing.

'Tash, Tash,' Moira came into the ladies. 'Are you okay? Shay was concerned and asked me to make sure you were alright.'

I forced a smile on my face. 'Yeah fine,' I replied washing my hands for something to do.

She leant up the vanity until looking at me. 'Small world hey?'

'Small world indeed,' I confirmed, I could see her looking at me so I helped her out. 'Affair number two.'

'Oh,' she touched my arm. 'Don't let it spoil your day, it's in the past, it's the future that's important.'

I thought for a moment, she was right, why should I be ashamed? Sam had cheated, I hadn't and it was a long time ago.

'Come on, they'll be waiting for us,' she gave my arm an encouraging squeeze.

I did as she said, thrusting back my shoulders and holding my head high. They were still at the bar, Jemma conspicuous by her absence. 'Hey sweet,' Shay was looking at me troubled.

'I'm good,' I held his hand needing the comfort.

'Tash, I am so sorry,' Alan passed my drink to me. 'I had no idea.'

'It's no big deal,' my smile grew. 'To be fair to Jemma she didn't know Sam was married, he told her he lived with his sister.

The crowd went '*Oh*'.

'She came to the house and thought I was his sister, she couldn't apologise enough when she found out I was his wife and we had two kiddies,' I felt the need to explain. 'It wasn't her fault.'

'But your brother?' Alan still looked embarrassed.

I held up my hand. 'Our Dale used to be a player. It would be more difficult to find a women Dale hasn't slept with than has.'

Again the '*Oh*'

'Still she could have been more tactful,' Emma said. 'In front of the kids as well.'

'Where is she?' I hoped she hadn't felt the need to leave because of me.

'Outside having a ciggie,' Jenny tutted. 'Come on let's go to the table, they are waiting for us to be seated.'

We trooped after her, Shay and I bringing up the rear. 'If Jemma tries anything on with you, I will drop kick her into next week,' I told him quietly.

'Behave Tash,' he shook his head. 'I've more taste than that, I've got the woman I want.'

I smiled as we sat at the end of the table facing each other, Troy next to me. 'We're putting Jemma the other end, just in case,' he told me beaming.

'I'm so over it,' I shrugged and I was, it was Sam's weakness not mine.

'Glad to hear it,' he looked up as Jemma came back and sat sheepishly at the other end of the table.

I gave Shay as soft smile as I picked up the menu, he reached across to take my hand as we looked at the food on offer. I caught Moira eyeing us proudly, it made her day when Shay and I made a go of it which was really nice because I'm not sure I would want Jamie to have an older girlfriend, although if it kept him out of trouble I could be persuaded.

The meal went without a hitch, Troy keeping me and Shay highly entertained. When it was over we sat at the table relaxing. 'Do you want a drink beautiful?' Shay pulled his chair round so he was sitting next to me.

'Can I have a latte please?'

He nodded going to the bar as Jemma sidled over to me. 'Sorry about earlier,' she put one hand on the back of my chair.

'Don't worry about it, it was ages ago,' I said charitably.

'I was just shocked to see you standing there with Shay, so you and Sam finally split up then?'

'Five years ago, he had another affair,' I replied. 'He married her, they've got a five year old daughter now.'

'Oh,' her face fell a little, maybe she had really liked Sam, thought he was something special. 'And Dale?'

'Finally settled down.'

'He was such a laugh,' she remembered.

'He still is,' I smiled as Shay brought my coffee.

'Listen up everybody,' Alan stood tapping a spoon against the side of his glass. We did, all looking at him expectantly. He cleared his throat nervously. 'As you know Moira and I have stepped out now for a year.

I smiled, what a lovely old-fashioned term, stepping out.

'And this morning I asked if she would do me the honour of being my wife and she said yes,' he beamed.

I gasped delighted, one hand flying to my mouth, what wonderful news. Shay had frozen next to me, that unreadable expression on his face, then he was on his feet going to his mom and hugging her.

'You don't mind son?' I heard her say.

'No,' he kissed her cheek. 'It's just grand.'

I joined them hugging Alan. 'Congratulations,' I trilled and then I turned to Moira and she kind of fell into my arms.

'You'll help me plan it all?' She whispered.

'Of course,' I was good at organising things.

'Thank you,' she touched my cheek and then we were swamped by Alan's family so Shay and I went to the bar for some bottles of Prosecco so we could do propose a toast.

'Are you happy they are getting married?' I wanted to make sure he was fine with it.

He turned to me beaming. 'Yes, she deserves this, she deserved it years ago.'

'Good,' we picked up the bottles and carried them back to the table, I even had a small glass.

Shay cleared his throat and took a deep breath, 'To mam and Alan, I'm so happy for you both. It's fantastic news.'

'To Moira and Alan,' we echoed, raising our glasses.

'Have you set a date?' Sara asked.

'The beginning of September,' her dad replied. 'At our age we can't afford to wait.'

That gave us roughly six months to organise it, not a problem.

'Where?' Lisa drained her glass.

'Not sure yet, we haven't discussed it yet.' Moira looked so nervous.

'Can I be bridesmaid?' Mya asked.

'Of course, sweetheart,' Moira gave her a cuddle. 'And Shay, you'll give me away?'

'Honoured to,' he smiled.

'Let's have another drink,' Alan looked the happiest man in the world.

We stayed another hour before we left before promising Moira I would go and see her the next day (the salon was closed on a Monday) and we could start the ball rolling.

Millie raced around us and we hurried up the stairs so we could change into our scruffs to take her a walk. As we did I thought how happy Moira and Alan looked, weddings could be lovely.

Mine and Sam's was a sombre affair, the local registry office followed by a meal in the pub, we couldn't afford anything else. My parents wouldn't contribute and Sam's mom disapproved of me so she wouldn't either, I didn't even have a wedding dress.

'Penny for them?' Shay asked as Millie stopped for a wee.

'Just thinking about Moira and Alan,' I replied.

'You're going to be in your element organising it, aren't you, you control freak,' he teased.

'Why am I a control freak?' I nudged him.

'Cos, you are, you like organising everyone, you're a natural mammy.'

'Is that a bad thing?' I frowned. Millie was still looking at what she had just done thinking where did all that come from? (FYI – big dogs do big wees).

'What? No, it's a wonderful thing,' he kissed my nose.

I frowned slightly.

'Put your face straight,' he said as we started walking again. 'It wasn't a criticism, nothing wrong with how you are, you're a natural nurturer Tash and I love you for it.'

'Thank you, I think,' I hooked my arm in his as we walked along the bank.

'So, Sam actually told Jemma that he lived with his sister?' He still couldn't quite believe it.

'Yep. It was nearly teatime and I was just sorting out Jamie and Lexi, Lexi had just finished school and the doorbell went and Jemma was standing there all fresh faced and innocent.'

'Had Sam told her where he lived?'

I shook my head. 'She had found out from one of his friends.' We stopped again for Millie. 'Anyway, she said "Is Sam in?" and I'm like "Who are you?" she looks me up and down and said "You must be his sister."'

Beside me Shay took a sharp intake of breath.

'I knew straight away then, Lexi and Jamie came toddling into the hall at that moment so I couldn't shout and I couldn't slap her. As calmly as I could I said, no actually, I'm his wife and these are his two children.'

'Shit,' he drew out the word.

'I've never seen anyone go so pale, she started apologising, saying she had no idea and I believed her, so I invited her in for a coffee.'

'You did what?'

'Sam was due home from work in the next ten minutes and I wanted to see the look on his face when he saw her sitting at the kitchen table.'

'Smart,' he sounded impressed.

'We were having a lovely chat when he walked in, I'd sent the kids in the living room to watch cartoons.'

'What did he say?' Shay hated how Sam had treated me.

'What could he say?' I asked as Millie stopped for another wee. 'Jemma called him a few choice names, slapped his face and left.'

'What did you do?'

'I threw him out.' It still hurt a little what Sam had done, not because I still loved him but the callous way he had treated the kids, he had hurt them as much as me with his affairs.

'But you had him back?' he tried to keep the disapproval out of his voice.

I nodded. 'He would come around to see Lexi and Jamie and I didn't want them getting upset every time he went back to his mom's where he was stopping. He swore he wouldn't do it again, swore it was me he loved.'

'And you believed him?' His voice was quiet.

'Not really, deep down,' I admitted. 'But I didn't want my children coming from a broken home.'

'So, you gave him another chance?'

'Everything was lovely at first, he really tried but it didn't take long for the rot to set in.'

'He was playing around?'

'Nothing I could prove,' I shrugged. 'Just gut feelings. He'd be late home from work, distracted.'

'Why would he want anyone else when he had you and two beautiful children?' Shay knew he would never want another woman.

'Sam covets what he can't have,' I explained. 'The fun for him is having to obtain it. Once he has it, he loses interest.'

'He is a bit of a bastard,' he frowned.

'He's a lot of a bastard,' I corrected him. 'Unfortunately, he is also the father of my children.'

'I know people back in Ireland who would knee-cap him,' he offered.

I laughed softly. 'I bet you do.' I was silent for a moment. 'So, what about you hun?'

'Me?' he asked as we walk steadily along the streets.

'Yes, you. You know all about my past but I know nothing of yours. Any love of your life's stashed away in Ireland?'

'No,' he shook his head.

'You have gone out with other women, haven't you?' I teased.

'Yes,' he laughed. 'Nothing ever serious though, I was saving myself for you.'

'Charmer,' I nudged him. 'Have you had many girlfriends?'

'Are you fishing?' He chortled.

'Yes, you've never told me anything. Including you I have slept with four men my whole life. There, that's my tally, what's yours?'

'Does it matter?'

I made him stop walking. 'I love you, I want to know all about you.' I looked up at him, the street lamps giving us a peculiar hue. 'Don't be secretive, please?'

He touched my chin. 'I'm not being secretive,' he said softly. 'There is truly no one that I have ever felt about the way I feel about you. I was just enjoying myself.'

'So, there's been a few?' My chest felt a little tight.

'There's been a few,' he admitted. 'But none that compares to you. Now matters, not the past, I love you Tash.'

I looked at him for a moment, the man that even my gay daughter calls shaggable Shay and I nodded. 'You're right, it's now that matters.'

'It is,' he confirmed and we carried on walking Millie.

'When I did Lauren's hair she said we ought to go to Hedgehog Cottage again.'

'Would you like that?' he asked.

'I would, it was such a nice couple of days.' All of a sudden, I felt tired and emotional and I didn't know why. It was happening a lot the last few weeks. 'I'd want to go in the summer though.' The only heating in the cottage was a log burner in the living room and two small blow heaters.

'We'll arrange it then,' he was quiet for a moment. 'I did think we could go abroad, have a holiday in the sun.'

'I can't even think about doing anything like that until Lexi has finished university,' I sighed.

He stopped walking. 'I'm not asking you to pay for anything. I'll sort out the holiday, I want to see you in a bikini.'

I looked at him puzzled. 'You see me in less than that all the time.'

He kissed me. 'I want to rub suntan lotion all over you and feel the sun beating down on our naked bodies as we make love on the sand.'

My mouth twitched. 'Can you do that when you are all inclusive?'

'Tash,' he scolded. 'I'm trying to be all sexy here.'

I kissed him again, it growing more intense as Millie pulled impatiently on her lead.

'Evening Tash,' a voice said beside me and I moved away from Shay guiltily.

'Hi Ken, you okay?' I blushed like a teenager getting caught with her boyfriend by her parents. 'How's the wife?'

'Good ta,' he answered jovially carrying on.

Shay laughed. 'Do you know everyone in the world?' Everywhere we went I always bumped into someone I knew.

'They come into the salon,' we began to walk again.

'I'm going to get some brochures tomorrow,' he decided. 'We'll have a look what's on offer.'

'Okay,' a holiday abroad, how nice would it be? The last holiday I had that was out of the country was before I met Sam, we just didn't have the funds when we were married.

'So, you'll come, if I arrange it?' He cast a sideways glance at me.

'Yes, of course.' I was looking forward to it already.

'And you won't try and back out saying you can't leave everyone for two weeks?'

'No, I won't.' I replied, two whole weeks of Shay, sun, sea and sex, how wonderful.

'Dale and Bev can have Millie, they won't mind.' He continued.

No, but she might mind me having two weeks off work I thought but didn't say. 'They won't,' I agreed.

'Excellent,' he looked pleased with himself as we carried on walking Millie. I took his hand, realising how lucky I was. I also knew that I would contribute in some way, I liked to pay my way.

We walked the dog all the way around the perimeter of the park before heading back home. Locking the front door and drawing the curtains against the evening, we lounged in front of the TV and did nothing.

Four

Monday was my day off, the salon didn't open but since Shay had started stopping on a Sunday, I got up Monday mornings to do his breakfast. He kept telling me not to, that I should have a lie in but I enjoyed doing it. Scrambled egg on toast with a side order of bacon for him this morning.

'What have you got there?' He asked, fussing Millie and sitting at the table.

I smiled at him, dressed in his royal blue overalls that I had lovingly washed and ironed, his lush dark curls scrapped back into a top knot and his ever-present stubble on his chin, he was my gorgeous man.

He picked up the brown sauce bottle waiting for me to answer and shook it over his eggs.

'I'm going to Moira's later,' I replied. 'We are doing wedding stuff.'

'I know that beautiful, but why are you taking all the stationary?'

I touched my pile of things one by one. 'A4 pad to do our lists, pens, highlighters, post-it notes,' I took a breath. 'Dividers, so we can find everything easily and a folder to put it all in.'

'You are so loving this,' he laughed.

'Moira is going to have the best wedding ever, I promise you.'

'I have no doubt of that,' he had faith in me. 'My little control freak.'

I gave him a brilliant smile. 'Steak and chips for tea okay?'

'You have to stop feeding me so well,' he chuckled, eating his breakfast.

'I like looking after you,' I drank my tea, I hadn't had breakfast, I didn't feel very hungry. 'Millie, bed!' She had snuck to Shay's elbow, trying to get her nose on the plate.

She sulked off, giving me the evils, she had already eaten breakfast the greedy mare. I sat and watched him as he ate and again thanked my lucky stars for the way everything had turned out.

'What time are you going to my mam's? He asked.

'She said about one. She and Alan are going to look at engagement rings this morning.' I yawned discreetly.

He finished his breakfast, taking his plate to the sink. 'I'll do it,' I took it from him. 'You've got to get to work.'

He smiled putting his arms around me and rewarding me with a deep kiss, his hands going to the cheeks of my bum and cupping them tightly. 'Thanks, dahling,' he whispered.

I smiled back, wishing he didn't have to leave for work straight away. We had a very good sex life, more than good in fact I'm sure that was why I felt tired a lot of the time.

He released his hold on me, getting his wallet and taking out several twenty-pound notes. 'Here,' he thrust them in my hand.

'What's this for?'

'For you,' he knew I would try and get out of taking it.

'Well it can't be for services rendered I didn't shag you last night,' I joked.

He laughed softly. 'Put it to the food, electric, I don't care just take it.'

'You don't have to pay board,' I pushed it back to him.

'Take it beautiful,' his tone was more forceful. 'Please. I'm here nearly all the time.'

I did so reluctantly, he wasn't wrong. The only night's I didn't see him was a Tuesday, when he had a night in with his mom and Friday's when he went for a pint with Dale. 'Thank you.'

He picked up his keys to his truck. 'I'll see you later. Don't forget Dale and I are going to the gym for an hour when we finish work.'

'I won't,' he and Dale enjoyed the gym.

'So, it will be getting on for six-thirty when I get home.'

I loved how he called my house home. 'I'll be here,' I walked with him to the front door, watching as he pulled away from the house. God, I did love him.

An hour later I was ready to take Millie her morning walk and we headed towards the park again, re-treading the path and the three of us had walked the previous night.

She pulled me along as she always did, she was such a big dog. I was trotting along nicely when I heard someone shout. 'Hello darling, fancy a shag!'

I turned indignantly ready to give whoever it was a right mouthful and perhaps I would even set big dog on him. In one of the cul-de-sac's I could see a breakdown truck with a baldly man standing next to it.

'Excuse me?' I was incensed.

'I said do you fancy a shag?' he repeated slowly.

'You cheeky bastard!' I cried, marching towards him with Millie leading the way. He was about to get a piece of my mind.

He started laughing and then Shay appeared from the other side of the truck. 'Your face Tash,' he had tears in his eyes. 'Classic.'

'Very funny,' I muttered blushing.

'Tash, Ray. Ray, Tash,' he introduced me to this boss.

'Hello love, Shay told me to shout it so punch him,' he gave me a huge grin as he patted Millie. 'Beautiful dog.'

'Don't call my Tash a dog,' Shay joked.

Ray shook his head used to his employee. 'How do you put up with him?' He asked me.

'In short bursts,' I replied with a smile. 'What are you doing here?'

'Breakdown,' Ray indicated to the house.

I looked across at the detached house with an irate looking bloke standing outside. 'I'd better let you get on.'

'I was saying to Shay earlier we should all go bowling one of the nights, we haven't had a staff outing for ages.'

'Sounds like fun, count me in.' I smiled. 'Come on big dog, let's leave the workers to it.'

'Nice to meet you Tash at last,' Ray did seem like a nice man.

'You too,' I smiled again.

'See you later beautiful,' Shay pulled himself into the truck.

I waved pulling Millie away and making my way home. I put the first load in the washing machine, mixing my clothes with Shay's, what a lovely metaphor.

Tidying around I hummed softly, happy in my world. When it was time I left for Moira's, my stationary supplies in my Lidl carrier. I was so looking forward to organising everything, Shay was right, I was a control freak.

Moira hustled me inside when I arrived at her house with my bag of stationary, she still looked on cloud nine and I was so happy for her. If anyone deserved to be happy than she did after bringing Shay up alone.

'Oh Tash!' She cried. 'There were so many rings to choose from.'

'Have you decided yet?' I asked with a smile.

'Yes,' she flashed her left hand under my nose.

'Oh Moira, it's so beautiful.' Small diamonds surrounded a larger ruby on a yellow gold band.

'Ruby is my birthstone, July,' she informed me.

'It is so gorgeous,' I held her hand admiring it.

'I can't believe I'm getting married,' she looked so content that my eyes filled with tears. 'What's the matter?' she asked concerned.

'I'm just pleased for you.' I sniffed. 'Ignore me, I seem to be all emotional at the moment, I don't know what's wrong with me.'

'Its being in love that does it,' she teased.

'It must be.' I took off my coat going into her neat kitchen.

'Tea?' She filled the kettle, flicking the switch.

'Please,' I lay my stationary out on the table.

Moira turned, a smile breaking out across her face. 'I knew you'd do it properly.'

'I like organising things,' I blushed a little.

'You know sweetheart, I'm so grateful for you helping.'

I blushed a little more. 'I'm happy to.'

'I class you as my daughter Tash,' she came to stand by me. 'I couldn't ask for anyone better for my son.'

'Thank you,' I gushed, fresh tears in my eyes, even my own mother never classed me as a daughter. 'That is so lovely.'

'Are you sure you're okay?' She looked at me in alarm.

'I just feel very tearful at the moment,' I admitted.

'Are you still worried about Jamie?' I had told her what an absolute shit he was being.

I nodded. 'I just don't know what to do about it. Shay is trying so hard to build a relationship with him and Jamie is being so rude. Lexi gets on well with Shay, it's not a problem at all.'

'The only thing you can do is to be patient,' she told me wisely.

I was quiet for a moment. 'I don't think Sam's helping.

'You're ex-husband?'

'I was suspect he's turning Jamie against me.'

'Why would he do that? He has a wife and wee daughter, what could he possibly gain from it?'

'I think he just likes causing trouble,' my tone was bitter.

'Have you asked him if he is?' She made the tea and brought it to the table.

I shook my head. 'Our Dale has but Sam pretended he didn't know what he was on about.'

'Let them get on with it sweetheart,' she advised. 'They'll need you before you need them. Anyway, how is that son of mine, I didn't have much chance to catch up with him yesterday.'

'Sorry, I'm monopolising him,' I did feel a little guilty how much time he was spending with me.

'It's lovely to see him so happy and settled. I never wanted him to be like me, by himself.'

I smiled, picking up the A4 pad and a pen. 'Shall we start?'

'Yes,' the note of excitement was back in her voice and she kept glancing at her engagement ring. 'Now I called Moseley Old Hall this morning.'

'It's lovely there,' I cut in. Moseley Old Hall wasn't that far from us, I can remember Sam and me taking the children. The house itself was nearly five hundred years old with historic gardens that would just be beautiful for wedding photographs. If my memory served me correctly Charles II hid there when he was fleeing from the loyalists, hark at me hey.

'We went a couple of weeks ago for something to do and I just fell in love with the place. They have a place called The Barn that is authorised for wedding ceremonies, it holds sixty-two, so we've provisionally booked it.'

I clapped my hands together. 'Excellent,' in my neat hand I put "Wedding Venue" and Moseley Old Hall, sixty-two guests. 'Will it be enough though?' I fretted taking a sip of tea.

'Plenty big enough,' she assured me. 'It's just close family and friends,' she hesitated for a moment. 'Do you think Dale and

Bev will come and Lexi and Belle? Jamie too of course, just so my side doesn't look too sparse.'

'Of course, they will. Well Jamie might not be but the others definitely.'

'Tell them to put it in their diaries, eighth September.' She beamed.

'I will, now invitations. I could make them, I used to do a lot of card making.'

'Are you sure it won't be too much trouble?'

'Not at all. Now you need to decide on a colour scheme. So, what I'll do is we'll list everything we need to organise and then we can tick off one by one as we do them.'

'That's a grand idea,' she made more tea. 'It is going to be wonderful.'

I agreed, spreading different coloured pens across the table so I could co-ordinate it all.

We worked till five and I left with promises of calling her if I had any more ideas. She made me take the folder home with me as she didn't want Alan seeing anything, she wanted it all to be a surprise.

I was preparing dinner when Shay arrived, kissing me and fussing Millie he asked. 'Was mam okay when you saw her?'

'Very excited still. She has her ring, it's gorgeous,' I chatted. 'We got a lot done but it is going to take some time planning. They want to get married at Moseley Old Hall.'

'Where's that?'

'I'll show you,' I was cooking, steak, chips, egg and mushrooms. 'It's lovely.'

'I'll nip up and have my shower,' he headed for the stairs, he was sweaty from the gym.

'Okay hun,' I laid the table, feeding Millie as everything cooked.

By eight we were all done and ready to take Millie for her walk. I enjoyed the half hour away from the TV, Shay and I caught up on each other's days.

'I got some brochures,' he chatted as we skirted around. 'We'll have a look at them later.'

'Great,' I was looking forward to a holiday now he had suggested it.

We stopped as Millie did her business. 'Ray said you are a very pretty woman and you could do so much better than me.'

I laughed softly. 'Tell Ray he's right.'

'We arranged the bowling night for two week's Saturday, is that alright for you?'

I thought for a moment. 'Yes, I can't think of anything I have to do then.'

'Excellent,' he wanted me to meet his work colleagues, there were three other men who worked and one woman. 'It should be fun.'

'Should be,' I agreed hoping they all liked me.

Five

Millie and I arrived at the salon just after eight-thirty, she had usual sniff around while I made coffee. I always got to work a little earlier than I really needed to, I liked a moment's quiet contemplation before we got busy.

Bev arrived at eight-forty-five, looking like she had just got out of bed. 'Rough night?' I asked as I made her coffee.

She sat at her station, pulling out her make-up bag and plugging in the straighteners. 'We overslept, bloody alarm never went off.'

'Oh dear,' I stood behind her and did her hair while she put her slap on.

'Thanks Tash,' she smiled gratefully.

'Alan and Moira are getting married,' I told her.

'How wonderful,' she did look pleased. 'Is Shay okay about it?'

'Yeah fine. She told me to tell you to keep the eighth of September free, it's a Saturday.'

'Oh, bless her, no need to ask who's organising it all for them,' her smile was sweet.

I grinned, she knew me so well.

'You'll be next,' she predicted.

I shuddered. 'Not me honey, I'm never getting married again.'

'You would if Shay asked you,' she finished her make-up and finally turned her attention to Millie, who was looking most put out due to the lack of fuss.

'No, I wouldn't,' I sat at the reception desk. 'You'll never guess who Alan's daughter is though?'

'Who?' She sipped her coffee.

'Jemma Coles,' I told her quivering at the memory.

'The Jemma Coles? The Jemma Coles who had an affair with Sam? She gasped.

I nodded. 'I nearly died especially when she announced to the whole pub that she has slept with my husband and my –.' I stopped abruptly.

'Don't worry,' Bev gave me sad smile. 'I know she slept with Dale too, remember?'

'Sorry,' she did seem to have lost some of her confidence, she was worried Dale would go back to his old ways. 'You don't have to keep fretting that Dale's going to go off. Seriously he is so happy with you, I've never seen him so content.'

'I just wish I could get it into my thick skull,' she groaned.

'You will,' I assured her, quickly changing the subject. 'Sam wants to take Jamie to Thailand.'

'And Lexi?' She was glad of the conversation change.

'Funnily enough he didn't mention Lexi, which isn't going to please her one bit.' I pulled a face.

'He's punishing her for liking Shay,' she said wisely. 'He is such a knob.'

'I'm thinking along the same lines,' I admitted. 'Why is he being like it Bev?'

'I've told you why, he wants you back.'

'Why now though?' She was as bad as Shay.

'Because you're with Shay,' she checked the time, nine-o-five, Carling was late again. 'Sam likes the unobtainable.'

'Sam can fuck off,' I said forcibly.

'That's my girl,' she praised.

'Shay wants us to go abroad on holiday.'

'That'll do you good, it's been ages since you had a proper holiday, even if it was just a week in a caravan,' she looked out of the window as Carling arrived in her Fiat 500.

'Sorry hun,' she bustled through the door but at least she had her tunic on, she usually didn't bother wearing it.

'Make a fresh one,' Bev instructed, she never told her off about her lax time keeping.

She did as she was asked and we stopped talking about private things, Carling was liable to tell the whole world, we chatted about more mundane things.

'Seeing Shay tonight?' Bev asked as we stood side by side doing our customers.

'Never do on a Tuesday,' I replied. 'Jamie's coming for his tea though.'

'Still no better?' She mouthed to me.

I shook my head. I really didn't know what to do about it.

She gave me a sympathetic smile as we carried on working, I adored my job and I loved working with Bev, as I said earlier I cherished my life apart from how Jamie was being.

We shut at five and I hurried home, Jamie was due at six and I wanted to be showered and changed before he arrived. A beef stew was cooking in the slow cooker and I thought after supper we could take Millie for a walk and perhaps talk properly for once.

I fed big dog and then set the table. After I had changed I sat in the living room, praying that my son wouldn't cancel.

My mobile pinged and I picked it up – *Hope you had a good day sweetheart. Hope all goes well with Jamie. Miss you + luv u loads xxx*

I smiled like a teenager, Shay was such a smoothie. I texted back. *U only saw me this morning lol. Thank you, me too. Luv u loads 2 xxx*

I heard Jamie's key in the door and I hurried into the hallway. 'Sam,' I said seeing my ex-husband with our son.

'I've got all the details on Thailand,' he waved a folder in the air.

'Dad can stop for tea, can't he?'

I hesitated, I didn't want him to but Jamie would be annoyed with me if I didn't let him. 'You're dad's probably too busy and Meera will wonder where he is,' I said brightly, trying to get out of having him there.

'She's taken Safi to her mom's, they're staying overnight.'

'Oh okay,' shit I wouldn't be able to get out of it now. I went into the kitchen setting another place. 'It's only beef stew.'

'Your beef stew?' Sam took off his expensive leather jacket putting it on the back of the chair.

'I made it yes,' I answered, I really didn't want him there.

'I love your cooking, it's one of things I miss about you.'

I had no desire to know what the other things he missed about me were. 'Have a seat and I'll dish up.' It was strange having Sam sit at the table, almost like old times. He was sitting in the seat he always sat in, although it was a different chair now.

'No Paddy tonight?' Sam leant back on his chair watching me as I got dished the food up and I was glad that I had my old jeans, vest and cardigan on, my hair scraped back into a ponytail and no make-up on.

'*Shay* doesn't come round on a Tuesday and will you please stop calling him Paddy? It's getting on my nerves,' I banged the dish of stew in front of him and did the same to Jamie who was sniggering next to his dad.

'Sorry,' the look on his face told me that he wasn't in the least.

I sat opposite them, not feeling very hungry at all as Sam chatted about this and that. Jamie too was talkative telling me about school and how he was joining a football team. I felt a certain degree of sympathy for him, the poor kid just wanted his mom and dad back together. I just wished he would realise why we could never make a go of it again and stop punishing me.

Sam took another spoonful of stew. 'This is amazing,' he praised, dunking in a chunk of bread.

'Yeah mom, it's good.' Jamie aped his dad.

'Thanks boys,' I had to be polite. We carried on chatting until we had finished eating and then Sam and Jamie did the washing up and I nearly passed out with shock.

'Can I go and see Freddie?' Jamie was getting restless.

'Who's Freddie?' I hadn't heard of him before.

'He's in my year at school,' he replied.

'Fine,' I hoped Sam would go as well.

'Thanks mom,' he got his coat.

'I'll come and pick you up,' Sam told him.

'You know Freddie?' I frowned slightly.

'Yes, he's a good kid,' he replied. 'Shall I make coffee?'

'I'll make it,' I took the kettle from him. 'Please come for your lunch Sunday,' I said to my son.

'Will Paddy be here?' he asked.

I bit my tongue. 'It doesn't matter if he is, just come for lunch.'

He shrugged making his escape and I turned to Sam. 'I thought you were going to have a word with him about this?'

'I tried,' he replied but I knew he was lying, he had no intention of soothing the waters.

He took his coffee into the living room, sitting on the settee. I plumped for the chair even though I usually sat where he was. 'Come and sit by me Tash so I can show you everything,' he indicated to the folder he was holding. I did so reluctantly, wishing he would just go home.

He went through all the print offs he had brought with him. I had to admit it looked amazing, five stars hotels, trips to ride on elephants and visiting monkeys. They were also going to Khoa Phing Kan where they had filmed *The Man with the Golden Gun*, Sam was a huge James Bond fan.

'It looks great,' I admitted. 'Are you taking your daughter as well?'

'Of course Safi's coming with us.'

I stared at him with narrowed eyes. 'I'm talking about your other daughter, Lexi, remember?' My tone was like ice.

He flushed a little. 'Lexi is busy at university.'

'Not in August,' I argued. 'This is going to hurt her.'

'Lexi won't take a blind bit of notice,' he said confidently.

'You really don't know your own children do you?' my voice was harsh.

'She wouldn't want to come with me,' he stated. 'She's all you at the moment.'

'Is that what you resent?' I asked sharply, was he looking down my top as he spoke to me, the cheeky git.

'It would be nice if she visited once in a while,' he dragged his eyes away.

I flushed pulling my cardigan around me. 'She's the same as Jamie, damaged by us,' I felt tearful again. 'I always swore that my kids wouldn't go through what I did.'

'We do our best for them despite our divorce,' he stated. I'm sure he was definitely looking at my boobs. That was Shay's fault, making me paranoid that they were getting bigger.

'Lexi isn't going to be happy that you are taking Jamie on a holiday of a lifetime but not her,' I reiterated.

'Well perhaps she can go with you to,' he picked up the brochures that Shay had brought home. 'To the Costa del Sol.'

I snatched the brochures from him. 'Don't be sarcastic.'

'I'm not,' he gave me a charming smile. 'I just think she might enjoy going with her new stepdaddy.'

'Sam,' I cried. 'You are such an arsehole.'

'We had some good holidays though didn't we Tash?' he took no offence at my words.

'I wouldn't compare a week in a cramped caravan with two weeks in Thailand.'

'But they were special, I was with you and the kids,' he looked straight into my eyes.

I looked away quickly. 'It was a long time ago Sam.'

'I think about if often,' he moved a little closer to me and I shifted uncomfortably in my seat.

'Sam,' I warned softly as Millie shot up, a loud bark escaping from her.

'Shit,' Sam cussed as Shay appeared in the living room.

'Hello,' I said quickly, blushing even though I had done nothing wrong.

'Hey,' he replied, a pissed off expression on his face.

Sam gave him a big smile. 'Hi Shay,' he raised a hand.

'Hey,' he replied quietly, going into the kitchen with Millie.

'Oh I don't think Paddy very happy,' Sam chuckled.

'Stop it,' I scolded as Shay called me to the kitchen. I got up to go to him, just what was he doing here, I never saw him Tuesday.

'What the feck is he playing at?' Shay demanded, his eyes flashing angrily.

'He came to discuss Jamie's holiday,' I kept my voice low.

'I don't like it Tash,' his tone was gruff. 'As soon as I saw his car outside I thought what the fuck is he doing here?'

'I don't like it either. I thought he'd go when Jamie left for his friends,' I defended myself.

'He's playing you,' his brow furrowed into a frown.

'Don't start this again,' I whispered, weary of it.

'Me start?' he shook his head. 'When I walked in he was looking at your tits. Tell him to go.'

'I can't,' I couldn't cope with ructions at the moment.

He stared at me for a moment. 'Fine, I'm going to bed.'

'Shay,' I followed him to the door as Sam came into the kitchen, he walked past him without a word.

Sam watched his retreating back. 'Bloody hell I thought Jamie had come back for a minute.'

'What?' I asked distracted, Shay never came back on a Tuesday, so why tonight? Almost like he had a sixth sense that Sam would be with me.

'Bit childish storming off to bed,' he laughed. 'But then, he is only young.'

'It's getting late Sam,' I shook my head.

He took the hint. 'See you soon love,' he kissed my cheek.

I let him out and he went to his white Audi Q5, I didn't wait for him to get in the car before I shut and locked the door. Letting Millie out of the back so she could do her business I worried what Shay would say. As much as I wanted to I couldn't cut all ties with my ex-husband, not with having the children in common.

Millie came back in looking none too happy, the poor girl had forgone her walk. Turning everything off I went upstairs with a heavy heart. Going into the bathroom I brushed my teeth, took out my ponytail and put on the pink sexy nightie that I had brought for our mini-break in Lytham.

Shay had looked really pissed off so I needed to creep. Walking into the bedroom he was in bed, lying on his back, that livid expression still on his face. 'See you soon love. Fucking wanker,' he spat.

'Stop it,' I felt tired. 'I didn't expect you tonight.'

'Evidently,' his tone was dark.

'Please don't,' I got into bed, lying next to him.

'I know Sam's game,' he was really angry. 'He doesn't come near the house for five years since the divorce and now he thinks he can pop in whenever he wants.'

I kept quiet, not daring to tell him Sam had his supper with me.

'He wants to cause trouble,' Shay continued to rant. 'He's the one poisoning Jamie against us.'

'I don't disagree with anything you've just said,' I replied softly. 'But I don't want Sam though.'

'He was looking at your tits Natasha, your tits,' he turned moodily from me so I snuggled up to him. If he acted like this than Sam was achieving exactly what he had set out to do.

I stroked his face, pushing myself against him, my fingers tracing his lips. He caught my hand. 'I'm not really in the mood.'

I gave him what I hoped was a sultry look. 'You will be when I've finished with you.'

He couldn't resist giving me a little smile as I lay on him, kissing a trail from his chest to his stomach, muscles twitching under my lips. I moved down the bed disappearing under the covers.

I had never given Shay a blow job before, I had come close before Christmas but then things had happened and me thinking that Deep Throat had already got there first had stopped me doing it but that was about to change.

I kissed his stomach and the top of his thighs, my touch light. Taking a deep breath I took him in my mouth and he groaned softly. Judging by the way he was moving and the noises he was making I think I was doing something right.

Unfortunately it was also very hot under the duvet and eventually I had to come up for air, much to his frustration. 'Shit beautiful,' he breathed, flipping me over so he was above me. 'You are insatiable.'

I smiled softly, I knew he wouldn't be mad with me for long. He pushed my hair away from my face. 'Only I'm allowed to look at your tits.'

'Shush,' I held a finger to his lips.

He took it in his mouth, sucking gently on it. I pulled him to me kissing him impatiently. 'Love me,' I whispered.

He got a condom out of the bedside table and put it on. He paused before entering me, his eyes never leaving mine as we made our beautiful, special love.

Afterwards I lay in his arms feeling gratified. 'I was surprised to see you tonight.'

'I was missing you and I wanted to see you,' he answered.

This was silly, if we both wanted to be together all the time then why shouldn't we be? 'If we have sex like this when I'm not expecting you then you can drop in more often.'

He tilted himself away from me. 'You don't mind me just turning up?'

'Shay,' my voice was soft. 'You don't have to go home if you don't want too, even on a Friday when you see Dale you can always come back here'

He looked at me uncertain for a moment. 'Are you asking me to move in with you?'

'Do you want too?' I asked shyly.

He thought for a minute. 'I want to know that when I finish work you are here waiting for me. I want to build this future with you.'

'Then I'm asking you to move in with me,' I simplified.

'Once I do, I'll never leave,' he cautioned.

'I wouldn't want you to,' I kissed him gently.

'Then I want to,' he replied returning it.

'Will your mom be okay with it?' I fretted.

'Yes,' he assured me. 'She'll be happy.'

'I'm placing all my trust in you, please don't hurt me,' I looked openly into his eyes.

'I would never hurt you,' he swore solemnly.

'Then we do it soon?' Now I had made my mind up I didn't want to wait.

'This weekend?' he suggested.

'Excellent,' I snuggled against him, we had taken the next step. The only thing I had to do now was get Jamie on side. At least Sam may finally get it into his thick skull that Shay and I were serious about each other.

'Happy?' he asked kissing the top of my head.

'Very,' I replied snuggling closer.

Six

I got to work the next day, early as usual and for once Bev was already there. 'Morning,' she said thrusting a cup of coffee in my hand and giving Millie a head rub.

'Morning,' I beamed feeling happy but a little nervous at the same time.

'You look annoyingly cheerful,' she cocked her head to one side.

'I am, I think,' I sat at the reception desk. 'Shay's moving in with me.'

'That's great,' she gave me a hug. 'When?'

'The weekend,' I put my head in my hands. 'I hope I'm doing the right thing.'

'You know you are, so when did you decide?'

'Last night,' I watched Millie as she walked around the salon, sniffing everything.

'I didn't think you saw him on a Tuesday?' she reached under the counter bringing out a packet of bourbons. 'Breakfast,' she explained.

'You are going to have to start getting up earlier,' I laughed pinching one. I hadn't had a bourbon biscuit since I was pregnant with Jamie. I would eat them with gherkins and yes, I know how disgusting that was. 'I don't *usually* see him on a Tuesday but he dropped in last night.'

'That's nice, he really can't keep away from you.'

'It was a bit awkward actually, Sam was there,' I pulled a face.

'Sam!' she looked at me in surprise. 'What the hell was he doing there?'

I grimaced. 'He came to talk to me about Thailand, he had his supper but Shay does not know that.'

'You're an idiot feeding him,' she chided.

'I know, Shay was not impressed. In fact, he was downright angry,' I pinched another biscuit.

'I don't blame him,' she shook her head. 'I would be too.'

'He accused Sam of looking at my tits.'

'To his face?' she asked aghast.

'No, he said it to me.' I dunked the biscuit in my coffee. 'He keeps saying they are getting bigger and it looked like Sam noticed.'

She looked me up and down. 'They do look bigger.'

'Don't you start, I know I've put weight on.' I shifted on my stool. 'My tunic's getting a bit on the tight side, do you fancy going to Zumba.'

She thought for a moment. 'We could do, it's better than the gym.'

'That's what I said to Shay.'

'I can't believe that you and him are going to live together,' she smiled again, happy for us.

'Me neither, what if we don't get on?' I felt a little panicked.

'Tash,' she gave me a patient look. 'You and Shay are meant to be together. I have never known two people more suited. Just enjoy it and anyway financially you'll be so much better off.'

I hadn't thought of that.

'Make sure he pays his way,' she warned sunnily. 'I know you, you're a soft touch.'

'He gives me money towards the food already.'

'It's a win, win situation then,' she grinned as Carling arrived for work on time for once. 'Say congratulations to Tash, she and Shay are making it official.'

She went pale. 'You're getting married?'

'No,' I tried not to look smug, poor Carling still had a crush on him. 'We're moving in together.'

'Oh,' she tried to rally a smile. 'That's great.'

'Thank you hun,' I beamed. 'I'll make a fresh round of coffee,' I called Millie to me and went in the back room, closing the child gate that kept her out of the salon when we were open.

I made the coffee and took them into salon. 'We're busy today,' Bev was flicking through the diary.

'I like being busy,' I put everything I needed on my station. 'I'm going to tell Jamie about Shay when I finish work, I'm not looking forward to it.'

'I wouldn't be either, he's not going to like it you know,' she said as Carling messed with her mobile.

'Don't,' I groaned picking up my own mobile and ringing Lexi.

'Hi mom, everything okay?' she asked.

'Are you up and about already?' the clock read nine.

'Just because I'm a student that doesn't mean I laze in bed all day,' she sniffed.

'Yeah you do,' I teased.

'Okay,' she admitted. 'I've got a lecture at ten.'

'Thought as much,' I paused for a moment. 'Lex how would you feel about Shay moving in with me?'

'About time,' she answered. 'Have you asked him?'

'Yes, last night, he's moving in the weekend. Are you sure you don't mind?'

'Mom,' she threatened, she had told me time and time again to just do it.

'It'll always be your home,' I said softly, I didn't want her to think otherwise.

'I know it will, to be honest though mom when Belle and me finish Uni then we're going to get our own flat, we're used to living together now.'

'I'm pleased for you honey,' I said. 'But both you and Belle will always be welcome, don't forget that.'

'I won't mom,' her answer was soft. 'Have you told Jamie yet?'

'I'm going to drop by your dad's later, wish me luck.'

'You're going to need it,' she retorted. 'Tell Shay I'm happy for you both. My mom and shaggable Shay shacked up together.'

I laughed softly. 'Thank you hun, love to Belle. Love you loads.'

'Love you too mom, see you Sunday.'

'See you Sunday,' I closed the call.

'Was Lexi okay?' Bev asked as our first customers arrived.

'Pleased for us,' I smiled going to my first lady.

'That's good,' she readied herself for the day.

I arrived at Sam's after dropping Millie at home just after five-thirty, his Audi was in the driveway but Meera's Qashqai wasn't.

I knocked on the front door and Sam answered looking like he had just stepped out of the shower. 'Tash,' he said surprised. 'Are you okay?'

I gave him a tight smile. 'Sorry Sam, I should have called first. Is Jamie here?'

'Yeah, he just doing his homework,' he stood aside to let me in.

'Thanks,' I walked inside waiting in the hallway as Sam called Jamie from him room.

'So, has Paddy got over his paddy?' Sam asked with a sly smile.

'Very droll,' I looked up as Jamie came down the stairs. 'Hi love, had a good day at school?'

'It was okay,' he shrugged, not coming near me in case I tried to hug him.

'Can I have a quick word?' I screwed up my courage.

'I'll disappear,' Sam went to walk away.

'No, it's fine, it won't take long.'

'Can I get you a drink?' he offered.

'No, I'm good,' I was nervous though, it was ridiculous I was the adult.

'Go through to the lounge then,' Sam herded us in the room.

I perched myself on the edge of the chair. 'Jamie, I just wanted to tell you that Shay is going to move in with me this weekend.'

'What?' He screwed his face up as Sam sat there his own face like stone. 'That's disgusting.'

'Jamie,' I warned, wishing Sam would back me up. 'Don't start.'

'Well you moan I don't come and see you and then you ask Paddy to move in,' he cried. 'You won't see me at all now.'

'Sam?' I looked to my ex-husband for support but he just stared at me.

I gathered up my handbag, blinking back the tears. 'It's time you grew up Jamie,' I snapped. 'You're sixteen not six.'

He gave me a look full of attitude.

'I love you Jamie, so much but I can't cope with what you're doing at the moment.' I stood ready to go.

'What do you expect him to do? Sam asked his tone hard. 'You're choosing some bloke over him.'

I turned angrily. 'Don't you dare preach to me!' I was incensed. 'Not after what you did.'

'What does that mean? He challenged me.

'Three times while you were married to me, living with your children you choose a woman over all of us,' I spat, holding up my fingers. 'Three times.'

'It's not the same,' he dismissed me.

I turned to Jamie. 'If you want to strop, then strop at him.' I pointed to Sam. 'You know what? Forget it, just bloody forget it.'

'Don't be like this Tash,' Sam said quickly.

'You are such a bloody hypocrite,' I exploded. 'What right do you have to judge me after what you did?' I looked at Sam, my eyes flashing angrily.

'I'm not judging you,' he retorted but I could tell by his face he was.

'Yes, you are.' I retorted. 'You're sitting there like you've done nothing wrong.

'Mom shut up,' Jamie stuck up for his dad.

'Shut up,' my blood was boiling nicely thank you. 'Do you know your precious father had his first affair when I was seven months pregnant with you?'

'Dad?' Jamie looked at him unsurely and I felt a little guilty, I had never told him that little gem before.

'Leave it Tash,' I could see he was beginning to get annoyed and quite frankly I didn't care, I had protected him enough over the years.

'I know your game Sam,' I warned. 'I know exactly what you are up to. You think I don't know that all this nastiness that comes out of our son's mouth hasn't come out of yours first? What a wonderful role model you are.'

'You're out of order.' Sam pointed a finger at me.

'I'm out of order?' I gasped. 'I'm not doing anything wrong with Shay, we're not hurting anyone. It's not as if he has a wife and I'm breaking up their marriage.'

My words stung him which is exactly what I wanted. He stared at me, his mouth twitching angrily.

'The trouble with you Sam is you always want what you can't have,' I continued. 'You've always been the same.'

'When did you get like this?' he spat.

'What, not a pushover anymore?' I was running out of steam. I looked at my son who was sitting there with an identical expression to his father. 'You both need to get used to Shay living with me because the situation isn't going to change. We are together, deal with it.'

'He's no good for you. You will never have with him what we had,' Sam shook his head.

I looked at him flabbergasted, he really was delusional.

'There was nothing like you and me,' he stood, taking a step towards me. 'There is nothing like you and me.'

'Oh my God,' I cried. 'Do you really think it was so good between us? I could take you back this instant Sam and you would screw me over once again, you can't help yourself. At the end of the day you *never* loved me enough not to hurt me.'

'And you think Paddy does?' he scoffed.

I pulled the strap of my bag over my shoulder. 'Yes, I do.' With all the dignity I could I muster I walked from the house, not looking back.

Who did Sam think he was, who did Jamie for that matter? Getting into my car I started the engine and pulled away from the kerb. Jamie would come to me first, I refused to bend to him anymore. It hurt though, a real gut-wrenching hurt. The tears began to fall unheeded and I kept having to blink them away so I could see where I was driving.

I turned into my street, seeing the reassuring sight of Shay's truck parked outside my house. I parked up and hurried inside, trying to dry my tears.

'Hey sweet,' he greeted me then stopped dead. 'Have you been crying?'

'No,' my voice cracked and the tears began to fall again.

'Hey what's wrong?' he held me tightly.

'I,' I took a deep breath. 'I went to tell Jamie that you were moving in and he is being a little shit.'

'What did he say?' his voice was gentle.

I was still crying. 'He said he won't come here at all now.'

'Tash,' his tone was still tender. 'If it's going to cause problems then I won't move in, we'll wait until Jamie comes around to the idea.'

I looked up at him sadly. 'I don't want to wait, do you want to wait?'

'Not at all,' he answered.

'I am not letting Jamie dictate what I'm going to do with my life,' I said, not daring to tell him what Sam had contributed to the argument. 'I did that for too many years with Dale.'

He put his hands either side of my head, kissing my lips gently. 'I want to be with you,' he whispered. 'I want to live with you and be here for you. You mean everything to me and as long as it causes no heartache for you then you will always have me.'

'Thank you,' I kissed him back.

'Cup of tea?' he moved to put the kettle on.

'Please,' I gave Millie a love. 'Have you fed her?'

He nodded, busying himself with the drink. I still felt emotional, tears in my eyes. I couldn't see a solution to the problem but frankly I didn't want to have to choose between either of them. I couldn't not be with Shay, it just wasn't an option.

'Here you go,' he gave me a mug of tea, a browned-off expression on his face.

'What's wrong?' I asked sitting at the kitchen table.

'Nothing, I'm grand,' he sat next to me and attempted a smile.

'Love?' I prompted. 'I can tell something is by your face.'

He hesitated for a moment. 'I'm not having it Tash,' he replied. 'If Jamie keeps upsetting you like this then I'm going to have to say something to him. I'm not having him stress you out all the time, I care about you too much.'

'Please don't,' I reached for his hand.

He took mine. 'I mean it sweetheart, I know he's your son and only sixteen but really he is old enough to not act like a child.'

'I know,' I didn't want any more arguments.

He looked at me for a long moment. 'Sure, you still want me to move in?'

I squeezed his hand. 'Yes, more than anything.'

'Good,' he pulled me to my feet. 'Come on let's sort out some food.'

I nodded wiping my tears away. 'What did your mom say?'

He laughed softly. 'She is over the moon, we have to go for supper tomorrow.'

'She's not angry with me is she?' I didn't her to think that I was taking her son away from her.

'No,' he tapped my bum lightly. 'I just told you, she's pleased.'

'Good,' I managed a smile as we sorted out our meal.

Seven

Dinner at Moira's went well, she fussed around us and I was happy that she was pleased that her son was moving in with me. Alan was there too and we chatted away about the wedding.

I had told Bev about my run in with Jamie and Sam and she said she was proud of me having a go at my ex-husband, even if I was about sixteen years too late. I did have a little cry when I was telling her but as she said I couldn't let him rule me and he was just like Dale was at that age.

That thought depressed me, did I have to wait another seventeen years before Jamie became a decent human being like I'd had to wait with my brother? She was great all week though, keeping me cheerful when I got down about the situation with Jamie, so by Saturday I was full of excitement with a soupcon of trepidation. This was it, there was no turning back, Shay and I were going to live together for real. Yikes!

I hadn't seen him since Thursday, he was busy packing all his things up ready for Dale to help him move today. Judging by his texts though he was more excited than me.

I had taken Millie to work with me to make sure she didn't get in their way, even though she didn't usually come to the salon on a Saturday. I hurried home after we had shut, with Bev following me in her car, we were all going to share a take away to celebrate.

'Exciting isn't it?' Bev grinned as she took Millie from me so I could get my bags and lock the car.

'I'm so nervous,' I admitted going up the path.

'You'll be fine,' she tried to get Millie to stop pulling on her lead.

I walked into the hallway and nearly fell over the boxes and bin liners that littered the floor. 'Looks like he's definitely moved in,' she smiled again, taking off Millie's lead and stepping daintily over them.

Going into the kitchen it seemed equally full of boxes and black bags and I bit down on my lip. 'Alright Tash?' she gave me a sideways glance, she knew I liked things neat and tidy.

'Yeah,' I stepped over a box. 'Tea?'

'Please,' she took off her coat.

Poor Bev was on driving duty, Shay had picked Dale up earlier to help him move in. I made the tea and we went into the living room where they were sprawled on the settee, a bottle of lager in their hands and more boxes littering the floor.

'Here's me dahling,' Shay declared on seeing me as Millie went to greet them. 'My house buddy.'

'There's stuff everywhere, is it yours?' it was a stupid question.

He nodded, the bottle of lager raised to his lips.

'Oh,' I forced the smile on my face. 'I thought your mom was moving in as well the amount of stuff there is.'

Bev and Dale tittered, they knew my OCD only too well. 'No, just me,' he replied innocently.

'I've made some space for you upstairs,' I tried again.

'I'll sort it out tomorrow, Dale and me are knackered,' he gave me his beautiful smile.

My brother gave me a warning look, what did a few boxes matter for just one day? There weren't just a few boxes though, there were lots. 'Okay,' I sat on one chair, Bev taking the other.

'Are we having Chinese or Indian?' Dale smiled sweetly at Bev.

'I don't mind, what does everyone else want?' she replied.

'Indian,' Shay declared, jumping up to get the menus from the drawer in the kitchen.

'Everything okay sis?' Dale gave me a huge smile.

'There are boxes blooming everywhere,' I whispered.

'Don't start nagging him,' he warned. 'Chill a little.'

I nodded reluctantly. 'Fine, I'll keep it shut,' I replied as Shay came back into the room.

'Everyone choose what they want,' he sat on the arm of my chair, passing me the menu.

'Chicken Tikka, pilau rice and cheese naan please,' I answered promptly passing the menu to Dale.

'You're so boring sis, you always have the same,' he ribbed.

'So?' I took a sip of my tea as Shay put his arm around me and kissed the top of my head.

'Will you call it in?' he asked Dale. 'They can never understand my accent.'

'No worries,' he turned to Bev. 'Write down what everyone wants will you love?'

I passed her a notebook and pen and she made the list in her untidy hand. When it was delivered we sat around the kitchen table, eating the food with a nice cooling lager.

Dale and Bev had decided to leave the car at mine and get a taxi home, so she could have a drink. The four of us fitted together perfectly, Dale and I had always spent time together, we were more than close.

We sat in the living room after, chilling and chatting and I was so good ignoring all the boxes and bin bags that littered the floor even though I was itching to put them in their rightful place myself. They left at eleven and we made our way wearily to bed for our first night of officially co-habiting.

Sunday morning came and along with it Lexi and Belle for their roast dinner. 'Oh mom,' she gave me a sombre hug as she surveyed the mess on the floor. 'How are you coping with this?'

'I'm not, it's everywhere,' I admitted. 'He hasn't unpacked a single thing yet.'

'Where is he?' she smiled at Belle who was trying not to laugh at the distress on my face.

'Surveying the shed to see how much room there is for his tools,' I shuddered.

'You can only just about get the lawnmower in there,' she took off her coat. 'I'll go and say hello.'

Walking outside to the small garden Millie came bounding over to see her. 'Hello big dog,' she patted her. 'Morning Shay!'

He came out of the shed on hearing her. 'Morning dahling, how ya doing?'

'Fine thanks,' she peered inside, mindful of the spiders, there really wasn't any room at all.

'We need a bigger shed,' he said wiping his hands on his old jeans. 'It's a pity there isn't a garage.'

'You know if you don't pack your stuff away mom will have an absolute cow turn,' she advised with a smile.

'She'll be good,' he returned it.

'Oh, bless you Shay, bless your naivety and your twinkling Irish charm but you have a lot to learn and I will show you the way,' her smile grew as she added. 'I just wanted to say I'm so glad you've moved in with my mom, she's really happy and I can't remember her ever being truly happy before.'

'You can't?' he couldn't keep the surprise out of his voice.

She shook her head. 'She always seemed a little sad when she was married to dad as if she was worried that something bad was going to happen. It was only when I got older I knew why, not that she's ever said much about his affairs,' Lexi too looked a little sad. 'Now though, she's happy.'

'That's good to know,' he meant it.

'However, she will not continue being in a good mood it you don't put your shit away,' she laughed, leading the way back to the house.

But he never did and by Sunday evening when there was just the two of us again I had to bite my tongue so hard to stop myself nagging him that it was a surprise I didn't cleave it in two.

'Hey beautiful,' he whispered when I sat next to him on the settee and I knew that look, he was after some nookie.

'Hello,' I forced a smile. If I had to move one more bin bag or step over one more box then I wouldn't be responsible for my actions. There just wasn't the room, especially having such a big dog, she took up enough floor space.

He pulled me to him, kissing me as he hand went caressed the top of my leg. 'Shay,' I started trying to stay focused.

'Yes sweet,' he hand moved to my boobs.

I moved away and he had a look of surprise on his face. 'If you don't move those boxes and bags then I am going to put them all outside in the rain.'

He held my hand. 'You wouldn't do that dahling, you love me.'

Fine, then let me put it like this. If you do not unpack your things and put them neatly away in their designated places that I have provided for you then I am *never* having sex with you again. They are driving me mad!'

'You not have sex with me again, never, you love it too much,' he sounded confident.

'I'm not kidding,' I used my mommy voice.

He looked at me with his unreadable expression on his face that he was so good at and then he dived from the settee like a whirlwind, picking up his stuff and tidying them away.

I laughed loudly, the things men would do if they thought they wouldn't get any nookie. Millie ran around barking and trying to join in the fun, nearly succeeding in tripping him over.

Going upstairs I found him frantically putting clothes onto hangers. 'Right,' I took them from him. 'I've made my point, I'll empty the rest tomorrow,' I pulled him down on the bed. 'Now, where were we?'

Eight

So Shay had moved in on Saturday and it was now Wednesday and so far, so good. There were still a few boxes littered about the place but my threat to withhold sex had worked and between us most of the things were neatly in the places I had allocated for them.

It was truly lovely having him there and knowing that he wasn't going home. I still worried about Jamie, that went without saying but he had chosen to stay away.

'Tash,' Carling sidled up to me. 'Have you got any tampons in your bag?'

I finished putting the plastic bag on my customers head to help her colour along, (honest, I'm not a serial killer) and settled her on the sofa with a magazine before going into the back room.

'I don't use tampons but I should have a pad,' I got my handbag, looking in the zipped section where I usually kept them.

'Thanks, Bev hasn't got any,' she looked a little flushed.

'No, she won't have,' I replied. Bev had the coil fitted years ago, not for her the monthly curse. I was thinking of having one fitted myself, save on the condoms.

'I've usually got some but I'm early this month,' she explained.

I shook my head, some things you did not need to know. 'Here you go,' I pulled one out giving it to her.

'Thanks babe,' she took it from me, disappearing into the staff toilet.

I looked again in my handbag with a frown. The feminine hygiene products I had were Morrison's home brand, I hadn't shopped there since before Christmas, why hadn't I brought any others?

Leaning up the breakfast bar I tried to work out the last time I'd actually had a period. I could remember I had one the day Bev and Carling came to tell me that the baby wasn't Dale's. That's why I was going to give Shay a blow job because we couldn't do anything else but I chickened out in the end, but after that I couldn't recall.

Bev came into the room, putting the kettle on. 'Hun,' I turned to her, my heart hammering in my chest. 'When did you come to tell me that Fallon's baby wasn't our Dale's?'

She pursed her lips. 'About two weeks before Christmas, the Sunday, why?'

'No reason,' I murmured going to the reception desk and picking up the appointments diary, flicking through the pages I tried to work out the weeks with mounting dread. I could not have missed two periods without even noticing, only I could. I was so caught up with Shay and the problems with Jamie and Sam that I hadn't even realised.

Bev was just making us all a cup of coffee when I went to her. 'I've got to pop out,' I mumbled, my face burning.

'What about your lady?' she frowned.

'The colour will take at least forty-five minutes and my next customer isn't due yet,' I picked up my handbag and Millie, thinking it was time to go home, tried to follow me. 'I'll be ten minutes big dog,' I assured her.

There was a pharmacy on the Coppice Farm estate and I hurried there, looking at the vast array of pregnancy tests on offer I picked the one that claimed to be the most accurate and paid for it with shaking hands.

Going back to the salon, I locked myself in the toilet, peeing on the stick. Luckily I had to go, it was nerves I think, if I was pregnant then it would make so much sense. My weight gain, my boobs getting bigger, how up and down I was emotionally.

'Tash, your coffee's getting cold,' Bev shouted through the door.

'In a minute,' I replied preoccupied as I timed the test with my gorgeous Radley watch that Shay had brought me for Christmas.

It would be negative, of course it would. Shay and I were always careful, a condom every time, even when we were pissed. The time was up, shaking like a leaf I looked at the test blankly for a moment. No, it couldn't be, it had to be wrong. Positive! A smile broke across my face, we had made a baby, I don't know how but we had done it together.

Then reality hit me like a ton of bricks. I could *not* have a baby, I was forty-two years old and already the mother of two teenage children. Opening the door I called to Bev, I needed to talk to her.

'What?' she shouted back.

'Can you come here a minute please?' I tried to keep the panic out of my voice.

She came to me muttering under her breath. 'I've got a customer Tash, what is it?'

I pulled her in the cubicle, shutting the door. 'What are you doing?' she cried.

'Look!' I thrust the white plastic stick at her.

'What's that?' she tried to back away but it was a little cramped.

'Look!' I repeated shoving it under her nose.

'It smells of wee Tash!' she batted my hand away.

'Please Bev,' I gave it to her once again and she took it reluctantly.

'Is this a pregnancy test?' she demanded.

I nodded mutely.

'So you are-.'

'Pregnant,' I finished for her.

'Oh my God!' she cried and I shushed her.

'Don't,' I could feel my eyes fill with tears. 'What am I going to do?'

'What do you mean?' she looked at me perplexed.

'I can't have a baby,' I wrung my hands nervously. 'I'm too old, I already have two children.'

'I thought you and Shay were careful.'

'We are, we always use a condom,' I felt like I was going to pass out.

'Well something has gone wrong,' she had on her compassionate face.

'I thought it would be just the two of us to think about,' I continued dazed. 'My kids don't need me anymore like they did and I thought Shay and I could go on holidays and just enjoy ourselves. Babies were not in our plans, I have had to bring kids up since I was ten years old, I can't go through it all again.'

'Are you sure the test is right?'

I shrugged. 'It would make sense.'

'You have two choices hun. You have the baby or you have an abortion, either way you need to talk to Shay,' she reasoned.

'I can't do either,' panic engulfed me.

'You have to tell him,' her voice was firm.

'This wasn't part of our new start,' I moaned.

She looked at me for a long moment. 'Go home and sort this out.'

'What am I going to do?' I whispered.

'I can't tell you what to do,' she replied. 'You are a born mother Tash, it's what you do best.'

'That's no help,' I chided.

'Go home and talk to Shay.'

'My customers,' I faltered.

'I'll see to them. Carling can do the blow dries, she's good enough now.' Impulsively she gave me a hug. 'Whatever you decide I'm here for you. Personally I think it would be the icing on the cake for you and Shay, it's not my decision though, it's yours.'

I nodded opening the loo door. 'He only moved in Saturday,' I felt numb. 'And now I have to tell him this.'

'I know babe, call me if you need me,' she hugged me again.

I nodded stiffly, putting the lead on Millie and going to my car. It seemed to take an age for Shay to come home from work and then he was in the kitchen, seeming to fill it with his presence.

'Had a good day beautiful?' he asked kissing me.

I stepped away from him. 'Sit down please.'

'This sounds serious,' he had a look of puzzlement on his face.

Going to the sink I began to absently wipe it down, my nerves threatening to go off the scale. 'Tash?' he prompted with trepidation.

I turned to face him, my heart threatening to burst out of my chest. 'We need to talk.'

'About what?' he slumped at the table. 'Is this to do with Sam?'

'What? No,' I screwed up my face, still keeping a distance between us.

'What is it then?' he demanded. 'Is it Jamie?'

I couldn't get the words out at first and then they came out in a rush. 'I'm pregnant.'

He laughed delighted. 'That's,' then he saw my face and stopped. 'You're not pleased?' it wasn't a question.

'I can't have a baby,' I cried. 'I'm forty-two years old, I've had my kids.'

'Sweet,' he tried to interrupt me.

'No,' I held up my hand. 'I just can't.'

'Don't I get a say in this?' his voice was full of hurt.

I looked at him sadly. 'No,' I was trying and failing not to cry.

'What?' he pushed back his chair, an irate look on his face. '*Our* baby Tash, not just yours.'

I forced myself to look at him. 'My decision and mine alone.'

'So I have no say in whether you keep *our* baby or kill it?' his tone was harsh.

'Don't,' I sobbed. 'It's going to be me having to bring it up by myself when you decide it isn't what you want, or when you come home smelling of another woman's perfume.'

I could see the muscles working in his face as he tried to reign his temper in. 'Why the fuck did you ask me to move in with you if that's what you think of me?'

I couldn't answer him so he tried again. 'Our baby Tash, ours. I'm not going to screw around on you, stop thinking that I am.'

I turned away, I just couldn't look at him. He moved to me, pinning me against the sink. 'I. Am. Not. Fucking. Sam!' he forced the words out, his breath searing my ear. He was right behind me and I could feel the anger radiating from him.

'I just can't,' I repeated, my heart breaking. 'I can't have a baby.'

He was frozen for a moment and then he moved, grabbing his car keys and going out the door.

Millie whined coming to stand by me. 'Shay!' I screamed but his truck was pulling away from the kerb. Sitting on the chair I began to sob loudly, it wasn't how I wanted it to be. Dale arrived a few minutes later, a concerned look on his face.

'Have you spoken to him?' he sat next to me.

I nodded miserably. 'Bev told you?'

'Yes she did, she's worried about you? What did Shay say? Was he happy, angry?'

'He was happy, I think,' I felt ancient. 'At first.'

'That's good then,' he tried to sound enthusiastic.

'How can I have the baby Dale?' I cried. 'How?' 'Easy if you want to,' he replied.

I turned away, he would never understand.

'Tash,' he pushed. 'Sis, tell me the truth, do you want this baby?' I couldn't answer. 'What was the first emotion you felt when you found out you were pregnant?'

'Leave it Dale,' I warned.

'I know you,' he argued. 'Be honest sis, what was the first thing you felt?'

I hesitated for a moment, I couldn't change my mind.

'Tell me,' he insisted.

I faced him, tears falling down my face. 'I was happy,' I reluctantly admitted.

'So why are you not going through with it?' his voice was gentle.

'How can I have a baby?' I challenged. 'After what Sam did, he said that the reason he cheated on me all those times was because I was never there for him, that I was too involved with the kids.'

'Sam would have said anything to make *you* feel guilty and try to get you to take the blame for what *he* did. Shay isn't like that. Do you have any idea when Shay and I go out on a Friday how many beautiful, stunning women come on to him?'

I shook my head that was something else to worry about.

'Lots, he is a handsome man, and he politely turns them all down because of you.'

'I just can't,' I repeated freaking out.

'He loves you Tash, give him some credit for not being like Sam,' Dale was adamant. 'You're a fool if you lose him over this.' He looked at me shrewdly for a moment. 'Unless it isn't his.'

'What?' I was shocked he would even suggest such a thing.

'Well is it?' he probed.

'Dale!' I really didn't need this.

'Well?' he raised an eyebrow.

'Of course it is,' I slumped in my chair.

'You haven't been messing around with Sam have you?'

'No,' I could have slapped him for the insinuation. 'I'm not you.'

'Cheers for that sis, I have changed you know?'

'Sorry,' I mumbled.

'It you want this baby then just have it,' his tone was soft again.

'How can I? What if he leaves me and I end up a single parent?' That thought was just too heart-breaking.

'One: he is not going to leave you and two: worst case scenario it does all go tits up in a few years' time then you won't be alone. You'll have me and Bev, Lexi and Belle. Plus do you really think that Moira would turn her back on her grandchild? You'll have plenty of support. Just don't do something you will regret please?'

My eyes sought his. 'Six months ago if I'd told you that Shay had gotten me pregnant you would have broken his neck.'

'I would,' he agreed. 'But I'm a different person now, thanks to Bev.'

'I'm glad you're happy,' I was crying again.

'And I want you to be happy too sis. Go to him and the pair of you have this baby,' he reached for my hand.

'I'm so scared,' I whispered.

'We're all scared if something,' he sounded so wise. 'I'm scared of seeing a pretty young girl and not being able to resist her. It doesn't stop me trying my hardest with Bev never to hurt her though. If I'm scared it matters.'

I looked at him proudly. 'You know I'm beginning to like you.'

'Er, haven't you always liked me?' he pulled a face.

I shook my head. 'I've always loved you but how you were, I never really liked you sometimes,' I explained. 'But I do now.'

'Thanks, I think,' he stood enveloping me in one of his bear hugs. 'Shall we go and find him?'

I groaned, still scared. 'Yes,' going upstairs I washed my face. I looked haggard, I was going to be such an old mom. When I re-joined Dale in the kitchen he had his car keys in his hand.

'He'll be at a pub, I know I'd need a pint. Sure this is what you want? Once you've told him you're keeping it you can't change your mind, that wouldn't be fair.'

'Yes, I'm sure it's what I want.' My first emotion on knowing I was pregnant was, as I said to Dale, jubilation, didn't that tell me everything I needed to know?

'Come on then,' he steered me out the door and to his car. 'More bloody expense at Christmas and birthdays,' he teased. 'Another snot nosed brat calling me Uncle Dale.'

I tried to laugh but it was hard. 'What if he tells me to sod off?'

'Behave Tash, he would never say that to you, for some strange reason he's bloody besotted with you, poor bloke. If I hadn't brought him into the salon that day he'd still be out enjoying himself without a care in the world. Now look at him, got a cougar for a girlfriend and he's going to be a dad, I feel so responsible.'

'You know I said I was beginning to like you, well I lied.' We pulled away from the house.

He laughed loudly. 'That's more like my sister.'

We drove around a few pubs until Dale spotted Shay's truck on the car park of the Lancaster. 'Do you want me to come in with you?' he offered.

I shook my head. 'No, I need to do this by myself but thank you anyway.'

'Call me later so I know you're okay,' he hugged me tightly.

'I will,' I replied.

He stroked my hair. 'My big sister knocked up by my best mate.'

'Yep,' I forced a smile. 'Don't tell anyone yet will you? Moira and the kids need to know first.'

'I won't and I'll tell Bev not to either. I don't envy you having to tell Jamie though.'

I grimaced. 'Don't, it's going to be horrific.'

'Just keep focusing on Shay and the baby.'

I nodded getting out the car. Walking inside I could see Shay sitting at a table away from the main area, slouched over a pint of lager that sat untouched in front of him. Screwing up my courage I headed over to him. 'Shay,' I began softly.

He looked up and to my dismay I could see tears in his eyes. 'I think you've said everything you need to say,' he sounded crushed.

I sat next to him, wishing I could have a drink as well, I certainly needed one. 'I was wrong,' I kept my voice low. 'I do want to meet this baby we've created. I want to see if it has your hair, your eyes, your beautiful smile. I just want to hold it. I panicked, I am just so scared.'

He looked at me with his lovely brown eyes. 'Don't play with me.'

'I'm not,' I reached awkwardly for his hand. 'It was just a knee jerk reaction. I am too old, I've already done my bit with children, I wanted some me time but,' I paused trying to keep the tears away. 'This is precious, this is ours. When the test was positive my first thought was how happy I was,' again I paused.

He watched me, letting me gather my thoughts. 'And then me being me all I could think about was the negatives. Sam played around.'

'Do you have to mention Sam?' he cut in.

'Please let me talk. Sam played around because he said I was too involved with the kids, that I had not time for him. What if you think the same?'

'For the hundredth time I am not Sam nor would I ever be like him. I love you, truly love you, isn't that enough?'

I realised it was, all I needed was the love of the man next to me to be happy. 'Yes, it's enough,' I replied.

'So we are going to have this baby?'

'If that's okay?'

He moved closer, bringing his arm around me. 'Yes,' he whispered, burying his face in my hair. 'Come on let's get out of here, are you in your car?'

I shook my head. 'Dale dropped me off.'

'Dale?'

'I'm sorry love, he and Bev know. You should have been the first person I told but like I say I freaked out.' I did feel bad about it now.

'What did he say?' his voice was thick with emotion.

'He talked some sense into me,' I smiled softly.

'I owe him a pint then,' he stood leaving his lager. 'Let's go home.'

I got up also and hand in hand we walked to his truck.

Nine

I woke at six the next morning a little disorientated, Shay's side of the bed was empty and it took me a while to gather my thoughts. We had said little to each other when we had returned home the previous night, we just lay in each other's arms, contemplating silently how our lives were going to change irrevocably.

I got out of bed, pulling on my dressing gown. Shay was in the living room, a mug of tea on the coffee table and fussing Millie absently.

'You're up early,' I said sitting.

He turned at the sound of my voice. 'Hey beautiful,' he sounded tired.

'What are you doing?' I rubbed Millie's head, sitting next to him.

'I couldn't sleep,' he replied. 'I've already taken Millie for a walk.'

'I bet she enjoyed that,' I felt a little un-nerved. Was he having second thoughts?

'Do you want another tea?'

'I'll do it,' he got up quickly, disappearing into the kitchen as I leant back against the settee. He returned with two steaming mugs.

'I'll make an appointment at the doctors today,' I chatted to make things normal, he seemed preoccupied.

'It's a good idea,' he agreed, taking my hand. 'Tash.'

'What?' I whispered, please don't let him have changed his mind now that my own was made up.

'Thank you,' he reached out to touch my cheek.

'For what?' I lay my hand over his.

'I never thought I would have the chance to be a father,' he stopped for a moment. 'My choice was to be with you and I knew that meant not having children and that was enough because I love you but now.'

'Now?' I whispered.

'I can't believe it's going to happen,' tears filled his eyes. 'And I am so thankful.'

'Oh love,' I hugged him to me glad he was happy. 'I need you now more than ever.'

'I'm here,' he kissed me and I kissed him back. God, I was horny. Usually when I was pregnant I went off sex, I just wasn't interested, which was one of the reasons Sam told me he had strayed.

'Come back to bed,' I pulled him up, continually kissing him.

He allowed me to lead him up the stairs, in the bedroom I pulled off his jumper, my hands running across his chest.

'Tash, is it okay?' He was worried.

'Yes,' I breathed. 'Just don't put your full weight on me.'

He still looked a little doubtful, bless him. I pulled him on top on me, my hands unrelenting all over him. Shedding my own night clothes, I freed him from his jeans.

Automatically he reached into the bedside table for the condoms. 'We don't need them anymore,' I smiled, my hand building up the friction.

He groaned, pushing himself between my legs and then he was inside me and it felt like we had more connection than ever before. I don't know if it was not using a condom or my pregnancy but I could feel every fibre of him.

We rocked against each other, him careful not to lie on me. Every sensation was amplified, every touch electrifying.

He came loudly, clasping me tightly. 'Shit beautiful,' he breathed.

'You like?' I smiled, pushing the curls away from his face.

'I like,' he grinned, moving of me and holding me tightly.

'Me too,' I lay across him. 'You know I'm going to be big soon?'

'I know,' he kissed my nose.

'We're going to have a baby Shay, you and me,' I still couldn't believe it.

'Made with love,' he snuggled against me.

'Can we not tell anyone until we've had the scan?'

'Why?'

'I just want to know everything's okay.' I explained.

'It will be but we'll get used to it ourselves before we tell anyone,' he promised. 'Tash.'

'Yes love,' I said as I played with his hair.

'How did you realise you were pregnant?'

'Something Carling said so I went to get a test from the pharmacy and did it at work,' I answered.

'Have you kept it?'

I curled a lock of hair around my finger hoping our baby had his hair. 'Yeah.'

He gave me a patient smile. 'Can I have a look at it?'

'What? Yeah course,' I dived out of bed going to my handbag and took it out. 'There you go,' I went to his side of the bed to give it to him.

He caught me around the waist burying his head in my stomach. 'You have a bump already,' he trailed kisses across it.

'I just thought I was getting fat,' I admitted. I felt a little self-conscious standing there in my altogether.

'You're beautiful,' he whispered. 'Hey in there, I'm your daddy.'

My eyes filled with tears and I reached down to caress his face. 'And although you are a bit of a surprise we will love and cherish you,' he continued. 'Me and your mammy will be the best parents ever.'

I reached down to kiss the top of his head and he took the test from me, a look of amazement on his face.

'Does it smell of wee?' I asked.

'Wee?' he gave me a puzzled smile.

'Bev said it smelt of wee when I showed it to her yesterday,' I explained.

He laughed softly before growing serious. 'Would you really have had an abortion?'

I moved away, pulling on my dressing gown. 'I don't know,' I answered truthfully. 'No, probably not. Would you have left me if I had? Would it have been the end of us?'

He thought for a moment. 'It would have tested me. I don't think I would ever understood it,' he was equally truthful.

I lay back by him. 'Let's not talk about it, it isn't an option now.'

'Okay. Jamie isn't going to be happy.'

I shrugged, he really was concerned about how Jamie was being. 'He's going to have to get used to it.' I was adamant.

'I don't want you to get stressed,' he stroked my hair. 'When you tell him. I'll come with you.'

'I think it would be better if I told him by myself.' I replied.

'We're a couple sweet, a partnership,' he tried to be patient.

'I just think I'm better going by myself,' I knew it was the wimp's option.

'Beautiful,' he had a warning in his voice.

'Just go with me on this one,' I pleaded. 'We need to tread carefully.'

'You're too soft on him,' he chided.

'Let me do it my way,' I kissed him. 'We should get ready for work.'

'I suppose,' he yawned. It's going to kill me not to tell anyone.'

'You can talk to Dale,' I pulled myself away.

'I can, can't I? I'm going in the shower first,' he shot past me.

'What do you want for breakfast?'

'Just some toast will be fine,' he replied.

By eight-forty I had arrived at the salon with Millie, Bev was already there and the kettle was on. She beamed on seeing me. 'Everything okay?'

'Perfect,' I smiled. 'I take it Carling wasn't in yet?'

'You are joking, it's much too early,' she replied. 'I can't believe you're pregnant Tash.'

'Me neither, I always worried that Lexi would come home pregnant or that Jamie would knock a girl up and it's me.' I laughed.

'How's Shay?' She took the decaffeinated tea bags from me, I had to look after myself now.

'Stunned but over the moon.' I giggled. 'I think he'll make a good dad.'

'I think he'll make an excellent one,' she agreed. 'When are you going to tell people?'

'When I've had the first scan, which reminds me I need to call he doctors.'

'Do it now before Carling arrives.' She made the tea.

I managed to get an appointment with my doctor at four pm and Bev said I could leave early.

I dropped Millie off at home and hurried to the surgery. I had known my doctor since the children were born, she had a son the same age as Lexi and as they had been in the same year at school and we used to chat at the school gates.

Her name was Doctor Charvi Desai but was universally known as Vee, which is what I called her. 'Hi Tash,' she greeted me with a huge smile.

'Hi,' I took a seat by the side of the desk so I was sitting to the side of her feeling nervous.

'Kids okay?' She brought my notes up on screen.

'Fine and yours?'

'Good, all doing well,' she looked at me over the top of her glasses. 'Now what can I do for you?'

I hesitated for the slightest moment. 'I'm pregnant.'

She failed to hide her shock. 'Are you sure?'

'I've taken a test and it's positive.'

'Right let's get you booked in with a midwife. How far gone do you think you are?'

'Around ten weeks,' I answered vaguely.

'We'll get a scan arranged and then we'll get a more accurate date. Are you and the baby's father together?'

'Yes,' I was a bit put out. 'We live together.' What did she think that I would get pregnant by some random bloke?

'I heard on the grapevine that you were seeing one of the mechanics from Ray's Garage?' When I nodded she continued. 'It's not the big baldy one, is it?'

'No that's Ray, Shay's got dark curly hair.'

'Irish?' She raised an eyebrow and I nodded again. 'Very nice.'

'I think so,' I agreed.

'And is he pleased with the pregnancy?' She was typing away on the computer and I wondered if under "Father" she was typing "Fit".

'He's over the moon,' I smiled.

'And you?' Again, the look over the top of her glasses.

'Not at first,' I admitted. 'I did think about having an abortion for all of five seconds.'

She nodded understanding, then looked at me with a critical eye. 'Are you sure you're only ten weeks?'

I shrugged. 'That was my last period.'

'I think we'll get the scan sorted ASAP. It's going to be different now from when you had your first two.'

'In what way?'

'You are, what we term in the medical profession, a geriatric mom.' She tried not to smirk.

'I'm only forty-two,' I was most put out.

She laughed softly. 'Sorry Tash but that's what you are,' leaning back in her chair she continued to smile. The midwife will call you tomorrow, I'll make sure of it.'

'Thanks Vee,' I knew she wanted to be certain I was cared for.

'I'll see you soon because I want to keep an eye on you too,' she stood touching my arm. 'Congratulation Tash and can I just say you must be bloody mad to have to do it all again.'

'I know,' I smiled picking up my handbag. 'See you soon Vee, love to the family.'

'Yours too,' she replied and I left saying goodbye to the receptionist on the way out.

Calling into Lidl I picked up some jacket potatoes for supper and hurried home, Shay arrived about five-thirty still grinning like the cat who'd got the cream. 'How did you get on at the doctors?' he asked.

'Fine, everything is done by the midwife now so Vee, my doctor, is going to arrange it all tomorrow.

'Did she give you another pregnancy test?' He fussed around me.

'No, home pregnancy tests are as accurate now as theirs so they take your word for it. They'll send me for a scan, you'll come with me, won't you?'

'Of course, you don't have to ask,' his voice was full of excitement.

'The scan will give us a more accurate idea of when the baby is due,' I explained.

'But you think about ten weeks?'

I nodded. 'And I think I've worked out when it happened,' I smiled.

'When?' He was curious as he made me a cup of decaffeinated tea.

'Do you remember Christmas Eve, Eve?' I laced my arms around his waist, resting my face on his back, he smelled of the garage.

'Yeah, we made love in front of the Christmas tree, it was wonderful hot sex,' although I couldn't see, I just knew he was smiling.

'The pound shop condoms?' I reminded him.

He turned delighted. 'You tight arse,' he cried. 'Look at the trouble you've got us in for the sake of a couple of quid.'

'The trouble *I've* got us into?' I dug him in the ribs.

'Yes,' he put his face inches from mine. 'You and your gammy condoms.'

'What does gammy mean? I asked, I wish he'd speak English.

'Useless,' he grinned.

'They were not gammy and it is not my fault,' I defended myself. 'It's not me who's got sperm that can penetrate rubber.'

He laughed loudly as my mobile began to ring and I moved to answer it. 'Hi sweetheart,' I said.

'Mom!' Lexi spluttered. 'Do you know where dad is taking Jamie?'

I pulled a face at Shay, this was the phone call I had known would happen. 'Yes,' I admitted.

'Why didn't you tell me?' She sounded hurt.

'I chickened out. I knew it would upset you,' I answered truthfully. 'Plus, your dad can do his own dirty work.'

'He won't take me because I get on with Shay,' she fumed. 'He is such a childish arsehole.'

I couldn't argue. 'We'll sort something out, maybe we could go away.' I tried to soothe her, really wanting to tell her about the baby but wanting to keep it between Shay and me also, just for now.

'You shouldn't have to,' she sounded so upset. 'I hate him mom, really hate him.'

'Don't Lexi,' I played peacemaker, giving Shay a shake of my head. 'He's still your dad.'

'How can you stick up for him after what he did to you?' She demanded.

'Love,' I began softly. 'It's all in the past. Just don't do something you'll regret.'

'Me regret?' She spat. 'He'll regret it when he doesn't see me anymore.'

'Is she okay?' Shay asked concerned, he could hear her from where he was standing.

'Shay wants to know if you are alright.' I cut in.

'At least he cares,' she seemed to have run out of steam.

'I care too,' I reminded her.

'I know mom,' she sighed. 'I take it the little shit is going?'

'What do you think?' I answered.

'He behaves like a brat and gets rewarded,' she was tearful now and I didn't know what to say. 'It's not the holiday that's bothering me, I wouldn't want to go without Belle, it's the fact that he never even asked me. Like I don't matter to him, only Jamie and Safi do.'

'You matter to the people who are important,' I assured her.

'I know,' she sounded so down.

'Tell her to come with Belle Saturday, we'll have a takeaway and a movie,' Shay raised his voice.

I relayed the message. 'Aw mom, he is so lovely,' she laughed softly. 'Tell him we will but only if I can choose the film.'

'I will,' I promised. 'Is Belle with you?'

'Yeah, we're just about to cook some food.'

'Okay,' I paused. 'Don't let dad get to you, it's what he wants.'

'I won't,' she replied. 'I'm glad I've got you mom.'

'You'll always have me.' I did love my daughter.

'I know. We'll see you Saturday, I love you.'

'Love you too,' I answered and then she was gone.

'So she's not happy about Thailand?' He looked in the fridge for something to accompany the jackets.

'No. How can he take one without the other?'

'Because he's a bastard,' Sam was never going to be his favourite person.

'I can't believe him,' I felt so angry. 'Him and me are going to have words.'

'Leave it sweet,' he advised. 'She's got us.'

'Even though you're having one of your own?' I was testing him.

He turned from the fridge. 'Lexi is just as important,' he clarified. 'She's yours and I want every part of you.'

'Where did I find you from?' I whispered tearfully.

'We found each other,' he replied that gorgeous smile on his face.

I went to him, taking him in my arms and kissing him. 'Let's go to bed.'

'Aren't you hungry?' He raised his eyes.

'It can wait.' I breathed.

'We made love this morning are you always like this when your pregnant?'

I shook my head. 'I usually go right off sex,' I admitted. 'I don't know what it is with you though.'

'I'm flattered,' he kissed me again.

'You should be. So, do you want to go to bed?' He nodded so I led up the stairs.

'I'm still concerned I'm going to hurt you or the baby though,' he was a worry wart.

'Love,' I kept my voice level. 'If you think I'm not going to have sex for the next six months then you can think again.'

'Fair enough,' he began to undress me and I watched him intently. He kissed my stomach, talking softly. 'Hey little baby, can you shut your eyes and ears to this bit? I would appreciate it.'

I giggled, straddling him, I could feel how much he wanted me and I wanted him equally. As small part of me was waiting for the bubble to burst, I had never felt this happy in my whole life, except when I had my children of course.

His hands caressed my breasts, bigger now as they prepared for the arrival of our baby. His mouth closed over the buds, teasing them and I arched my back, every sensation magnified.

'Beautiful,' he breathed, manoeuvring so he was inside me.

Moving my hips against him I leant backwards so my hands were flat on the bed. He groaned loudly, hands on my hips, setting the pace. I just couldn't get enough of him.

We came together and I got off lying by his side. 'I can't wait to tell everyone about the baby,' he lay his hand gently on my stomach.

'Neither can I,' I admitted, although I knew not everyone would be happy for us.

Ten

My scan came through for late Friday afternoon the following week and we both arranged to finish early from work. It was our late night at the salon but Bev assured me that she and Carling would cope.

I would be relieved when it was done and we could tell people, it was killing me keeping quiet, especially with Lexi and Moira.

We arrived in plenty of time for the appointment, Shay was a bag of nerves but I felt strangely calm. 'Are you okay? I asked him as we waited to be called.

'Yeah,' he took my hand.

'It'll be fine, I've done it all before,' I said breezily.

He looked at me with a touch of annoyance. 'But I haven't.'

'Point taken,' I forgot it was his first time, I had to make it feel special for him.

'Natasha Turner,' I heard my name and I stood excitedly, pulling Shay with me.

We were led into a small room and I needed the loo due to the pint of water I had drunk an hour before to help with the scan.

The nurse had me lie on the bed as Shay took the chair next to it. 'The doctor will be with you shortly,' she said closing the door.

He began to look around the room, foot drumming nervously on the floor, as the door opened once more a young girl came in. 'Hello,' she trilled. 'I'm Doctor Kate Banner.'

'Hello,' I answered unsurely, she could not be a doctor, she didn't look old enough to have left school. 'I'm your sonographer and I'll be talking you through your scan,' she looked at her notes. 'Natasha and?'

'Shay,' he replied. 'How ya doing?'

'Good, thank you,' she pushed her glasses up her nose reminding me so much of Belle. 'You must be the daddy,'

'I am,' he confirmed.

'Right, let's show you your baby,' she placed tissue all around my stomach and I pulled up my top. She picked up the tube of gel. 'This is cold,' she warned.

I braced myself, was it nearly seventeen years since I had gone through this with Jamie, it seemed less.

She spread the gel over my tummy chatting away. 'This is the first one I've done by myself, I've always had someone with me before.'

Shay and I exchanged glances, trust us. 'Don't worry though,' she continued. 'I am fully qualified.'

I smiled politely at her as she got the hand-held transducer and began to move it over my stomach. As she fiddled with the screen I felt Shay take my hand.

'There we are', she said pleased. 'Listen,' she did what she had to do to make the heartbeat audible.

'Is that the baby?' Shay asked amazed.

'Yes, nice and strong,' she replied as he held my hand tighter. 'Now look at the screen.'

We did as the black and white image appeared and there it was, our first glimpse of our baby. 'Wow,' Shay breathed as the doctor went through the checks she had to do.

'Absolutely perfect,' she smiled. 'Everything as it should be.'

I breathed a sigh of relief. 'Okay Natasha I would say you weren't far wrong with your dates, you are twelve weeks pregnant, I would give you a due date of twenty-third of September.'

'Wow,' Shay said again, a giggle escaping his lips. 'I am so happy.'

'Bless,' I turned to him. 'Are you crying?'

'No,' he pulled a face, blushing a little.

'Yes, you are,' I teased.

The doctor went through some other things that we needed to know but I don't think Shay heard a word, his eyes never left the screen.

'Do you want a copy of the picture?' she asked.

'Please?' I replied as she gave me some tissue to wipe the gel from my stomach. 'Can we have two please?'

'They are five pounds each.'

'That's fine, daddy will pay,' I smiled cheekily.

He looked at me indulgently getting his wallet. We left New Cross ten minutes later, Shay guarding the scan picture's as if his life depended on it. Calling into Sainsbury's on Bentley Bridge we picked up something for tea and I lost him, I found him a few moments later in the clothes section. 'What are you up too?' I smiled.

'Look,' he held up a pack of romper suits. 'Shall I?'

'If you want too,' I grinned.

'What size?' he looked a little lost.

'Nought to three months,' I replied taking them from the stand. 'You can never have enough vests and bibs too.'

'I didn't know that, I am going to be such a shite dad,' he looked so crestfallen.

'No you're not, you are going to be a fantastic father,' I kissed him, not caring who was about. 'I love you.'

He held me with his intense stare. 'I love you too. Shall we invite mam and Alan Sunday for lunch and break the news to them?'

'Good idea, I'll do lamb.'

'Lamb?' he raised an eyebrow. 'I have vests and bibs to buy.'

'Tightwad,' I teased.

'Correct,' he grinned.

'Do you want to call in the salon on the way home and show Bev the scan?' I suggested when we got to the checkout.

'Do you want to?' he asked as we waited patiently to be served.

'I'm bursting to show someone,' I replied.

He caught me around the waist, a big grin on his face. 'Me too,' he admitted.

'Shall we then?' my hand fell to my stomach, I was definitely getting a little bump.

'Yeah,' the checkout girl began to scan our grocery. Shay had stuck a pack of vests and a pack of bibs in the trolley as well as the romper suits as well as a rattle shaped like a doughnut.

We paid for our purchases and headed for the salon. By a stroke of luck our Dale was also there, sweeping hair up from the floor. 'Hi,' I called as we went through the door.

'Big sis,' he cried on seeing me. 'And me best mate.'

'I'm impressed, I didn't realise you knew what a brush was,' I teased.

'I'm helping the missus out,' he beamed. 'She's just in the loo.'

'Where's Carling?' I sat on the settee.

'Gone, she going out tonight so Bev let her finish early,' he replied. 'How did the scan go?'

Shay gave him a huge grin, taking the picture carefully from his coat pocket. 'Look.'

Dale took it from him, calling Bev and she came tottering in. 'What have you got there?'

'The scan picture,' he showed her.

'Oh my God, let me see,' she stood next to him. 'It's wonderful, what's that?'

I peered at the photo. 'What's what?'

'It looks like there is an aura or something around the baby.'

I looked closer. 'That *is* the baby,' I shook my head.

'Oh, I can never tell. So what due date have they given you?'

'They said the twenty-third of September,' Shay had that thrilled look about him.

'What about the sex?' Dale was still trying to work out the scan.

'The doctor said its fine, we've just got to be careful,' I replied. 'I think Shay's worrying that he's going to poke the baby's eye out with his Pina Colada.'

Dale blanched. 'I meant the sex of the baby.'

'Oh,' I blushed. 'We can find out at the twenty week scan.'

'You could always try reverse cowgirl if you're worried about hurting Tash in the missionary position,' Bev said to Shay helpfully.

'What's that?' Sometimes I was so naïve.

'Well Shay would have to lie on his back.'

'My sister!' Dale cried covering his ears with his hands and humming loudly.

'Sorry,' she giggled and I joined in as Shay looked thoughtful.

'Any way we'll leave you to it, we just wanted to show you the scan,' I beamed. 'And by Tuesday the whole world can know.'

'When are you telling everyone?' Dale had stopped humming.

'Moira and Lexi Sunday and I'll go and see Jamie Monday,' I answered.

'She won't let me go with her to tell Jamie,' Shay pulled a face.

'Tash knows how to handle it,' he said confidently.

Shay looked doubtful and I felt doubtful but neither of us wanted to spoil the occasion.

'Right, see you tomorrow,' Bev was ready to go home.

'You will,' I replied and we too went straight home, Milly bowling us over in her excitement.

'Careful,' Shay reached out to steady me.

'It's okay,' I'm nearly always falling over her, I'm used to it,' I patted her head.

'You have to be cautious now,' he gave me a concerned look.

'Stop worrying, I'm not made of china.'

'I know,' he smiled going into the living room and putting the scan picture pride of place on the fireplace. 'I still can't believe I'm going to be a dad.'

'You'll believe it when it's screaming its head off at three in the morning,' I said darkly.

He turned to look at me, a cheeky grin on his face. 'It'll make a change from you screaming your head off when I'm giving you a good going over.'

'Hey,' I flushed laughing.

His smile increased. 'I'm not complaining, I like making you howl.'

I blushed harder, sorting out supper for us and after we sat snuggling watching old episodes of Friends.

By ten-thirty I was shattered but still excited by what was to come. 'Come on daddy time for bed,' I declared.

He looked at me delighted. 'Daddy, I adore that, it makes feel ten feet tall.'

I let Millie back in, ensuring the back door was secure. 'Get up those stairs now,' I playfully smacked his bum.

He scooted up the stairs, 'Natasha Turner you are carrying child, behave yourself.'

I held out my empty hands. 'I'm not literally carrying a child yet, I've still got a free hand to smack your arse.'

'Turner is Sam's name, isn't it?' He looked thoughtful for a moment.

'Yeah, why? I went in the bathroom to brush my teeth.

'Nothing,' he came up behind me, hands clasped around my waist. 'How tired are you?'

'Just a little sleepy, why?' I brushed my teeth vigorously.

He nibbled my ear. 'Shall I show you what a reverse cowgirl is?'

I turned, toothbrush poised at my mouth. 'How do you know what it is? Have you ever done it?'

He became evasive. 'Do you want me to show you or not?'

'Is it fun?' I was terrible, being jealous of his past sexual conquests, after all how many different positions were there, you were always going to do the same.

'Everything we do is fun,' he waited until I had rinsed my mouth before taking my hand and leading me to the bedroom.

Quickly he shed his clothes and lay on the bed. 'Come here,' he whispered. 'Take your clothes off.' I turned away blushing. 'Now, do a striptease for me,' he urged in his clit throbbing accent.

'No,' I felt too self-conscious. It was alright for him lying on the bed starkers with muscles in all the right places.

'Do it for me,' he was persuasive.

Shaking my head, I pulled my jumper over my head and hurriedly pulled off my trousers. 'Slower,' he said.

'I am not doing a strip, taking off my bra and pants I joined him on the bed.

'Spoilsport,' he teased as we kissed and cuddled for a while. 'Sit on me,' he instructed. 'But face away from me.'

'What?'

'Come on,' he giggled. 'Just straddle me.'

I looked at him doubtfully, it felt less like making love then having a test, I just hoped I passed. I did as he said and oh my! What a wonderful position for a woman.

My only gripe was that it wasn't very intimate, but the penetration – wow! Anyway, Shay was right, he did make me howl.

When we were done we lay side by side catching our breath. 'So?' He kissed my stomach. 'Did you enjoy it.?'

'Yes,' my face was flushed.

'Good,' again he kissed my tummy. 'Night, night little baby, sleep tight.'

'Night daddy,' I answered for the baby. He laughed softly and we fell asleep in each other's arms.

Eleven

We invited Moira, Alan, Lexi and Belle for lunch on Sunday, so we could tell them the good news. We had brought lamb, which I did with mint gravy, new potatoes, veg with tiramisu for afters.

Shay seemed like he was going to burst with happiness, fussing around me and laying the table, ready for us to eat.

Moira and Alan arrived at one, Lexi and Belle a couple of minutes behind them.

'Lamb?' Lexi sniffed the air. 'Have you won the lottery?'

'Kind of,' I smiled mysteriously, giving them all a glass of wine and getting myself an orange juice.

She looked at me puzzled and I herded them into the living room where Shay was waiting with Millie. Moira hugged her son as Alan shook his hand and the girls fussed Millie.

'Lexi wants to know if we've won the lottery doing lamb for lunch,' I informed him.

He smiled taking my hand. 'Tash and I have something to tell you.'

'You're getting married?' Lexi asked hopefully.

'No,' I pulled a face, then straightened it as Shay looked at me hurt, I motioned that he should carry on.

He took a deep breath, looking at me lovingly. 'Tash and I are going to have a baby.'

'Shay Albie Flynn, are you telling me the truth?' His mom cried.

'He is.' I confirmed. 'I'm twelve weeks pregnant.'

'Oh my sweet baby Jesus,' she stood unsteadily, enveloping us both in a hug, tears falling down her face. 'Oh my.'

She held me so close, I felt like I was suffocating. Taking a step back I turned my attention to Lexi. 'Sweetheart?'

She got up hugging me tightly. 'It's great mom,' she whispered.

'Are you sure?' I needed her to be happy for us.

'Positive,' she turned to hug Shay. 'I'm going to be a big sister again.'

'You are,' I stroked her hair gently. 'But you will always be my baby.'

'I know,' I smiled. 'So that's why we're having lamb.'

'It is a celebration,' I smiled back.

'Have you thought of any names?' Belle too looked happy for us.

'Accident,' I joked lamely.

'Alan laughed. 'When are you due?'

'The twenty-third of September,' I answered.

'But that's only two weeks after the wedding,' Moira chaffed. 'We should change the date.'

'Its fine,' I assured her. 'I went nearly two weeks over with Lexi and Jamie.'

'We know,' Lexi began to ape. 'You're a pair of ungrateful brats. Twelve hours I was in labour with you Lexi, forty-eight with Jamie.

'Oi,' I warned, that was what I always said to them when I was angry.

She laughed hugging me again. 'We were worth it though, weren't we?'

'You were,' I kissed the top of her head.

'Oh, nearly forgot,' Shay picked up the scan picture from the fireplace and passed it to his mom.

She took it from him with a gasp of delight as Lexi and Belle peered over her shoulder.

'I can never work out what goes where,' Belle admitted as Shay pointed out where everything was.

'It's so lovely,' Moira was beginning to fill up again.

'Mam?' Shay put his arm around her.

'I'm just so pleased for the pair of you and pleased for myself. I'm going to be a gran.'

'You are,' I smiled, my own mother wouldn't be over the moon at the news and I was glad Moira was like she was.

'Come on,' Lexi put her arm through hers. 'Let's help mom cook lunch.'

She paused. 'You know sweetheart I'm fond of you too. You are like a granddaughter to me.'

'Oh,' Lexi hugged her tightly. 'Thank you, even my real nan's never think that.'

'Come on then,' Moira beamed.

'I can cook lunch,' I always cooked lunch.

'Tash, let us spoil you,' Belle pushed her glasses up her nose.

I pulled a face as Shay laughed, he was right, I was a control freak. 'Come on expectant mother, put your feet up.'

'I can't do nothing for the next six months,' I hissed.

'Oh, I can find you plenty to do,' his voice was loaded with suggestion.

'That's what got me into this mess in the first place,' I smiled.

He laughed, holding me close. 'Mom is going to drive you mad.'

'I don't mind it's nice. My own mom won't be anything like it, at least Moira is pleased.' I took his hand.

'She is more than pleased,' he confirmed. 'Are you sure you don't want me to come with you to tell Jamie?'

A cloud passed over my face. 'No, I need to do it myself.'

'Sure?' I could tell he was concerned.

'Positive,' I kissed him again. 'Let's go and join the others.'

He nodded and we went into the kitchen and spent a wonderful few hours talking about the baby and the future, it was so good. I had to enjoy it because telling Jamie was going to take the shine off everything.

Monday seemed a long time coming and I timed it so I arrived at Sam's around five. I really wasn't looking forward to this, after telling the others I knew that it wasn't going to be the same.

'Tash,' Sam greeted me at the door. 'Meera's home.'

What did he think? That I didn't want to see him if his wife was at home? 'That's okay,' I replied. 'I've something to tell Jamie but I need to tell you too.'

'You're not marrying Paddy are you' his smile never quite reached his eyes.

'Grow up Sam,' I growled going inside. They were all in the lounge watching and old episode of the Simpsons. I felt so nervous as I sat down.

'Are you okay Tash?' Meera looked at me expectantly.

I nodded, my eyes going to my son. 'I just need to tell Jamie something.'

'Do you need some privacy?' She asked.

'No, its fine,' I needed her there, she would back me up if no one else would. 'It's something you all need to know about.'

'That sounds intriguing,' Sam was staring at me.

'Jamie,' I began unsurely. 'You have got to know how much I love you and that is never going to change. From the moment I knew I was carrying you I have loved you with all my heart.'

He scowled, not liking me talking to him like that.

I took a deep breath. 'Shay and I are going to have a baby.'

Silence greeted my announcement, then Meera was on her feet and hugging me. 'Oh Tash, that's wonderful news.'

'Thank you,' I returned the hug gratefully.

'Is it going to be my brother or sister like Jamie and Lexi?' Safi gave me a cuddle too, bless her.

'Absolutely not,' Sam answered for me, his tone harsh.

'I shot him a look, he'd made Safi tearful. 'More like a cousin,' I kissed her cheek.

'Did you plan it?' Sam had gone a little green around the gills.

'No,' I admitted, blushing a little.

'He's trapped you,' he stood agitated. 'The conniving little shit.'

'Sam, can't you just say congratulations?' Her tone was weary.

I looked at her embarrassed, poor Meera, she deserved so much better than him. I turned to my son. 'Jamie?' I don't know why I was holding my breath but I was.

'It's disgusting,' he spat. 'You're too old to have a baby. You'll never get rid of him now.'

'I don't want to get rid of him,' my eyes filled with tears, why couldn't he even pretend to be happy for me?

'Does Lexi know?' Sam asked quietly.

'Yes and at least she's pleased for us,' I tried not to sound bitter. 'Please Jamie, don't cause ructions over this. I love you, I will always love you. You will always be my little baby.'

'But I won't will I?' He pointed to my stomach. 'That thing will be.'

'That's enough Jamie,' Meera snapped. 'If you can't say anything nice to your mom then keep your bloody mouth shut.'

I was shocked, I had never heard her speak to either of my children in that tone before.

'Well he's right,' Sam chimed in. 'How can you be pregnant by him, you've only know each other for five minutes. He'll be a cloud of dust before the baby's first birthday.'

I stood feeling tearful. 'I'm going, I just wanted to tell you all.'

'You don't have to go Tash,' Meera cut in.

'I do,' I just wanted to get back to Shay.

'Don't upset yourself,' she soothed.

I battled to stop the tears falling as I turned to my son. 'I just wanted you to be happy for me, for us. Having Shay doesn't mean that I don't love you anymore. Having this baby isn't going to change the way I feel about you.'

He scowled back at me.

I shook my head, picking up my handbag and Meera followed me to the front door, 'Don't let them upset you.'

'I'm sorry Meera, Sam should have more respect for you than what he shows you,' I could have killed him.

She shrugged indifferently. 'You of all people should know what Sam like.'

'I do,' I admitted, as an afterthought I took the scan picture from my handbag. 'It's only you that will be interested.'

She took it from me. 'Oh, Tash it's fantastic. Are you really pleased?'

'I am, it was a shock at first but now,' I paused. 'Shay's so happy, I wish my son was too.'

'He'll come around,' she rubbed my arm, absently. 'I've gotten really fond of you Tash, and I'm very happy for you both.'

'Thank you,' I was quiet for a moment. 'You know when I found out that you were pregnant and Sam was going to marry you, I hated you.' I confided in her.

'I don't blame you, I would have done too,' she leant up the doorframe.

'Lexi was so excited though about the baby, so excited to be a big sister again.' a tear trailed down my cheek and I brushed it away absently. 'When I brought her and Jamie to the hospital the day you had Safi, I wasn't even going to come in.'

'But you did and I felt a mixture of emotions. I was euphoric at having Safi but nervous that you were there. If I'd have been you I would have hated me too.'

'You looked so young and so unsure my heart melted a little.'

'You showed me how to bathe her,' she smiled softly at the memory.

'I love Safi,' I smiled back. 'She's a beautiful little girl.'

'She is,' she agreed.

'Don't let Sam get away with his games,' I didn't want to see her hurt.

'We all know what games he wants to play,' she had grown sad.

'Just take care of you and Safi and I'll see you soon.' I hugged her briefly.

'I've booked the table for Lexi's birthday,' she told me. 'The Chase Gate, Saturday thirty-first of March, is that okay?'

'Yes, thank you,' Lexi's birthday was the second of April, I really didn't want her on the first of April and I had crossed my legs so I gave birth to her at twelve ten in the morning luckily. Sam had cried buckets, our marriage had seemed solid then.

'I've spoken to Lexi today, I don't think she's bothered about celebrating her birthday.'

'She's a little upset about Thailand,' I admitted.

'I told Sam it wasn't right to ask Jamie but not her,' she coloured a little.

'It's not your fault,' I said kindly. 'And thank you for organising the table.'

'And you're bringing Shay?' She tilted it head. 'Don't let those shits stop you.'

'I won't,' I pulled a face. 'Shay's with me now whether Jamie likes it or not. I spent years giving in to Dale, I don't want to make the same mistake again.'

'Good for you, the tables booked for six-thirty.'

'I'll make sure we are all there,' I dug the car keys out of my handbag. 'See you hun.'

'Night Tash and give my love and congrats to Shay, he seems a really nice man and I'm thrilled for you both.'

'Thank you, take care.' I drove home wishing Jamie would be better and realising that Shay was right about Sam's intentions. Why would Sam think for one minute that I'd want him back and to make it so obvious in front on his wife too?

I was crying again, all my bloody hormones but I ached for my son to be home with me, to be pleased about Shay and the baby but they were empty wishes.

I pulled up just as Shay arrived home, he had gone to the gym with Dale. 'How did it go?' He asked, then he saw my face.

I shrugged going into the house and fussing Millie as he followed me inside. 'Sweet?' He asked softly.

'What do you think?' I got myself a glass of water wishing it was wine.

'Oh dahling,' he took me in arms. 'I'll go and talk to him.'

'No, don't,' I hadn't the stomach for any more arguments.

'He shouldn't keep doing this to you,' he sounded irritated. 'What did he say?'

'You don't want to know,' I sat at the kitchen table.

'Oh, I do,' he sat next to me. 'I want to know exactly what he said.'

'Please love,' I said quietly. 'Can we just forget it and concentrate on the baby?'

He reached out to touch my cheek, saying softly. 'Okay beautiful.'

'We're going out for Lexi's birthday on the thirty-first of March, Meera has arranged it at the Chase Gate,' I said. 'You will come won't you?'

'I wouldn't miss it for the world.' He said grimly.

I gave him a weary look. 'No trouble Shay, its Lexi's birthday.' I warned.

'I know,' he took my hand. 'Did you tell Sam about the baby?'

'Yes, he was there. Safi got all excited wanting to know if it would be her brother or sister like Lexi and Jamie.'

His smile was small. 'What did Sam say?'

I hesitated just long enough for Shay to narrow his eyes. 'He didn't say a lot,' I lied badly.

He grunted not believing me but not pushing it either. 'Let's sort some food out.'

'I'm not really hungry,' telling Jamie had robbed me of my appetite.

'You have to eat.'

'I will later,' I began to cry again and he knelt before me, taking me in his arms.

'Come on sweetheart,' he soothed.

'Why has Jamie got to be like this?' I sniffed. If I was truthful it was what Sam had said was concerning me more. He was helping to make Jamie the way he was, why was he so against Shay? Did he truly believe that I had any feelings left for him after what he had done to me?

'I don't know,' he stroked my hair. 'I wish I could do something to make it better, I feel it's my fault.'

'It's not,' I leant against him.

'If I wasn't with you – '

'He'd still be a shit,' I felt so tired.

His hand went to my stomach, rubbing it gently. 'We'll work it out, I promise.'

I nodded tightly, thinking it would never be sorted.

Twelve

I was still upset when I arrived at work the next day about Jamie but at least now everyone could know, it no longer had to be a secret. Bev was already there when I walked in with Millie, a mug of decaffeinated coffee waiting for me.

'How did it go?' She asked saying good morning to big dog as I hung my coat up.

I shuddered. 'Don't ask,' I sat at the desk, yawning discreetly.

'That bad?' Her voice was caring.

'Oh, Jamie reacted exactly how I expected him to so there was no surprise there. No, it was Sam who shocked me.'

'Sam?' She brought out her compact mirror to check her make-up.

I told her everything he had said and she sat there listening with her mouth agape. 'I know both me and Dale have always had our suspicions that he wanted you back but to do it in full view of Meera.'

'I was so embarrassed.' I admitted.

'Didn't she say anything? I'd have punched his bloody lights out.'

'She didn't say a thing while I was there, whether they had words after, who knows? She seems almost accepting of it.'

Bev thought for a moment. 'Perhaps she thinks its karma. She took Sam from you so she thinks Sam wanting you again is her punishment.'

'She didn't really take Sam from me, she merely distracted him. I threw him out remember?' I pointed out.

'I wonder if you hadn't, where you would be now? She mused.

'In an asylum,' I smiled bitterly. 'He would have driven me mad.'

'Do you have any feelings left for him at all, I'm being nosey,' the smile she gave me was huge.

I didn't answer for a moment, eventually I replied. 'I still think he's a good-looking man but no before you say a word, I do not fancy him.' I paused. 'And up until I met Shay we were getting on really well, I even liked him a little.'

She pulled a face. 'That's the truthful answer,' my look was prim. 'After all I did love him once.'

'He is so jealous of Shay being with you and he is going to get much worse now you're pregnant. Talking of Shay, what did he say about it all?'

I reddened a little. 'I didn't tell him what Sam said I just couldn't face the row it would have caused.

'You should have told him,' she chided. 'It looks a bit suss keeping things from him.'

'I know. Anyway, shut up now, Carlings just pulled up,' I stood taking the empty mugs to the sink in the back room.

'I need to talk to her about your maternity leave, were you going to tell her today?'

'Yes,' I knew Bev wasn't looking forward to not having me in the salon and I felt a little bad about leaving her in the lurch.

'Morning,' Carling breezed into the salon.

'Morning,' I came into the main area. 'Someone looks very chipper.'

She actually beamed at me. 'I have had a wonderful weekend.'

'What did you get up to?' Bev stood stretching her back.

'I went shopping to Merry Hill.'

'You sure know how to party,' I teased.

She ignored me. 'I went into Schuh to look at the boots and I met him.'

'Met who?' Even I was smiling at her excitement.

'Hi name is Aaron and he is gorgeous,' she leant her elbows on the desk, a dreamy expression on her face. 'We spent Sunday and yesterday together.'

'He's not some poor cow's husband, is he?' Bev was sceptical.

'No,' she looked hurt. 'He's my age actually works at the Express and Star in advertising.'

'He's a sale rep,' I smiled, a gob on a stick.

She got out her phone to show us his picture.

'He is a handsome chappie,' I approved, her good mood was catching.

'Lovely,' Bev agreed peering over her shoulder. 'Carling we need to have a chat.'

She was immediately on the defensive. 'I haven't been late for ages and I've got my tunic on.'

'It's not that,' Bev looked at me.

I shifted on the stool. 'Hmm Carling I'm pregnant.'

She looked at me sharply. 'You and Shay are going to have a baby.'

I nodded. 'Yes, so I'll be going on maternity leave and it will be up to you to help Bev.'

'It will mean a slight wage increase.' Bev added.

'You and Shay are going to have a baby?' She repeated.

'Yes,' I pulled a face. 'Why?'

She blushed. 'Nothing, it's lovely.'

I felt a little smug, she had a huge crush on Shay. 'It's a bit of a shock.'

'But a nice shock though,' she had rallied a little.

'Yeah,' I said softly. 'So, you fancy being a proper stylist?'

'Yes,' she beamed.

'I've asked Lexi and Belle to come to the salon Friday night and you can cut their hair, just a nice straight forward trim. 'I'll help you all I can. Practice makes perfect.'

'Thanks Tash,' she smiled.

'I'm relying on you Carling,' Bev warned her. 'Don't let me down.'

'She'll be fine,' I felt like being nice to her, I was tired of people being funny with me.

'Oh, here's baby daddy,' Bev pointed to the window as Shay and Ray parked up the breakdown truck outside.

I smiled as they came into the salon, a big smile on Ray's face. 'Shay's just told me Tash, I had to come and say congratulations.

'Aw thank you,' I beamed as he hugged me.

'Seriously though love, you're a beautiful woman you could have done so much better.' Ray teased.

'I know, I took pity on him,' I smiled at Shay.

'Hey,' he grinned back, winking at me.

'Do you mind what you have?' Ray leant against the reception desk as Carling sat on the settee filing her nails.

'I really don't mind, I have one of each,' I replied amused how Shay's boss was having a good look at Bev.

'I don't mind either, as long as it's healthy,' Shay cut in.

'Are you still up for the bowling Saturday night?' Ray asked.

'I sure am,' I was looking forward to it.

'You're not going to actually bowl now, though are you?' Shay frowned at me

'Of course, I am,' I smiled at him beatifically.

'Tash is a really good bowler,' Carling piped up. 'Do you remember the last time we all went bowling?' She asked me. 'You wiped the floor with the lot of us.'

'That's what Shay's worried about,' I teased.

'No, I'm not,' he frowned deeper.

'You are, you have a competitive streak a mile wide,' I grinned.

'Shut up,' she shook his head. 'I've left the doughnuts in the pickup truck.'

'Aw you've brought us doughnuts?' Bev asked playfully.

'I've brought the expectant mammy a treat,' he dug the keys out of his overall pocket. 'I'll go and get them.'

I followed him outside, leaving Ray to drool over Bev. Shay looked over his shoulder. 'Where are you going?' He asked playfully.

I drew level with him. 'Can't a girl follow her man if she wants too?'

He gave me his beautiful smile, taking my hand. 'Have you seen how Ray's looking at Bev?' He chuckled.

'I have, that's why I've come out of the way,' I replied. 'Isn't he married?'

'Yes, for years to Rita. You'll meet her Saturday night.'

'Shay leant into the truck bringing out a tray of Krispy Kreme doughnuts. 'Oh, baby likes,' I praised taking them from him. 'Thank you hun,'

'You're welcome,' he grabbed me gently, mindful not to knock the doughnuts out of my hand and kissed me deeply. I returned his kiss, we were both lost in the moment. Eventually we came up for air and I remembered we were in the middle of a car park right by the salon. 'Look how red you've gone,' Shay teased.

I flushed more, feeling a little embarrassed. 'I think that's the first time we've ever kissed like that in broad daylight, I'd forgotten where I was for a moment.'

'That's nothing to what I really want to do to you,' he whispered.

My nethers twitched, 'Later Tiger,' I grinned, pupils dilating.

At that a voice cut into our "moment", Bev and Ray were hanging out the door of the salon.

Ray was wolf whistling as Bev shouted. 'Put him down, you don't know where he's been,' which just made me blush more.

'Oh,' I called back. 'I know exactly where he's been.'

Shay gave me a cheeky grin, tapping my bum. 'You sure do dahling.' Holding his hand, we walked back to the salon.

'Oh, shall I put the kettle on?' Carling took the doughnuts from me.

'Please,' I replied as our first customers began to arrive.

'Come on Shay,' Ray said. 'Time, we weren't here or they'll be doing our hair.'

'I could polish your head,' Bev looked at his bald palette with a smile.

'If I wasn't married I'd let you,' he said appreciatively.

She giggled coyly as Shay and I exchanged amused glances. 'See you back at home,' he said. 'And don't drink too much tea.'

'It's decaffeinated,' I protested.

'It's still not good for you,' he wagged his finger.

'Are you and Dale going to the gym?'

He shook his head. 'Not tonight, I'll come straight home,' he fussed Millie.

'Okay, I'll start supper,' I went to my first lady and caped her up. 'See you Saturday Ray.'

'Congratulations again love. Ladies,' he doffed his cap and they left.

'He is going to be murder,' Bev chuckled.

'Who?' Carling asked taking my lady to the basin.

'Shay with Tash being pregnant, he's worrying about you picking up a bowling ball now.'

'I'll soon knock it out of him.' I vowed.

'He can keep buying doughnuts though,' Carling smacked her lips, sugar caked on them.

Thirteen

I concentrated on the job in hand, breathing in sharply as I tried to pull the zip of my jeans up.

'What are you doing?' Shay looked at me sprawled across the bed.

'Trying to fasten my jeans,' I panted with exertion. I think I had to admit defeat, it just wasn't going to happen.

'You'll squash the baby doing that,' he scolded. He went to his wardrobe picking out a red jumper and pulling it over his curls.

'It's alright for you,' I moaned. 'I have nothing to wear.'

'Put a dress on, that nice maxi one,' he fetched clean socks from the drawer.

'I am *not* wearing a dress with bowling shoes.

'You don't have to bowl,' he pointed out.

'Shut up Shay,' I pulled a face. 'I'm not going.' I could feel myself beginning to sulk.

'Why?' He looked gorgeous as usual with the minimum of effort.

'Because I've got nothing to wear,' I groaned. 'I'm not going.'

'You've got to have *something* to wear,' he went to my wardrobe opening the doors.

'Nothing fits,' I really felt like throwing a tantrum. 'If I'm like this at twelve weeks then what am I going to be like at six months?'

'We'll get you new clothes,' he promised.

'That isn't going to help me tonight is it?' I was an ungrateful little madam.

'Hey, I'm trying to help here,' he was put out and I couldn't say I blamed him.

I harrumphed, getting off the bed and getting a lace out of his boots. 'What are you doing?' He asked. 'I'm going to make my jeans fit,' I threaded the lace through the button hole and the first loop of my jeans waistband and then tied it in a bow so there was a gap where the material didn't quite meet.

'Clever,' he said impressed.

'I feel like a bag of shit but it will have to do,' I pulled on a long jumper to hide the waistband.

'You look gorgeous,' he pulled on his boots, the one's I hadn't pinched the laces out of.

I sprayed my hair liberally with hairspray, I'd left it down and straight, hoping my full fringe would knock a couple of years off my age.

'Ready?' He put his wallet in his back pocket.

'Yes,' I picked up my handbag and the car keys. I was the nominated driver for the next few months, what joy.

'It should be a good night,' he was really looking forward to it.

We fussed Millie, giving her a treat before going to the Hollywood Bowl on Bentley Bridge. Everyone was already there and I took a deep breath, I always got a little nervous meeting new people.

'Here they are,' Ray greeted us, a pint of Guinness in his hand. 'Tash, my lovely lady wife, Rita.'

'Hi Tash, congratulations on the baby,' she trilled.

'Thank you,' I stood close to Shay.

'Nick and his girlfriend Rachel. Alison and hubby Carl and Rob and his significant other,' he raised his eyebrows. 'Will.'

'Hi,' I nervously fiddled with the handle of my handbag.

'Oh my God,' Will cried camply making me jump. 'Look at you, you are gorgeous just like Shay, you are going to make such a beautiful baby.'

'Er thank you,' I replied as he stroked my little bump.

'I did hope Shay was gay when he first started at the garage but alas no,' he laughed at the look on my face. 'Only teasing, I wouldn't do that across my lover.'

I smiled unsurely as Rob pulled him away with an apologetic look on his face.

'Come on,' Ray instructed. 'Let's find our lane.' We dutifully changed into the bowling shoes. 'So how are we going to play this?' Shay had got himself a lager and me a water.

'Shall we split into teams?' Nick suggested. 'Garage verses spouses?' He began to press buttons on the screen.

'Okay by me,' Alison replied, she was the receptionist cum bookkeeper, a homely looking woman around sixty.

'Are you sure you're okay to bowl?' Shay whispered and I shot him a look of annoyance.

'I'm picking up a bowling ball not knocking up an extension,' I retorted.

'Fine, bowl then,' he drank his lager as I hoped my jeans would stop up.

We began the game and Carling wasn't wrong, I was bowler extraordinaire, three strikes in a row and it earnt me a high five from Will. Shay on the hand wasn't doing very well at all, his first bowl went into the gutter next to the lane.

I laughed at the look of disgust on his face. 'You might have super sperm but your bowling's shite,' I whispered.

'Shite?' He raised his brow. 'That's fighting talk Natasha Turner.'

'Bring it on,' I leant into him, enjoying the contact.

He moved away picking up his ball and sending it down the alley. 'Oh, what a shame you only knocked down six,' I teased.

'If you weren't plugged I'd put you over my knee and smack your arse.' His voice was low in my ear.

'What's plugged?' I asked touching his fingers gently.

'Pregnant,' he grinned.

'That is a horrible word,' I chided as my turn came again.

Another strike! I was on a roll, I could be modest but what the hell, I had put our team well in front.

'I wish you were on my team,' Nick had a fed-up expression on his face. 'I thought you could bowl Shay?'

'I'm just having a bad day,' he said defensively.

I smirked taking a sip of water, looking around. Bloody hell, there was Fallon, the woman who tried to trick my brother in believing her baby was his. She was with a man but she wasn't bowling she was just sitting there heavily pregnant looking bored. I wondered what lies she had spun him? She would be no different now than when she had tried to fool Dale, the cow.

I didn't even mention seeing her to Shay she just wasn't worth it.

'Another drink?' He asked draining his lager.

'No thanks hun,' I replied. 'I'm just going to the ladies.

'Okay, I'll get me one.'

I left them going to the loo, I peed a lot now, it was always the same. I flushed the chain coming out of the cubicle and washing my hands. I heard the door of the other cubicle and glanced in the mirror, Fallon was at my shoulder.

I turned staring her out at she glared back at me. I shook my head, going to walk away but she looked me up and down and said. 'I heard that stupid Irish fucker had knocked you up.' She gave me a look of pure distaste before heading for the door.

I followed her, the cheeky cow. 'At least it's his, I haven't got to blame it on someone else because the father doesn't want to know.'

'Oh, you think your something else you do, you stuck up cow,' she snapped.

'Me think I'm something else,' I asked incredulously. 'If you weren't pregnant I would knock you into next week.'

'Ditto,' she snarled.

I didn't see Ray come out of the gents and go straight to Shay. 'I think Tash is in a spot of bother by the ladies.'

'The baby?' He said in a panic coming to me and stopping dead when he saw Fallon and I exchanging insults.

'You'll keep,' I promised her.

'Looking forward to it,' she growled.

'You won't be,' I itched to slap her pretty little face.

'Tash, come on,' Shay appeared in the corridor. 'She's really not worth it.'

Fallon gave him a withering look. 'Go on Natasha run along.'

I glared at her but followed Shay back to our lane. 'Feisty little thing your missus.'

'Sure is,' he grinned at me as I bobbed my tongue out at them. 'Tash and Fallon have a little history.'

'A little?' I screwed up my face.

Will came over to us, sitting next to me. 'So, Shay said you're a hairdresser?' He asked fanning himself with a piece of paper.

'Yes, I started off as a Saturday girl when I was at school,' I replied. I liked Will with his bleach blond hair and numerous piercings. In his twenties he wore skinny jeans and a tight white t-shirt without an ounce of fat on him.

'I'll come and see you, see what you can do with this,' he motioned to his hair.

'Why do you fancy a change?' I smiled.

He nodded. 'Rob like's blondes which is why I dyed my hair.'

'I think Rob would love you whatever colour your hair was,' I caught sight of Fallon again giving me the evils from across the room.

'Someone you know?' He whispered leaning into me.

I scowled. 'She tried to trick my brother into believing that baby she's carrying was his.'

'What an absolute bitch!' He cried staring at her.

'As soon as I've had this baby I'm going to knock her into the middle of next week.' I predicted.

'I love you,' Will squeezed my arm. 'No wonder Shay is so taken with you.'

'Taken with me?' A smile sprung to my face.

He nodded sagely. 'Shay doesn't say a lot but he adores you and having his baby has made him ten feet tall.'

I was pleased, it was always nice to hear it from someone else. 'I must admit I thought my baby days were behind me but I am looking forward to it.'

'It'll be lovely,' he looked at me critically. 'You are going to be my new best friend,' he decided. 'You are so beautiful.'

'So are you,' I twinkled.

He laughed delighted as Shay came over to us. 'Are you two bowling or what?' He asked.

'Patience big boy,' Will answered camply fluttering his eyelashes at him.

'Stop tormenting Shay.' Rob joined us passing his beloved a pint of cider.

'Come on then Tash, what's that short for?' He pulled me to my feet.

'Natasha,' I let him pull me up.

'That's much classier, I shall call you Natasha from now on.'

'I'd rather you didn't,' I kept my smile in place. 'It reminds me of my mother.'

'Like that is it?' He seemed to know without my saying anything.

'Yeah, when am I going to be introduced to Sue?' Shay put his arm around me.

'I was going to go in the week, you can come with me if you want,' I reached up to kiss his cheek.

'I will,' he held me tighter.

'Are you lot going to bowl?' Ray come meandering.

'Lead the way,' I declared.

For the next hour we carried on bowling, the spouses wiping the floor with the garage workers.

'I can't believe you won,' Shay moaned pulling on his coat.

'Stop sulking,' I laughed checking I had my car keys. 'Carling told you I was good at bowling.'

'I didn't realise how good,' he pulled a face. 'Have you enjoyed yourself?'

'I have, let's go and see big dog,' I took his hand as we said goodbye to everyone with promises to meet up soon.

'You know why you beat me tonight?' He said as we made our way to the exit.

'Why?' I did feel content.

He cast me a sly glance. 'It's the Irish in you.'

I laughed, smacking his bum. 'You and your Irish sperm.'

He joined in the laughter as we walked past Fallon and her "new" fella. 'Bitch,' she hissed.

'Slag,' I retorted as Shay pulled me away.

'Oi,' he chuckled. 'All this fighting talk is giving my mickey a hard on.'

'What's a mickey?'

He whispered in my ear. 'My prick.'

'Oh,' I laughed loudly as he grabbed me around the waist. 'Shall I put my foot down and get you home?'

'Yeah,' he pulled me along until we reached the car.

As soon as we got home I saw to Millie, then I rushed upstairs telling Shay I needed a wee.

Shay was wondering where I had gotten to when I emerged in the living room in my beautiful pink nightie that was now getting a little tight but still serviceable.

'Are you coming to bed?' I asked switching off the living room light.

He looked at me standing there and licked his lips. I walked over to him, walking in what I hoped was a provocative manner. It was no good, I felt quite self-conscious though and I began to giggle.

Shay looked at me amused. 'What are you laughing at?'

I shook my head. 'I'm trying to look sexy and failing miserably.'

Shay regarded me for a moment. 'You're doing okay from where I'm sitting.'

I sat by him on the sofa in the semi-darkness, the only light coming from the hallway. I stroked his face tenderly. 'I can't believe how lucky I am.'

Shay took my hand. 'It's me who's the lucky one.'

'You are such a smoothie,' I smiled, kissing him deeply, hands running across his chest and I pulled his jumper off.

He nuzzled my neck, gently biting my ear lobe as I dipped my head to his chest.

'Where's Millie?' he asked huskily.

'Still outside,' I breathed.

'Excellent,' he pulled me across him, so I was sitting astride him.

'Okay?' He asked his hand resting lightly on my stomach.

'Very,' I kissed him again, moving against him.

'Do you think we could have too much sex?'

I thought for a moment. 'Naw,' I grinned. 'You can never have enough.'

Fourteen

'Get changed,' I ordered sorting out Millie and tidying up the kitchen.

Shay looked down at the blue shirt and smart jeans he wore with a frown. 'Don't I look presentable enough?' He was a little worried about meeting my mom after everything he had heard.

'You do and there lies the problem,' I screwed up my face. 'Go and put your overalls on.' Mom would take one look at him dressed like that and her eyes would pop out of her head.

'I am not putting my overalls on to meet your mam,' he laughed softly. 'I don't want her thinking you are shacked up with a fella that has no pride in himself.

'Fine, go like that,' I tutted. 'But if she makes a pass at you, it's your own fault.'

'Your mam would not make a pass at her daughter's boyfriend.'

I gave him a knowing look. 'Wouldn't she? You have no idea what mom's like, Dale and I aren't exaggerating you know.'

He gave me his beautiful smile and I could tell he still didn't believe she was as bad as we said she was. Picking up his car keys he said. 'Let's go visiting then.'

I groaned wondering why I was even bothering to tell her about the baby, she did a wonderful job of ignoring Lexi and Jamie so I doubted this one would be treated any differently.

'Come on,' he held out his hand and I took it walking to his truck we waved at our neighbours and then climbed in.

We arrived at moms too quickly, it would have suited me better for us to take a week to get there. She would love Shay on site, she'd always been a sucker for a good looking man. To be fair though she was a stunning woman, especially when she was a younger. I could remember when I was little, before she had left home, watching her as she styled her hair and put her make up on.

I thought then that she was the most beautiful woman in the world and I ached for her to pay me the slightest bit of attention. I didn't get any of course, she would exit in a cloud of perfume leaving me with my baby brother and drunken father. Back in the present I blinked away the tears, the memory was so powerful. Mom was oblivious to me as I craved her to give me just the slightest iota of praise.

'You okay sweet?' Shay asked taking my hand briefly.

I gave him a sad smile. 'Yes, we won't stay long.'

'I don't mind if we do,' he replied wanting everything to be right.

'Maybe you don't but I do,' I directed him to a parking space and he killed the engine then we got out.

He gave me an encouraging smile. 'Let's go and tell the expectant gran the good news.'

'She's not going to like it,' I warned as I knocked the door of the flat. 'She's not like Moira.' Mom answered, the low cut blouse she wore leaving little to the imagination. Tight skirt, black tights and high heels completed the look. Her shoulder length blonde hair was bleached and immaculately straightened. She did it herself, she told me I wasn't a good enough hairdresser to be trusted with her hair.

'Natasha,' she looked at me with a touch of alarm. 'What are you doing here?'

'I've come for a visit,' I plastered the smile on my face.

'You never come to visit,' her look became suspicious.

I came clean. 'I've got something to tell you.'

'I'm off out soon, it's Wednesday, I always go up the club,' she made no move to let me in. 'Paul's picking me up in a bit.'

'I thought his name was Dave?' Well it was at Christmas. I could never really keep up with her love life, not that I took much interest.

'That was the one before,' she tutted.

I shook my head. Well are you going to let us in, we won't stay long?' I enquired.

'Us?' she peered around the door, her eyes lighting up when they rested on Shay as predicted.

'Yes us,' I repeated and she moved aside to let us in. 'Mom, this is Shay. Shay, this is my mom,' I did the introductions.

'How ya doing Mrs Wilkins?' he said politely as we stood in the hallway.

'Oh it's Sue, please,' she trilled, indicating that we should go in the living room. We did so dutifully and winced at the state of it, housework was never one of her strong points. Clothes were strewn on one chair, mugs littering the surfaces and a layer of dust so thick I could have written my name in it. 'So you are Natasha's young man?'

'I am,' again the courteous tone.

'Well,' she sat on the sofa, patting the cushion next to her. 'Sit by me.'

I tried not to smile as I cleared the chair of clothes, dumping then ceremoniously on the floor. Shay did as he was bid, sitting next to her like a good little boy.

'He's a looker Natasha,' she told me approvingly. 'You are just like me, always had an eye for a good looking bloke. You should have visited earlier.'

I blanched at the thought, the last thing I wanted was to be compared to my mother, especially by my mother.

She turned to Shay. 'I went out with an Irishman once, the sex was out of this world.'

'Mom!' I hissed sinking down in my seat, she was so bloody embarrassing. Shay sat there lost for words and I could have cheerfully killed her, I just knew she would be like this.

'You don't mind do you?' she flashed Shay a flirty smile.

I cleared my throat. 'Mom, we have some news. I, I mean we, are going to have a baby.'

She gave me a look of pure disgust. 'I thought you looked like you'd put weight on.'

I felt my heart contract, couldn't she be pleased for me, just once? 'No, I'm nearly fourteen weeks pregnant.'

'You are too old to have a baby Natasha,' she chided.

'We're very happy Sue,' Shay cut in quickly, seeing the hurt on my face.

'And you're too handsome to be tied down with babies, you should be out having fun. I wish I'd never had kids to tie me down, I would have been so much better off.'

'You'd never guess you had kids the way you act,' I retorted and immediately bit my tongue.

She shot me an irritated look. 'Trouble with you Natasha is that you take life much too seriously. Shay would be better off with someone more like me, he'd have more fun,' she fluttered her eyelashes at him and he looked at me with alarm. 'Can I get you a tea or a coffee?' she leant towards him, giving him a liberal view of her cleavage.

I shook my head. 'We're going in a minute,' I answered for him. She never offered me a bloody drink, I always had to make own, once I'd tackled the washing up that is.

'I really can't believe you are having another child,' she looked at me exasperated. 'Didn't you learn anything after having Lexi and Jamie?'

I pulled a face as the door went again and she got up quickly scurrying into the hall. 'I told you what she was like,' I gave Shay a shrug off my shoulders.

He let out a long breath. 'She's certainly something else.'

'Quite,' I replied as she reappeared with a shifty looking bloke who didn't look much older than me.

'Paul this is my daughter Natasha and her boyfriend Shay,' she introduced us indifferently.

'Hey Paul,' Shay had his friendly voice on.

'Hello,' I was a little more guarded. I'd had some spectacular run in's with mom's various boyfriends over the years.

'Hi,' he replied full of cockiness, just her type. 'I can see you're the image of your mom, dazzling.' He gave me the once over, sitting down as if he owned the place.

'Do you want to see the scan photo before we go?' I wouldn't hold my breath.

'No, you're alright, they never look like anything to me,' she replied and I tried to quash the hurt.

'Scan photo? Paul pricked his ears up.

'Yes, my stupid daughter has only gone and got herself pregnant again even though she's much too old,' she screwed her face up.

'Thirty-two isn't that old,' he replied amicably.

My head swivelled in his direction. 'I'm forty-two, not thirty-two,' I corrected him.

Paul in turn, looked at my mom. 'You told me you were fifty-two and you had your daughter when you were twenty.'

'Fifty-two!' I guffawed loudly. 'She wishes she was fifty-two, she pushing sixty-three.'

'Natasha!' she cried and I felt a certain sense of pleasure.

'How old are you?' I asked Paul as Shay sat there entertained.

'Forty-five,' he mumbled looking a little green around the gills.

'Oh,' I drew out the word. 'Well we'd better make tracks, we've got to go and see dad.'

Shay jumped up, following me to the front door. 'Nice to meet you Sue,' he called over his shoulder. 'You too Paul.'

'Yeah, see you soon,' I tittered, glad to be out of there.

As soon as we got into the truck I began to giggle. 'Fifty two! Who's she trying to kid?'

'She looks good for her age though sweet to be fair,' he played the diplomat.

'Don't tell me you fancy her?' I teased.

'No,' he protested. 'I'm just stating fact. You and Lexi are both like her.'

'And I thought you loved me,' I pouted. 'Fancy saying that I'm like my mother.'

'I do love you,' he started the engine. 'It was a compliment, of sorts.'

'Well brace yourself again because you are about to meet my dad. Just don't have a drink if he offers you one because you won't come out of there sober and you'll be lighter in the pocket,' I cautioned.

'I'll be good,' he followed my directions to dad's flat.

'Jaysus it stinks in here,' he gasped as we walked up the stairs to the lift.

'It's not the best place in the world to live,' I admitted banging the letter box.

'I thought you had a key?' he looked around the dimly lit corridor.

'I've left my bag at home,' I banged again, then peered through the letterbox. 'It doesn't look like he's in, the place is in darkness. He's probably at the pub.' He never used to go to the pub on a night as far as I knew, all his drinking was usually done in the daytime.

'Which pub, we'll go and find him,' he offered.

'I'm not trawling around pubs trying to find him, it's not as if he will be interested anyway. We'll call another time.'

'Let's head for home then,' he took my hand and we walked back to the truck.

As he drown us back I thought about my mom, what did I ever do to deserve the parents Dale and I were lumbered with? At least the baby would have Moira, she was going to be a loving gran.

'I can't believe how uninterested your mam is,' he shook his head.

'I didn't expect anything else,' I admitted leaning my arm over the back of his seat and playing with his curls.

'You deserve better,' he said forcibly.

'I have better. I have you and my kids, well perhaps not Jamie now. Moira and Alan, Dale and Bev, even big dog. I'm happy with my life,' I moved my hand to his leg, rubbing it gently.

He glanced at me, a huge smile on his face. 'That's sweet,' he lay his hand on mine until he had to change gears.

I moved it a little higher. 'Stop it,' he gasped. 'I'll crash the fecking truck.'

'Stop what?' I asked innocently, my hand now on his crotch and rubbing gently.

He looked at me again, before quickly turning his attention back to the road. 'I'm to doing anything at all,' I began to undo his jeans, feeling reckless.

Without a word he turned the truck abruptly into the small car park opposite The Mitre Pub. Coming to a halt up the far corner he killed the engine. 'You want to play?' he asked softly.

I giggled, slipping my hand inside his jeans. 'Yes,' I whispered.

Undoing his seatbelt, he leant towards me, unclicking my own. The only illumination came from the streetlight on the roadside, the pub having shut down some months previously.

I unzipped him slowly, holding back my hair as I dipped my head down, trailing my tongue along his length and I could feel him trembling.

'Shit Tash,' he lightly rested his hand on my back as he leant against the seat, eyes closed in bliss.

I smiled inside, moving a little so I could take him in my mouth, I was getting quite the fellatio expert, they would be calling me Deep Throat soon.

Shay groaned in appreciation as I took him deeper. Teasingly I stopped, moving up to his lips and kissing him, my hand now keeping up the friction, making him groan more. 'I love you dahling,' he whispered, kissing me again.

'You'd better,' I smiled heading back down, this was *fun*, it was *risky*. My tongue rolled over his tip as he flexed his hips, groaning again.

Suddenly there was a knock on the driver's window, startling us both. Shay looked out noticing the hi-vis jacket. 'Shit Tash, it's the police. Stay where you are.'

My heart began to palpitate, the first time I threw caution to the window we get copped by the police, typical. Shay leant forward so he was hiding me from view as he undid his window.

'Everything okay sir?' the policeman asked.

'Fine thank you, I just pulled over for a minute.'

I recognised his voice, I had done his wife's hair for years, and they knew Meera. Ignoring Shay's hand pushing me down I sat up. 'Hi Sunil,' I smiled. 'Sorry I asked Shay to pull over, I felt sick and I've been sitting with my head between my knees to try and stop it.'

He peered through the window. 'Hi Tash, I thought that was if you felt faint?' he frowned.

'Really? No wonder it hasn't worked,' I thought fast, blushing furiously.

'The missus said you were with pup. How are you?'

'Little bit of sickness but apart from that fine,' I smiled sweetly.

'Well you take care,' he took off his helmet off, giving us a nod of his head.

'You too Sunil,' I beamed, waiting until the patrol car had disappeared from view before bursting into a fit of the giggles.

Shay looked at me laughing also. 'That was fecking close.'

'Oh my God! Do you think he knew what we were doing?' In the semi-darkness I was still blushing.

'Probably,' he touched my face tenderly.

'We'd better go home,' I bit my bottom lip nervously. 'They might come back.'

'Let's get out of here then,' he zipped himself up still grinning.

As he drove us home I gently rubbed his leg, I couldn't really believe how randy I was with this pregnancy, I was like some kind of rampant nympho. I followed Shay up the path and as he unlocked the front door my hand went to his groin, grabbing it gently.

Spilling into the hallway, we began to kiss again as Millie came out of the living room to greet us. We danced around a little, the kisses becoming more urgent, hands all over each other. Millie, thinking it was a game, tried to join in, barking loudly and jumping up us, I groaned pulling away from him.

'I'll just let her out,' calling her to me I opened the back door and she went sprinting up the garden. Coming back I closed the door to the living room, finding Shay in the kitchen, half sitting, half leaning on the kitchen table.

Smiling I went to him, undoing his jeans and kneeling in front of him, carrying on where I had left off. He moaned loudly, fingers raking my hair and then he pulled me to my feet, hands fumbling under my skirt, taking down my tights and knickers.

With a grunt he lifted me up so he was taking all my weight as he thrust into me, it was a good job the blinds were closed. I gasped loudly as he movements became more urgent, then we collapsed on the kitchen floor laughing loudly. 'Wow,' I rained kisses on his face. 'That was.'

'Fabulous, wonderful, fantastic?' he suggested helpfully.

'All of them,' I agreed.

'You howl more thank Millie does,' he teased.

'I hope you don't do that to big dog,' I giggled.

He grinned stroking my hair. 'Does it get any better than this?' he asked.

Raising myself on one elbow I stared into his gorgeous face. 'I don't think it does,' I sighed contentedly. 'Mug of Ovaltine?'

'Perfect and I'll see to big dog.'

Fifteen

I sang "Happy Birthday" slightly off-key when Lexi arrived with Belle just after five thirty. She had taken her present the week before so she could open it in the morning,

'Aw thanks mom,' she beamed as I kissed her cheek. 'And thank you for my presents.'

'Did they fit okay?' I gave Belle a hug.

She undid her coat showing off her new skinny jeans and cold shoulder top we had brought her.

'You look gorgeous,' I complimented her.

'Do we really have to go?' She pulled a face.

'Yes,' I'd had this conversation with her earlier on in the day.

'But it's my birthday, I should be able to celebrate it how I want,' she groaned.

'It was nice for Meera to arrange it,' I checked my bag making sure I had everything.

'Yeah lovely,' she muttered and I shot her a look as Shay joined us in the kitchen.

Lexi, let out a low whistle. 'Looking gorgeous Mr Flynn.'

Shay grinned. 'Happy birthday dahling, are you having a good time?'

'It would be better if it was just the four of us going out,' she pulled a face. 'You look very nice though.'

Shay preened a little. 'It doesn't hurt to make an effort,' he was dressed in black skinny jeans and a cobalt blue jumper. He'd even got me to do his hair and his stubble was carefully trimmed. He wanted to look better than Sam, I knew that without him saying.

'Shall we?' I asked, I was driving and it was the first time I had driven Shay's truck, I much preferred my Clio.

We arrived at the pub in plenty of time, Lexi and Belle looking like they wanted to be anywhere else.

Shay had treated me to a new outfit when we had brought Lexi's presents. A long jumper dress in bottle green, black tights and knee-high boots, and for once I felt dressed up.

'You look lovely Tash,' Belle walked with me. 'Really blooming.'

I linked my arm in hers as Shay and Lexi walked in front. 'I feel blooming,' I admitted, everything at the moment was going nicely, thank you.

Sam, Meera and Safi were waiting for us in the bar area and I hoped that tonight would go without a hitch.

'Hi,' Meera greeted us with hugs and kisses, Safi wanting to rest her head on my stomach and talk to the baby. Shay and Sam shook hands politely as Lexi accepted her presents with a thank you.

'Where's Jamie?' I asked taking my mineral water from Shay.

Sam looked a little sheepish. 'He's not coming.'

'It's okay mom,' Lexi pre-empted my reaction.

'It's his sister's birthday,' I scowled.

Sam shrugged annoyingly as Bev and Dale arrived. 'Hey birthday girl,' Dale gave her a present with a kiss on her cheek.

'Thanks Uncle Dale, Aunty Bev,' she beamed.

'What are you drinking?' Sam cut in between me and Shay.

'Lager and a red wine Sam,' Dale replied going up to the bar with him.

'We got a taxi,' Bev explained.

'I wish I could have a drink,' I moaned.

'You're having something better,' Meera smiled.

'True,' I smiled casting a glance at Shay, he did look tasty tonight. He in turn was watching Dale and Sam up the bar, his trademark unreadable expression on his face.

'You okay?' I asked softly.

He turned, his serious expression replaced by a smile. 'I am.'

'Good,' I took his hand as Sam and Dale came back to where we were waiting.

'So, I said to him,' Sam was telling my brother a tall story by the sound of it. 'I wouldn't, would you?'

Dale laughed politely as Sam freewheeled his arms about, catching me in the stomach. I winced, taking a step backwards.

Shay gave him a killer look. 'Careful,' he snapped.

'Sorry ay I paddy.'

I grasped Shay's hand. 'Are you okay?' He asked.

'Yes, leave it,' I said quietly.

He glared at Sam once more. 'Sorry Tash,' Sam put a hand on my arm. 'I didn't realise you were behind me.'

'I'm okay,' I moved away from him.

'Mrs Turner,' the waitress came over to us and both Meera and I answered "Yes."

'Sorry,' I mumbled, smiling at Meera, my face flushing a little.

'Your table is ready.' The waitress led the way. We sat down, me next to Shay, as the waitress gave us the menus.

Shay was sitting there with a thoughtful expression on his face. 'Penny for them?' I asked.

'Trying to work out how to keep my temper in with your man there,' he inclined his head in my ex's direction.

'He's not worth it,' I prayed he would keep the peace. 'What are you having?'

'Have what you want, I'm paying,' Sam cut in laying his wallet on the table.

'No, we'll go halves,' I said firmly.

'Rubbish,' he gave me a brilliant smile. 'I can get my daughter's birthday meal.'

I pulled a face at Bev who was sitting opposite me and she gave me an "ignore him" look.

'Dale,' he called. 'Guess what we're having for the games room.'

'What?' Dale asked politely.

'A genuine Space Invader game, can you remember them?'

'Vaguely,' he replied.

'You do, that holiday you came on with us to Borth, we couldn't get you off it,' he recalled. 'Jeez you had some holidays with us, didn't you?'

Dale took a long drink of his lager, not answering.

'Right, has everyone got a drink?' He got to his feet. 'Before we order I just want to say a few words.'

'Dad, sit down,' Lexi heckled.

He ignored her. 'Twenty years ago, today Tash gave me the precious gift of our daughter, Lexi Mae. Thank you so much Tash,' he raised his glass in my direction. 'We are so proud of everything she has achieved, she is a fine young woman.'

Shay put his arm across the back of my chair and leant into me. 'Pity he isn't proud enough of her to take her to Thailand with them,' he whispered and I had to agree.

'So happy birthday to our precious daughter, Tash we do make beautiful children,' he raised his glass.

I looked at Shay uncomfortably, seeing the annoyance on his face but fair play he stood also, raising his own glass. 'Happy birthday Lexi Mae.'

'Thanks uncle Shay,' she teased as we all toasted her, they did get on well.

We ordered our food, the conversation turning to everyday things as Shay kept us entertained.

'Mom can I have a copy of the scan photo?' Lexi asked. 'I want to show my friends at Uni.'

'Of course, you can,' I replied glad that she wanted one.

'I can't believe how big you are for fourteen weeks.' she smiled.

'She is having one ginormous baby,' Bev said.

'I think I am,' I rubbed my stomach, still quite unable to believe that Shay and I were going to be parents.

'It's good Irish sperm,' Shay smiled charmingly at her. 'It reaches the parts other sperm cannot reach.'

'Er Safi,' I said pointedly, the little mite was watching Shay fascinated.

'Sorry,' he held his hand to his mouth. 'I am going to be a crap dad, the baby's first word will probably be feck.'

'I don't think that's true for one minute,' Meera gave him a dazzling smile.

'It takes more than good sperm to be a father,' Sam's tone was curt.

Shay narrowed his eyes so I tried to defuse the situation. 'So,' I looked at Meera. 'Will you have anymore?'

She pulled a face. 'I'd love another one.'

'We've gone through this,' Sam snapped. 'What's the point of bringing more children into the world?' He downed his drink.

Meera looked down at her glass and I thought I could see tears in her eyes, Sam could be such an arse.

'I can't wait for the baby to be born,' I chatted away. 'I'm really hoping it has Shay's hair.

'Shay has fab hair,' Bev agreed.

'Don't I have fab hair?' Dale asked her.

'You have lovely hair Uncle Dale,' Lexi grinned. 'Just not as nice as Shay's.'

Shay flicked out his curls. 'Why thank you.'

'A good cut would do it the world of good.' Sam rubbed a hand over his own short style.

'A qualified hairdresser now are you dad?' Lexi asked bluntly. 'Shay looks pretty cool.'

I bit my lip, as Shay moved closer to me.

'So, have you told Sue and Paul the *good news*?' Sam wanted to know.

'Mom knows, dad wasn't in,' I replied.

'Do you remember when you told Sue that you were having Lexi? She nearly cried at the thought of being a Nan,' he signalled to the waitress to buy more drinks. 'She made a pass at me.'

'Sam!' Meera cried embarrassed.

He shrugged it off. 'Tash knows what her mom's like, she doesn't take any notice.'

'Maybe not, but I do,' Lexi tersely. Her relationship with her dad had really hit rock bottom.

Luckily the food arrived and conversation ceased as we tucked in. 'Try this,' Shay held out a piece of steak and ale pie on his fork and I took it from him.

'That is really nice, I should have had it,' I looked down at my lasagne and chips.

'You can have half of it, if you want?' He offered.

'No, you eat it,' I pushed a curl away from his forehead, I did love him.

'You two are so sweet together,' Meera sounded envious.

'We are, aren't we?' Shay grinned.

'It's really lovely,' she looked at Sam, who did not look impressed at all.

'Shay is going to show me how to dance the Irish jig,' Lexi informed us.

I turned to him, a smile on my face. 'The Irish jig?'

He nodded, that serious expression on his face. 'I could give Michael Flatley a run for his money.'

'This I've got to see,' Bev stated.

'Me too,' Meera giggled, Shay was quite a hit with the ladies.

'No, it's true,' he lay down his knife and fork. 'The place I grew up in Cork was quite rough, so my mam decided I should go Irish dancing lessons to keep me off the streets.'

'Oh my God,' I laughed.

'I'm pretty good,' he kissed me quickly, not worried about anyone seeing us.

'And one day he's going to take me and Belle to Ireland,' Lexi continued.

'Ireland?' Sam sneered. 'The party capital of the world.'

'At least he's asked me,' she retorted.

I shook my head, she was still angry with her dad about Thailand.

'So, Paddy,' Sam finished his meal. 'Can I get you another drink?'

'I'll get you one mickey.' Shay stood going to the bar.

'Mickey?' Sam looked puzzled.

'It's what Irish men call their pricks,' Dale informed him gleefully.

I hid my smile as I watched Shay disappear to the gents and Sam took the opportunity to sit in his vacated seat.

'Hey Tash,' he gave me his most charming smile.

I returned it politely, wondering how rude it would look if I just got up and moved. 'Why didn't you make Jamie come tonight?' I challenged.

'You know what he's like, he would have just kicked off,' he draped his arm over the back of my chair.

'You said that you were going to talk to him,' I reminded Sam.

'And I will.'

I knew he was lying though, Sam was doing a bang-up job of adding fuel to the fire.

'Anyway,' Sam's voice was low. 'You look really beautiful tonight.'

'It's being with Shay, it suits me,' I retorted.

He looked at me cynically. 'I don't think Irish boy will stick around.'

'You don't have to, I do, I retorted.

He went to touch my face but I batted his hand away. 'Darling,' his voice was charming, the kind of voice that years ago would have me taking him back in an instance. 'Just say the word and I'll take you and the baby on.'

'What?' I asked in disbelief, had I just heard right.

'It's always been you and me, we are meant to be together.'

'Oh my God,' I cried, my voice equally low. 'Your wife and child are here.'

'It's how I feel,' his eyes sought mine.

'I can't believe you just said that.'

'Think about it,' he urged. 'We can be a family again. I'll bring Safi with me; our kids would certainly approve.'

I was totally speechless and I could tell by the expression on Bev's face that she had heard everything. Shay came back from the gents, joining Dale at the bar. I glanced at him, he was ordering more drinks and I could tell but his face that he was unimpressed with how close Sam was sitting to me, he'd be even less impressed if he knew what Sam was actually saying to me.

'Think about it darling. Take your time, I'll be here for you,' Sam was saying. 'Paddy isn't for you and deep down you know it's true. I still love you Tash, you have to realise that.'

I looked at him sadly. 'You really are an arsehole, If Meera had any sense she would chuck you out and be with someone who deserves her.' I stood needing Shay but before I left him I bent down towards him, my face merely inches from his. 'Now just fuck off and leave us alone. You would be the last person on earth I would want to be with.'

'Darling, don't,' he went to grab my arm but I dodged him going to the bar.

'You okay beautiful?' Shay asked giving me a mineral water.

'Yes,' I could feel my cheeks burning as Meera joined Sam at the table, Safi playing with Lexi and Belle.

'Sure?' He said. 'You look a little flushed.'

I shrugged off the question. 'Can we go after this one please? I'm feeling a little tired.'

'No worries,' he looked at his watch, it was still early. 'I'm not sure if Lexi and Belle will want to go yet though.'

'They are meeting friends up town in a while, then they're getting a taxi back to ours.' I was feeling guilty, as if I had done something wrong.

'Sure, no problem,' he gave me a curious smile.

'Thanks, I'm just going to the ladies.'

I scurried away, I was avoiding Sam really. What was he thinking, saying those things to me?'

Bev came sidling over to me as I washed my hands at the basin. 'I can't believe what Sam said to you.'

'I thought you could hear him, the wanker,' I answered darkly.

'Shay would go ballistic if he knew. What make Sam think you'd want him back? You haven't been encouraging him, have you?'

'No!' I said sharply. 'Why would you think that? I am perfectly happy with Shay thank you.'

'Sorry hun,' she patted my arm. 'I know you are.'

'We're going in a while, I can't sit here with him any longer. Why would he do it with Meera here too   ?'

'You know what a bastard he is, as we've said before Sam likes the unobtainable.'

'I just feel sorry for Meera and Safi.' I replied.

'You should tell her what he's saying to you,' her words were forceful.

I turned to her feeling tearful. 'I couldn't hurt her like that, think of Safi.' I straightened my dress looking at myself in the mirror.

'You're too soft,' she shook her head. 'Come on, I'll protect you from randy ex-husbands.'

'Thanks,' I grimaced as we walked bar into the bar, to my discomfort Shay and Sam were practically sitting on each other's laps. What if Sam said something? Shay would flatten him.

'Tash,' Sam gave me his most charming smile. 'Did you hear the joke about the Englishman and the Irishman?'

I glared at him. 'Shay are we ready to go?'

He nodded. 'But first I want to hear Sam's joke,' he turned to him, folding his arms.

'He doesn't know any jokes,' Dale rested his hand on his ex-brother in laws shoulder. 'Do you Sammy boy?'

He faltered for a moment. It isn't that funny actually,' he replied.

'They rarely are,' Meera was holding a yawing Safi on her lap.

'Shay?' I was really ready to go.

He nodded standing. I went to Lexi giving her some money and telling her to have a good night.

'Don't wait up mom,' she kissed my cheek.

'I'll keep my phone on just in case,' I fretted.

'We'll be fine, there's a load of us going.'

'Okay, be careful,' I warned as Shay and I said our goodbye's.

As I drove home I could see Shay keep casting glances at me. 'You okay?' He asked eventually. 'You seem very quiet.'

'I'm fine,' I answered quietly.

'Are you sure?' He tilted in his seat.

'Yes, I'm just tired,' I tried to force a smile.

'What were you and Sam on about earlier, you looked pretty intense,' he kept his voice casual.

'Just about Jamie not turning up. You'd think he'd have made the effort for his sister's birthday.'

Shay agreed but he wasn't stupid, he knew it something more. I was glad to get home and Millie was certainly pleased to see us.

I looked at the clock, it read ten. I knew it was Saturday night and we usually had a late one but I hadn't lied when I'd said I was tired.

'I think I'll go up,' I still felt a sense of uneasiness.

'I'll be up in a minute,' he hugged me.

'You don't have to, it's early.'

He smiled sweetly. 'Early night will do me good.'

I lay in bed as he joined me and we cuddled together. 'Are you sure you're okay?' He asked kissing the top of my head.

'Yes, I'm just tired,' I snuggled closer. 'That's all.'

He traced a finger along my cheek. 'I know something's playing on your mind, please tell me.'

I hesitated. 'You'll hit the roof if I do.'

'Tell me sweet, you're worrying me now.'

I took a deep breath, telling him exactly what Sam had said to me, I couldn't keep it from him.

'Who the fucking hell does he think he is?' he cried sitting up in bed.

'He's just being a pain,' I tried to soothe him. 'We'll take no notice.'

'He's a fecking eejit, I'm here and I have no intention of leaving you so why the hell does he think he can say things like that to you?'

'Like you say he's an idiot.'

'He needs sorting out!' He was angry.

'That's the reason I didn't want to say anything,' I said. 'Forget it please, I told him to fuck of anyway.'

'If he keeps pushing it I will say something,' he warned. 'I just don't know how he's got the nerve. I could understand it more if I'd done a runner and not bothered about you or the baby.'

I sat up also, kissing his soft lips. 'I love you and that's all that matters.'

He attempted a smile. 'I love you too but it's not on beautiful.'

'Just leave it, please.' I rubbed my stomach. 'We have more important things to concern ourselves with.'

Shay declined to comment and I knew it wasn't the end of it.

Sixteen

By Monday I was still steaming about what Sam had said to me at Lexi's birthday meal and Shay wasn't overly impressed either. I could see the pair of them coming to blows if I didn't do my upmost to keep them apart.

I sighed fussing Millie absently, I was making proper Irish Colcannon, Moira had given me the recipe and I was going to serve it with thick rashers of unsmoked bacon, yummy!

I looked at the piece of paper Moira had written out for me, I needed spring onions and I didn't have any. Turning off the potatoes I picked up my bag and car keys. 'I'll be ten minutes bit dog, I just need to pop to the shop.'

She stared at me as if to say. "I don't have a clue what you are on about but I'll wag my tail anyway."

Lidl was virtually empty and I was going back to my car when I heard someone shout my name. I turned with a sinking feeling, Vince, my dad's drinking buddy was bearing down on me.

'Natasha, hello,' he gave me a sickly smile. 'Have you seen your dad?'

'Not since Christmas,' I replied, he knew we rarely saw each other. 'I did go around to his flat Wednesday night be wasn't in. I thought he was out with you.'

'I haven't seen him since last Tuesday,' he did look concerned.

I took a step back, he stank of beer and looked at my watch. It was four-thirty, Shay wouldn't be home until five-thirty and I had a horrible feeling in my stomach. I needed to go and check his flat.

'Come on, we'll just go and make sure everything's okay,' I decided.

He nodded relieved. I had known Vince for years, he'd always seemed to be around. When we were in the car I cracked the window even though the day was cool, the smell of booze was making me feel a little sick.

Climbing the stairs to dad's flat my heart was beating ten to the dozen, dad *never* missed going to the pub, ever.

'Dad!' I called banging on the door. Nothing. 'Dad, its Natasha!' I tried again.

I looked at Vincent, my stomach rolling. 'It doesn't look like he's in.'

'Do you have your key?'

I nodded taking it from my bag reluctantly. Inserting it in the lock I took a deep breath and opened the door. 'Oh my God,' I gagged, the smell was horrendous.

Without thinking I pushed open the living room door. 'Natasha!' Vince cried propelling me backwards and into the hallway. 'Don't look.'

But it was too late, I had already seen. My dad was in his chair, head bent forward as if he was asleep but he wasn't. His body and face purple and bloated.

'Call for an ambulance!' Vince instructed going back into the room.

I fumbled to get my phone from my bag, the battery nearly dead. 'Which service to you require?' The pleasant voice asked after I had dialled nine-nine-nine.

'I'm not sure,' I stuttered. 'It's my dad.'

'What's wrong with him?' Her voice was reassuring.

'I think he's dead,' I blurted out. What did I mean think? I knew he was. 'We found him in his flat.'

'What's your name?' She asked softly.

'Natasha Turner,' I replied.

'And the address?'

I gave her all the details she needed and she told me to stay where I was and wait for the emergency just as my battery died.

'Natasha?' Vince was by my side.

'He's dead, isn't he?' I asked bluntly.

'I'm so sorry,' he seemed like he didn't know what to do.

'I'm going to be sick,' I gasped, turning my head and bringing up everything I had eaten that day. The smell of decay was all around me.

'I'm so sorry,' Vince repeated, rubbing me back lightly.

I seemed to take an age for anyone to come as we waited outside for them then the police and the ambulance arrived at the same time.

'Natasha Turner?' The policeman asked and he looked all of twenty.

I nodded, numbness spreading all through my body. Vince spoke to them, I don't think I was capable. I listened as if I was in a bubble, it just didn't seem real.

Vince was telling them he had seen him last Tuesday and I found my voice, telling them that Shay and I had called Wednesday night and had gotten no answer.

'To be fair, he looks like he's been there a while,' the policeman said and then immediately looked contrite.

'He drinks a lot,' I said nervously playing with the strap of my bag. 'Could that have caused it?'

'I don't know,' the policeman answered. 'There will have to be a post mortem.'

I gagged again, I didn't want my dad cut up. 'Are you okay?' He asked concerned.

'I'm pregnant,' I answered, my hand on my stomach as if I was protecting the baby from the horror. 'I just feel sick.'

'Sorry,' he gave me a sympathetic smile.

'I need a drink,' Vince rubbed his chin nervously.

I glared at him, convinced that was what had sent dad into his early grave, he was only sixty-three. We were there about another hour and then they said we could go but they would be in touch.

'I'll drop you somewhere,' I said to Vince. I felt lost, I should have been crying, wailing, but I felt nothing, just numb.

'Drop me at The Angel, I really need a drink,' he said.

I nodded, Vince wasn't my concern but Dale was, I would have to tell him. I dropped Vince at the pub with promises to let him know when I heard anything and let him know when the funeral was.

I tried Dale's flat first but he wasn't there so I headed to Bev's. She opened the door immediately. 'Tash,' she cried on seeing me. 'Tell your brother not to be such a male chauvinistic pig, men can do the ironing.' She stopped dead, seeing my face. 'What is it?'

I shook my head going inside, Dale was sprawled on the settee, a big sloppy grin on his face. 'Sis, tell Bev women are so much better at ironing than men.'

'Dale,' Bev inclined her head towards me.

He sat up, the smile disappearing. 'Sis?' He said, concerned.

I flumped on the settee. 'Dad's dead.'

'What?' He frowned.

I looked without really seeing him. 'I found him in his flat earlier, me and Vince. The police came.'

'Shit Tash,' Bev put her arm around me. 'Are you okay?'

'Yeah,' my answer was weak. I looked at my brother. 'Dale?'

He shrugged. 'What do you want me to say? He never bothered about us Tash.'

'He is your dad,' I cut in.

'In name only,' Dale countered. 'He was the same as mom, neither of them could give a flying fuck about us.'

'Don't speak ill of the dead,' Bev chided.

'He glared at her. 'They don't deserve our tears, either of them.'

'I think he's been dead a while,' I still felt disorientated. 'Shay and I went around Wednesday night and couldn't get an answer and Vince hadn't seen him since Tuesday.'

'How awful,' Bev sat next to Dale unsure what to say.

'Why did you go Wednesday?' he wanted to know.

'We were going to tell him about the baby,' I replied sadly.

'Why?' he stood agitated. 'He's never bothered with Jamie or Lexi, why would you think the one you're carrying now would be any different?'

'I don't know,' my voice was small, Dale seemed so angry.

'Do you need anything babe?' Bev asked me softly, glaring in my brother' direction.

I shook my head. 'I have to get home, I need a shower, all I can smell is death on me.'

'Shall I come with you?' she gave me a half smile.

'No, thank you,' I looked at the clock, it was after seven. 'Are you going to be okay Dale?'

'Course I am. Don't you go getting upset about this,' he warned. 'He isn't worth it, he's never been worth it. He has *never* been a proper dad to us, ever.'

I looked at him in dismay before walking to the front door with Bev. 'Take no notice of him, he just doesn't know how to react,' she said sympathetically.

'Will you look after him please?' I fretted, he was always my concern.

'Of course I will. Call me if you need anything, even if it's just a chat,' she paused. 'And I don't expect you in work tomorrow.'

'I'll be there,' I wouldn't let her hug me, not with the smell of dad's flat all over me. 'Thank you.'

By the time I got home it was seven-thirty and I could see Shay in the kitchen window peering outside. 'Where the feck have you been?' he demanded when I went into the kitchen. 'I come home, the tea's half cooked, Millie's hungry and you're nowhere to be seen?'

'My dad died,' my voice was barely audible.

'What?' had he just heard correctly?

I told what had happened and he listened intently. 'Why didn't you call me?' he frowned.

'My battery died after I called nine-nine-nine,' talking of which I got my mobile and put it on charge.

'Well why didn't you call when you got to Dale's?'

I turned to him wearily. 'You know what Shay for once you weren't the first thing on my mind, funnily enough.' As soon as the words left my mouth I regretted them.

He moved to hug me but I pushed him away, I stank of my dad's flat, the smell almost overwhelmingly sweet, like when you threw up because you had drunk too much. I gagged, trying desperately not to throw up again as I stripped off my clothes where I stood, trying to keep Millie away from me.

'What are you doing?' he cried, hurrying to close the blinds.

'I smell, it's all over me,' I shoved the clothes into the bin, I never wanted to wear them again.

'Sweet!' he cried distressed.

'I need to shower,' I pushed past him, going upstairs. I turned the shower to as hot as I could stand it, letting the water cascade over me, cleansing me.

I must have stood there for twenty minutes, my eyes tightly shut, and replaying the glimpse I had gotten of my dad's putrefied body again and again. Dressing in jogging bottoms and an old t-shirt of Shay's I ventured downstairs, my hair hanging wet around my face.

'Do you want something to eat?' Shay asked, the same concerned look on his face that Bev had when I was round hers.

'I'm not hungry,' I replied going into the living room and hugging big dog to me.

'You have to eat something sweet,' he followed me, putting an arm around my shoulder as Millie tried to lick his face.

I looked up at him. 'Can I have a cup of ginger tea please? I feel sick.'

'Sure,' he kissed the top of my head, going into the kitchen as I sought the comfort of Millie once more.

I curled up on the settee, staring at nothing. I just didn't know how to feel, surely when your dad died you should at least shed a tear but I couldn't, I just felt odd. Shay brought my tea and placed it on the coffee table, realising how the whole thing must have knocked me sideways.

Sitting next to me, he gathered me in his arms. 'I'm so sorry about your dad sweet,' his Irish accent was soft.

I nodded. 'Thank you,' I replied because that's what you did. You thanked people for their condolences. 'And I'm sorry too, I should have called you, I shouldn't have left you worry. I'm sorry about snapping at you as well.'

'Don't worry,' he kissed the top of my head, resting his chin there. I could feel his heart beating and I closed my eyes feeling safe.

'It was horrible,' I said quietly. 'I can still see him Shay, all bloated and.'

'I know,' he soothed. 'It's going to be alright, I promise.'

'They think he was dead for days.'

'Will there be a post mortem?' he asked and I nodded.

'What if he was there Wednesday night, what if he was dead and I just walked away?' panic began to sweep me.

'Shush,' he held me tighter.

I struggled out his grip. 'What if he wasn't dead?' my eyes were bright. 'What if he was still alive and I could have helped him?'

'What if's will drive you crazy,' he pushed damp hair from my face. 'It isn't your fault, I'm not having you beating yourself up about this.'

'If I'd had my key with me we could have gone in, I could have saved him,' I groaned dismayed.

'Enough,' he held my face in both hands. 'We don't know that.'

I stared at him for a moment, he was right of course, how could I have known? I nodded again, leaning my head against his shoulder, taking comfort from him. 'Whatever's got to be done, I'll help you,' he pulled me closer. 'How was Dale?'

'Indifferent,' my voice was slightly muffled by his jumper. 'He has no time for either of our parents. Dad wasn't very nice to him when he was young. I think dad resented my mom for leaving an eight year old child with him, that's why I looked after him. Dale said I shouldn't be wasting my time on either of them.'

'I'm beginning to agree with him,' he frowned.

'I'll have to clean out his flat, God knows what I'm going to do with his stuff,' I fussed.

'We will *all* clean out the flat, Dale included,' he corrected. 'I know a couple of bloke's, they'll take the furniture away for us if we want.'

'It's not any good,' I sighed. 'Shit I need to tell the kids.'

'Are they close to him?' Shay was confused, he didn't think that they were.

'Well, no,' I admitted. 'But I still have to tell them.' Reaching for my mobile I called Lexi first.

'Hi mom, you okay,' her voice was sunny.

'Not really love,' I replied. 'I've got some bad news love, grandads dead.'

'Oh right,' she paused for a moment. 'How?'

'Not sure, Vince and I found him this evening, it looked like he'd been dead for a while.'

'Shit mom, are you okay?' she was immediately concerned.

'I just feel sick, the smell wasn't very nice,' I answered as Shay passed me my herbal tea and I took a sip.

'Yak! Is Shay there?'

'Yes, he's here,' I smiled slightly at him.

'I don't know what to say,' he admitted. 'I mean it's sad that he died but that's it.'

'I know honey, he never bothered with you so you never really knew him,' I sighed. 'I just need you there at the funeral.'

'Of course,' she replied. 'Are you going to be okay mom, do you need me to come over because it's not a problem.'

'I'll be fine,' I stifled a yawn. 'Shay will look after me and I'll see you Sunday.'

'See you Sunday mom, love to Shay. Love you loads.'

'Love you more.' I finished the call. 'There is not going to be one tear shed at his funeral.'

'You reap what you sow,' he told me wisely.

I declined to answer, dialling Jamie's number but it went straight to voicemail so I called the landline at Sam's, hoping that Jamie or Meera would answer. Unfortunately Sam did. 'Hi Sam, its Tash. Is Jamie there please?' I kept my voice as polite as I could as Shay listened closely.

'No, he out, why?'

'He's not answering his mobile,' I clicked my tongue impatiently.

'He never does,' Sam had his most charming voice on.

'Shit,' I said under my breath.

'Something important?'

I could picture him sitting on his recliner, cordless phone in one hand not at all worried about what he had said Saturday, secure in the knowledge that I would always come round to what he wanted, simply because I had in the past.

'I found my dad dead today, I just wanted him to know.'

'Paul,' he sounded genuinely shocked. 'How?'

Briefly I told him what had happened. 'Bloody hell darling, do you want me to come round to you?'

'No, thank you, I'm fine.'

'Is Paddy with you?' there was an undercurrent of meanness in his tone.

'Of course he is,' my answer was short.

'You need someone with you who knew Paul, so you can talk about him.'

'Why would I want to talk about him?' I screwed up my face. 'I don't need to talk about him at all.'

'That's not healthy darling.'

I cringed, I hated how he kept calling me darling. 'Anyway will you tell Jamie please? I have to go.'

'I will and look after yourself. I am so sorry for your loss,' he did sound sincere.

'Thank you,' I threw the mobile on the chair.

'Gobshite,' Shay said darkly. 'What was he saying?'

'Shut up,' I smiled softly.

'Well the blokes a maggot,' he declared.

'I'm not going to disagree with you,' I pulled my legs onto the settee, laying my head in his lap.

'That's because you know you can't,' he stroked my hair. 'You look knackered beautiful, are you going to eat anything?'

'No, thank you. Do you want anything?' I suddenly realised that he hadn't eaten either.

'I'll sort something, don't worry,' he carried on stroking my hair.

I got up quickly. 'Let me do you something,' I needed to be useful.

'I'll do it,' he caught my hand.

'I want to,' I insisted.

'Beans on toast then,' his smile was caring.

'Great,' I laughed softly. 'But if you hold my head under the covers like you usually do when you fart you'll now be gassing you child as well, think on.'

He chuckled, he did find it highly amusing. I made his supper still feeling numb and out of sorts, all I could see was my dad's dead face.

He ate it hungrily and then we tidied away and I resumed my position on the settee with my head on his lap. I couldn't even tell you what we were watching on the television, I was running through a mental list of everything that would have to be done.

'Okay beautiful?' he asked for the hundredth time as he kept up the hair stroking. 'Do you want anything?'

'No, thank you.'

'Sure?' he moved his feet, Millie had decided that she wanted to lie on them.

'Yes,' I looked at the clock, it was nine-thirty. 'I'm going to turn in.'

'Okay sweet, I'll sort Millie out,' he waited for me to get up, planting tiny kisses on my stomach. 'Sleep tight baby Flynn.'

I smiled kissing the top of his head. Going upstairs I got ready for bed, I was shattered but I doubted that I would sleep. I heard Shay coming upstairs and Millie settling down for the night in her basket and then he was in the bedroom bearing gifts of Ovaltine.

I smiled watching as he undressed and got into bed. 'Thank you hun, you are good to me,' I said gratefully. 'I do love you so much and I'm so glad that you're here,' I paused for a moment. 'I'm sorry I haven't been good company tonight.'

'It's not a problem,' he placed his hand on my tummy and I snuggled against him.

Seventeen

'Shay!' I screamed, sitting bolt up in bed. 'Shay! Turn the light on!'

'He did, looking at me groggily. 'What's wrong, is it the baby?' He said panicked.

'He was here,' I cried, clinging onto him.

'Who was here?' He held my arms. 'Jaysus you're shaking.'

'My dad, here was here. He was standing at the edge of the bed, just watching me.'

'It was just a dream sweetheart, he tried to calm down but it had seemed so real.

'His face was all discoloured and bloated and he was just staring at me.' I fell into his arms.

'It's just a figment of your imagination, you're bound to be upset. Do you want a glass of water?'

'No, thank you,' I looked around my bedroom fearfully, convinced at what I had seen.

'You need to sleep beautiful,' he lay down forcing me to do the same, it was ten past one. 'Come on.' He held me close as I tried to get my breathing under control.

I spent the rest of the night dozing, every time it seemed like I would go to sleep I would jerk myself awake.

By the time Shay got up for work the next morning I had done him a full English breakfast to make up for the lack of sleep last night.

'You should have stopped in bed,' he said as he attacked his breakfast hungrily. 'And why do you have your work clothes on?'

'Because I'm going to work,' to be fair it was just a purple top I was wearing, I could no longer fit into my tunic.

'Is that a good idea?' he frowned slightly.

'I'm better off at work,' I replied sipping my herbal tea. He showed his disapproval instead of saying it but I ignored him. Sitting at home by myself would do me no good at all.

'If it gets too much come home,' he carried on eating.

'I will, I just want everything to be normal.'

'How did you sleep?' He was watching me closely.

'Fine,' I turned my attention to Millie.

'Sweet,' his tone held a warning.

'Shit then,' I admitted. 'I tossed and turned all night, it's a wonder I didn't keep you awake.

'You did,' and to be fair and he did look tired. 'Have you eaten anything?'

'Not yet but I will before you start nagging me.'

'Be sure you do because I will check with Bev that you have.'

I bobbed my tongue out at him and he gave me his beautiful smile. 'Have you finished?' I took the plate when he nodded as he went upstairs to finish getting ready for work. He came down ten minutes later, hair in a man bun and teeth all brushed.

'Call me if you need me,' he gave me a cuddle.

'I will,' I promised, kissing him lovingly. 'Thank you.'

'What for?' He touched my cheek.

'Just for being you,' I let him go, he was going to be late for work if he wasn't careful.

He smiled again, giving Millie a head rub before hurrying to his truck. 'Come on big dog, let's go to work.' I said, she knew what that meant, she loved being at the salon with all the different customers fussing her and bringing her dog treats, it's a wonder she wasn't the size of a house.

We arrived at the salon even earlier than usual so I was surprised to find Bev already there along with Carling.

'Tash, what are you doing here?' She asked.

'Working,' I replied as Millie caught Carling a treat with her nose in the groin area. 'More to the point what are you both doing here this early?'

'I didn't think you'd be in,' Bev chided.

'Yeah,' Carling gave me a sympathetic smile. 'Sorry about your dad babes.'

'Thank you hun,' I gave her a nice smile. 'How's Dale?' I asked Bev.

'He's fine, he's gone to work too,' she replied.

'I know it seems strange but I haven't shed one tear, not one.' I shook my head sitting at the reception desk as Millie mooched around the salon.

'Shall I make you drink?' Carling asked.

'I would love a cup of proper coffee.'

'Are you allowed?' Bev gave me a suspicious look.

'Only if Shay doesn't find out,' I smiled as my mobile pinged. 'Oh, talk of the devil.' I read his text, he was going to drive me mad checking up on me all day.

'Is he okay?' Bev asked as Carling disappeared in the back to make the drinks.

'He's been great.' I answered, then I hesitated for a minute. 'Should I be crying?'

'Do you want to cry?' Bev asked.

I shook my head. 'No, I don't think I do.'

'Then it's fine not too.' She smiled sweetly at me for a moment then her face grew serious. 'Deal with it the best way that suits you, there is no right or wrong way. The only way Dale will cry over this is if we punch him in the mouth.

I nodded as my phone pinged again, Jamie, saying he was sorry about grandad. My eyes filled with tears, my son had actually bothered to send me a text to say something. A phone call would have gone down better or even a personal visit but a text would have to do.

'Tash?' Bev was looking at me concerned.

'It's from Jamie,' I looked at her.

'About time,' she stated gruffly. 'That kid is one ungrateful little shit.'

'He is,' I agreed as I text back asking if he was alright and that I loved him loads. My mobile stayed infuriatingly silent, maybe Meera had made him send the message?

'Now, are you sure you're okay to work? Bev chaffed.

'Yes,' I drew out the word. 'I have got to phone the council and the benefits office though.'

'Not a problem, do what you have to do,' she replied as Carling brought the drinks. I have to say my coffee was delicious.

In between my customers I did the phone calls I had to make. 'We've got a month to clear the flat,' I said feeling dead on my feet.

'Shall we do it Sunday?' She suggested.

'I don't except you to do it,' I replied.

'Hun, am I not your brother's better half?' She asked and I nodded. 'We're sister in law's practically, family.'

I smiled suddenly. 'I have to admit you are one of the few of Dale girlfriend's that I have actually liked.'

'Ah sweet, I'm touched,' she wiped away an imaginary tear.

I smiled again, it fading as I saw my mom approaching the salon. 'What the hell does she want?' I hissed.

She walked inside, all mutton dressed as lamb, her stunning features pinched with spite. 'Well that's nice isn't it?' She said by way of a greeting.

'What is?' I asked tiredly, my mother I could do without.

'I went to my local shop this morning to get some ciggies and the bloke behind the counter told me about Paul.'

I sighed finishing off my customer, this I didn't need.

'You should have told me Natasha, I shouldn't have had to hear it from a stranger.'

'I really didn't think you'd be interested,' I retorted getting my customer her coat and taking her money. With a smile I bid her goodbye.

'Sue, I have a salon full of customers,' Bev said pointedly.

Mom snarled at her. 'And you! I don't know how you've got the nerve to talk to me corrupting my son.'

'Corrupting your son!' Bev spluttered.

'Mom,' my tone was forceful. 'This is neither the time nor the place. I'll come and see you later.'

'Well look at her,' she threw a look at Bev. 'It's disgusting with my little boy.'

'Your little boy!' I choked, the absolute brass neck of this woman.

'What did I ever do to deserve kids like you two?' She was going for the sympathy vote with the other customers. 'You never think of me ever, and as for your children, they don't even give me the time of day. You should have told me about your dad.'

'You left Paul over twenty-five years ago, why are you bothered?' Bev was angry.

'I had to leave that man, he was mentally abusing me.' Fake tears came into her eyes.

'Bollocks,' Bev retorted as our customers watched with interest. 'You left him and your children.'

I couldn't take them with me,' she wiped away her phony tears.

I was suddenly livid. 'You didn't want to take us with you! You were quite happy to leave your eight-year-old son with his drunken father.

'You were there,' she defended herself.

Oh God, we'd had this argument so many times. 'He needed his mother, not his sister. He cried for you every night, he just wanted you to hold him but you wouldn't.'

'I couldn't,' she leapt in.

'You wouldn't,' I repeated firmly. 'You've never been a mom to either of us. Everything you do is just for show.'

'You snobby little bitch,' she spat at me.

'That's better mother,' I goaded. 'Come on show everyone your true colours. You're nothing but a dirty slag. You never deserved me and Dale. You have two beautiful grandkids that you have no interest in and another on the way. You are going to die a bitter lonely old woman, you selfish cow.'

She moved quickly, slapping me across the face as everyone gasped.

'Out!' Carling stepped forward, her petite figure trembling with indignation. 'Just get out. How dare you hit your pregnant daughter, you old skank.'

In the back-room Millie began to bark as I looked at Carling flabbergasted.

'Carling's right,' Bev squared up to her. 'Get out of my salon now.'

Mom hesitated for a moment then flounced out of the salon as Carling steered me into the back-room. 'I'm going to fucking kill her,' I fumed.

'Shush,' Carling soothed. 'Think of the baby.'

'I can't cope with her.' I fumed as Shay arrived popping in on his lunch break to see how I was doing, quickly Bev filled him in on what had happened.

'Sweet,' he tried to hold me but I pushed him away.

'Don't,' I stepped away from him. 'I've had enough. I've finished trying to get one iota of anything from her. She has crushed me time and time again, well no more.'

'Tash,' he held out his hands, 'Calm down, think of the baby.'

'Calm down,' I spluttered. 'It's okay for you, you've got Moira, you don't know what it's like to have parents like mine.'

He looked a little wounded. 'Sweetheart,' he tried again. 'She doesn't mean anything, you have us.'

'I'm finished with her. She didn't give a fuck about my dad.'

'I know,' he managed to hold me. 'She's not important.'

Millie came to me, leaning her large body against my legs. 'You need to let it all out,' he kissed my head.

'Please Shay, just leave me alone, stop fussing over me. I need to deal with it all in my own way.' I didn't realise how hurtful my words were, I'd truly had enough.

He stepped away as Bev and Carling gave me a pitying look. 'Fine, I'll see you at home then.' He would give me some space, I seemed liked I needed it.

I nodded, blinkered to how I had hurt him. Without another word he left.

'Tash,' Bev said softly. 'It's not his fault.'

'I'm not blaming him,' I snapped.

'Aren't you?' she asked sadly. 'Your next lady's here.'

I nodded taking a deep breath. 'Carling.'

'Yes?' She looked at me jaded.

'Thank you for what you said to my mom.'

'She was bang out of order,' she frowned slightly. 'She shouldn't have hit you.'

'No, she shouldn't,' I agreed. For the rest of the day I hardly spoke. I think we were all relieved when it was time for me to go home.

I banged about the kitchen, knowing I should do something to eat but I had no appetite. Shay would nag me and as much as I loved him I just couldn't cope with it at the moment, for the first time ever, I wished he was going home to his mom.

I heard his key in the front door and I groaned softly and then Moira was in the kitchen taking me in her capable arms.

'My dahling,' she held me close. 'I am so sorry about your da. How are you my angel?'

'Okay,' I replied as she held me at arm's length.

'No, you're not, as any fool can see. 'Sit, sit,' she plonked me at the table taking the plastic container from her son. 'You are going to eat, there are two of you to think of now and then you are going to talk to me.'

'I don't want any fuss,' I muttered.

She cocked her head to one side. 'I'm not fussing, I'm doing it because I think the world of you and you have had a deep shock. Go and have your shower son and leave us girls be.'

He did and she decanted the contents of the plastic box into an ovenproof dish and put it in the oven, then sitting next to me. 'It must have been a grand shock finding him like that.' She took my hand.

I nodded mutely. Why couldn't my own mom do what Moira was doing?

'And I wager that you don't know how to feel, that you haven't even cried.

I shook my head.

'And what kind of daughter doesn't cry when her da dies?' she tightened her grip.

I looked away ashamed as she leant towards me. 'Shall I tell you what kind of daughter?' She continued. 'The kind who has never known a father's love. You don't have to waste your tears on him. He did nothing in life for you. Stop feeling guilty my sweetheart, he should feel guilty not you.'

'He was my dad though,' I whispered.

'In name only,' she cried. 'Anyone can be a father, can create a baby. It takes someone special to be dad.'

She was making perfect sense.

'And your mother,' she literally spat the words out. 'If I see that fecking woman I'll slap her myself.' She got up to make tea. 'Bother with those who love you, don't waste your time and energy on those who don't, promise me.

'I promise.' I said meekly.

'That's my girl,' she brought my tea to the table, winking at me. 'It's leaded,' her word for caffeinated. 'You've had a trauma just don't tell the baby police, if he,' she inclined her head to the ceiling. 'Asks it's decaffeinated.' I gave her a proper smile, she was so lovely.

'I'm inviting myself for supper too, I hope you don't mind,' she fussed Millie. 'You are one fecking big dog.'

I smiled again. 'Of course I don't mind.'

'Now what have you got planned for Monday?'

I thought for a moment. 'Nothing, it's going to take a while for the post mortem so I can't arrange anything, funeral wise, yet.'

'Shall we get ourselves off for some wedding shopping?' she was trying to cheer me up.

'I'd like that,' I sipped my tea.

'I have to get my boy something for his birthday too.'

'So do I. I haven't a clue what though. We have the twenty week scan on his birthday, we can find out the sex of the baby if we want to.' It was nice just chatting.

'Do you want to?'

'We haven't discussed it yet, I'd quite like the surprise but if Shay wants to we will.'

'Don't let him have it all his own way,' she cautioned good-humouredly.

'I just want it to be special for him, being his first.' I rubbed my stomach distracted still thinking about my mother.

'He couldn't be any happier,' she touched my cheek. 'Now point me in the direction of the dishes.'

'I'll get them,' I went to stand but she shook her head.

'You are putting your feet up,' she said so I told her where everything was as Shay re-joined us in the kitchen.

'Okay?' he asked bending to kiss the top of my head.

I nodded, taking his hand as I felt a twinge in my tummy.

'She is, I'm looking after her tonight,' Moira smiled.

I put his hand on my stomach and he looked at me puzzled for a moment then he felt it. He stared at me, a big soppy grin on his face and I smiled back. Without a word he cupped the back of my head, kissing me gently.

'What?' both Moira and Millie were staring at us.

I called her over, placing her hand next to Shay's. 'Is that?' she asked excitedly.

I nodded. 'That's the first time I've felt he or she kick.'

'It's just grand,' she had tears in her eyes.

'It's fantastic,' he held his hand there but it looked like that was it for now. 'Special.'

'It is,' I agreed, in a horrible two days it was a little ray of sunshine.

'I can't wait to meet the baby,' his mom chatted. 'Did you ever imagine that you would have any more?'

'No,' I replied. 'I thought my days of changing nappies were over, well unless I had grandchildren. Although I can't see Lexi having any.'

'I met Lexi yesterday, well her and Belle.'

'Did you?' she hadn't said anything when I told her about her grandad but I suppose she hadn't given it a thought.

'Yes, we chat on Snapchat,' Moira looked pleased with herself that she used technology. 'Anyway I mentioned that I was at Birmingham yesterday and they didn't have any lectures so I treated them to their lunch.'

'That's really kind of you,' I was pleased how they all got on.

'Anyway Saturday I am going on a march with them,' she brought the oven dish out of the oven.

'What kind of march?' I asked, watching as Shay helped his mom.

'A gay rights march,' she answered gleefully.

Shay guffawed. 'You do know what a gay rights march is?'

'Of course I do, I'm not an eejit,' she began to ladle the stew into the dishes. 'I have my rainbow t-shirt with a unicorn on to wear. I'll make sandwiches and we'll have a grand old time.'

'A rainbow t-shirt?' Shay gave me an amused look as he brought the dishes to the table.

'It's going to be a great day. I love the bones of those two, they are such good girls.' She sat at the table.

'You do know that they are together as in girlfriend and girlfriend, don't you?' I wasn't sure she did.

'Natasha Turner I am only sixty-four and I am not senile. Of course I know that they are a couple,' she chastised me.

'Sorry,' I flushed as Shay grinned.

'We had a boy in the village, in Quin. He was a lovely person, I went to school with him. Johnny Baxter was his name and as camp as a field full of tents, he didn't try to hide it,' she remembered. 'One night he got the shite beaten out of so badly by some lousy maggot gay bashers.'

'Bastards,' I said quietly, if anyone touched my daughter because of her sexuality, I'd rip them a new one.

'I've told you before Tash, it was a small minded village. They wouldn't approve of you and Shay living in sin.'

'Was the boy okay?' I asked concerned.

'He was, but he left for Dublin as soon as he could and we never saw him again.'

'That's awful,' I tasted a little of the stew and it was good, but unfortunately my appetite was still poor.'

'You had a gay friend at school as well didn't you son?'

'Yes, Michael,' Shay was eating his stew as if I hadn't fed him for a week.

'I was very proud of my son, he was his friend even when some of the other boys picked on him. Michael was very fond of Shay.'

'He fancied me,' he grinned between mouthfuls.

'Shay Albie Flynn!' Moira reprimanded.

'I like that name, Albie,' I ate a little more stew.

'It is his dad's name,' Moira looked a little sad. 'I wanted to give him something of his dad's.'

I gave her a sympathetic smile, no one had an easy life. Moira had spent years by herself because the man she loved she couldn't have. It was quite tragic but at least she had Alan now and seemed happy.

We ate our supper, me managing more than I thought I would. I felt like the Queen of Sheba as Shay and his mom washed up as Millie and I watched. The doorbell rang and I got up to answer it, Dale and Bev were standing there. 'Why didn't you use your key?' I asked.

'It doesn't seem right now Shay lives here,' he replied.

'Don't be daft,' I smiled as they followed me inside.

'Can you imagine me letting myself in and finding you flat on your back, legs akimbo with me laddie?' he teased. 'I'd need counselling.

'Dale,' I hushed him. 'Moira's here.'

He chuckled going into the kitchen. 'Mrs F!' he cried waltzing her around the room.

'Dale,' she cried laughing. 'How are you?'

'Wonderful, as you know,' he replied. 'I just wanted to see how Tash was, Bev told me about mom.'

I grimaced like I had a bad taste in my mouth.

He became serious. 'I can't believe she slapped you.'

'The baby kicked earlier,' I didn't want to waste my breath talking about it anymore.

'She can fuck off now, I have totally finished with her. If she dropped dead tomorrow I wouldn't give a flying fuck.'

'Dale,' I warned gently.

'Never mind Dale,' he rounded on me. 'Stop being such a soft touch sis. You don't need her, she certainly isn't bothered about you.'

'I know,' I sat at the table as Shay made more tea.

'Have you heard anything about dad?' he asked.

I shook my head. 'I can't do anything until the results of the post mortem.

'We are going to help clear his flat Sunday,' Bev cut in.

'Are we?' he screwed up his face.

'Yes, we are,' she answered firmly. 'We are not leaving everything for Tash to do.'

'I wasn't going to,' he too sat at the table.

'So what kind of funeral will you have for your da?' Moira joined us at the table as did Shay.

'We'll take him to the tip,' Dale said darkly.

I ignored him. 'Just the crem and then maybe a little do at his local. A few sandwiches or something like that.'

'We are not having a do for him,' Dale still seemed so angry. 'Why the fuck are you bothering?'

I was beginning to lose my patience. 'I am not having people say we did not do our best for him.'

'For that waste of time?'

'Dale,' Bev said softly, she could see how upset I was getting again.

'It's a reflection on both of you,' Moira's tone was gentle. 'Tash is right, just because he never did the right thing by either of you doesn't mean that you have to stoop to his level.'

'I know what you're saying Mrs F,' Dale had the upmost respect for Shay's mom. 'But the old scrot just does not deserve it.'

'We are still doing it though, regardless of what he was like,' my voice was firm.

'You are such a walk over,' Dale shook his head. 'Anyway we've brought you a present.'

'You have?' I cheered a little, I did so like presents.

He nodded passing me the carrier bag he was holding. I took it and peered inside, a giggle escaping my lips.

'What have you got there?' Shay looked over my shoulder.

I brought out packets of bourbon biscuits and a couple of jars of gherkins. Dale gave me a brilliant smile as Shay and Moira looked at me puzzled. 'I know it's disgusting but when I was pregnant with Lexi and Jamie I craved gherkins and bourbon biscuits together.'

'You're right, that is disgusting,' Bev gagged.

'It tastes lovely,' I argued.

'I wouldn't want to snog you after you ate that combination,' she tittered.

'I have to say I agree with Bev,' Moira stifled a yawn. 'Now are you going to be alright sweetheart?' she asked me.

'I will,' I smiled, she was such a lovely person.

'Good, I'll make my way home then. Alan is coming round at nine, he's been babysitting,' she stood.

'I'll take you home,' Shay stood to.

'We'll drop your mom home,' Dale cut in. 'You stop where you are.'

'Thanks,' he was glad not to have to go out, he wanted to get settled. 'Gym tomorrow?'

'Yeah, usual time,' Dale replied giving me a big hug. 'See you soon sis.'

'See you bruv,' I kissed his cheek. 'If I hear anything about dad I'll let you know.'

'Okay, thanks,' he went to the kitchen door.

Bev followed him as did Moira, Millie milling around our legs. Shay put his arm around my waist as we went to see them out, it was a little squashed in the hallway.

Moira paused, putting her hands either side of my face. 'You are a beautiful person, you deserve better than the parents you were given. I am proud that you and my son are together and so grateful that I am part of your family and you are part of mine.'

'Thank you,' I whispered tearfully.

She turned to Dale. 'You too lovely, I'm proud of you both.'

He hugged her tightly. 'Mom and dad mean nothing to me. Tash brought me up, no one else.'

We watched as Dale's car pulled away from the kerb before going back inside. 'I think we'll buy a dishwasher before the baby arrives,' Shay began to pour hot water into the bowl.

'Can we afford one?' the thought of buying everything we needed for the baby was beginning to concern me a little.

'We need it,' he held out his hands. 'Look at them, red raw from all the washing up I have to do.'

'Stop moaning,' I stood poised with the tea towel ready to dry up the mugs he was washing. 'You're just spoilt because your mammy used to do everything for you.'

He smiled, it fading as he looked at me. 'Your face is still marked.'

'It'll go,' I replied with less concern than I felt.

'I feel so fucking helpless,' he cursed. 'If a man had slapped you I could go and beat the living daylights out of him but I'm not into hitting women.'

'It's okay,' I put my arms around his waist, resting my head on his back. 'I'll live.'

'It isn't okay though,' he argued, his voice tense. 'It kills me to think she can hurt you and I can't do jack shit about it.'

I held him tighter. 'Don't beat yourself up about it, I expected nothing less from her. She'll get her comeuppance, trust me.'

He turned slightly, a look of doubt on his face. 'I suppose,' he replied.

Eighteen

I was still wracking my brains as to what to buy Shay for his birthday the following night as I prepared a delicious supper of spag bol and garlic bread. Shay had gone to the gym with Dale and I was glad they were close, it made things a whole lot easier. The baby had moved again last night as we lay on the bed and Shay was feeling ten feet tall, I thought his hand would be stuck to my stomach all day.

The doorbell rang and I cussed under my breath going to answer it. 'Sam,' I said in surprise.

'Hi darling,' he gave me a bunch of flowers, not a cheap bunch either, one of those fifteen quid bouquets from Sainsbury's. 'I am so sorry about your father.'

'Thank you,' I answered stiffly, reluctantly taking the flowers from him.

'Coffee?' He kind of pushed past me before I could answer.

I followed him into the kitchen, banging the flowers onto the worktop.

'How are you?' He sat at the table.

'Absolutely fine,' I replied putting the kettle on. 'Why wouldn't I be?'

'Well,' he pulled a face. 'You found your dad dead Tash, that's got to be a shock.'

'A little,' I made us both a decaffeinated coffee, luckily Shay wouldn't be back for at least fifty minutes so hopefully Sam would have drunk his coffee and slung his hook by then.

Sam was watching as I moved around the kitchen. 'You look radiant, pregnancy has always suited you.'

Never stopped you looking elsewhere though I thought but did not say. 'How's Jamie?' I asked out loud.

'He's good, doing his homework as we speak.' Sam took his mug of coffee from me.

'Have you managed to talk to him?' I sat opposite him, hand resting on my stomach.

He became vague. 'I don't see much of him at the moment.'

'I thought you said he was at home, doing his homework,' I contradicted.

'He is,' he looked as Millie came into the kitchen going to him for a bit of fuss. 'I don't know what you want with a dog this big.

'She's lovely,' I would have said night was day just to disagree with him.

He looked thoughtful for a moment. 'How's Dale taking it? He asked because he thought he ought to.

'He truly is not bothered,' I replied as I saw Shay's truck pull up outside, what was he doing back so early?

He came into the kitchen still in his overalls, hair in a manbun and he hadn't shaved for a few days.

'Hey Shay,' Sam greeted him jovially. That's an interesting look you are sporting.'

'Hi,' he replied shortly, kissing me on the mouth but there was no feeling behind it.

'I thought you were going to the gym?' My stomach flipped over.

'Dale got a puncture so we were messing about with that and decided not to go,' he got himself a coffee.

'I've just come to offer my condolences,' Sam indicated to the bouquet of flowers.

'Yeah, sad times,' he stayed leaning up the sink his trademark unreadable expression on his face and I prayed that he wouldn't start any trouble after I had told him what Sam had said to me at Lexi's birthday meal.

'He was a character though your old dad,' Sam turned to Shay. 'He caught me and Tash in her bedroom having some,' he paused for a second. 'Some fun and I didn't know where to put myself. Paul didn't bat and eyelid, just asked if I had a tenner I could lend him.'

I cringed, this was going to cause a row I could do without.

'Then there was the time we drank all his cans of beer, I thought he was going to put me in traction,' Sam continued to reminisce.

Shay's face hardened, it told him all he needed to know about my dad. He didn't care about someone screwing his daughter but he went ballistic about the same man drinking his beer, bastard.

'We had some good times didn't we Tash?' Sam turned back to me, smiling softly.

I scowled, I knew exactly what games he was playing. He liked to think that Shay would feel out in the cold because he couldn't join in. He was making it loud and clear that he was a part of my past that Shay would never be privy too.

Making sure I sounded disinterested I replied. 'Not really, my dad was vile and hardly ever sober. When he was at home he was usually passed out on his bed. I have no fond memories of him.' I took a breath. 'The only time he really came home was when he'd run out of money.'

Sam's mobile pinged and he looked briefly at the screen before ignoring it.

I hoped Shay would go for his shower so I could get rid of Sam but no such luck.

'You're too hard on your dad Tash.' Sam said. 'At least he wasn't breathing down your neck all the time.' His mobile went again.

'I think you have selective memory,' I chided as Millie made herself comfortable on Shay's feet.

His phone pinged again. 'Someone's impatient,' Shay's tone was soft but deadly.

He picked it up peering at the screen. 'It's only Meera.'

'She's probably wondering where you are,' could he be making it more obvious? Why didn't he just go, Shay was beginning to look very unhappy.

He answered me. 'You're right, I'd better go.'

Yes, just fuck off,' I thought. 'I'll see you out.' I stood, casting a helpless look in Shay's direction, I just knew we were going to argue once he had gone and I hadn't the heart for it.

We walked into the hallway, Sam pausing at the door and giving me a smile that in a previous life would have made me do exactly what he wanted.

'I meant what I said at Lexi's birthday darling,' his voice was low. 'I would take you back and the baby on in an instance. I've never stopped loving you, more than Paddy ever will.'

'Stop it,' my words were forceful. 'Please Sam.'

He declined to reply, kissing my lips gently before I could move away. I took a few steps back praying that Shay was still in the kitchen.

Walking to his car he turned. 'Let me know when the funeral is, I'd like to pay my respects.'

I pulled a face, shutting the front door and going back to Shay. He had his back to me, washing his hands with deliberate movements. Millie came around my feet wanting her food.

Taking a deep breath, I said. 'Are you okay love?'

He turned off the tap, picking up the towel to dry his hands. 'Not really. I'm sick of him being here. He always seems to be here when he knows I'm not.'

I picked up Millie's bowl, pouring in her food. 'I think you're being a little paranoid.

He finally faced me, his brown eyes nearly black with anger. 'No, I'm not and you know it. I should have been the one bringing you flowers, not him.'

My heart dropped, I didn't care for his tone. 'I can do without this. I've got so much to do, so much to think about. I don't even want the flowers.' With that I picked them up and threw them in the bin.

He looked a little contrite, retrieving them. 'Have the flowers. I suppose they were given for the right reasons.' He tried to give them to me but I batted them away.

I was suddenly angry, not so much with Shay, I'd feel the same way but he always had to start an argument when Sam was involved.

'I don't want the fucking flowers,' I snapped. 'Sam would love this, causing squabbles between us. It's what he's trying to do.' I took them going to the garden waste bin outside and dumping them unceremoniously inside.

I felt jaded, bone weary as I went back to the kitchen to continue with supper. Shay was still by the sink and as I went to walk past him he grabbed my waist.

'I'm sorry,' he said meekly. 'He just infuriates me'.

'It's what he wants.' I started to cry, big fat salty tears.

'Don't cry sweet, I hate to see you upset. I just don't want him keep popping up in our lives.'

'What am I supposed to do? He's the father of my children.' I sniffed loudly.

'Which he uses to his advantage time and time again.'

I stared into his face. 'I give up I don't know what you want me to do.'

'Tell him,' his tone was a little forceful.

'I have told him,' I rushed to defend myself.

'Maybe you need to be more assertive.'

Great, now I was too polite, I just couldn't win. I tried to wriggle out of his grasp but he held me tight. 'I can't be rude, I have to get on with him for Lexi and Jamie's sake.'

'You're too nice that's your problem,' he touched my cheek gently. 'He's a gobshite. I love you so much and it kills me the way he's treated you and continues to treat you. He has no respect for either of us. He thinks he can sit in my home, coming onto you in front of me and it's perfectly acceptable. He thinks that what we have is nothing that you would choose him in a blink of an eye.'

I was still snivelling. 'I love you'.

He pulled me against him, resting his chin on the top of my head. 'I know you do dahling.'

'Then don't let him get to you,' my voice was muffled by his clothes.

He moved so he could look at me. 'Shall we have supper? And don't tell me you're not hungry otherwise I'm going to put you over my knee and smack your arse.'

I smiled even though I was still upset. 'I'll have that for dessert,' and we both laughed.

Together we cooked the spag bol, sitting at the table to eat it. 'Going back to what you said earlier you haven't got to do everything by yourself, I'm here now.'

'I know and I'm grateful.' I tried to eat my food but my appetite was still poor.

We ate in silence, me trying to work out how I could deal with Sam and coming up with a big fat zero. I had to be careful, he had already managed to turn Jamie against us and I didn't want to make things worse.

When we had washed everything up Shay announced that he was going for his shower and I sat in the living room trying to find something to watch on the tv.

I didn't want Sam coming between us. Why now, after five years, did he think he could do this? I know he got bored, he had done when we were married. Sam loved the chase. Loved deciding he wanted something and going all out to get it.

I had turned him down so many times when we had first met. I was never going to leave Dale, it was always going to be me and him but Sam was charming and clever. He had pursued me relentlessly, promising that he would take on my little brother as well as me.

I had believed him, no one had paid me so much attention before, he made me feel so wanted. The first time we had slept together he had smothered me with his weight, telling me how lucky he was, how he would never leave me, never hurt me. How he would give me the life I deserved. Empty promises.

I jolted back into the present, he was a lying, manipulative little shit and my heart went out to Meera and Safi.

I needed Shay, going upstairs I heard him turn the shower off and I pushed open the bathroom door. He stood with the towel around his waist, wet curls on his head.

'Hey,' he gave me his beautiful smile.

I returned it. 'Are you happy?' I asked softly.

He cocked his head to one side and looked at me puzzled. 'Where has that question come from?'

'All we seem to be dealing with is shit.' I felt so washed out. 'My dad, Jamie, my mother, Sam. We just seem to keep arguing.'

He smiled again in the steamy bathroom. 'Little disagreements not arguments,' he corrected. 'It's shit that people keep throwing at us, not that we are creating ourselves. Anyway,' his smile grew. 'Look at the making up we do.'

I went to him, hooking my arms around his neck. 'We don't have to fall out to do that,' I kissed him intently.

He kissed me back, fingers raking my hair. 'In answer to your question I am extremely happy,' a tilt of his head. 'Is this baby hormones and your insecurities kicking in?'

'Might be,' I answered wryly. 'Anyway, you need to talk, with Sam.

He ignored me, growing serious. 'Every single day I thank my lucky stars that I came into the salon with Dale. If I had met you any later then someone else may have got to you first and snagged you and we would never have this.

'Who would have snagged me?' I doubted it.

'Oh,' he looked vague. 'Perhaps a handsome solicitor called Harry.'

'Who?' I was puzzled.

His laugh was light. 'Don't you remember? Dale's birthday, he chatted you up and gave you his card.'

'Oh yeah,' I grinned.

'I have a confession to make,' he looked bashful. 'I took his card from the fireplace so wouldn't call him. I didn't want to share you with anyone else.'

I was flattered. 'I wondered where that had gone. 'I wasn't going to call him you know?'

'I know,' he kissed me again.

I ran my hand along his chest, curling the hair around my fingers before going lower, cupping him as the towel fell to the floor. 'I need you Shay,' I whispered.

'You've got me,' he ran his hands down my back.

'No,' I breathed. 'I mean really need you.

His kisses became urgent, breathing more rapid as we danced towards the bedroom, never breaking contact.

Tumbling onto the bed he was above me, planting kisses all over my face. 'You are insatiable,' he whispered grinning. 'And I love you for it.'

I ran my fingers through his hair, holding him to me. Gently he pushed my legs apart with his knees. 'Me insatiable?' I teased, taking him in my hand. 'Look how nice and hard you are already.'

He nibbled my ear. 'It's your own fault, you drive me wild, I only have to look at you.'

'That's how I feel about you,' I murmured pressing myself against him.

He eased into me, filling me up, both of us emitting a groan. We began to move together, there nothing else in the world. 'God, I love you,' he breathed.

I nuzzled his neck, a light sheen of sweat on our bodies. 'I love you too.'

He moved his head, taking my nipple is his mouth, his hand seeing to my other one. Our love making just seemed to get better and better, we really were as one. When we were done, he lay by myside, kissing the mole I had just above my belly button and making me squirm.

'Does that tickle? He asked.

'Yeah,' I stroked his hair feeling content.

He lifted himself up onto his elbow. 'Marry me Tash.'

'Sod off,' I retorted, thinking he was joking.

He looked at me mock hurt. 'What? You don't want to marry me?'

I shook my head, hell would freeze over before I got married again.

'But I'm not that bad looking and I have my own car.'

'Shut up,' I kissed him. 'Come on let's go and keep Millie company and find something shit to watch on TV.'

Nineteen

It had been a long week, I knew I wouldn't hear anything about my dad just yet but I really wanted too. I needed to get the funeral out of the way so I could concentrate on the baby and the future.

I was getting big, I was only four and a half months pregnant, what was I going to be like at eight months?'

I finished putting the colour on my ladies' hair as Carling brought me a mug of herbal tea, staring at my burgeoning mid-drift critically.

'What?' I asked, getting the magazine for my customer.

'You look ever so big Tash,' she said without preamble.

I flushed slightly. 'I know, with Lexi and Jamie you could hardly tell I was pregnant until I was about seven months.'

'It's a different father,' Bev cut in.

I hadn't thought of that, with both my two I'd had identical pregnancies, no trouble all the way through and then labours from hell. Thinking about it I didn't have a craving for bourbons and gherkins either. With this one it was prawn cocktail crisps.

'Different sperm if it's different dads,' my lady looked up from her magazine. 'Stands to reason, it's going to be a different pregnancy.'

I gave her a bright smile, I didn't know her from Adam, she was a new customer, nosey mare. Although to be fair we were talking in front of her.

Bev smiled looking out of the window. 'Oh my God,' she cried making us all look in the same direction.

I did take a double take. Dale and Shay were riding around the car park on a pair of bikes waving at us.

'Where the hell have they got those from?' Carling was watching them with amusement.

'I don't know,' Bev looked at me.

I gave her a shrug, I'm pretty sure that Shay didn't have a bike when I left for work this morning. He was riding past the window, no hands, waving manically at me.

'Is that baby daddy?' My lady asked.

I shook my head. 'I've never seen him before in my life,' I replied as Carling tittered.

'Look at him,' Bev watched as my brother did a wheelie, caught the back wheel on the kerb and fell off. 'Oh my God.'

'He used to do that all the time,' I told her. 'He broke his arm once doing it. You'd think by now he would have realised he can't actually do them.'

We watched as Shay skidded to a halt, helping Dale up. They pushed the bikes to the salon and leant them up the outside wall before coming inside.

'Where have you got those bikes from?' Bev asked, brushing dirt off my brother's coat.

'From the garage, Ray found them out back,' Shay gave me his beautiful smile.

I looked at him, hair scrapped back in a man bun, his beard coming on a treat (he was a lazy shaver now he had snared me) and he wore a black parka with a furry lined hood, (he looked like a teenager, I looked like a granny in comparison).

'And what are you going to do with them? Bev asked primly.

'We're going to the pub on them,' Dale laughed. 'Come on Bev, do you want a backy around the car park?'

She giggled following him outside and Shay gave me a coy smile. 'I'd offer you one but it wouldn't work,' he thought for a moment. 'I could always get a basket for the front, you could sit in it like ET.'

I growled at him, I missed out on all the fun as Bev cocked her legs over Dale's bike and he sped around the car park with her shrieking in delight.

'What are they like?' Mrs Norton, one of our favourite old dears tittered. 'It's been ages since I could get my leg over on a bike.'

'I used to pinch Lexi's,' I admitted. 'If I was a bit short on petrol.'

'That I would have loved to have seen,' Shay smiled. 'So, is it okay if I go to the pub with Dale?' He gave me his puppy dog eyes.

'Fine but just be careful on the bikes, I don't want the police telling me you've gotten flattened under a ten-tonne truck because you were drunk in charge of a bicycle.' I warned.

He smiled again. 'I'm only going to have a couple. I'll cook tonight.'

Great wasn't I suffering enough from heartburn.

'Thanks.' I forced a smile. 'Just be careful.'

'Tash chill a little,' he applauded as Bev and Dale came back into the salon. 'At least, you managed to stay on it for more than five minutes.'

'It was weighted at the back,' he joked earning him a slap around the head from Bev. 'What time are we meeting at dad's tomorrow?' Dale asked, rubbing the back of his head.

'Ten,' I replied squatting on the stool by the reception desk.

'That early?' He pulled a face.

'You know what dad was like, it's probably going to be a big job.' I said patiently.

'Do you think we'll find a stash of money in the sugar jar?' He looked hopeful.

'No,' I answered shortly.

He laughed. 'No, you're probably right, come on Shayster, let's leave them to it.'

'Be careful.' I warned, I wasn't convinced they should be drinking and riding, I was such a stick in the mud.

Bev watched as they left a smile on her face. 'God, I do love him,' she said softly and then turned to me blushing. 'Sorry Tash.'

'What have you got to be sorry about, I'm glad you do.' I smiled going back to my customer.

They got back from the pub unscathed and we spent a quite evening in front of the TV. I wasn't looking forward to cleaning my dad's flat, it was a job I could do without.

By the next morning my nerves were all over the place but I couldn't quite figure out why.

'Ready?' Shay asked dressed in his scruffs.

'Ready,' I confirmed as he picked up the box of cleaning products that I was taking with me. I rubbed Millie's head going to the door and opening it for him.

We got to the flat at the same time as Bev and Dale, the April day was filled with weak sunshine and I took a deep breath as I opened the door.

'Oh my God!' Bev gagged, it still smelt ripe in the flat.

'That is not nice,' Shay agreed as the three of them looked to me.

I sighed going inside. My first job was to open the windows and then I looked around. I had never noticed how bare the flat was, minimalist in its furnishing.

'Where do we start?' Dale looked lost, some of his bravado disappearing.

'They're coming to pick the furniture up at two,' Shay massaged my shoulders knowing it was hard for me.

'Kitchen then,' Bev said firmly. 'You boys can start in the bathroom.'

'I'm not going in there,' Dale pulled a face.

'Do as you're told,' she smiled lovingly at him.

'Come on, let's leave the ladies to the kitchen,' Shay picked up some of the cleaning stuff and headed for the bathroom. Dale pulled a face following him reluctantly.

Bev and I went into the kitchen and I cringed, it was filthy. Cans all over the work tops, food going mouldy on the plates. She looked at me with sympathy in her face.

'We'll sort it babe,' she said softly.

'How could he live like this?' I demanded. 'Why would he live like this?'

'It was what he wanted, you can't change that.'

I shook my head, pulling on a pair of marigolds and taking a bin liner from the stash I had brought with me. Without a word I began to empty the plates and cans into them.

'The dirty bastard!' Dale appeared in the kitchen. 'You want to see the state of the bathroom.'

'No, we don't,' I retorted.

'No, we don't,' Bev echoed making gagging noises, the kitchen was bad enough.

Dale leant against one of the units watching us. 'You shouldn't have to do this sis,' his voice was soft.

'Yes, I do,' I contradicted. 'We're not him Dale, we'll never be him.' Anyway, don't leave Shay cleaning the bathroom go and help him.'

He grumbled under his breath, leaving us be. Bev opened one of the cupboards and grimacing. 'Did he ever just run a wet cloth around?'

'No, that's why I'm such a clean freak.' I replied.

'I understand you so much better now,' she began to empty it just a few pieces of crockery, nothing matching.

I walked with trepidation to the fridge, taking a deep breath, I opened it, sadness threatening to overwhelm me. All that was in there, food wise was a lump of mouldy cheese and a plastic bottle of soured milk. There was, however half a dozen cans of Banks's bitter.

'I'll have them if you don't want them,' Dale was behind me.

'I was going to chuck them in the bin,' I turned to him with a frown.

'Waste not want not,' he beamed.

I sighed. 'Why aren't you helping Shay?'

'He wants to know if you've got a pneumatic drill to get the black from the toilet bowl.'

'Oh my God,' Bev gagged again. 'That's disgusting.'

'Bang some bleach down it.' I advised. 'It's up to the council then.'

By one we had nearly finished, there really was that little in the flat to sort. His clothes I had divided into two piles, things that could go to the charity shop and stuff that a homeless person would be too picky to have on their backs.

'Do you want anything to remember him by?' I asked Dale.

'Why the fuck would I want to remember that old bastard?' he asked.

'Don't Dale,' Bev chided softly.

'I've got a flask in my bag,' I changed the subject. 'Does anyone want a hot chocolate?'

'You are such a girl scout,' he teased. 'Have you got anything to eat?'

'Kit Kat's, I replied. I'd brought plastic cups as well, I didn't want to drink out of his mugs.

We sat at the small dining room table, drinking and eating the Kit Kat's. 'Do you think he's here?' Bev asked looking around the room.

'Like a ghost? Dale scoffed.

She scowled at him. 'Humans are full of energy, it has to go somewhere.'

'Nah,' he shook his head. 'We're like a light switch, once we're dead that's it nothing, like we've just been switched off.'

'And here was me so looking forward to spending my eternity with you.' Her tone was biting.

'I thought I saw him, the night I found him. He was standing at the bottom of the bed.'

'Dirty pervert,' Dale shook his head.

'It was just a bad dream sweetheart.' Shay rubbed my shoulder. 'You scared the bejaysus out of me when you screamed though.'

'It seemed so real.'

Bev shivered drinking the last of her hot chocolate. 'Well I believe in them and I wouldn't want to live here knowing this is where he died.'

'Me neither,' I admitted as Shay's mobile began to ring.

'The lads are here,' he said and he and Dale disappeared out of the flat.

'Who are they?' Bev was peering out the window.

'Haven't a clue, just a couple of blokes that Shay knows,' I was ready to go home, I was all done in.

They came into the flat, two cheeky looking chaps in their late twenties.

'Tash, Bev, Chad and Kenny,' Shay did the introductions.

'Hello,' I smiled, they had very strange accents.

'Shall we get cracking?' Chad looked at me and Bev appreciatively, we still had it.

Dale and Shay helped them carry the spartan pieces of furniture to the flat bed lorry outside, it took several trips.

In between I managed to collar Shay. 'Are they gypo's?'

He gave me a sweet smile. 'The word you're looking for dahling is travellers.'

'Are they your relations?' How did he know gypo's?

'Cheeky,' he wagged a finger at me. 'No, they are Rita's relations, you know Ray's wife.'

'Rita's a,' I paused. 'A traveller?' She didn't seem like one although I doubt they walked around with badges on declaring the fact.

'She was but when she met Ray she settled in a house, she was very young.'

'Right,' I was thoughtful for a moment. 'They won't just dump the stuff on the side of the road, will they?'

He tapped the tip of my nose. 'Stop being a worry wort, they are under strict instructions to take it to the tip.'

'Okay,' I glanced around, everything was done, we could go home once the things had all been loaded onto the lorry.

Chad and Kenny came back for the last couple of chairs. 'Thank you ever so much for doing this,' I said giving them a tired smile.

'Not a problem for Shay's wan,' Chad replied I think he did all the talking, Kenny just seemed to nod.

'What's a wan?' Bev stifled a yawn.

'Woman,' Shay answered. 'It's an Irish word.'

'Oh,' she yawned again. 'I'm shattered.'

'Here,' Shay pressed some money into Chad's hand. 'Have a drink on us.'

He waved it away. 'Buy the baby something with it.'

'Cheers,' Shay put it back in his pocket.

'Thank you, that's kind.' I was touched.

'Right see you soon,' Chad said goodbye and Kenny nodded, then they were gone.

'They were nice pikeys,' Bev smiled getting our coats.

'Good blokes,' Dale agreed. 'Oh, what's this?'

'An old biscuit tin,' Bev replied. 'We'll sling it in the bin on the way out.'

'Have you had a look inside?' He went to retrieve it from the floor as I looked around the empty flat feeling lost. It truly was all over, he really was dead.'

Dale had got the lid off the tin and was peering inside. 'Tash,' he said softly holding out a photograph.

I gave him a puzzled look before taking it from him. It was a picture of me when I was four in my dad's arms. I had thrown my arms around his neck and we were both smiling for the camera, proper genuine smiles.

'It's the only photo he's got,' Dale kept his voice soft.

Numbness spread through me that was how it should have been, not how it was. 'Sweet?' Shay was looking at me.

I stared at him, my eyes bright with unshed tears. My dad was dead, he was gone, I could never make it right now, couldn't change anything now.

The sob tore through my body and I began to shake, tears falling now unheeded. Slowly I sank to my knees still clutching the photograph.

'Tash!' He cried alarmed, kneeling with me, capable arms holding me tight as I let out the grief I had for what should have been. 'Baby, it's okay.'

'He's gone,' I spluttered.

'I know baby, I know.' He planted kisses on top of my head.

'Sis, don't,' Dale was holding Bev, his own eyes filled with tears. 'Come on let's go home.'

Shay pulled me to my feet, hugging me tightly. I put the photo back into the tin, taking it with me.

'Don't get upsetting yourself,' Dale ordered, although he looked like he was going to cry himself. I wiped away the tears, not trusting myself to speak. 'Think of the baby and what you do have,' he continued wisely, hugging me.

We walked in silence to where we had parked, the boys carrying the cleaning things. Bev was going to drop off the bag of clothes to the charity shop tomorrow.

'See you Tuesday,' she gave me a hug. 'Phone me if you need me.'

'Thank you,' I whispered. 'And thanks for your help today.'

'Not a problem,' she kissed Shay's cheek. 'Look after her.'

We drove home in silence, Shay sensing that I didn't want to talk. Once home I saw to Millie and announced I was going for a shower, cleaning the flat had made me feel grimy.

I dressed in jogging bottoms and an old sweatshirt, going downstairs as Shay came up for his shower.

By the time he was done I was sitting outside on the small wall that separated the grass from the patio, my knees drawn up as far as I could. I needed fresh air, to clear my head. I had the beginnings of a headache.

Shay came out to me, straddling the wall behind me so he had a foot either side. His hands came around my waist, head resting on my shoulder. 'Okay?' He asked softly.

I shook my head fresh tears falling. 'I just feel so bloody angry,' I admitted. 'He had two lovely grandchildren and I bet half the time he couldn't remember their names.'

Shay stayed silent, what could he say?

'Why would he be like it Shay?' I asked sadly. 'Who could be a father and not want his children?'

'I don't know, I didn't have a father in my life.'

I turned so I was sitting side on to him. 'Do you wish you had?'

'I wish mam didn't have to struggle as much as she did bringing me up alone with no husband and family there for her,' he replied.

'Do you ever wonder what he's like?' I pushed.

'Curious, yes. I know I look like him but I wonder if I'm like him in other ways too.'

'You've got your mom's kindness and caring ways.' I brushed his lips with my own, an idea was forming in my mind.

'Yeah?' His smile was sweet.

'Yeah,' I confirmed. 'I love you.'

'Love you too,' he reached into his pocket bringing out the money he had tried to give Chad.

'What's this for?' I asked when he put it in my hand, there was fifty pounds.

'Buy something when you go to Merryhill tomorrow. Something for you or the baby or both and buy mam some lunch.

'Thank you,' I played with his curls.

'Talking of which shall we sort some food out?' he asked as Millie came to see where we were.

I nodded following him inside.

Twenty

I was looking forward to spending the day with Moira, I'd never done the whole shopping thing with my own mother. I had tried a few times but finally gave up when she said to me, 'Why would we want to go shopping together?'

After my mini meltdown yesterday I felt better, I had got it all out of my system. The biscuit tin had no other personal mementoes in apart from the picture. There was just his birth certificate and bizarrely enough he and my mom's wedding certificate. They had married just four months before I was born.

I made sure Millie was sorted, then I checked I had everything I needed before calling Lexi.

'Hi mom are you okay?' she asked brightly.

'I am love,' I replied. 'What are you up to today?'

'I'm going to study in the library,' she sneezed daintily. 'I think I'm getting a cold.'

'Bless you. Dose yourself up with Lemsip,' I advised. 'Now Lex I want to pick your brain.'

'That won't take long,' she chuckled.

'How hard do you think it would be to find a person in southern Ireland?'

She was immediately suspicious. 'Who do you need to find southern Ireland?'

'Shay's dad,' I answered, a touch of excitement in my voice.

'Don't go their mom,' she advised.

'It would be a surprise for him,' I ignored her. 'He was only saying last night that he was curious about him.'

'No,' she was firm.

'Anyway, when I see Moira today I'm going to discreetly pump her for information,' I chatted.

'I really don't think you should or if you insist on poking your nose in then you should talk to Shay or Moira first,' she was the voice of reason.

'It wouldn't be a surprise then if I did that would it,' I laughed lightly. 'Anyway, I'm not saying I'm going to do it, I don't even know his last name.'

'Do you know his first?' She asked.

'Albie, Shay's middle name,' I replied. 'So, do you think it would be easy to find him?'

'Relatively, if we know where he lives, his age and full name.' She sounded confident.

That was food for thought. 'Okay love, speak to you tomorrow, I've got to go and pick Moira up.'

'Don't do anything silly,' she warned. 'Give Moira a hug from me. Love you loads.'

'Love you too,' I hit the off button making my way to Moira's. She was in the window looking for me and I waved as I got out of the car.

'How are you and my grandchild? She trilled when she opened the door.

'We're good thank you,' I replied.

'How did the flat cleaning go?' She chatted as she got her coat and handbag.

I told her about the photograph and how I had cried and she gave me a hug, it was lovely having her in my life.

'Let's go and do some serious shopping,' she declared.

We arrived at Merryhill, it wasn't too busy and I had my sensible shoes on as I had a feeling we were going to do a lot of walking.

'So, what are we looking for?' I asked.

'An outfit, shoes,' she began.

'Sexy underwear? I teased.

She gave me a flirty look. 'I've already got them.'

'Go Moira,' I cheered, I hoped I still had a good sex life at her age.

'Now hat or fascinator?' She stopped outside Debenhams.

'Fascinator,' I replied promptly. 'But we need to pick your dress first just to make sure.'

So, Debenhams was our first port of call and we trawled around the dresses with Moira seeing a few that she liked bit it was such a big decision that I cautioned her to have a good look around and not rush into anything. Although until we had the dress we couldn't get the accessories.

We walked around the shops, Moira trying on a variety of outfits until I declared it was time for lunch. 'Shay's treating us,' I informed her.

'He's a good boy. Eat Central?' She suggested.

'Sounds good to me, what shall we have?'

'I just fancy a jacket potato,' she found a table as I went to order, cheese and coleslaw for Moira on her jacket and cheese and chilli for me. Plus, a nice cup of tea, I allowed myself one proper tea or coffee per day.

I carried them to the table, taking of my coat and hanging it on the back of the chair.

'What have you got to get?' She asked.

'Shay's birthday present and something to wear for dad's funeral.'

'Have you seen a wedding outfit yet?' She tucked in her potato hungrily.

'I've seen loads of dresses that I would love to wear for the wedding if I wasn't pregnant. I'm going to be nearly eight and a half months, I think I'll wait till nearer the date before I buy anything, I don't know how big I'll be.'

'You'll look stunning whatever you wear,' she smiled kindly. 'You know I can't wait for the baby to arrive, I'm so glad that Shay has a chance to be a father.'

'He'll make a brilliant dad,' I predicted.

'He'll be there changing the nappies, doing the night feeds,' she chuckled.

'And I'll let him,' I grinned. 'I'm so glad that I've got him.'

'He's the lucky one,' she countered. 'Some of the girls he used to date, well if he'd come home and told me he'd gotten them pregnant I'd have grounded him for life.'

'What were they like?' I tried to sound casual but I was curious.

She gave me a knowing look. 'Not as beautiful and as kind as you are.'

I blushed looking down at my meal. 'I think he'll spoil the baby rotten,' I smiled.

'That's what father's do,' she was quiet for a moment. 'I often feel sorry for Shay not knowing his da. I ask myself if I was selfish not telling Albie about him, not letting Shay know him.'

'You did what you thought best,' I replied.

'Albie would have made wonderful father, he always wanted children you see? His wife couldn't have any. Quin was such a catholic place though, she shuddered. 'If I'd have told him about Shay then he would have had the dilemma of acknowledging him which would have him ostracized or divorcing his wife to be with me which was against his beliefs.'

'He couldn't have been that devout though if he had an extra marital affair,' I said without thinking. 'Sorry.'

'No, I agree,' she gave me a smile. 'I loved him dearly Tash but I knew I was making the right decision walking away. I never thought he would leave his wife you see, never thought I deserved him too. It broke my heart though, it was such a hard thing to do and I loved him very much. It was only when I met Alan that I felt truly over him.'

I filled up, what a lonely life she must have led. 'What would your name have been if you had married him?'

'Cassidy.'

'Moira Cassidy. Shay Cassidy,' I said the names out loud.

She smiled. 'I'll be Cole's when I marry Alan. Moira Coles, if I was at school the kids would call me "arseholes"

I began to titter, she could be quite funny.

She laughed too. 'Oh, but Shay is so like his dad. Same hair, same smile, same temperament. He even walks the same. Albie always treated me like a lady same as Shay does you. He'll never hurt you Tash, not like your ex did.'

'No, he won't,' I just had to keep convincing myself.

'He was so gorgeous though, just like my son. He was our postman, he moved to Quin just after his wedding, his wife had family in the village. We would exchange the odd word at first and then we started to talk, I mean really talk.'

I lay down my knife and fork, my plate clear and leant forward enjoying listening to her.

'Then one thing just led to another,' she looked away blushing.

'What would you do if your paths crossed again?' I asked sipping my tea.

She giggled like a teenager. 'My stomach would just flip like it did all those years ago. He had a head of dark curls just like my boy. Sometimes I glance at Shay and just for a split second I'll think its Albie standing there.'

She was quiet for a moment. 'I wish Shay had known him. I haven't done a bad job though have I bringing him up on my own?'

I looked at her, this woman who had taken me to her heart and wanted nothing in return. 'I think you've done a wonderful job,' I said softly.

'Thank you,' she went quiet again. 'I think if they did meet then they would like each other.'

'Do you?' My brain was going into overdrive, surely that made what I had discussed with Lexi earlier something to really consider. What a wonderful surprise that would be. I would talk to Lexi, get her to help me track Albie down.

'I do,' she finished her tea. 'Shall we carry on with the shopping?'

I nodded pulling on my coat. I got a pair of black maternity trousers and a black blouse from Next which would do for the funeral and I brought Shay a nice pair of jeans and a slim fit cable jumper in Royal blue that he would look so shaggable in I could hardly wait for his birthday, from River Island.

Then in Clintons I saw a little teddy bear with "Happy Birthday Daddy" and even a birthday card with "Happy Birthday from the Bump" on.

We also ended up back in Debenhams to have a second look at one of the dresses she had seen earlier.

'Try it on again,' I suggested and she hurried to the fitting rooms as I looked at all the beautiful dresses that were too slinky for me to get into. I was going to look like a hippopotamus at the wedding.

'Tash?' Moira called me.

I turned she was wearing a shift dress with a long coat over the top both in a pale pink delicate lace.

My eyes filled with tears. 'You look beautiful.'

'Really?' She looked unsure. 'I really like it.'

'It's gorgeous, such a delicate pink,' I watched as she gave me a twirl. 'Dove grey shoes and a matching fascinator would look a treat.'

She stared at the mirror. 'I'm going to have it.'

'I would.'

'Shall we look for shoes?' She looked so excited.

'Yeah,' I smiled feeling knackered but wanting to sort Moira out.

She changed back into her clothes and we went to the shoe department where we found a fab pair of court shoes and as a bonus we found the perfect fascinator.

Weighed down with bags we walked past Mothercare. 'Shall we?' Moira asked.

I nodded, I still had the money that Shay had given me. There was so many lovely things in the shop but I decided to be practical, a changing mat, vests, bibs things like that.

Moira had disappeared around the other end of the shop coming back with a bottle steriliser, pack of baby bottles and a multipack of baby wipes. 'Can I?'

'No, you've got a wedding to pay for,' I couldn't let her spend her money.

'If I can't treat my grandchild then it's a bad job,' she teased playfully. 'Babies are expensive enough.'

I gave her a big love. 'Thank you, it's more than my own mother will do.'

'The woman's a fool, she doesn't know what she's missing.' We paid for our purchases and decided it was time to head home, I wanted to text Lexi the details about Shay's dad before he got home. Plus, my feet were killing me.

By the time we reached Moira's it was a little after four. 'Are you having a cup of tea?' Moira asked.

'I'll get home if you don't mind, Millie will be platting,' I helped her get the shopping from the boot.

'Of course.'

'Will you keep the baby things here please, I don't want to tempt fate.' I asked.

'Of course, I will,' she picked up all her bags.

'Thank you for today Moira, it's been really nice, I've really enjoyed it,' I kissed her cheek. 'And thank you for the baby things.'

'You're welcome and no, thank you for a lovely day, you are such good company Tash, my son is very fortunate. Speak soon.'

'We will,' I got back into the car and with a wave I drove home.

I was knackered when I got home, Shay would have to see to big dog, I couldn't take her a walk if my life depended on it. I put the kettle on I would have a nice cup of herbal tea and quick lie on the settee.

I was fast asleep with Millie lying on the floor next to me Shay got home.

He stood watching me for a few minutes thinking how peaceful I looked lying on my back my stomach swollen with our child. A feeling of complete and utter love washed over him and then Millie ruined it all by waking up and barking a greeting.

I shot up, dribble at the corner of my mouth.

'Hello beautiful,' he said fussing big dog.

'Hello handsome,' I wiped my mouth discreetly with the back of my hand.

'Have you had a good day shopping?' He sat next to me on the settee.

'It's been great, I didn't realise how tired I was though,' I yawned loudly.

He put his arm around me. 'I tell you what I'll take Millie a walk, you relax and I'll pick up some fish and chips, I can tie her up outside.'

'That would be great, can I have chicken and mushroom pie though please?' I asked.

'Mammy can have anything she wants,' he kissed me.

'Moira has brought us some things for the baby, a bottle sterilizer and some bottles she's keeping them at hers.' I told him. 'She's spoiling us.'

'I'll take a look next time I'm there,' he seemed pleased. 'Did she get her outfit?'

'Oh love, it's stunning,' I enthused. 'She is going to be beautiful bride.'

'She is,' he agreed. 'Are you okay you look a little down?'

'I'm fine,' I shrugged. 'I just keep thinking I'm going to look horrible at the wedding. I'll be huge and there really isn't anything nice for me to wear. All the dresses I liked were definitely not for pregnant women.'

'You my dahling will look beautiful whatever you wear. You would look stunning even in a quilt cover, you are daft Tash.'

I narrowed my eyes, what a copout. Right I thought disappearing upstairs.

Going into the airing cupboard I stripped off my clothes tying the duvet cover around me like a toga dress, as an afterthought I put the pillow case on my head. Let him see now if he thought I looked good in a duvet cover now.

I tried to control my laughter as I headed back downstairs. Shay was still in the living room, a mug of tea in his hand. 'What the feck!' He exclaimed.

'Well how do I look?' I gave him a twirl. 'It's my outfit for your mom's wedding.'

'You are a nutter!' He cried.

'Er excuse me you're the one who said that I would look good in a quilt cover.' I smiled.

'Have you got anything on under that?' He was looking at me appreciatively.

'Might have, might not,' I teased.

'Take it off,' he tried to smile.

'Make me,' I challenged.

'What?' He took a step towards me.

'I said if you think your man enough make me,' I smirked.

He took a step towards me and I fled up the stairs giggling, Millie joining in with a bark.

He was hot on my heels as I went into our bedroom, laughing loudly. Roughly he pulled me against him. 'You're an eejit,' he said kissing me.

'I thought you were fetching fish and chips?'

He pushed me down gently on the bed and I watched as he shed his clothes quickly. He was such a beautiful man.

Laughing he climbed on the bed, untangling me from the quilt. 'Look at you,' he breathed kissing my stomach. 'Hello baby, your mom has been buying you things and your gran too.'

He moved up the bed kissing me deeply. 'Shall I go to the chip shop now?'

'Only if you want a punch,' I threatened.

He laughed, lying between my legs. 'Marry me,' he said.

'Sod off,' I pushed him away.

'Don't tell me to sod off,' he chided. Pushing forward he filled me with him.

'Shay,' I groaned, nails raking his back.

'Nice?' He moved against me.

'Yes,' I breathed moving with him.

For the next half hour, we made our beautiful love.

Twenty~One

I picked up my dad's death certificate on the eleventh of April and the main cause of death was Alcoholic Cirrhosis. I googled it as soon as I went outside and basically, he had drunk himself to death.

Standing in the car park I felt so angry that I could have exploded. The one man who should have loved and neutered us had turned his back on Dale and me and had his most lasting and intimate relationship was with alcohol.

Shay could see I wasn't happy as soon as he got home and I gave him the death certificate to read. 'He was nothing but a drunken bastard,' I fumed. 'He could have had so much if he hadn't loved the booze more than anything.'

'I know sweet,' he gave me a cuddle and I did feel sorry for him. This was supposed to be an exciting time for us and he had a pregnant girlfriend who seemed to be in a permanent bad mood.

'Bev said I can nip in and out tomorrow, I need to arrange the funeral and the do after,' I told him.

'Is Dale going with you?' He fussed around Millie.

I shook my head. 'He hadn't offered.

'You don't wait for him to offer,' he pulled a face. 'You tell him. If you're going to see the funeral director than he can sort out the pub.'

'I don't mind,' I replied weakly.

'Well I do,' his tone was firm. 'You do enough Tash, I'm not having you stressing about this. If you arrange the funeral then he arranges the wake.'

'He won't be arsed,' I predicted.

'He's going to have to be, it's only fair,' I could tell he wasn't in the mood for me to argue.

'Fine, I'll phone him now,' I picked up my mobile calling my brother, he answered quickly.

'Alright sis?'

'Yes, I've got dad's death certificate, we can get the funeral sorted now.'

'What did the old bastard die of?' He asked without tact.

'Drink basically,' my answer was short.

'Now there's a surprise,' he retorted.

'I'm going to see the funeral people tomorrow, any preferences? Music at the crem?' I asked.

'Ring of Fire,' he laughed. 'Because that's where he is, down below.'

'Don't,' I scolded. 'As soon as I have the date and the time I will let you know and then you can go to the Angel pub in Wednesfield and arrange a little do after. Ask them if they can put a bit of a buffet on.'

'We are not having a "party" for him,' his tone was bitter.

'Yes, we are and it's not a "party",' I scolded. 'We are going to do right by him, even if he never did right by us.' Shay was looking at me as if to say "don't back down".

I heard a voice in the background and then Dale said. 'Fine, Bev and me will sort it.'

'Thank you,' I said gratefully, closing my eyes briefly. 'Are you okay?'

'Yeah, are you?' his answer was full of bravado.

'I am, I'll call you tomorrow,' I smiled at Shay sadly. 'Bye.'

'See you sis.'

'He's going to sort it then?' Shay asked when I put my mobile on the table.

'Yes, Bev will help him,' I smiled again. 'Sorry I'm being such a miserable cow.'

'I'm used to you being a miserable cow,' he teased resting his hands on my shoulders and kissing the top of my head. 'I'll go and have my shower.'

I spent a couple of hours at the funeral directors the next day and they were so helpful. I decided on a bog-standard cremation in the cheapest coffin they had, after all he was going to be burnt and he would have preferred me to buy everyone a drink rather than spend the money on a fancy wooden box that much I did know.

Luckily, we were having financial help for the funeral, neither Dale nor I had much in the way of savings, me less so now with Lexi at university.

So, everything was set, the funeral was to take place on the twenty-seventh April, a Friday. The time was eleven am just in time for pubs to be open when it was finished, how apt.

The day of the funeral was dull and drizzly, with a cold chill in the air. I found out my old herringbone winter coat that I couldn't fasten but at least it looked respectable.

Shay had to lend a black suit from Nick at work, he didn't own a suit of any description, but he did buy a new white shirt and black tie.

He did scrub up nicely. 'You okay?' he asked coming into the bedroom.

I turned from the mirror. 'Bit nervous,' I admitted. Going to him and straightening his tie. 'You look very handsome in a suit.'

'Do I?' He smiled. 'Thank you.'

'Shaggable Shay,' I teased.

'What?' He gave me his special smile.

I shook my head, finding out my black handbag. I was glad both he and Dale had promised to wear suits, I just hoped Dale would keep his word. No one was going to say we didn't care.

I looked at my watch and then looked out of the window, 'Bev and Dale are here with Jamie,' I hurried down the stairs, Belle and Lexi were keeping Millie amused in the kitchen.

'Don't get dog hairs on your trousers,' I warned going to the front door and letting them in. They had arrived in a taxi, Alan had kindly offered to take Belle to the funeral with them.

'Sis,' Dale hugged me tightly and I was glad to see he had indeed put a suit on and Bev had trimmed his hair.

'You okay?' I stroked his cheek before turning to my son. 'Jamie, I'm glad you're here,' and at least he looked relatively decent with his school trousers and shirt on and a black Harrington jacket.

He allowed me to hug him which surprised me but when Shay joined us he slinked off to his sister. 'Sorry,' I mumbled to Shay feeling a little embarrassed.

'It's okay,' he shrugged, pulling Millie away from Bev's skirt.

'I'm going to swing for him,' Dale said angrily.

'Not today babe,' Bev but a restraining hand on his arm.

I went to the window looking out for Moira and Alan, they had promised to get here before the hearse and car arrived. 'Do you think mom will turn up?' Dale stood by me, looking very smart and I was proud of him.

'I bloody hope not,' I retorted, 'I haven't seen her since the day she slapped me round the face.'

'And I haven't seen her either.'

'I hope no one's told her when it is,' I chaffed, that was all I needed, her turning up.

'She wouldn't dare show her face,' Bev assured us as Moira and Alan arrived.

'You okay love?' Alan gave me a hug then he shook Dale's hand.

'I'll be glad when it's all done,' I admitted, I really liked Alan.

'Sweetheart,' Moira gathered me in her arms. 'You are going to be fine trust me.'

'Thank you,' I leant my head against her shoulder enjoying the comfort. I don't know what I would have done without her these last few weeks.

'You're welcome,' she took a step back tapping my arm. I smiled turning back to the window, my nerves increasing.

I breathed a sigh of relief as the hearse pulled up along with the funeral car. Shay and Bev were coming in the car with me, Dale, Lexi and Jamie, as our partners it was only fitting.

'Time to go sweet,' Shay stood behind me.

I nodded reluctantly as we all gathered our things and trooped to the front door. 'You go first Shay,' I said quietly, I wanted to run upstairs and hide under the duvet.

He shook his head. 'You, Dale and the kids need to go to the car first.' He said softly. 'It's how it's done.'

'Oh,' I began to tremble again as I opened the front door.

Moira pulled Shay to one side. 'Keep an eye on Tash son, she's shaking like a leaf and I don't want her getting too upset.'

'I will,' he promised following them outside and nodding a greeting to Joe, our next-door neighbour.

Moira and Alan followed, while Belle secured the house.

The journey to the crem seemed to take forever before we were pulling up outside the chapel. I stared at the coffin, a spray of white flowers on the top, I still couldn't believe that my dad was in there dead.

I could see Moira and Alan parking up and I knew that we had to wait until everyone had arrived before we could go in. I wasn't expecting many people though, dad's side of the family had lost touch with him years ago and I hadn't wasted my time letting them know of his death. His drinking buddies would probably come on the bus if they came at all and I wasn't particularly bothered one way or the other.

Shay took my hand, giving me an encouraging smile. 'Soon be over sweet.'

I nodded my eyes going back to the coffin.

As Moira, Alan and Belle arrived so did Sam and Meera. Sam wasn't in the best of moods, he had wanted to go to the funeral by himself but Meera had insisted on accompanying him.

'It looks like they've arrived all ready,' Meera pulled her coat around her.

'We'd have gotten here earlier if you had stopped trying to decide which coat to wear and had just chosen one.'

She looked at him hurt. 'Will you stop shouting at me?'

He ignored her. 'What's Paddy doing in the car with her?' He demanded. 'He shouldn't be in there, he didn't know Paul.'

'He's there for Tash,' she hated how jealous he was of Tash's new love, it made her feel insecure.

'For now,' he growled. 'The thick paddy bastard.'

Belle coughed pointedly behind them and Sam turned as Moira pulled herself up to her full height. 'That's my son you're calling names,' she pointed an angry finger at him. 'Thank yourself lucky we're at a funeral.

With that she took Belle's arm, walking towards the chapel. 'Who the feck is that?'

'Lexi's dad and his wife,' Belle replied, trying not to smile, Moira could be a feisty lady when she wanted to be.

Behind them Sam and Meera kept a safe distance as they made their way to the funeral party.

Twenty~Two

I sat in the car and took a deep breath. 'Ready?' Shay asked softly, sitting opposite me. I nodded as the men from the funeral directors opened the door and he got out first, taking my hand to help me from the car. The others followed and a sombre air hung over us.

Taking Jamie's hand (I was surprised he let me) we began to filter into the chapel. 'I'm okay mom,' he protested. 'I don't need you to hold my hand.'

'It's not for you, it's for me,' I replied with a sad smile.

Following the coffin slowly we were directed to the front row and sat Bev, Dale, Lexi, Jamie me and Shay. I felt better having everyone around me, it showed the world that although our father couldn't give a monkey's fart it didn't stop *us* being a united family.

A hand touched my shoulder and I turned quickly, Moira was behind me and I was glad.

The official came and we turned to the front, my dad's coffin slightly off centre. 'Good morning,' he said giving us a professional smile. 'Thank you all for coming.'

I looked around, there was about twenty of us, more than I thought there would be.

'Friends,' he continued. 'We are here today to honour the life of Paul Henry Wilkins. A funeral is an opportunity to join in taking leave of someone we have loved but it is more than that.'

I felt Shay take my hand and I turned to give him a tight smile, my eyes filling with tears.

He continued with the ceremony, when he got to the part when he said. 'He will live on with your memories and remain a member of your family through the influence he has had on you and the special part he played in your lives.' I began to cry quietly my head bowed.

Shay tightened his grip on my hand passing me a tissue as Jamie rubbed my arm in a comforting gesture. I looked along our line and was surprised to see Bev was also crying, I didn't even think she liked my dad, it was probably just the sadness at a wasted life.

'Paul was father to Natasha and Dale and grandfather to Lexi and Jamie,' he smiled at us as Dale and Lexi sat there stony faced. 'And I'm sure he took pride and comfort from his cherished family.'

Dale shook his head, stretching out one leg. 'Now can I ask you to take a quiet moment to remember Paul and if you have a religious belief perhaps say a quiet prayer.'

We did and I closed my eyes remembering all the bad things, the drink, leaving us short of money when mom left, laying into Dale in one of his drunken rages because his son had done something wrong at school. I truly could not think of one good memory.

'Would you please stand for the committal,' he smiled again.

'You're doing brilliant dahling,' Shay whispered as we stood.

My smile was sad as I squeezed his hand. I just wanted it to be over now. I wanted to get on with our life.

'To everything there is a reason and a time to every purpose on earth, a time to be born and a time to die. Here in this last act, in sorrow but without fear, in love and appreciation, we commit Paul Henry Wilkins to his natural end.'

My sobs became a little louder, I still couldn't believe that he was gone without any chance of reconciliation, of finding something between us. Dale and I were his children, surely we must have meant something to him?

He continued. 'We have been remembering with love and gratitude of a life that has ended. Let us return to our own homes and to our work, enriched and inspired by these memories.'

The curtain began to close around the coffin and an elastic band felt like it had wrapped itself around my chest.

The silence in the room was overpowering as Shay motioned for us to leave the chapel. He was so good, taking care of us. I could see Sam and Meera sitting three rows back and his eyes seemed to be boring into me. I looked away quickly putting my arm around Jamie.

We went outside and had a look at the funeral spray that had sat on top of the coffin. Next to it was a beer can fashioned from flowers, I stooped awkwardly to read the card.

'Who sent that?' Shay was next to me.

I grimaced. 'Sam and Meera,' I replied shortly. Sam always had to show off, to go one better, tosser.

'Really?' he frowned.

'I don't know why, he hadn't seen him for years and they never got on anyway.'

Shay pursed his lips and I prayed for a peaceful day. 'Mom,' Lexi cuddled me. 'How are you?'

'I'm good,' I kissed her cheek, stroking her hair.

'Tash,' Meera stood in front of me, a hand on my arm. 'I know how you and your dad were not that close but I am sorry.'

'Thank you,' I nodded. 'And thanks for coming.'

'Tash,' Sam folded me in his arms. 'I can't believe he's gone.'

I pushed him away expecting him to burst into uncontrollable tears going by the look on his face.

'Thank you for coming Sam,' I said as politely as I could. 'And thank you for getting Jamie here.'

'I threatened him,' he ruffled his son's hair affectionately. 'Ah Lexi, I thought you'd emigrated.

'Not now dad,' she said shortly going to Moira and Alan.

I gave him a smile that never reached my eyes and took Shay's hand joining them. 'So that's the ex,' Moira linked her arm in mine. 'Not a bad looking fella.'

Shay might have actually growled as his mom shook her head. 'Just saying,' she smiled. 'Doesn't mean he isn't a total fecker though.'

'Natasha,' Vince had arrived. 'A good send off for your old man.'

'You're all coming to the Angel aren't you?' I asked. 'There's a bit of a buffet on.'

'Of course, we all will,' he paused looking at my tear stained face. 'It was never yours or Dale's fault. Paul was never meant to be a father.' He bowed slightly, hurrying away.

'Come on love,' Moira steered me towards the funeral car. 'It's nearly done.'

I felt drained when we arrived at the Angel, Shay ordering the drinks. 'Whisky?' I raised an eyebrow.

'It's that kind of day,' he put his hand around my waist, looking over at my ex.

'Leave it hun,' I said wearily.

I'm not going to say a word, I promise,' he assured me. 'Jamie what are you having?'

'Cola please,' he replied and at least he had remembered his manners.

'Who is this handsome young man?' Moira joined us at the bar with Alan in tow.

'This is Jamie,' I answered.

'Isn't he lovely?' Moira exclaimed as he went bright red.

'He is,' I confirmed smiling. 'Jamie this is Shay's mom and her fiancé Alan.'

He mumbled a hello as Moira took his arm. 'Come with me and tell me all about yourself,' she ordered. 'I bet you have all the girls after you at school.'

He looked at me helplessly as she steered him to a table at the corner. 'Now Jamie,' she said. 'As you know Shay and I are Irish and do you know what the Irish people drink at a wake like this one?'

He shook his head.

'Why whisky of course. So, what do you say, are you man enough?'

'Yes,' he nodded eagerly.

'Just don't tell your mom,' she warned going to the bar.

'Your mom has kidnapped Jamie,' I told Shay.

He smiled warmly. 'She is really good with kids, she'll have him eating out of her hand in no time.'

'You think?' I asked doubtfully.

'Oh yes,' he replied as Alan called him.

'Natasha, can I get you a drink?' Vince appeared at my elbow.

'I'm good thank you,' I replied. 'I'm glad you all came.'

'It was the least we could do,' he replied as we were joined by a couple of men I didn't know but I could tell they were dads drinking buddies.

'Sorry about Paul,' the one said as Dale made is way over.

'Thank you,' I replied politely.

'He was a good bloke, do anything for anyone,' he carried on.

'Except for his own family,' Dale said bitterly.

'Shut up,' I warned.

'Well it's true,' he retorted. 'Mac don't know what he was like. The only thing he was interested in was a beer glass.'

I couldn't argue, Dale was right. I felt weary, I wanted to go home but Shay was talking to some people I didn't know a glass of whisky in his hand.

'Babe, how you holding up?' Bev sidled up to me.

'Knackered,' I admitted. 'I've had enough now.'

'I think Shay's enjoying his whisky.'

'He's Irish,' I teased. 'Any excuse will do.'

'Tash,' she laughed. 'Don't be so naughty.'

'It's true,' I rubbed my stomach without thinking.

'Baby dancing?' she asked and I nodded. 'Poor Meera, Sam's just abandoned her.' Bev was looking over at her. 'Should we go and talk to her?'

'I suppose we should, I do not miss being married to him. The only person he ever thinks of is himself.'

We meandered over and she looked pleased to have someone to talk to. 'You look really blooming Tash,' she smiled as we sat down with her.

'Halfway through now,' I stifled a yawn. 'I feel so knackered I can understand why they call older mom's geriatric mothers.'

She smiled again. 'Well you don't look knackered. Is Shay still excited?'

'Like a dog with two tails,' Bev answered for me. 'That baby is going to be spoilt rotten.'

'Why not?' she looked a little sad.

'You okay?' I asked softly.

'Usual,' her smile was tired.

'Thank you for coming today, it means a lot,' I hated to see her so down, I knew exactly how low Sam could make you feel.

'You've always been good to me Tash, it's the least I can do,' she looked at her watch. 'I have to go and pick Safi up from school.'

'Is she okay?' I loved their daughter to pieces.

'She's fine, she wanted to come today to see her aunty Tash.'

'Oh, bless her, tell her I'll see her soon.'

'I will, bye.'

'Bye,' we echoed as we watched her go to Sam, they exchanged a few heated words and then she had gone.

'Bugger,' I cursed. 'I thought Sam would have gone with her.'

'Still worried something will go on with Sam and Shay?'

'I am, Shay's on the whiskey and Sam's downing pints like they are going out of fashion.'

'If they start hitting each other with their handbags we'll leave them to it.'

I grimaced looking around the room my eyes resting on where Jamie and Moira were sitting. 'Who's that?'

She peered over taking an interest in the young girl talking to them. 'I have no idea, oh Moira's on her way over, you can ask her.'

Shay's mom had a beaming smile on her face as she joined us. 'Oh, Jamie is such a nice young man.'

'My Jamie?' I asked bewildered. *A nice young man* would not be the way *I* would describe him.

She nodded. 'Did you know he had a girlfriend?'

'No,' I was a little put out that I didn't, I was only his mother after all.

'Her name's Abbie Davies,' she indicated her head in their direction. 'That's her, isn't she a beauty? She's sixteen, lives with her parents in the next street to Jamie and they are at school together. Her father owns his own parcel delivery company and she loves the soaps and Strictly Come Dancing.'

'How long has she been here?' Bev asked.

'Oh, about five minutes,' she replied breezily, ordering two whiskies and a diet cola.

'She arrived five minutes ago and you found all that out?' Bev chuckled. 'You missed your vocation Moira, you should be working for MI5'

Shay came behind me, resting his hands on my shoulders. 'How ya doing beautiful?' He enquired.

'I'm good thanks,' I turned my head to give him a smile. 'Jamie has a girlfriend.'

'He does?' He looked over at the table.

'She's lovely,' Moira smiled. 'Come and say hello.'

We did as she gave Jamie one of the glasses of whisky. 'It's a wake,' she told me firmly. 'Jamie is an honorary Irishman today and we are sending your dad off Irish style.'

I clamped my mouth shut, he wouldn't get another one. 'Abbie, this is Jamie's mom Tash and my son Shay, they're having a baby together.'

She smiled at me shyly. 'Hello.'

'Hi,' I gave her my best smile. 'It's nice to meet you.'

'How ya doing?' Shay tilted his glass at her, he did sound merry, bless him.

Jamie sat there looking a tad pleased with himself and who could blame him. She was such a pretty young thing and clearly besotted with my son. She had beautiful dark skin, deep brown eyes and perfect white teeth. Her shoulder length hair chemically straightened.

'You never said you had a girlfriend,' I tried not to sound like I was complaining.

He shrugged infuriatingly, taking a discreet sip of his whisky, scared I was going to whip it away from him. I just hoped he was being sensible.

Spying Sam by the bar I went marching over to him, what else was he keeping from me? 'Did you know that Jamie had a girlfriend?'

He nodded paying for his pint. 'They've been seeing each other for a couple of months.'

'Why didn't anyone tell me?'

'You're too wrapped up with Irish boy to notice anything,' he said resentfully.

'Don't start,' I growled. 'He should have told me.'

'Careful Tash. You know Paddy will chuck his toys out of his pram if he sees you talking to me,' he looked so arrogant.

'Piss off Sam,' I snapped. 'Leave him alone.'

'Look at you Tash,' his eyes moved up and down my body. 'Knocked up by him, God hope the baby doesn't have any of his genes.'

'Not this again,' I hissed. 'Change the record Sam and think of your wife for once.'

'I can't stop thinking about *you*. I still love you darling, that's never gone away,' he lowered his voice slightly. 'I can't help how I feel.'

'It's my dad's funeral. I don't want to hear this shit anymore.'

'Well tough because you going to hear it,' his voice was charming. '*I* never wanted to leave you, you made me go.'

'You were screwing someone else!' I struggled to keep my voice quiet.

'It didn't mean anything. You are the only one who ever meant anything,' he pressed.

'Oh God,' I said weakly. 'Please just stop it, I can't do this.'

'I would *never* have left you and the kids. I didn't want to marry Meera, I had to when she got pregnant. It's you I've always wanted.'

'I am not listening to this bullshit,' I went to walk away but he caught my arm.

'You have to listen,' his eyes sought mine. 'Don't be with him, be with me.'

I leant forward. 'Get it into your thick skull Sam that I love Shay, really love him.'

'Tash,' he tried to interrupt.

'No,' I held up my hand. 'I thought I knew how love felt, what is was when I was with you but I was wrong. What you and I had doesn't even touch what Shay and I have. He treats me so much better than you ever did and I hope and pray that we grow old together.'

'You'll be old before him, he'll soon find some young girl that takes his fancy.'

'Can you hear yourself?' I asked angrily. '*You* shit all over me not once but three times and there may be more that I just don't know about. Now I'm warning you Sam, leave us alone or I'll tear your world apart.'

'You wouldn't,' he really thought he could still wrap me around his little finger.

'Try me,' I challenged. 'If you don't leave us alone then I will give Meera chapter and verse on what you keep saying to me.'

'She wouldn't believe you,' he tried to sound confident.

'Wouldn't she?' I left him with that quandary going back to the others not noticing Moira by us.

Sam took a large gulp of beer as Moira squared up to him. 'You never learn, do you?' She stated. 'Leave them alone, they're happy.'

'What has it got to do with you?' He said with distaste. 'Nothing, so just keep your nose out of things.'

'I has everything do to with me, he's my son and I love Tash like a daughter,' she said annoyed. 'And I tell you now if you keep bothering her then it won't be Tash or my son that will swing for you, it will be me. I heard enough of your mouth back at the crem.'

She pointed an angry finger at him before coming back to me and Shay. 'Okay mam?' He asked. 'What were you talking to Sam about?'

'Just passing the time of day,' she winked at me. 'Tash shall we get more drinks?'

'Okay,' I really was ready to go home. 'Jamie can have pop.'

'Mom,' he groaned as Shay grinned.

'I was having whisky at his age and it never did me any harm,' he said his voice slightly slurred.

'Really?' I raised an eyebrow following Moira to the bar.

'I've had a word with your man,' she informed me ordering more drinks.

'My man?' I asked puzzled.

'I heard what Sam was saying to you.'

Oh shit, that was all I needed. 'Moira.'

She stopped me. 'I heard what you said back to him and thank you Tash. I know Shay feels exactly the same. Your ex is a wasteless fecker but I'm pretty sure he won't bother you again.'

'Thanks Moira,' I smiled hoping she was right.

'You're welcome sweetheart.' She tapped my cheek.

We spent another couple of hours in the pub and it was getting on for six when we finally decided to leave. Lexi and Belle were heading back to Birmingham, they were out for a friend's birthday the next day.

I collared Lexi by the door. 'Love, you know we were talking about Shay's dad.'

'Leave it mom,' she advised. 'He won't thank you.'

'Humour me,' I answered shortly. 'His name is Albie Cassidy and he lived in Quin just outside Dublin. Oh, and he's about the same age as Moira.'

'Dahling,' Shay winked at me on the way to the gents.

'Do you think he heard?' I panicked.

'No, he's a little pissed,' she replied. 'I still don't know.'

'I just want to see if he still lives there, that's all,' I half lied.

She kissed my cheek saying reluctantly 'I'll see what I can do.'

'Thanks love,' I hugged Belle. 'Watch how you go, text me when you're home safe.'

They nodded in unison, going to catch the bus into Wolverhampton. Jamie and Abbie were also going, Sam having left with a very strange, determined expression on his face.

'Please come and see us Jamie,' I practically begged. 'I miss you. Bring Abbie too.'

'We will,' she assured me and I had to admit I did like her. I hoped she would be a positive influence on him.

'Bye you two,' Shay had returned from the gents. 'Be good.'

Abbie gave him a lovely smile as Jamie merely nodded but at least he wasn't rude or pulling a face.

'Hey dahling,' Shay turned his attention to me.

'Hey,' I echoed. 'Shall we go and sort big dog out?'

'We'll drop you,' Alan had his car keys on his hands.

'That's okay, thank you. Bev has got to pick her car up so we've ordered a taxi.' I replied.

'Yes, I'm going to get piss head home,' she nudged Dale. 'So, I can have a glass of wine without worrying about getting me lado home.'

We said our goodbyes and headed home but not before I gave Vince thirty quid telling him to buy everyone a drink for our dad. Dale moaned at me but I ignored him.

By the time Shay and I were alone it was a little after seven. I fed Millie as he got himself another whisky, it was a good job he wasn't at work tomorrow.

'I love you Tash,' he was all drunk and loving.

'Love you too,' I cut us sandwiches I couldn't be bothered to cook.

He came behind me, arms around me, rocking us. 'Hey beautiful.'

'Hey,' I smiled, I'd only ever seen him drunk a handful of times before.

'Love you,' he nuzzled my neck.

'I know you've just told me.' I replied. In fact, by the time he had consumed another few glasses and fallen to sleep on the settee he had said it fourteen times.

I came down from the toilet to find him lying on his back, mouth open snoring.

I did contemplate waking him up, I really did but I didn't want to be kept awake all night by his snoring, I had work in the morning.

Getting a fleece blanket, I covered him up, first taking off his shoes and tie. He looked so gorgeous, he always did. I thought I should be angry at him for getting drunk at dad's funeral but truthfully, I could never be angry at him really, he always made me laugh in the end.

I felt guilty when I got into bed and realised how nice it was to spread out. I fell straight into a dreamless sleep only to be rudely awoken at four in the morning by Shay getting into bed and putting his cold feet on me.

'Oi!' I cried shooting upright.

'It's your own fault,' he grumbled. 'You left me downstairs, I woke up freezing.'

'I covered you with the fleece.' I lay back down.

'When I woke up Millie was lying on it. Why didn't you wake me?'

'I tried but you were flat out,' I fibbed. 'And you were snoring.'

He wrapped himself around me. 'My head's banging.'

'It's your own fault,' I chided. 'Now shut up and go to sleep.'

He muttered under his breath as I tried to drop off again.

Twenty~Three

I could hardly believe it was nearly three weeks since my dad's funeral. Today though was a double celebration day, Shay's thirty-third birthday and also the day of the twenty week scan, cue happy smiley face.

Shay was still asleep so I went downstairs to feed Millie and make tea and toast. We were both off work today so after our nine-thirty appointment at the hospital we were going to Moira's and she and Alan were taking us out for lunch.

Going back upstairs I placed the tray onto the floor, kissing my sleeping prince awake. 'Happy Birthday to you!' I sang in my off-key voice.

He opened one eye grinning. 'Morning beautiful.'

'Tea and toast for the birthday boy,' I announced.

He pulled himself up, leaning against the pillows. 'Thanks sweet.'

I picked up the tray, putting it on the bed as we tucked into breakfast. 'We have yet to decide if we want to know the sex of the baby, we can find out today if we want too.'

He thought for a moment. 'I don't know, what do *you* think?'

'You decide, it's your first,' I smiled, he was so excited.

'It's a difficult one. Part of me wants to but part of me doesn't.'

'It might be fun not knowing until the actual birth,' I mused.

'Then that's what we'll do,' he really did look ridiculously happy.

'Oh nearly forgot, your presents,' I reached under the bed taking out the gift bag.

'For me?' he asked opening it. 'Aw thanks Tash, they're great.' He held up the jeans and jumper. 'I'll wear them today.'

'Baby asked me to give you this too,' I passed him a smaller bag.

He took it from me with a puzzled smile, reading the card, *Happy Birthday Daddy from the Bump* then he unwrapped the teddy bear with *Daddy* on the front. 'It's great,' he looked a little tearful, bless him. 'I wish he or she were here now.'

'The little mite will soon be putting in an appearance and you'll be wishing for peace and quiet,' I teased.

'I won't,' he put down the bear taking me in his arms. 'You have other presents too.'

'In a while,' he muttered kissing me.

'Are you after another present from me?' I asked coyly.

'I might be,' he chuckled, kissing me again. 'You have to make love to me on my birthday, it's the law.'

'Is that right?' I smiled. 'And what did you do last year when you didn't know me?' I was being nosey.

'I used my right hand,' he beamed.

'Nice,' I giggled loudly. 'What are you like?'

'Handsome and witty,' his smile grew, then he looked at me out of those beautiful come to bed eyes. 'Sit on me,' he said huskily. 'It's my birthday.'

I straddled him, it was the least I could do for the birthday boy. He pulled my nightie over my head so I was naked. 'Look at you,' he breathed. I was five months pregnant and felt huge but he was looking at me like I was the most desirable woman in the world. 'You are so beautiful.' I filled me with him, moving slowly against him, my hands caressing his chest. Taking my time I enjoyed every moment and I think he did too.

I hadn't lied to Sam at my dad's funeral, what Shay and I had did eclipse anything that had gone before. He could be a raucous little bleeder when he got going though, bless. Afterwards we lay in each other's arms and I have to say I had never felt so content.

'Did you say there were more presents?' he asked like a big kid.

'Yes,' I got them from under the bed.

'It's like Mary Poppins's bag under there. Come Christmas I'll know exactly where to look,' he declared.

I watched as he opened his present from Lexi and Belle. 'Single malt Irish whisky and the good stuff too,' he was pleased.

'For some bizarre reason they really like you,' I teased, they had spent a lot of money on it, more than I would have done for a bottle of alcohol.

Dale and Bev had brought him a pair of trendy boots, they seemed to like him too. 'I am going to look the smartest daddy-to-be ever,' he was pleased.

'Talking of which, it's time to get ready.'

We arrived at the hospital in plenty of time, chatting until we were called in. I lay on the bed, Shay in the chair next to me holding my hand. 'I hope the picture's clear.'

'It should be,' I replied. 'I just hope everything's okay.'

'Of course it will be, look at you, you're glowing.'

'The size of me I'm convinced I'm having an elephant,' I rubbed my tummy.

'It's good Irish-.'

'Sperm,' I finished for him, with a giggle. 'I know, you keep telling me.'

The door opened and sonographer came into the room. 'Hello,' she greeted us warmly. 'I'm Doctor Beddows and you are Natasha and Shay here for your twenty week scan?'

I nodded as Shay's excitement grew. 'I've gone through your notes and today I'll be looking for any abnormalities with the foetus.'

'Okay,' I said quietly, holding my breath a little. Both Shay and I had agreed that if there was anything wrong with the baby then I would still go ahead with the pregnancy. We couldn't get rid of it just because it wasn't perfect.'

'Do you wish to know the sex?' she asked smearing jelly all over my stomach.

'No, we want it to be a surprise,' Shay answered.

'How lovely,' she nodded, beginning to run the transducer over my skin. 'So many want to know before the birth now but its fun having the surprise.' She stopped abruptly staring at the screen.

'Is everything okay?' I asked timidly, neither Shay nor myself could see the screen.

She frowned looking at my notes. 'Can you just confirm your full name please?'

'Natasha Eileen Turner,' my voice was shaking.

'And your address?'

I told her, panic beginning to grip me as I held Shay's hand tighter. 'Please tell me what's wrong, you're scaring me.'

She looked at us with a furrowed brow. 'Er I'm not sure how to tell you this.'

'What?' nerves made Shay sound sharp.

She turned the monitor to us and there, clear as day, were two babies on the screen. 'Two?' Shay gulped.

Two,' Doctor Beddows confirmed.

We exchanged alarmed glances. 'No one said anything about two,' I finally managed to say.

'I really don't know what to say, I can't imagine how it was missed at the twelve week scan.'

The world went a little dim as I tried to process what we were being told. Twins, how would I ever cope with two babies?

'On the positive side everything is progressing how it should be, both babies are completely healthy and about the right size for twins of this age.' She went through some other checks and pointers but she might as well be telling us they had purple skin and pink spots because we were in too much shock to take anything in.

'So basically,' she was saying. 'Two sperm have attached themselves to the uterus wall at the same time.'

'Double top,' Shay muttered under his breath and I swear there was a hint of a smug smile on his face.

'It's like having siblings at the same time,' she finished.

We listened a little more and then the appointment was over and we left clutching a picture of the scan that Doctor Beddows hadn't charged us for, our ears ringing with her apologies and the parents-to-be now of not one but two babies.

Shay took the car keys from me, I don't think he trusted me to drive and we in the car in complete silence for a few minutes. 'Twins then hey?' he said eventually.

'Yeah two,' I still felt panicked not to mention a little faint. 'No wonder I'm so bloody big,' I swallowed loudly. 'Two babies are going to mean two of everything.'

'That's what twins usually mean,' he muttered staring out of the windscreen, then reality seemed to hit him. 'Twins,' he repeated dazed.

'Yes,' I was shaking.

He started the car and we drove to Moira's in silence. What would I do if he left me? I would be a single mother of two babies!

One baby wasn't so bad, it was doable, but two. Oh my God! I couldn't just get rid of one, rent it out.

I was going to be a mother of four! Count them four! Three doesn't sounded that bad. Hi, how many kids do you have? Three? Oh that's a nice number instead I'll have to say four. As Shay would say shite!

Moira and Alan were waiting for us to arrive. 'Happy birthday son!' she cried, watching as we both sat on the settee in silence. 'What's wrong?' she clasped her hand to her throat.

'Was everything okay with the scan?' Alan too looked concerned.

I looked at them. 'Two,' I said numbly.

'Two?' Moira repeated. 'What are you blathering on about?'

'We're going to be the proud parent of twins,' Shay clarified.

'Twins!' she was as shocked as us. 'How?'

'Well we had sex,' he began.

'Oi!' she pointed a warning finger. 'You know what I mean?'

'I can't believe it,' I stumbled over the words. 'She said she doesn't know how it was missed at the twelve week scan. It's going to be so expensive, I mean really expensive.'

'It will be fine,' she put a comforting arm around me. 'From a purely selfish point of view I think it's absolutely wonderful.' She gave me a kiss on the head.

'It is,' Alan agreed. 'And we're here to help, don't forget that.'

'Thank you,' I replied as next to me Shay began to chuckle. 'Are you getting hysterical?'

'No,' he cried, pulling me to my feet and waltzing me around the living room. 'We're having twins beautiful! You and me, it's fantastic!'

'It is?' I had to admit his enthusiasm was catching.

'Yes,' he kissed me lovingly. 'It's going to be perfect. I'm here, I'm not going anywhere.'

It was as if he could read my mind and I smiled lovingly at him. 'It's certainly a huge birthday surprise.'

'The best one I could have wished for,' he assured me.

Moira and Alan were beaming at us as I sat back down out of breath and got my mobile from my bag. 'Who are you calling?' Shay asked.

'Lexi,' I replied and she answered almost before it rang. 'Hi love, how are you?'

'Good mom, are you? Did the scan go okay?'

'Everything it as is should be except for one thing.'

'And what's that?'

'We're having twins. Surprise!' I trilled.

'Good one mom,' she giggled.

'I'm not joking,' I said mildly.

She screamed down the phone. 'Oh my God! That's brilliant!'

'You don't mind then?' I asked.

'It's fab, honestly mom. Is Shay there?'

'He is, we're at Moira's,' I smiled at him.

'I've found his dad,' she whispered. She knew I couldn't reply so she continued. 'He still lives in Quin, I've got his address.'

'That's great,' was all I could say but it was turning out to be a good day.

'Put Shay on mom,' she said.

I held the phone to him. 'Lexi wants a word.'

He took it from me. 'Hello dahling, thanks for my whisky and thank Belle too please.'

'Happy birthday baby daddy,' she laughed. 'How are you feeling?'

'Like the cat's that got the cream,' he admitted. 'When you come Sunday we'll celebrate.'

'Absolutely,' she agreed. 'Enjoy your day.'

'Cheers sweet, you too,' he gave me back my phone.

'And now we are going to celebrate our good news,' Moira announced.

I nodded picking up my handbag, butterflies in my stomach, we had found Shay's father.

Twenty~Four

Everything was arranged, Lexi and I would fly to Ireland on Saturday morning, we would stay overnight at the only pub in the village and seek out Albie Michael Cassidy. Lexi was not convinced we should be doing it but I told her she didn't have to come with me, I was perfectly capable of going by myself.

She retorted that she wouldn't trust me to even find Ireland by myself which I thought was a little uncalled for. So I had three days to wait until I could be meeting Shay's dad, yay! Now to the job in hand, Lexi had insisted that we use her bedroom as a nursery for the twins and I needed to sort it out and today being Monday and my day off was the day to do it.

Twins, I still couldn't get my head around it. Although Lexi had pointed out that I wasn't being a good mother to our unborn children by lying to their father about where we were actually going on Saturday. I had told him it was a pampering weekend at the Park Hall Hotel but as I then counter pointed out it was for the greater good.

I had told Meera about the twins and she was really pleased for us. I had seen Jamie a few times but he had never mentioned it and so I hadn't either. I should not be so scared at upsetting him, I really annoyed myself with it.

My own mom? Well I haven't even bothered telling her, I hadn't seen hair or hide of her since the day in the salon when she had slapped me, the old cow and frankly I didn't want to see her.

I began to pack things away in boxes, hauling them to the shed with Millie trying to help but just succeeding in getting in the way. I would keep it all in the shed for Lexi to go through, she might want it for when she and Belle get their own place.

The day flew by and by the time Shay came home from work I was hot and sweaty and my back was beginning to ache. 'What have you been up to?' he eyed the boxes still to be taken to the shed suspiciously.

'Clearing the nursery,' I replied breezily.

'Tash,' he said annoyed. 'You do not hump boxes about in your condition.'

'Stop fussing,' I dismissed his words.

'Fussing! You are five months pregnant.'

'Yes pregnant, I haven't got some serious disease, I am quite capable.'

'You do not do heavy lifting,' he pointed a finger at me.

I pulled a face, bobbing out my tongue.

'Don't defy me Tash about this or I will smack your arse,' he warned.

I smiled cheekily at him. 'Promises, promises.'

He grabbed me around the waist, giving me a kiss. 'You have a precious cargo, if you want anything doing you wait till I get home.'

'I'm not a weak feeble woman you know?' I responded.

'You are one of the strongest women I know, just humour me, please?'

'Fine,' I sighed, kissing him again, my hand on the cheeks of his bum, planting tiny kisses all down his neck.

He held me a little away from him. 'Should we? What if I hurt you?' He was driving me nuts with his gentleness. When we did make love you would think I was made of china and if he pushed a little too hard then I would shatter into a million pieces, he was so careful.

I rolled my eyes. 'You won't, I promise,' I caressed his cheek. 'Are you going off me?'

'What? No, I'm not going off you. Please don't think that.'

'Are you sure?' I did worry after Sam and what he did to me when I was pregnant with Jamie.

'Positive,' he said firmly.

I laughed softly, cupping him with a gentle squeeze. 'We'll just cuddle then.'

He gave me a knowing smile. 'I'm going for my shower.'

I nodded taking out the lasagne that I had made for supper and putting it in the oven. He seemed to be gone a long time so I went upstairs to see where he was. He was lying on the bed wrapped only in his towel when I went into our bedroom.

'I've been waiting for you,' his voice was sexy.

'I thought you were worried about hurting me?' I raised an eyebrow.

'You've told I don't have to be, he said softly.

I smiled sitting next to him on the bed and we kissed and cuddled. God I loved him so much, I hoped that if Lexi and I did get to meet his dad then he would be happy.

'Hey beautiful,' he breathed, hands snaking up my top.

'I'm all hot and sweaty,' I really could do with a shower myself.

'Just how I like my woman,' his hands moved to my pregnancy bra, which I had to say was not the sexiest lingerie in the world, just as the doorbell rang. 'Who the feck is that?' he asked disgusted.

'I won't know until I answer it,' I got up reluctantly, going downstairs as Millie began to bark.

Dale and Bev stood on the doorstop. 'Hey sis, we were bored so we thought we'd come and see you.'

'I'm flattered,' I pulled a face letting them in as big dog went ballistic, she loved them to bits.

'Plus Bev didn't feel like cooking so I said to her I know who's always got food in,' his smile was cheeky.

'Ignore him,' she put down her bag.

'Lasagne and garlic bread with salad?' I tempted.

'Perfect,' he grinned. 'Where's the Shayster?'

'Upstairs,' I replied checking the food, I didn't add that they had interrupted our nookie as well.

'We went shopping today,' Bev passed me the carrier bag she had in her hands. 'We brought some things for the twins.'

'Aw, thank you,' I took it from her. I peered inside, it was full of cute little outfits that I just bet Bev had loved buying. 'They are gorgeous, you shouldn't have done.'

'That's what I said to her when I saw how much it had come to,' Dale joked. 'I've brought the daddy some lager.'

'Did I hear someone say lager?' Shay came into the kitchen.

'Shayster,' he cried. 'You look like you need a drink.'

'Looks like I'm driving then,' Bev gave a resigned sigh.

We ate thirty minutes later, then retired to the living room. Shay kept giving me licentious glances as he messed with his mobile. A few seconds later mine tinged and I looked at the message. **Hope they don't stay all night, I want my dessert xx**.

I sent him a smiley face back and tried to concentrate on what Bev was saying. 'A pamper weekend, I am so jealous. It will be lovely for you.'

'You should go too, Tash and Lexi wouldn't mind would you sweet?' Shay gave me a smile.

'Not at all,' I stumbled over the words, knowing if she said she wanted to then I would have to come clean about what I was up too but to be honest I didn't want her knowing until we had come back.

'I can't go, someone has to man the salon,' she teased.

'Sorry hun,' I smiled catching Shay looking at the clock. He did it off and on for the next hour as we talked about everyday things. I really did enjoy their company but I had to admit clearing out Lexi's bedroom had left me knackered.

By ten Shay was faking that many yawns that I had a fit of the giggles. 'Keeping you up?' Dale asked pointedly.

'Busy day,' he stated, with a grin.

'I must admit I'm tired too,' I cut in.

'Cleaning out Lexi's bedroom today, humping heavy boxes to the shed,' Shay ratted on me. 'I've threatened her.'

'Sis, you need to take better care of yourself,' Dale scolded.

I waved away his words. 'In a couple of months I'm not going to feel like doing anything, so why I can I will.'

'Fair enough,' he conceded, more used to my stubbornness then Shay was. 'Are you ready babe?'

'I am,' Bev stood. 'Let the lovebirds go to bed.'

I saw them out before going upstairs to have my shower. By the time Shay came to bed I could feel sleep trying to steal me away. He could see how knackered I was as he lay behind me and wrapped his arms around me. 'I still haven't had my dessert,' he whispered.

I smiled sleepily. 'Will tomorrow do?'

'Yes,' he kissed the back of my neck. 'Don't forget.'

'I won't,' I promised. 'I love you.'

'Love you too sweet.'

Twenty~Five

'This is a really bad idea,' Lexi said as we trundled our way through the deserted picturesque village, small colourful houses either side of an immaculate village green and just one pub at the end of the single road. The *Monks Well*, our destination.

'Shut up,' I huffed, she was beginning to sound like a stuck record, it was all she had said since we had gotten off the plane.

'You should call Shay and tell him what you are up to,' she pulled a face.

'It wouldn't be a surprise then, would it?' I said through gritted teeth as the first penny sized rain drops began to fall.

'He is going to hit the roof when he finds out,' she predicted, hurrying to the pub, leaving me behind.

'Will you just shut up?' I snapped, trying to catch up with her. 'I've paid for you to have a nice trip to Ireland and all you can do is moan.'

'You are going to be in so much shit when he finds out,' she sounded like she was the mother and I was the daughter.

'Lexi,' I warned as we went into the bar, a few of the locals taking an interest in us.

'Can I help you ladies?' the barman asked.

'We have a twin room booked in the name of Turner,' I gave him my best smile.

'Oh yes,' he matched it with his own. 'Come up and I'll show you to your room.' He took both suitcases with ease, going up the rickety stairs he went to the end of the small corridor, opening it with a key.

Pushing it open, he stepped inside flicking on the lights, it was a little dark in the room. It was small too, with twin beds neatly made, a small table and two chairs under the window that looked out onto the village.

'Is this okay?' he asked with his Irish lilt, twinkling his blue eyes at me.

I took off my coat. 'Perfect thank you.'

'Breakfast is served between seven and nine-thirty, we also do lunchtime and evening meals. We're the only place in the village where you can eat actually,' he looked at me, his face dropping a little. 'I'll leave you to settle in.'

'Thank you,' I trilled, picking up my small case and putting it on the bed.

'He was totally checking you out,' Lexi grinned. 'Until he realised you were pregnant. You are a cougar extraordinaire.'

'Shut your face,' I retorted, looking out of the window. 'Do you fancy exploring the village?'

'Hadn't you better touch base? Tell the expectant daddy that we have arrived safely at our *spa weekend*?' she was heavy on the sarcasm.

I pulled a face going into the bathroom, no service on my mobile. 'Can you get a signal?' I called through the open door.

She checked her phone. 'No,' came the reply.

'I'll have to call from the bar, I think I saw a phone there.'

Lexi cocked her head, listening to the noise drifting up from the bar. 'He's going to think it's a very lively spa.'

'You didn't have to come with me you know,' I was getting a tad fed up of her disdain.

'Oh I did,' she told me. 'Someone has to keep an eye on you.'

I looked at my beautiful daughter, who I loved with every fibre of my being. 'I should have made you catch the ferry instead of treating you to a plane ride. It would have taken hours to get here then.'

She bobbed her tongue out at me. 'Come on let's go and case the joint then.'

I pulled on my coat and picked up my handbag before heading to the bar. 'Could I use your phone please? I can't get a signal on my mobile.

'Of course,' the barman passed me the handset and I dialled Shay's number from memory. 'What are you wearing?' I perved when he answered.

'Hey dahling, I didn't recognise the number,' he sounded pleased to hear from me.

'Neither Lexi or I can get a signal,' I explained. 'I'm using the hotel's phone.'

'It sounds very noisy,' he said puzzled.

'You know what these places are like,' I answered quickly. 'I just wanted to say we are here safe, you enjoy the peace and quiet.'

'I'd rather you were here nagging me,' he teased. 'At least I won't worry if I don't hear from you.'

'It's only for one night,' I smiled. 'Anyway I'd better go. Give Millie a big hug and I love you loads.'

'Love you too sweet, hi to Lexi, you both take care,' he ended the call.

'He okay?' Lexi was waiting for me impatiently.

I nodded. 'He sends his love,' I did feel bad lying to him but it was special circumstances and hopefully it would all turn out wonderful in the end.

At least it had stopped raining which was good, no wonder Ireland looked so green. From what I could work out Quin consisted of one main road with just a few houses each side of the green. There was also the obligatory church and cemetery with a colourful six foot statue of the Virgin Mary standing outside.

'Look at that,' Lexi said trotting over to it with me following. 'How ugly is that?'

'Shush, that blasphemous,' I stood in front of it doing a kind of curtsey.

'What are you doing mom?' she asked baffled.

I blushed. 'Genuflecting, it's what Catholic's do.'

'You're not a Catholic,' she pointed out, shaking her head.

'So?' I shrugged, walking into the cemetery. We had brought a bunch of flowers with us just in case we found Moira's parents grave. It was the least we could do.

'Jaysus,' Lexi used one of Shay's favourite sayings.

'That is also blasphemous, especially in a cemetery,' I scolded looking at my watch, it read two. We walked around the grounds for a while, reading the inscriptions on the graves, some were really old.

'Mom!' Lexi called excitedly and I hurried over to her. 'I've found it.'

She had indeed. Moira's parent's double grave, it just had to be, she had never really mentioned her mom and dad and I never really liked to ask but the headstone read:

Fiona Moira Flynn
&
Colm Francis Flynn

Lexi lay the flowers on the grave and I bent awkwardly to tidy it. 'What are you doing?' I asked her.

'Taking a photo of the grave so we can show Moira, I think she'd like to see it. That's if she ever talks to us again when she finds out what *you've* done,' she replied cheekily.

I ignored her. 'Hello Mr and Mrs Flynn,' I chatted. 'I hope you don't mind us bringing you flowers. Your daughter is a really lovely woman and she's doing so well. She's getting married to a lovely man. Her son, Shay, well he's someone very special, I wish you'd known your grandson.'

'Mom, you are just weird talking to a gravestone,' Lexi tutted helping me up.

'I'm just being civil,' I retorted. 'There's nothing wrong with that.'

'Come on let's get this over with,' she said grimly, wishing she had put her foot down and forbade me to come over to Ireland or better still ratted me out to Shay.

We walked back into the street, Lexi checking the piece of paper in her hand. 'He lives at number eighteen,' she looked at the houses in front of us.

I nodded, my heart hammering in my chest. We walked for a little bit before she stopped dead in front of me. 'Lexi,' I rebuked, bumping into her.

'Mom,' she whispered, pointing to a house across the road.

My eyes followed her. A grey haired man was in the front garden, his back was to us but the stance of his body was so familiar. Taking a deep breath I crossed the road quickly, my daughter following.

'What are you doing?' she hissed. I shushed her, I just wanted a closer look. 'Don't,' she cried.

He turned at the sound of her voice and my blood ran cold. I was looking at Shay in thirty years' time, no doubt about it.

'Shit,' Lexi clung to my arm.

'Good afternoon ladies,' he said pleasantly. 'Dodging the rain are you?'

'Yes,' my voice came out as a croak.

He cocked his head to one side, giving us the same beautiful smile that Shay always did. I just couldn't get over how alike they were, he would never be able to deny parentage. 'Now that isn't an Irish accent and we don't get many visitors in Quin, in fact I can't remember the last time,' he smiled again. 'Are you both lost?'

I just couldn't find my voice, I felt so tongue-tied.

'We're just having a look around,' Lexi answered hesitantly.

He nodded taking us in. 'Mother and daughter by the look of you.'

'Yes, we've just come from the cemetery,' she was trying to sound normal but the shock of seeing how alike Shay and his dad were was one I could not describe.

'Are you looking for anyone in particular?' he asked looking at us more closely.

I finally found my voice. 'We are actually looking for Albie Cassidy,' the words were out before I could stop them.

'You've found him but I'm sure I'm not dead, well not yet anyway,' he became wary. 'How can I help you?'

No, it was no good, the words had disappeared again and I stood there opening and closing my mouth like a goldfish.

Lexi glared at me, shaking her head. 'We are friends of Moira Flynn.'

He caught his breath loudly. 'I haven't heard that name in so many years,' he looked dazed. 'Is she well?'

'Very well, thank you,' Lexi replied and I was glad that she had come with me. I felt queasy now that I had opened up this particular can of worms and I reached for the garden wall to steady myself.

'Are you okay?' he asked concerned.

'I just feel a little woozy,' I stuttered.

'My mom's pregnant,' Lexi explained.

'Who's this Albie?' a kindly looking woman appeared from nowhere, startling me. Shit was that his wife?

He turned to her, a look of confusion still on his face. 'They say they are friends of Moira Flynn,' he pointed at me. 'Your wan's pregnant and feeling a little unsteady on her feet.'

'How far gone are you?' she asked softly.

'Five and a half months,' I managed to reply.

'Come in, come in,' she flapped her hands at us. 'You look like you are going to faint dead away. Let me get you some water.'

'Thank you,' Lexi replied for me, taking my arm and propelling me forward.

We went into their neat bungalow and Albie sat us on the patterned sofa and his wife fetched me a glass of water. When we were all sitting down he said. 'Well you know my name and this is my wife Niamh but we don't know yours.'

'Sorry,' I held my glass like a life saver. 'I'm Natasha Turner and this is my daughter Lexi.'

'Is Moira in any trouble?' he was still mystified to why we had turned up.

'No, far from it,' Lexi could see that I was struggling. 'She's very well, happy. Getting married in September to a lovely man called Alan.'

'That's good,' he replied and silence filled the room, this was harder than I thought it would be.

'So you're Moira's friends?' Niamh said eventually. 'And you live by her here in Ireland?'

'No,' I shook my head. 'We live near Wolverhampton, West Midlands in England.'

'Why don't you give them your postcode too?' Lexi muttered sarcastically and I glared at her.

'So how do you know Moira then?' Albie was curious.

'She moved to England three years ago with her son,' Lexi explained.

'Son? So she married and had a child then?' he asked.

We exchanged looks. 'Not exactly,' Lexi admitted. 'She had Shay thirty-three years ago.'

I cringed as both of them did the maths in their heads. 'Thirty-three years ago?' he repeated looking dazed.

'Yes,' I mumbled as Niamh looked at her husband.

'Perhaps,' she began. 'It would be better if we started again and you both came out with what you are trying to say instead of going around the houses? But first a cup of tea, I have a feeling we'll need one.'

I pulled a face, the babies kicking as Albie stared at us, the same unreadable expression on his face that Shay was so good at. 'So your wife knows about Moira?' Lexi asked for something to say.

'Niamh is my second wife, my first wife passed away and I didn't want any secrets between us this time.'

'Oh,' I fell silent as we waited for her to come back with the drinks.

'Well here we are,' she bustled back into the room, the cups on a tray. 'Are you okay having tea with the baby and all?'

I nodded mutely, I needed a strong cup of something. She poured and settled back next to her husband.

My daughter was looking at me, urging me to just come out with what I wanted to say and I cleared my throat nervously. 'When Moira left Quin,' I began. 'She went to live with her friend in Cork.'

'I tried to find out where she had gone but no one seemed to know, not even her parents,' he interrupted. 'She just upped and left.'

'She didn't tell her family where she was going,' I replied. 'She had to leave, she was three months pregnant.'

He went ashen. 'Why didn't she tell me?'

'She had no desire to break up your marriage, plus her parents were pressuring her to give the child up for adoption once it was born.' I was shaking.

'But she didn't?' Niamh was staring at her husband. 'She kept the child?'

'Yes,' I answered softly. 'As I said she moved to England with him three years ago.'

'It was my child?' Albie was looking at me with his beautiful brown eyes.

I nodded. 'Moira was convinced it was the right thing to do for everyone concerned,' my words were hushed. 'She brought Shay up all alone.'

'And she has asked you to come and tell us now?' Niamh looked as shocked as her husband.

'No,' Lexi spoke. 'Moira doesn't know we are here and neither does Shay. I told mom it was a bad idea.'

Et tu Brute? That's it Lexi, stab me in the back, I thought.

'She should have told me,' he looked stunned. 'I have a son.'

Niamh took his hand. 'It's a bolt from the blue,' she confessed.

'I can imagine,' Lexi took an interest in her cup of tea.

'I'm sorry,' I put down my own cup standing. 'Lexi is right, it isn't a good idea. I just didn't think it through properly. I thought it would be nice for Shay to know his dad and for his dad to know him. I really shouldn't have interfered, please forgive me.' I was getting myself in a right tizzy.

'You can't spring this on me and just walk away,' Albie stood also.

'I'm sorry,' I blustered, bursting into tears.

'Mom,' Lexi was by my side, giving me a hug.

'I'm sorry,' I repeated, snivelling I turned to her. 'I just wanted to do something nice. I never gave Moira a thought, how she would feel about it. I just wanted Shay to get to know his dad now that he's going to be a father himself.'

'He's going to be a dad?' Albie gasped and if I thought someone couldn't look more shocked than when I announced he had a son then I was wrong, he did.

Lexi rolled her eyes. 'Sit down mom,' she ordered then taking a deep breath she said. 'Mom and Shay are together as in boyfriend and girlfriend, they are going to be parents in September.'

'It's a good job neither of us have a dicky heart,' Niamh murmured.

'So the baby, it's my sons?' Albie didn't seem to be taking things in, must have been the shock.

'We're having twins actually, surprise!' I joked weakly.

'Sweet baby Jesus,' he gasped, leaning back against his chair.

'Bit of a shock I expect,' Lexi was queen of the understatement.

We sat in silence for a while as Albie and Niamh took it all in. 'Mom's hearts in the right place, it's just a pity her brain isn't,' Lexi said eventually.

I threw her the evils, looking down at the carpet.

'I think I need another cup of tea,' Niamh got up. 'No, not tea, whisky.' She went into the kitchen.

'So you came all the way from England to seek me out?' he still looked bewildered.

I blew my nose noisily, nodding. 'Like I said it seemed like a good idea.'

Niamh came back with three glasses of whisky and an orange juice for me. 'So twins then?' her voice was bright, in fact it was overly bright.

'Non identical, we decided not find out what sex they are until they are born,' I answered. 'I didn't want any more kids, I have Jamie, who's sixteen, as well as Lexi. As you can probably tell I'm older than Shay. Anyway just before Christmas I brought some condoms from the pound shop and one must have split and,' I pointed to my stomach. 'Voila.'

'Mom!' Lexi slid down in her seat. 'People do not need to know about the condom splitting.'

I smiled sheepishly as Niamh took a long drink of whisky and asked. 'So have you seen each other for long?'

'Since last September, well kind of. It wasn't really serious then,' I babbled. 'I'm ten years older than him and he is my brother's best mate and one day they came into the hairdressers where I work, cos that's what I do, I'm a hairdresser. Anyway I thought he was just gorgeous and we began to see each other on the quiet, although Lexi did know, then we split up. I was really worried about the age gap, still am in a way. Plus I wasn't sure if it was just sex between us.'

'Mom!' Lexi exploded, necking her whisky. 'You do not have to explain everything. Since September would have been a perfectly acceptable answer.'

I blushed, it was just nerves that as making me waffle. I sipped my orange juice wishing I had whisky too.

Albie was staring down at his glass. 'What's he like?' he asked quietly.

My eyes went to him, of course he would want to know what his son was like. 'He's lovely,' I said simply. 'He's gentle and kind and has a twinkly Irish charm that means you can't be mad at him for long.'

Niamh looked at Albie as if to say "I know exactly what you mean."

'He has a brooding look about him sometimes and you think he's in a mood with you but it's just his face,' I continued with a smile. 'He has a beautiful brown eyes and lush dark curly brown hair. Oh and he can grow a full blown beard in a week or so it seems.'

'All the Cassidy men can,' Albie chuckled softly.

'Most of the women too,' Niamh joked, still slightly flustered.

I smiled getting out my mobile from my bag and scrolling through my pictures, wanting to find a nice one of him. 'Here,' I passed him my phone.

He took it with trembling hands as Niamh looked over his shoulder. 'Jesus, Mary and Joseph,' she squeaked. 'He's the absolute spit of you.'

His eyes filled with tears as he looked at his son for the first time. 'He's a fine looking boy,' he whispered, his voice rusty.

Niamh had gone to the unit, taking out an old photo album and flicking through it until she found what she was looking for. 'Snap,' she said and I took it from her, it was a picture of Albie when he was roughly the same age as Shay was now, his hair dark, not grey.

'I can't get over it,' Lexi shook her head. 'Looking at you is like someone has put me in a time machine and I'm really looking to Shay in thirty years' time,' she told him. 'Oh I have something.'

She sat on the arm of the sofa, so they could both see her mobile's screen. I knew the video she was going to show them frame by frame, it was one of my favourites. Belle had taken it a couple of Saturday's ago. At first it is just me sitting on the settee, then Millie comes into shot.

'That's Millie, my uncle Dale's Irish Wolfhound that mom was only supposed to look after for a couple of days in October.

'She's a beauty,' Niamh smiled.

Then Shay is by my side, balancing a bowl of popcorn on my bump whilst telling Lexi and Belle why Fast and Furious 3 is such a pile of shite. He is so animated as he is talking to them, his laugh infectious. It ends with me yawning theatrically as if to say the conversation is boring me and he gives me a look of such utter devotion that I fill up every time I see it and then he kisses me before helping himself to a big handful of popcorn.

Albie started crying then, proper tears and I looked at Lexi alarmed. 'My boy,' he gasped. 'I've missed everything.'

Niamh held her husband tightly. 'Shush,' she whispered.

'I'm sorry,' I stood as quick as I could, all I seemed to be doing was apologising. 'I never wanted to cause you any hurt by coming here.'

'Perhaps we should go,' Lexi took her phone back.

'Maybe,' Niamh nodded. 'Where are you staying?'

'The Monks Well,' I replied giving her the envelope I had brought with me, photos of Shay and a copy of the twins scan picture plus my contact details.

'We go back to England tomorrow lunchtime,' Lexi informed them.

She nodded, seeing us to the door. Albie too wrapped up in his thoughts to even notice. 'Will he be okay?' I asked concerned.

'I'll make sure he is,' she smiled but it was a tired one.

'Shay's a mechanic,' I had forgotten to say.

'Albie enjoys tinkering with things.'

'And Moira gave him Albie as his middle name,' I added.

She nodded. 'I'll tell him. It's good to meet you Natasha, Lexi.'

'You too,' we echoed, beginning to walk back to the pub, staying silent until we were in our room.

'Well,' Lexi lay on one of the twin beds. 'That's one way to turn a person's world upside down. Good whisky though.'

I got on the other bed. 'I just didn't know what to do when he started crying.'

'Me neither,' she admitted. 'Poor man, don't you think you ought to phone Shay now and tell him what you've done?'

'You were with me,' I pointed out.

'Oh no,' she shook her head. 'You are in this on your own. I am merely here in a kind of bodyguard capacity.'

'I thought family were supposed to stick together?' I rolled onto my side, it was more comfortable.

'Only when you don't have stupid ideas. So are you going to speak to shaggable Shay?'

'No, and I don't think you ought to call him that anymore, not now we live together,' I needed to pull her up about something, especially when she had an infuriating way of always being right.

'Chill mom, I'm gay remember? I would be the last person who would want to shag him, even if he wasn't my near enough stepdaddy.' She checked her watch. 'It's only four.'

'I'm going to have a nap before we eat, if that's okay?' I felt dog tired.

'What am I supposed to do?' she whined.

'Go and explore the village or something,' I closed my eyes as she stomped from the room. Kids!

Twenty~Six

Lexi phoned Belle from the bar, filling her in with everything that had happened. She was of the same mind as Lexi, Tash needed to come clean to Shay now. 'Don't forget,' Lexi warned. 'If anyone asks, you know nothing. I'll see you tomorrow, love you.'

'Love you too,' Belle ended the call, feeling anxious. When Shay found out what Tash had done there would be fireworks for sure.

Lexi ventured out into the village, trying to kill time while her mom rested. She loved her so much, she had always made sure she was there for her daughter, telling her she could achieve anything she wanted, that she only had to put her mind to it.

Sometimes though her mom didn't think things through, she went headlong into situations without a thought of the consequences. This was one such time, what an absolute shock for Albie and Niamh.

'Hey Mr Cassidy, you have a thirty-three-year-old son that you knew nothing about and not only that but you are going to be a grandad to twins and how is your day going?' she shuddered as she walked along, stopping in front of the statue of the Virgin Mary by the church.

Glancing around to make sure no one was about she mirrored her mother's earlier actions, genuflecting self-consciously. 'Hey Mary,' she began. 'Or should I call you Virgin Mary? I'm not religious you see. Mom and dad had me christened and I go to weddings, christening's and oh funerals now I'm older but that's about it.

She paused gathering her thoughts. 'Please don't let Shay leave my mom over this,' it was what she was worried about. 'Mom isn't a bad person, scatty sometimes and dizzy all the time but she means well. She loves Shay you know, really love him. Dad hurt her so badly that I don't really think she'd survive if Shay did the same.'

She fell silent as a car went past before continuing. 'You being a catholic though I don't suppose you want to do us any favours. Mom's divorced, pregnant and living in sin. I'm gay and my brother's a total shit. Not exactly ideal for your faith,' she leant forward and said in a sociable whisper. 'And they were using condoms! So maybe it as an act of God, a gift?'

'Anyway if you could just help everything turn out okay in the end I really would appreciate it,' she high-fived the statue. 'Girl power and all that, amen.'

Laughing softly to herself she decided to carry on walking, trying to work out how they could keep all this from Shay so he didn't get angry with her mom.

'Lexi!' Niamh was bearing down on her, a worried look on her face. 'I was just heading for the pub, where's your mom?'

'She's having a lie down, the twins make her tired sometimes.'

'Do you have a moment love?' she asked softly. 'To come back to the house?'

'Of course,' Lexi was curious. She followed her, relieved to see that Albie looked a little brighter.

'Natasha is having a lie down,' Niamh explained to her husband. 'And Lexi was talking to the Virgin Mary.'

She flushed, unzipping her coat and sitting down. Considering it was late May it was still a little chilly in Quin.

'Would you like another whisky?' Niamh asked. 'We don't usually drink this much but it's been one of those days.'

'Please,' Lexi replied turning to Albie. 'How are you Mr Cassidy?'

'Better now thank you and you must call me Albie.'

She smiled unsurely, she would kill her mom for having a nap and leaving her to deal with this.

'Now,' Niamh bustled about before sitting down. 'Can we ask you a few questions now we've got over the shock?'

'Sure,' she downed half her whisky in one, even though the glass was nearly full.

'When is Shay's birthday?' Albie was holding one of the picture's that her mom had left with them.

'The fifteenth May, he's just turned thirty-three. That was day of the twenty week scan, when they found out it was twins. I think they were both in shock for hours, they only thought there was one baby.' I'm just like my mom, she thought, why answer with one word when twenty would do?

'Oh,' he was looking a little overwhelmed again. 'And he's a mechanic you say?'

'Yes, he works for Ray's Garage. He keeps my mom's old Clio going even though it looks like it should be condemned to the scrapyard.' Yep, just like my mom.

'He's happy though, with his life?' he was beginning to look tearful again.

'Yes. He and mom are really happy and we're all looking forward to the twins coming. Well my brother's being an arse, he always wanted mom and dad to get back together.'

'Have they been divorced long?' Niamh asked.

'Five years,' her face clouded over. 'Dad had affairs, he hurt mom quite badly and it took her a lot to trust Shay. He is the only man she's bothered with since dad left, she just never bothered before.'

'It's a shame,' she commiserated. 'It must be hard on you kiddies too?'

Lexi nodded, feeling herself fill up and she blamed the whisky.

'And Moira, did she ever marry?' she threw out the question casually.

'No, from what I can gather she threw all her energy into bringing Shay up. She gets married in September, on the eighth. I'm chief bridesmaid which means I get to look after all the little brats.'

'Little brats?' she frowned.

'Alan has five daughters and five grandchildren. All the grandkids are going to be bridesmaids or page boys.'

'And Alan's a good man?' Albie asked.

'He's lovely and they adore each other,' Lexi did wonder if she was saying too much.

'Do you think Shay will meet me?' he asked quietly.

It threw her for a moment. 'I don't know, mom would have to talk to him,' she replied tentatively, she didn't have a clue.

He nodded. 'I'd like to get to know him now I know he exists,' he took a deep breath. 'Why the feck didn't someone tell me at the time?'

'As mom said, Moira was thinking about your marriage and she didn't want to give her baby up and they would have made her,' Lexi said awkwardly, glad now that her mom wasn't with her, all full of emotions and hormones.

'That I can understand,' Niamh empathised. 'I would have done the same too.'

'I wish she had told me,' Albie sighed. 'My first wife couldn't have children she died ten years ago and I married Niamh four years ago.'

'I have a daughter Erin, she has a child,' Niamh chatted. 'We are going to end up with one hell of an extended family.'

'He is handsome isn't he?' Albie was looking once more at the photo he held.

'He is,' Lexi agreed warmly, it wasn't exactly the time to tell them she calls him shaggable Shay.

'And he treats you well?' he wanted to know.

Lexi thought for a moment. 'He doesn't try to be a dad to me which is good, I already have a dad even if he is a bit useless at times. Shay's more like a big brother, he makes me laugh and we gang up on mom.'

'That's good,' Albie was pleased.

'Where are you eating tonight?' Niamh enquired.

'At the pub, I suppose, there doesn't seem to be a lot to do in Quin.'

'Oh there was great excitement once when the cows got out of the farmer's field and blocked the road,' he twinkled his eyes at her.

She smiled warmly. 'I'm sorry, I just can't get over how alike you and Shay are.'

'That's okay,' he seemed pleased with the comparison.

'When your mom's awake bring her over and we'll eat together,' Niamh instructed.

'That's kind, thank you,' Lexi stood.

'I'm glad he's got people like you and your mom in his life,' Albie said.

'We do all get on great,' she confirmed. 'I'd better go and see how mom is.'

'Okay love, see you in a while,' Niamh smiled tiredly.

Lexi made her way back to me and I was still fast asleep, drool coming out of the corner of mouth. 'Mom!' she yelled making me jump.

'What?' I sat up disorientated. Where was I, where was my bedroom. Oh, I was in Ireland, shit.

'We've been invited to Albie and Niamh's for a bite to eat,' she informed me.

'When?' I frowned.

'Er, tonight. We go back home tomorrow,' she rolled her eyes.

'No, I mean when did they invite you?' I tried to keep my patience.

'Just,' she replied. 'I had a walk around the village and Niamh found me and I went back to their house.'

'Were they okay?' I wiped the sleep from my eyes.

'Yes, they asked me some questions about Shay, they seem nice,' she answered. 'I called Belle and she said you should tell Shay now too.'

'I'll see,' I answered vaguely.

'Albie wants to meet him.'

'It's Mr Cassidy to you,' I corrected, biting the skin around my thumbnail.

'He told me to call him Albie,' she pulled a face. 'I'm going to have a shower, I hope Niamh's a good cook.'

I nodded, sitting upright. I knew I would have to come clean to Shay about his dad but I wanted to do it in my own time. Although I liked them I wished I'd never got it in my head to come in the first place. I should be at home, snuggling up to Shay and watching something utterly crap on the tv.

Lexi came out of the tiny bathroom, just a towel wrapped around her. She had such a lovely figure, it was a crying shame that she hid it under jeans and baggy tops. 'Shower's free mom,' she paused looking at me. 'You okay?'

I nodded forcing myself into the bathroom, I wasn't okay, I just wanted to go home.

Twenty~Seven

It was strange for Shay to wake up Sunday morning without Tash digging him in the ribs and telling him to get up and make a brew. He lay on his back for a while staring at the ceiling, he really missed Tash when she wasn't with him, he never thought he would love anyone as much as he loved her. He hoped she was having a good time, she deserved a bit of pampering.

Bev and Dale had arranged to meet him at the pub for Sunday lunch so he didn't have to make do with something. His mom had asked to go to hers but you never got a pint with her dinners. His plan was to talk through some things with Dale, something he had in mind to try and soothe the waters a little where Jamie was concerned so Tash wouldn't stress so much about him. He wanted to tell her about it, what he had brought yesterday as a way of a bribe but he didn't know whether to call her and interrupt her last few hours at the spa.

What the hell, she wouldn't mind, now what was the name of the hotel? Park something. Park Hall Hotel that was it, he would call her and make sure she was okay and run through the plan with her before meeting Dale and Bev, he wanted to hear her voice too. He knew it was no good phoning her mobile, she had said yesterday that they couldn't get a signal

Finding the number he dialled it and waited for it to be answered. 'Good morning Park Hall Hotel, Emily speaking, how may I help you?' The voice was warm and friendly.

'How ya doing?' Shay fussed Millie. 'Could you put me through to one of your guests please, Natasha Turner?'

'One moment please,' he heard the sound of computer keys clattering and then she spoke. 'I'm sorry sir but we have no one of that name staying here.'

He frowned. 'How about Lexi Turner?'

Again the pause. 'No, I'm sorry we have no guests of either name.'

'Would you please check again?' he could feel he hint of panic trying to bubble to the surface.

'I'm sorry sir, we have no guests of those names here.'

'Thank you,' he hit the off button. He was so sure it was the right hotel so where the hell were they?

He tried Tash's mobile again but nothing, Lexi's was the same. He phoned his mom. 'Hey son,' she greeted on answering the call. 'Are you okay?'

'Can you remember the name of the hotel that Tash and Lexi were going too?'

'The Park Hall Hotel, why is there a problem?'

'I've tried to call Tash but they haven't got anyone staying there under the names of Natasha Turner or Lexi Turner.'

'Are you sure?' she was immediately concerned.

'Positive, I asked the lady to check, twice,' he fretted.

'What about Dale or Bev, would they know?'

'They thought she was going to the spa too. Where is she mam?' he was worried. 'Do you think it has anything to do with Sam?'

'Why would it have anything to do with Sam?' Moira was confused.

'What if he's sweet talked her round again? Convinced her to go back to him?' he could feel his agitation rising.

'Tash has more sense than that,' she dismissed the idea.

'Has she? Twice he has wormed his way back into her affections,' he couldn't see past it.

'She loves you!' Moira snapped, worrying where she could be. 'Would Belle know where she and Lexi are?'

'I could try her,' he was worried sick it was all to do with Sam.

'Let me know what she says,' Moira had an uneasy feeling.

'I will,' he ended the call, immediately calling Belle, it seemed to take an age for her to answer. 'It's Shay.'

'Oh hi Shay,' she sounded flustered.

'Where have Lexi and Tash gone?' he cut straight to the chase.

'The Park Hall Hotel,' she replied promptly.

'No they haven't, I've called the hotel and they are not even booked in there. Where are they Belle?'

'I can't hear you, I think there's something wrong with my phone,' she lied badly. 'I have to go.'

'Don't you dare hang up on me,' he warned. 'You know where they are, tell me! Are they with Lexi's dad?'

'No,' she cried, horrified that he would even think that. 'I don't know where they are,' she wasn't getting any better at lying.

'If you don't know where they are how would you know they are not with Sam?' he tried to catch her out.

She didn't answer. 'Tell me please dahling, I'm worried sick about them,' he begged.

She knew she had to tell him, she was too honest for her own good. 'They have gone to Ireland,' she answered quietly.

'Ireland?' he was flabbergasted.

'Yes,' in her room she cringed.

'Why have they gone to Ireland?' Of all the places he thought they were, Ireland was the last place he would have guessed.

'Please don't shout Shay,' she began nervously.

'Tell me now,' his accent became thick with emotion.

'They found your dad, they've gone to see him,' she rushed the words out.

He was so quiet that she thought for a moment that he had hung up.

'They've done what?' he was trying to hold his temper in.

'They've found your dad and they've gone to see him,' she repeated.

'I heard what you said,' he snapped. 'You *do not* tell them that I know, do you hear me Belle?'

'Yes,' she answered meekly.

'I mean it,' he was livid. 'Not a word.' He cut the call, grabbing his car keys and heading to his moms.

She was sitting in the living room agitated when he arrived. 'Do you know where she is?' she asked.

He nodded, slumping onto the chair. 'Yeah, I got it out of Belle.'

'So where have they gone?' she demanded impatiently.

He took a deep breath, picking at his thumbnail. 'Ireland.'

'Ireland?' she repeated stumped. 'Why are they in Ireland?'

He shifted uncomfortably in his seat. 'They've found my da, they've gone to see him.'

She reached out to steady herself on the arm of the chair. 'No,' she groaned. 'Please no.'

'I'm going to fucking kill her,' he said ominously.

Moira could hardly breath, the secret that she had kept for so long was about to come crashing out into the open. Tears began to fall as she realised how it was going to change everything.

'Mam,' he soothed sitting on the arm of the chair, holding her. 'Please don't cry.'

'Why would she do this without telling us?' she cried.

'I don't know,' he tried to comfort her. 'She has no right going behind our backs.'

'Doesn't she realise the hurt this will cause?' She couldn't believe that Tash would do something like this, that she would be so thoughtless.

'I am so fucking angry at her,' he fumed, his arms still round his mom. 'She knows what he meant to you, how you have struggled.'

Moira nodded, feeling like the wind had been knocked out of her.

'She lied to me! Bare faced lied to me too! How can I believe anything that comes out her mouth now?'

'Love,' she felt drained. 'Don't say that.'

'What am I supposed to say?' he exploded. 'She looked me in the eye and told me she was going on a spa weekend.'

Moira shook her head, not even beginning to understand Tash's thinking. 'Can you get me a whisky please?' she asked quietly.

'Yeah, sure,' this really wasn't about him at that moment, it was about his mom and how she was feeling. Going to the sideboard he poured her a stiff measure.

'Do you think he knows by now?' she began to cry again.

'Mam,' he said softly. 'It doesn't matter about him.'

'Wouldn't you like to know your da?' she dabbed at her eyes with the sleeve of her jumper.

He didn't answer for a moment, when he was younger he had wished his dad would come and find him, so he could be like his friends and have someone to teach him to play football.

As he grew up and Moira explained why she had done what she had he resigned himself to never knowing him. Part of him was curious though. 'You were my mom and my dad,' he clarified forcing a smile. 'Why would I need anyone else?'

She noticed that he had hesitated before answering. 'You have always been the best son a mother could ask for,' she sniffed loudly. 'Ah look at the state of me.'

'It's a shock, for both of us,' he rubbed his eyes. 'I thought Lexi would have stopped her, not gone with her.'

'Maybe she tried,' she shrugged. 'Knowing Lexi she's gone to keep an eye on her mother, I know I would have done.'

'I can't believe what she's done,' he took out his mobile.

'Are you going to ring her?' she sipped her whisky.

He shook his head. 'I'm texting Dale, we were supposed to meet for lunch but funnily enough my appetite seems to have deserted me.'

'Albie will be in shock too.' It was one of the few times she actually referred to him by name, it was usually Shay's father.'

He stared at the floor, not knowing what to say, she looked totally devastated. His phone pinged and he looked at it. 'It's Dale.'

'What will you say to Tash?' Moira was chaffing about that too, she loved her to pieces but this....

He shrugged, his face hardening. 'She lied to me and she's upset you,' his tone was harsh. 'I am so fucking pissed off with her.'

'Shay,' she scolded, there were too many swear words floating about. 'Just think carefully before you do anything rash. Think of those precious babies,' she knew how hot-headed her son could be.

He declined to answer. 'What time are they due back?' she asked.

Looking at his watch he replied. 'After three,' he replied picking up his truck keys.

'Where are you going?' she was troubled.

'I am going back to her house to wait for her to come home and see if she even knows what the telling the truth means.'

'It's your home too,' she corrected him, a jittery feeling filling her stomach.

'Is it?' he frowned, kissing her gently on the cheek. 'I'll see you later.'

'Son!' she cried, she didn't want them splitting up over this.

He ignored her, going to his truck and driving the short distance home. Millie raced around him and he decided to take her for a walk instead of sitting and thinking and waiting for his lying, deceitful girlfriend to come home. He pulled himself up sharply, is that really what he thought of Tash?

He would have said, up until a couple of hours ago, that she was the most honest person he had ever met but now? Look how she had deceived everyone about them seeing each other at the beginning.

'Come on Millie,' he called, taking her on an extra-long walk, trying to step out his anger but it just kept increasing.

It killed some time though and when he got home he sat on the settee with a glass of whisky sitting untouched on the coffee table and Millie lying at his feet. He looked around the room, seeing the little touches that they had brought together to make it theirs. They were trying to build a future together, but what now?

I was glad when Lexi and I arrived back at Birmingham airport. We had spent a lovely evening with Albie and Niamh, I really liked them. All I had to do now was convince Shay that he would too.

Shay, God I had missed him even though I'd only been away for one night. I loved him more than I had ever loved Sam, which was probably a bad thing to say but it was the truth. I put my hand to my bump, he was going to make such a wonderful father and hopefully the twins would have a decent grandfather too. I just couldn't wait for us to be parents. Albie had stared at the scan photo for an eternity, tracing the outline of the babies with his fingers. Poor man, it was so much to take in all at once.

Lexi got off the train in Birmingham, hugging me tightly. 'Let me know what Shay says,' she said and I nodded. I had decided to bide my time before I mentioned anything to him, test the water a little.

Getting off in Wolverhampton I caught the bus home. I just wanted to curl up with Shay and tell him how much I loved him. Millie came running into the hallway when I got home, nearly bowling me over. 'Hello love!' I called, taking off my coat and hanging it up.

No answer, but his truck was outside, frowning I went into the living room. Shay was on the settee, a glass of whisky on the coffee table. 'Hey you,' I grinned, so very glad to see him.

'Hey,' he echoed, his eyes bright. 'Has Belle called you?'

I fished my phone out of my bag. 'I don't know the battery's dead. Does she want me? Is everything okay?'

'Everything's fine,' he seemed a little jumpy. 'Did you have a good time at your *spa break*?'

'It was great,' I turned, not trusting my face not to give me away.

He stood slowly, standing in front of me. 'So dahling, what treatments did you have?'

'Oh you know,' my answer vague.

'No, I don't, that's why I'm asking you,' he did seem in a strange mood.

I faltered for a moment. 'The usual,' I risked a smile. 'Shall I rustle us up something to eat?'

He grabbed my arm. 'I called the hotel this morning, neither you nor Lexi were booked in.'

I blanched. 'You checked up on me?' I managed to stammer.

He put his face inches from mine. 'Where did you go?'

'Shay,' I began nervously, oh shit.

'Don't!' He hissed. 'Don't you dare lie to me again?'

Tears flooded my eyes. 'Please?'

'Please what?' he demanded. 'You looked me in the eye and blatantly lied to me,' he was so angry. 'Why should I believe a word you say now?'

'I went to Ireland,' the words were blurted out. 'I've met your dad.'

He stepped away from me, a look of pure disgust on his face. 'Why? Why would you do that?'

'I wanted to do something nice for you.'

'Nice for me!' He exploded. 'How is this *nice* for me?'

'Babe,' I tried to take his hand but he shrugged me off.

'My mam is in bits because of what you've done. You had no right, no right at all.'

'You knew I'd gone?' I thought he had only just found out.

'My mam Tash, what has she ever done at you?'

'I'm sorry,' I whispered.

'How dare you go behind my back!' He spat the words at me.

'I never thought,' I tried to defend myself. 'You said you wished you had known your dad and Moira said she wished you had too.'

'Don't try and justify it. My mam is crying her heart out!' He shouted making Millie bark. 'You are a lying, deceitful maggot!'

I felt numb, I had only thought about Shay meeting his dad, not how Moira would feel. I hadn't wanted it to be too late for him the way it had been with my own dad. 'Please Shay, I love you.'

'Do you?' he asked sharply. 'Are you sure about that? You won't tell Sam to leave you alone. Funny how he's always around when I'm not. What's the plan Tash? Have the best of both worlds or ride into the sunset with your ex once the twins are born?'

'Don't,' I was more than hurt, how could he even think that?

'I can't even look at you,' he picked up his keys existing the house.

I took a deep breath, trying to stem the flow of tears, the babies kicking furiously. I never envisaged this would happen, I had to see Moira.

His truck was gone when I went to my car and drove to her house. I needed to make things right but I really didn't know how. When she opened the door she looked as heartbroken as I felt. 'I'm so sorry,' It didn't seem enough but it was all I could say.

'Why did you do it Tash?' she asked as I followed her inside.

'Because,' I stopped, what could I say?

'You knew what he meant to me, how long it has taken me to move on with my life. I feel like you've ripped my heart out,' she sank into her chair.

Tears filled my eyes. 'I never meant to hurt anyone,' I sat on the edge of the other chair, legs shaking. 'I thought it would be nice for Shay to know his dad.'

'Don't you think if he had wanted to find his dad he would have done? He had all the details he needed,' she snapped harshly.

'I didn't think, I don't think,' my tears began to fall. I want everyone to have a happy ending but I always make it worse. I should have asked you both but I wanted it to be a surprise.'

'Well you succeeded there,' she retorted.

'I don't know how to make it right,' I was crying freely now. 'I would never hurt you, I love you. I always balls up,' I rubbed my stomach distracted.

She began to cry too, what a pair we were.

'I've cocked everything up,' I could hardly breathe. 'Shay hates me, he can't even look at me. I've lost him,' my sobs grew louder.

'You haven't lost him,' she said impatiently.

'I have,' I wailed. 'He called me a lying, deceitful maggot and he's right. I did lie, I didn't think of it as lie though.'

'What do you expect?' she asked. 'Did you think it would be like an episode of *Long Lost Family* and we would all cry tears of joy and embrace each other.'

'Yes,' I replied truthfully.

'Jaysus,' she swore. 'Has your life taught you nothing?'

'I just wanted to do something nice.'

'For my son or yourself?' she queried. 'Would it make you or him feel special?'

The pair of them really knew how to wound with words. 'I *never* do anything to make myself feel *special*. I just want to make other people happy.'

She looked away. 'You should have left well alone.'

'I wish I had,' I whispered.

'Alan will be here in a minute,' I think she wanted me out of her sight as well.

My heart contracted, he would hate me too. 'I'd better go,' I stood on shaking legs. 'I think Shay will come here. Please tell him I'm sorry and that I love him very much. I'm so sorry I hurt you too Moira.'

She didn't reply so I continued. 'We found your parents grave. We tidied it up and put some flowers on.'

Fresh tears appeared in her eyes and I had gotten to the door before she spoke. 'How was Albie?'

I turned tearfully. 'Like looking at Shay in thirty years' time.' Which was something would be doing now. 'He was lovely, really nice. He and his wife made Lexi and me welcome.'

'His wife?' she repeated, alarmed.

I nodded. 'Niamh is his second wife, his first wife died ten years ago.'

'Oh. What did he say about Shay?'

'He wants to meet him, he was very emotional. You are right, I should have left well alone, I've turned everyone's world upside down.'

She nodded her agreement. 'How did you leave it?'

'I said I'd call him, let him know if Shay will meet him,' my face screwed up. 'I've ruined everything and I've lost Shay for good.'

Sadly I hurried to my car, batting away the tears, absolutely and utterly heartbroken.

Twenty~Eight

I arrived home and there was only Millie to greet me, Shay nowhere to be seen as expected. 'Where is he?' I asked big dog but all she was interested in was her food.

I plugged in my mobile to charge it but in my tizz I forget to hit the switch on the socket so it didn't charge. I called Shay from the landline, leaving a tearful message asking him to come home.

I checked to see how my phone was doing a little while later and I cried again when I realised I hadn't flicked the switch, I felt so out of sorts. As soon as I switched it on my message alert went off about twenty times. I peered at the screen, Lexi was trying to get hold of me urgently.

I hit her number and she answered it immediately. 'Mom, where have you been? Shay knows.'

'I know he does, we've had a huge row and now I don't know where he is. I've upset Moira and we've had words and I've ruined everything,' I began to cry again.

'Oh mom,' she too sounded upset. 'Belle had no choice, she had to tell him.'

'Belle?' I was puzzled.

'He phoned Belle after he called the hotel, she's really sorry mom.'

I hadn't even give it a thought as to how he'd found out. 'Tell her not to worry,' I said. 'No point in everyone being miserable.'

'Do you want me to come home?' she asked softly.

'No, I'll be fine,' I didn't want Shay shouting at her too.

'I don't like you being this upset,' she tutted. 'I'm going to shout at Shay myself.'

'Don't,' I said wearily. 'You were right, Belle was right. I should have kept my nose out. Shay and Moira have every right to be angry with me,' I sighed. 'And now I've got to tell Albie that his son doesn't want to know. I've disrupted his life for nothing.'

'Oh mom,' she said. 'Call if you need me.'

'I will. Love you and tell Belle not to worry,' I blew a kiss down the phone.

'I love you too mom,' she answered.

I sat in the living room, hoping Shay would come home but he didn't. I left a zillion messages on his voicemail and about the same amount of text messages, but nothing. I did think about calling Moira but I wasn't her favourite person at the moment.

By nine-thirty I could stand it no longer, he wasn't coming home, it was finished. I was going to be a single mom to twins, I was scared shitless. They would only see Shay on a weekend and Moira would think I was such a bad mother and everyone would hate me.

Flopping into bed I felt shattered but I knew that sleep would not come easy. I lay there breaking my heart, smelling Shay's scent on his pillow as I hugged it to me. I must have fallen asleep about three, not waking until after eight. I bolted from the bed, he must have come back at some point because his work clothes were gone but that was all.

Had he stayed at his mom's? Picked up a woman and had a meaning less one night stand? No, that was a stupid thing to think, he wouldn't. Or would he? Sam had, he hadn't cared that I was carrying his child when he cheated on me.

I called Bev, even though she usually lay in bed until ten, this as an emergency. 'Tash do you know what the bloody time is?' she asked sleepily.

'Bev,' I sobbed. 'I need you.'

'What's wrong?' she was immediately awake. 'Are the babies okay?'

'Please can you just come over?' I pleaded.

'Give me half an hour but you'd better make me some strong coffee.'

'Thank you,' I ended the call, pacing the kitchen as Millie followed me, nearly tripping me over.

She seemed to take an age to arrive and then she was in my kitchen, face devoid of make-up and hair sticking up all over the place.

'What's up babe?' she scratched Millie's head. 'You look like shit, I thought pampering weekends were supposed to do you good?'

'Shay's left me,' I slumped at the table like a drama queen.

'Don't be stupid,' she looked shocked.

I told her everything and she sat there with her mouth open. 'You stupid cow!' she chided me. 'Why would you do something like this without telling them?'

'I thought it would be nice for Shay.'

'If you had told me what you were planning to do I would have stopped you,' she helped herself to more coffee.

'I truly wished I had.'

'Have you tried to call him?'

I nodded. 'And I've sent him loads of text messages.'

'Call Moira,' she found my stash of biscuits.

'I can't, she's too angry at me. I just can't face her,' I felt like a coward.

She looked at me frustrated. 'Stop being a wimp. Has he taken any of his clothes?'

'I told you, he must have come back for his work clothes.'

'If he was leaving you he would have taken more than just his work clothes, he's just chucking his toys out of the pram,' she stated. 'I'm surprised at Moira letting him stay at hers, she should have sent him home.'

'We don't know that he did stay there. Anyway she's angry at me, they probably spent last night drinking Irish whisky and slagging me off.'

'Hun,' she scowled at me. 'Don't let them do this to you. So you made an error of judgment, no one died. They'll come round.'

'They hate me now,' I howled.

'No one could have hated anyone more than you hated me when you found out about Dale and me but look at us now,' she said brightly.

I groaned, holding my head in my hands. 'I can't cope with this,' I cried as my mobile rang making me jump a mile. I looked at it before pushing it to Bev.

'What?' she poked the handset.

'It's Albie,' I hissed.

'Well answer it then,' she pushed it back to me.

'I can't,' I shook my head, what would I say?

'Just bloody answer it,' she ordered.

I grabbed it, pressing accept. 'Hi Albie,' I tried to sound normal.

'Hello Natasha, how are you?' he sounded nervous, bless him.

'I'm good thank you, how are you and Niamh?' I really wished I'd let it go to voicemail.

'We're fine,' he paused finding the courage to ask the question he wanted too. 'Have you spoken to Shay? I know you said that you'd ring me but if I'm honest I didn't want to wait.'

I promptly burst into tears and Bev took the phone from me. 'Albie, I'm Bev, Tash's best mate.'

'Why is she crying?' he asked concerned.

'Well, she's a little upset,' she admitted. 'Shay hasn't taken the news that she came and found you very well.'

'So he doesn't want to see me?' he voice was flat.

'They haven't exactly got round to talking about that, he was too busy shouting at her for not telling him what she was going to do,' Bev explained.

In my seat I cringed, Albie wold hate me now too for getting his hopes up.

'Moira isn't happy with her either,' she told him helpfully. 'Our Tash is a tad emotional as you can imagine.'

'Can I speak to her?' he asked.

'Hold on,' she covered the mouthpiece with her hand. 'He wants to speak to you.'

I blew my nose, taking the phone from her. 'I'm truly sorry Albie,' I whispered.

'I'm more concerned about you,' he sounded choked himself.

'I just wanted the two of you to get to know each other,' I didn't realise I had this many tears. 'I'm sorry I got your hopes up and disrupted you world for nothing.'

'Don't go concerning yourself with that,' again he paused. 'Can we keep in touch, you let me know when the babies are born?'

'Of course we can,' I was pleased he wanted to, he could come and meet his grandchildren, after all it didn't look like Shay was going to be around.

'We'll speak soon,' he assured me. 'Look after yourself and those babies.'

'You too,' I replied. 'Bye.'

'Bye dahling,' he said, sounding so like Shay.

I put the phone on the table still crying. 'Oh what a tangled web we weave when at first we do deceive,' Bev quoted.

'What?' I dabbed at my eyes with a tissue.

'It's William Shakespeare,' she informed me, with a thoughtful look. 'What are you going to do?'

'What can I do?' I said helplessly.

Bev stayed until lunchtime and then she left me to wallowing my own self-pity. I couldn't believe I was going to be a single mom to twins, why did I ever think this pregnancy was a good idea?

I couldn't cope with the silence, if Shay was going to leave me then I had to know. I would call him one more time and that was it. Sam had led me too much of a merry dance to put up with such nonsense from anyone else.

My heart was hammering as I pressed the button and his mobile rang out before going to voicemail. 'Shay,' I began. 'I don't know how many times I can say I'm sorry but this is the last message I'm leaving. I just need to know you're okay, I'm going out of my mind with worry. I know I shouldn't have gone to your dads and I'm sorry form the bottom of my heart for what I have done to you and your mom.'

I paused suddenly angry. 'If you are leaving then I want you to come and pick up your things now and have the guts and the decency to say it to my face instead of slinking away without a word. It's not fair on me.'

I closed the call shaking, what if he did leave? Should I have left the voicemail? Well it was too late now.

Shay got to his mom's a little after five-thirty, going straight from work. He couldn't face Tash just yet, he was still too angry.

'What are you doing here?' Moira demanded. 'Where's Tash?'

He shrugged taking off his work boots.

'Shay!' she cried. 'Have you argued again?'

'I haven't seen her,' he answered gruffly.

'But you said that you were going home when you left here last night.'

'Well, I didn't,' he cut in sharply.

'Oi,' she warned not liking his tone. 'Where did you go then?'

'I slept in the truck. Can I stay here tonight?' he looked all in.

'No, you can go home and sort this out with Tash.'

He went to reply but was interrupted by his mobile ringing. 'Aren't you going to answer it?' she asked pointedly.

'It'll go to voicemail,' his voice was thick with emotion as he stared at the screen.

'It's Tash isn't it?' she could have swung for him. 'How many times has she called?'

'Too many,' he stared moodily at the table.

'Stop being so childish,' she scolded as his alert tone went off to say he had a voicemail. 'Aren't you going to listen to it?'

He picked up his mobile reluctantly, his mom wasn't past giving him a slap when she thought the situation warranted it. He listened, then lay the phone back down.

'Shay?' his mom looked at him curiously. 'What did she say?'

'She's told me to go round and get my stuff.'

'Tash has?' Moira gasped, not believing it. 'Let me hear,' she took the phone listening to the message.

He got up fetching himself a glass of water. He was angry with her that's all, he had no intention of leaving. What if she meant it? Moira put the phone onto the table going to him and clipping him around the ear.

'Ow,' he'd forgotten how hard she could hit. 'What was that for?'

'Listen to it properly, she isn't telling you to leave, you eejit.'

He stared at his feet sulkily.

'She sounds distraught,' she chided. 'You've left her to stew without a word. She is carrying your babies, do you really think she needs this kind of stress?'

'She hurt you,' he cut in.

'She's sorry, she has said so a hundred times. This isn't about me now, the damage is done, we can't change the fact that Albie knows about you now. This is about the two of you, your future together. Do you love her?'

He looked at her sharply. 'Of course I do, from the moment I saw her.'

'Then why are you punishing her like this? She thinks you've finished with her, is that what you want?'

'No, I was never going to leave her, I'm just angry with her.'

'Go home Shay, where you belong.'

'Mam -.'

She held up her hand. 'Now Shay, go and sort this out and I will be checking that you have.'

He swore under his breath, pulling on his boots and not daring to defy her.

By four I thought that I would go out of my mind if I didn't do something so I began to clean my kitchen cupboards. I was on my wobbly stool, cleaning the top ones when Shay came in. He stood by the sink not saying a word.

When I felt the silence would suffocate me I had to speak. 'If you want to go, just go,' I said sadly. 'Please don't prolong the agony.'

'Go?' his voice was rusty.

I couldn't face him. 'I'll be okay,' my heart was breaking. 'You don't have to pretend, I won't stop you seeing the babies when they are born.'

'What?' His voice was sharp and it startled me, causing the stool to wobble precariously. I reached out to steady myself and he moved quickly, standing behind me, his hands holding my waist. 'Get down.'

'No,' I said childishly, squeezing my eyes tightly shut.

'You're going to fall, get down,' he repeated, still holding me.

The tears were threatening to fall again. 'I can't.'

He sighed impatiently, taking my hand and I stepped down shaking. 'Why?' he asked sounding as exhausted as I felt. 'Why do it?'

I sat at the table, taking a deep breath. 'When my dad died I realised that was it. We could never make our relationship any different now. Never have the chance to build bridges and be a father and daughter like we should have been. I have so much I should have said to him and now I'll never be able too. I didn't want you to be the same, I thought it would be nice for you to have the chance to know him.'

'It wasn't your place,' he said but at least he wasn't shouting anymore.

'I know but that's me Shay,' I felt sad. 'I try and make people's lives nicer.'

He stayed by the sink. 'You hurt my mam.'

I nodded bleakly. 'I regret that with all my heart but, oh I don't know what to say. To you or you mom. I can't change what I did, I can't take it back.' I looked down at my hands. 'I love you so much,' I began to cry, where was I finding all those tears from.

'I'm so angry at you,' he stated.

'I know, I would be too,' I agreed. I knew he was staring at me but I couldn't meet his eyes. 'Don't be angry at Lexi, she tried to stop me.'

I heard him sigh and then I did look up, hating the expression on his face, I couldn't read it. 'I'm so sorry.'

He nodded bluntly. 'I know.'

'I didn't mean to lie to you, I just wanted it to be a surprise.' Stop crying!

'I know,' he said again and silence filled the kitchen. Me sitting at the table and him standing, keeping a distance between us. 'What did he say?' he asked eventually.

'He was shocked at first,' that was a huge understatement. 'He wants to meet you.'

'What's he like?' he asked, his face giving nothing away.

'He's like you,' I replied wiping me eyes. 'Exactly like you, your mannerisms, everything. I really like him.'

He sighed stroking his chin. 'What did he say about the babies?'

'As I said he was shocked but he took it well. He found out he was going to be a dad and going to be a grandfather in the space of a few minutes.'

'That would be a shock,' he conceded.

'Where were you last night?' I asked, not really wanting to know the answer if it was one I didn't want to hear.

'I slept in my truck,' he replied, dark shadows around his eyes. 'I had to be away from you.'

I nodded. 'You don't have to stay because of the babies,' I told him miserably. 'Like I said I'll be fine, I'll have to be.'

Infuriatingly he looked away, his eyes going to the window. Why wouldn't he just tell me? 'Shay,' I began to sob again. 'I don't want to lose you, you are everything to me and not just because of the twins.'

'Stop,' he sounded worn-out.

'I'm not a bad person,' I babbled. 'I just want everyone to be happy that's all, I don't want to hurt anyone.'

'It's you flaw,' he shrugged.

'Yes, my flaw,' I agreed. I've had such a shit life that I want to make everyone's a fairy-tale.'

'Do you think your life is shit now?' his voice softened.

'Depends on what happens with us,' I looked at him sadly. 'Albie wants me to keep in touch with him, he called me earlier but I won't do anything that you don't want me to.'

He flicked the kettle on. 'I can't tell you what to do.'

'I've told him it doesn't look like he'll meet you,' I chewed on my bottom lip. 'I got his hopes up for nothing.'

He didn't reply, just carried on making tea, so I tried again. 'My dad had no choice, he choose to be a bastard to Dale and me, to not give us the time of day. Your dad didn't, up until two days ago he didn't even know you existed.' I looked out of the window, oh great, Moira was walking up the path. 'Your mom's here,' I said softly, trying to dry the tears.

He went to let her in and I could hear their hushed voices in the hall and then they were in the kitchen. 'I've come to see if you two are okay?' she took off her coat sitting down.

I glanced at Shay. 'I don't know,' I answered wretchedly, my hand resting on my stomach.

He turned away, making his mom a cuppa. 'Thanks son,' she said when it as placed in front of her.

I looked down at the table top, my stomach rolling with nerves. I sensed Moira staring at me and I shifted uncomfortably in my seat. 'I've told Albie that Shay doesn't want to meet him, I've sorted it.' I told her.

'Is that what you want?' she asked her son.

'I haven't said one way or another,' he replied with a shrug.

I bit my tongue, I couldn't seem to do anything right. Well I couldn't sit there any longer. I know Shay loved me but I had loved Sam too but it didn't stop me chucking him out and divorcing him though. I had royally fucked up.

'Millie needs her walk,' I said, going for her lead, making her race about.

'Tash,' Moira whispered softly.

I gulped back the tears. 'She hasn't been for a walk today.'

'But you haven't touched your tea,' she indicated to my mug.

'Its fine,' I sniffed loudly going into the hall and pulling on my coat. Without looking back I headed out into the evening.

I hurried along the road, Millie keeping pace with me for a change. Why was he making me suffer so much? Why couldn't he just tell me that it was over? I didn't deserve it, I hadn't intentionally set out to hurt anyone.

A cat ran across our path and Millie went to chase after it. I felt the lead got taut and I dug my heels in bracing myself but she was too strong. I tried to break my fall and protect my stomach at the same time, taking nearly all of my weight on my left arm and I cried out in pain as Millie washed my face with her tongue.

'Tash!' Mrs Evans, one of my very favourite customers, was beside me. She came into the salon once a week and I had done her hair on every appointment, baring holidays, for the last fifteen years. She was lovely. 'Have you hurt yourself? I saw you fall.'

'Yes,' I groaned, lying there like a beached whale.

'Come on love,' she tried to help me up as I hung onto Millie for dear life. 'She is such a big dog.'

'She is,' I agreed, struggling to my feet.

'Did you land on your tum?' she fretted.

I shook my head, wincing at the pain in my wrist, it really hurt.

'Come inside, I live just here,' she took my arm, the one not hurting. 'Bring the dog with you.'

I allowed her to take me inside her neat house, the furniture old but immaculate. 'I didn't know this was where you lived.'

'I've been here since I married in fifty-nine, I wouldn't want to live anywhere else,' she plonked me on the one of the kitchen chairs as Millie went off exploring and looked at me closely. 'Whatever's the matter dear?'

I gulped, unable to answer, a huge lump stuck in my throat.

'Sorry, it's none of my business,' she declared putting the kettle on. 'But you look like you could do with a strong cup of tea.'

'I shouldn't really.'

She gave me a dismissive look. 'I know you're pregnant but I drank tea with all of mine and it never did them any harm. These days you are too cossetted, it's not healthy.'

I tried to smile but only succeeded in crying again.

'My dear, things can't be that bad,' she lay her hand on my arm.

'They are,' I hiccupped.

'You live with Moira's son, don't you?'

'You know Moira?' I was surprised, Mrs Evans came in every week but she had never said.

'I know her vaguely, I see her at the bingo sometimes.'

'She's a lovely woman and I have broken her heart.'

'Why?' she tried to sound like she was not being nosey, making the tea she brought it to the table.

Falteringly I told her everything, she had that kind of face. When I had finished she was looking at me with pursed lips. 'It's nothing to do with me but if he is being like this with you, then he not worth your tears.'

I went to protest, Shay was so worth everything but I could see her point of view. Sam had made everything my fault, did I really want to go down the same route again?

Mrs Evans got up, fetching Millie some water. 'Let him stew,' she advised. 'Stay here and talk to me for a while.'

I nodded, I couldn't face going home just yet. Picking up my mug I winced at the pain in my wrist. 'Let me strap that up for you,' she fussed, enjoying having someone to look after.

Twenty~Nine

Shay and Moira sat in silence, the only sound the ticking of the kitchen clock. 'Tash has been gone a while,' she played nervously with the tissue in her hand.

He nodded, Millie's usual walk took about forty minutes and she had been gone an hour, plus it was beginning to get dark. 'Call her,' Moira chaffed. 'She was really upset when she left.'

He pointed to the work top on which my mobile sat. 'She's left her phone here,' he stood pulling on his coat. 'I'm going to look for her.'

'I'm coming too,' she needed to be doing something, she still felt shaken by Albie knowing now about his son.

'She always takes Millie the same route, she's a creature of habit,' he led the way, worried that something had happened to her. The roads were frustratingly empty, no sign of anyone.

'Where is she?' Moira cried, they had both come down so hard on her.

'I don't know,' he tried not to snap as he turned the corner just in time to see the tail lights of Sam's white Audi. 'Hey!' he cried, running after the car.

'Shay!' his mom called. 'What are you doing?'

'I fecking knew it,' he yelled. 'Fecking knew it.'

Moira finally caught up with him. 'What is it?'

He pointed, fuming. 'She's with him.'

'Who?' she was confused.

He turned to her angrily. 'That was Sam's car, she's with him!'

'Don't be an eejit,' she scolded.

'Well where is she then?' he demanded. 'I knew he'd charm his way back in.'

'Don't,' she felt close to tears.

He turned abruptly, heading back home. It had fallen fully dark now and he was out of his mind with worry. He called Bev and she answered straight away. 'Have you two sorted yourselves out or have I got to come and bang your heads together?'

'She's not with you then?' his heart dropped.

'Why would she be with me?' she puzzled. 'Have you two been bloody arguing again?'

'She took Millie a walk ages ago,' he was frantic. 'Mam and me have gone out looking but there's no sign of her. I saw Sam's car, do you think she's with him?'

'No I bloody don't,' she retorted.

'Then what is he doing around here?' Jealously was not letting him think straight.

'For God's sake!' She cried. 'Listen to yourself. My friend is absolutely heartbroken at the thought of losing you.'

'Bev,' he tried to cut in.

'Never mind Bev,' she sniped. 'It's about time you grew up a bit Shay. You are going to be a father and yet you are acting like a child.'

'Hey!' he cried offended.

'She didn't do it to hurt you or cause you pain. She did it because she loves you and what have you done? You've broken her heart and now you're accusing her of running off with her ex,' she was on a roll. 'Now you can sit there wondering where she is just like she has been the last night and today wondering where you were.' With that she cut the call, she couldn't be doing with talking to him.

Shay looked at his phone stunned.

'What did she say?' Moira was standing over him. 'Has she seen her, is she there?'

He shook his head, looking at his mom with bright eyes. 'What have I done mam? I've pushed her away.'

'Son,' she soothed rubbing his shoulder.

'I was just angry with her,' he felt tearful. 'Where is she mam?'

She shook her head, wishing she could answer.

I limped back with Millie about twenty minutes later, seeing Dale's car parked behind Shay's truck. I groaned, someone else to tell me what an idiot I was. Walking into the kitchen the three of them were looking at me with identical worried expressions on their faces.

'Where the hell have you been?' Dale demanded. 'Shay and his mom have been out looking for you everywhere,' he peered at me. 'You look bloody awful sis.'

I knew I did, my face was red and swollen from crying, I knew I looked a sight.

'You're covered in dirt,' Moira too looked concerned.

'Millie pulled me over,' I winced, taking off my coat.

'But where have you been?' Shay questioned.

Dale shot him a look. 'Have you hurt yourself?'

'A little,' I held my wrist gingerly. 'Mrs Evans took me in her house, she comes in the salon. Millie didn't mean to do it, she tried to chase a cat.'

'She's such a big dog,' Moira shook her head. 'Are the babies okay?'

I was annoyed, neither of them seemed concerned as to how I was. 'Don't worry, the brood mare didn't let anything happen to them.'

'Tash,' Dale warned softly.

'They're fine,' I flushed. 'It's taken the wind out of me, that's all.'

'I think it's about time I had her back,' Dale looked thoughtful.

'Had her back!' I cried. 'What do you mean?'

'It's time she came home with me, you weren't supposed to have her forever,' he replied.

I looked at him flabbergasted. 'I've had her since October.'

'But it wasn't forever,' he sounded reasonable. 'Look sis you're having twins, you ain't going to have the time or the space for her.'

'You live in a flat,' I pointed out. 'That isn't fair on her either.'

'Bev will let her live at hers,' he replied. 'I'm there nearly all the time anyway.'

'No,' I said bluntly as the three of them looked at me. 'I don't give things up because they're hard work sometimes.' That was a dig at Shay.

'Think about it sis, she could have really hurt you tonight. What if she hurt one of the babies?' he said.

'Millie wouldn't hurt a fly,' I flew to defend her as she lay on her bed, head resting on her paws and looking sad as if she knew what we were on about.

'Not intentionally,' he concurred. 'But she is a big dog and heavy, you would never forgive yourself or her if something happened.'

'He's right Tash,' Shay said quietly.

I stared at him coldly. 'I want everyone to go and leave me alone,' I began to cry. 'I mean it just go.'

'Don't talk to mam and Dale like that,' he rebuked me.

My tone was like ice. 'I mean you as well,' looking at the three of them I'd really had enough. 'And take the bloody dog with you.' With that I limped up the stairs, throwing myself on the bed sobbing. Two days ago my life was near enough perfect, the only blot on the landscape was Jamie. Now it looked a train wreck and it was all my fault.

'Tash,' Shay stood in the doorway. 'Don't cry.'

'Take the dog, take everything from me, I don't care,' I sobbed louder.

'Don't,' he stayed where he was.

'I thought I'd told you to go?' I forced my voice to be steady. 'Just leave Shay and I'll be fine by myself.'

'I don't want to go anywhere,' he came and sat on the edge of the bed, laying a hand on my shoulder.

I carried on crying. 'Everything's gone wrong,' I sniffed. 'I can't make it right and I want to so much.'

'I know,' he whispered.

I hiccupped, the twins having a game of football in my stomach. 'I, I,' the words just wouldn't come out.

'Shush,' he soothed, lying down and taking me in his arms. 'It's okay.'

'It's not though,' I cried. 'You're going to leave me, aren't you?'

'What? No,' he held me tighter. 'I'm just angry that's all. We're going to argue Tash, it doesn't mean I'm going to run away at the first sign of a problem.'

'Oh,' I just couldn't stop crying. 'It feels like you and your mom are ganging up on me.'

'We're not,' he shook his head. 'Mam's really worried about us both. I went to her yesterday and we really talked about things, about my dad.'

'Oh,' I repeated, waiting for him to tell me what had been said but he wasn't forthcoming and I didn't feel I could ask. 'I don't want Millie to go,' I felt desolate.

'I know you love her, I do too but Dale isn't wrong. We won't have the time or the space soon. Plus she moults like crazy and I'll be honest, I really don't want dog hair around our babies. She could have really hurt you when she pulled you over and it's not the first time she's done it,' he rationalised. 'If she lives with Bev then you'll see her every day because she'll be still coming to the salon.'

'I suppose,' it did make sense, I was struggling to remember to feed her, let alone walk her twice a day.

He took my chin in his hand, forcing me to look at him. 'I do love you sweet,' he whispered. 'More than I think you'll ever know.'

'I hope so,' I said quietly.

He kissed me, hands rubbing my back. 'You two!' Moira called up the stairs. 'Come down here now, I've made sandwiches.'

'I'm not hungry,' I confessed to Shay.

'When mammy makes sandwiches you eat,' he told me wisely.

I groaned, wishing they would go home and let me and Shay sort ourselves out. He pulled me from the bed and we went down into the kitchen.

'I know I shouldn't just help myself without asking but I also know you two haven't eaten,' Moira clattered around the kitchen filling Millie's water bowl.

'I said she could,' Dale grinned, tucking into his own sandwich. 'So Shayster, we'll pick up the car tomorrow.'

'What car?' I asked picking half-heartedly at my food.

'The Shayster has had a genius of an idea,' Dale beamed.

'I was going to tell you but,' he didn't need to finish the sentence.

'Jamie wants to be a mechanic, right?' Dale asked.

'Since he was little,' I agreed.

'Well Shay,' no,' he chuckled. 'You tell her mate, so clever.'

'Thanks,' he turned to me. 'I've spoken to Ray and he is willing to take Jamie on as an apprentice.'

At last some good news, so I said. 'But why are you on about a car?'

'I brought an old Corsa Saturday, I'll show Jamie how to do it up and for his seventeenth birthday we buy him his provisional licence and some driving lessons.'

'You would do that?' I was touched.

'Oh there is one condition,' he smiled for the first time. 'He tows the line, he gives you no more grief and we all play happy families.'

'How smart is that?' Dale chuckled.

'Thank you,' I whispered as my mobile began to ring, it was probably Lexi to see how I was. Oh no, it was Albie.

'Tash?' Shay was wondering why I wasn't answering it.

I stared at the three of them. 'It's Albie,' I floundered.

'Answer it,' Moira instructed softly.

I hesitated for a moment, then picked up my mobile, going into the living room. 'Hi Albie.'

'Natasha, I had to call and see if you were okay, you sounded so upset earlier.'

'I'm better than I was thank you,' I admitted.

'You sound better. I'm sorry I called, we were both worried about you,' he continued.

'I've really cocked up,' I said quietly. 'I've disrupted yours and Niamh's life and I've hurt people that mean so much to me. I love Moira, she's acted more like a mom to me these last few months than my own mom has in a lifetime. I didn't give her hardly any thought and I'll *never* forgive myself for that.'

I jumped startled as Moira took the phone from me. I hadn't even realised that she was in the room. Taking a deep breath she said. 'Albie, its Moira.'

I got up from the chair, going back into the kitchen to give her some privacy.

'Okay?' Shay asked, a puzzled look on his face.

'Your mom is talking to your dad,' I replied.

'That's a sentence I never thought I'd hear,' he attempted a smile.

'So shall we have Millie back tomorrow? Bev can have her off you at work?' Dale asked.

'I suppose,' I still hated the idea. Calling big dog to me, I buried my face in her fur, I would miss her so much.

'You can have visiting rights and play dates,' he tried to make me smile.

'Thanks,' I wanted to sulk again. We fell silent as we finished our sandwiches, then Moira came back giving me my phone.

'Mam?' Shay stood, going to her.

'I'm grand, grand,' she told him tearfully. 'I've had the conversation that I should have had with him thirty-three years ago.'

'What did you say to him?' he asked.

'A woman has to have her secrets,' she tapped his cheek as they embraced then she turned to me. 'Are we good Tash?'

I nodded hugging her too.

'Now, I have to go,' she picked up her coat. 'Alan and I have a guest list to finish.'

'Come on Mrs F, I'll drop you home,' Dale pulled on is jacket.

'Ah, you're a good lad,' she kissed my cheek. 'We discuss bouquets the next time we get together. You both come Saturday for a bite to eat.'

'Thank you,' I caught her hand. 'Are you sure we're still friends?' I cared about her so much.

She nodded. 'I have got something off my chest that has weighed heavily on me all these years, I'm just grand like I said.'

'Good,' I hoped we would all feel *grand* soon.

'Come on then Dale,' she smiled at him.

'See you tomorrow Shay, I'll pick you up at six.'

'Cheers,' he held onto Millie as my little brother gave me a big love.

'And you,' he said amused. 'Stop thinking you can make the world and everyone in it happier.'

'Sod off,' I warned, slapping his arm.

We stood at the window waving them off. 'I can't believe she spoke to Albie,' I said. 'I'd love to know what was said.'

'Sweet,' Shay looked at me as if to mind your own business. 'I'm going for a shower and then I'm going to bed. It's not comfortable sleeping in the truck.'

I nodded meekly. 'I'll tidy up.'

He gave me a smile before disappearing upstairs and I began to potter about whilst daring to breathe a sigh of relief. Hopefully we would be okay now and I wouldn't have to worry. I settled Millie down, giving her lots of hugs and kisses, I hated the thought of not having her and then I went for my own shower. What a few days, I could certainly do without the stress.

Shay was in bed, staring at the ceiling, one arm thrown casually above his head. I got in feeling exhausted. 'Mam seemed okay after she talked to dad, didn't she?'

'She seemed fine,' I tried to get comfortable, I was getting big.

He turned on his side so he was facing me. 'You were right what you said.'

'About what?' I snuggled into my pillow.

'Da had no choice did he, if he didn't know I existed?'

'None at all. I remember when I was a little girl, before Dale was born, I would fantasise that I had been kidnapped as a baby and sold to Sue and Paul. I used to wish that my real parents would find me and they would love and cherish me. That they had never stopped loving me or looking for me.'

'Really?' a smile played across his lips.

'I was about seven years old,' I defended myself.

'You really haven't had it easy, have you beautiful?' he said softly.

'People have had it much worse,' I shrugged. 'I just wanted a fairy-tale childhood that I could never have.'

'Our children will,' he predicted.

I traced his cheek with my finger. 'I was so scared that I had lost you.'

'I thought I'd lost you,' he countered.

'Lost me?' I was baffled. 'What do you mean?'

'I thought you'd gone somewhere with Sam the weekend when I found out you weren't at the hotel,' he explained. 'And tonight when mam and I went out looking for you I saw Sam's car. I was convinced you were in it.'

'Sam?' I said amazed. 'Why would I be somewhere with Sam?'

He turned on his back, pulling me against him. 'I keep thinking he's going to sweet talk you into giving him another chance.'

I shook my head. 'Never. I told you I was at Mrs Evans's, she was giving me tea and sympathy.'

'I know,' he took my hand.

'We are such a pair, you and me,' I kissed him tenderly. 'I'm more worried about you running off with some young bint.'

He thought for a moment. 'Well you never know,' he teased and I was glad that he was smiling again.

I stared at him for a moment. 'I've never felt as distraught as I've felt these last couple of days, I really thought we were finished and it was all my fault. All down to me.'

He turned on his side again, caressing my face. 'What's done is done. We look forward not back. We have so much to look forward to sweet. Our babies, mam's wedding and Jamie hopefully coming on side. I'll arrange for me and Dale to talk to Jamie over the weekend.'

I melted, how could I have risked what we had? I should never have got it in my head to interfere in things. 'I love you so much.'

'I know,' he smiled sweetly. 'I would find it hard not to love me too.'

'You big-headed git,' I laughed. 'Go to sleep.'

'Good idea,' he agreed and we fell asleep tangled in each other's arms.

Thirty

Shay told Tash not to worry about supper Thursday night that he was going to pop and see his mom, just to make sure that was okay after everything. 'How are you son?' she asked on seeing him. 'Are you and Tash sorted now?'

'We are,' he replied sitting at the kitchen table. 'And you?'

'Everything is as it should be,' she looked at him knowingly. 'So what's on your mind?'

'Me? Nothing,' he was always amazed that she could read him so easily.

'Get off with you,' she put the kettle on. 'What do you want to ask me?'

He took a deep breath, there was no point in beating about the bush. 'I want to meet him,' he answered quietly.

She exhaled her own breath, getting the mugs from the cupboard. 'I thought you might,' her tone was soft.

'I just don't want to do anything that would hurt you. I won't go any further if you don't want me to,' and he meant it, whatever his mom said was the way to go, was the way he would.

'He's your da,' she stated simply.

'And you are my world,' he looked at her like a little boy again.

'Tash and those babies are your world now,' she corrected.

'You will always be a huge part of it,' he said firmly. 'You were there when I needed a mom and a dad. You were the one who taught me right from wrong. Taught me how to ride my bike, picked me up when I fell off. I really don't want to do anything to upset you.'

Moira's eyes filled with tears. 'I took your father from you, I gave neither of you an option. You had no chance to know him.'

Shay listened, holding his cup in his hands. 'When I spoke to him Monday night I explained whey I'd done what I had,' she continued. 'And I think he understood. You should know him and I know he wants to get to know you.'

'I just need your blessing,' it was important to him.

Her face softened. 'You have it. I'm not going to deny I'm apprehensive about what will happen. Albie was the first man I lay with, the only man until I met Alan.'

He shifted uncomfortably. 'Maybe you ought to talk to Tash,' he wasn't sure he was the best person to talk about his mom's love life.

She smiled slyly. 'Don't worry, I'm not going into details.'

'Good,' he grimaced.

'What does Tash say about it all?' she sat down.

'I wanted to talk to you first, Tash is apt to have booked the tickets to Quin before I can finish the sentence.'

She laughed softly. 'She has a heart as big as Ireland. You know she and Lexi sought out my parent's grave? They put flowers on it and tidied it up. She is so lovely.'

His smile was gentle. 'She is. She is such a fantastic mother, the twins will be so cherished.'

'She is a good mom and she could have gone in such a different direction with the parent's she had.'

'That's why she wanted to find my dad, she didn't want me having any regrets like she has with her own,' he finished his tea.

'Has she seen that woman?' Moira wouldn't call Sue Tash's mother, she didn't deserve the title.

He shook his head. 'Sue doesn't even know its twins unless someone else has told her.'

Moira felt vexed, Tash deserved so much better. 'She's a hoor,' her tone was savage.

'I can't argue with you,' he wanted to get home and do what he had to do before he lost his nerve.

'And Jamie, are you dealing with that?'

'Dale and I are taking him for a drink tomorrow night, I'll sort it,' he sounded more confident than he felt.

'I like Jamie, he's a nice young man.'

'He liked you too, when you were giving him whisky,' his tone was cynical.

She shooed him away with her hand. 'Go home and speak to your dad,' she smiled. 'Alan will be here soon.'

'What does he think about all of this?' he had hardly registered the effect it would have on his mom's finance, which was pretty bad of him.

'He stays out of it,' she took the mugs to the sink. 'He supports me and he loves me but he never tells me what to do. I think he was a little concerned at first that I would call the wedding off.'

'You wouldn't?' he asked alarmed.

'No, I've put Albie on a pedestal all these years and I still do. He was the great love of my life but Alan is what I need now.'

He hugged her tightly. 'I love you,' he kissed her cheek.

'I love you too son,' she patted his cheek. 'Let me know how it goes and also don't let the ex-husband spoil what you are trying to do with Jamie.'

'That maggot?' he puffed out his chest. 'I'd like to see him try.'

Moira shook her head. 'Like father, like son. Now go.'

He grinned heading out the door.

By the time he got home I had given up trying to paint my toenails, it just wasn't going to happen with the twins in my tum. He popped his head around the living room door. 'Hey beautiful, I'm just going to grab my shower, I won't be long.'

'Okay,' I went to say more but he had disappeared. I grabbed the remote locking around the room. I missed Millie, she was literally such a huge presence. She had gone to live with Bev yesterday without as much as a backwards glance. Today, at the salon, she had fussed around me but gladly went home with Bev again. Sighing I tried to find something to watch on the television.

I was just shy of six months pregnant and I couldn't believe how fast the time was going. We had the nursery to finish and so much to buy for the little blighters that it was a little overwhelming.

'Hey,' Shay came into the room all fresh smelling.

'How's your mom?' I asked, moving the nail varnish so he could sit next to me.

'She's good,' he picked up the bottle. 'What are you doing?'

'I was going to paint my toenails but I can't reach,' I replied. 'Do you want anything to eat?'

'No, I'm fine thanks,' he was quiet for a moment. 'Phone him.'

'Phone who?' I was puzzled.

His beautiful brown eyes sought mine. 'My dad.'

I caught my breath. 'Are you sure?' I asked surprised.

His smile was nervous. 'Yes. Do this then I'll paint your toenails for you.'

'Seriously Shay, I only want you to do this if you are one hundred percent sure.'

'I am,' he confirmed.

I stared at him for a moment before picking up my mobile. Albie answered straight away and I could tell by his voice that he was glad to hear from me. 'Natasha, my girl, how are you?' he asked.

'I'm very well thank you and you and Niamh?'

'We've just had our supper and we're trying to decide what to watch on the ole box,' he was curious to why I had phoned.

'Albie,' I began softly. 'I have someone here who wants to talk to you.'

'Who?' his tone became shaky.

'Shay,' I answered passing him the phone. I stood to give them some privacy but Shay held me in place, his grip tight on my hand, he needed me with him.

'Hi,' Shay said nervously.

I could hear Albie inhale his breath and my eyes filled with tears. 'Hello son,' he said, his voice so full of emotion. 'How are you?'

'I'm grand,' Shay looked at me, unsure now what to say.

'It's so good to hear your voice,' he stopped trying to get his thoughts in order. 'I never thought,' he paused again, clearing his throat. 'I'm so glad that you want to speak to me.'

'I don't know what to say,' Shay admitted.

'No, me neither,' he confessed. 'There is so much I want to say.' Again the silence. 'If I'd known about you I would have found you.'

Shay didn't answer and my heart went out to both of them, this was so hard.

'I wouldn't have let you grow up with knowing me,' Albie continued. 'Your mam though, she did what she had to do, I understand it.'

'Yes,' Shay moved closer to me.

'So tell me about yourself, I want to know everything.'

I untangled my hand from his, he needed a stiff whisky. I got him one, willing them to talk to each other. 'Er,' he hesitated. 'I'm a mechanic and Tash and I are looking forward to being parents.'

'She's lovely and her daughter Lexi,' Albie cut in.

'They are,' he looked at me lovingly.

'I'm so glad they told me about you,' he rallied a little. 'So are you a footie fan?'

'I prefer rugby but Dale, Tash's brother, is trying to convert me.'

Albie chuckled. 'Me too, I prefer rugby,' he grew serious. 'I know all this is new, to both of us, but I would love to meet you, to get to know you properly.'

Shay closed his eyes. 'I'd like that too.' A tear slid down my cheek, bloody baby hormones.

'When?' Albie's voice was so full of hope that it broke my heart.

Shay looked at me and I mouthed "soon" and he nodded. 'As soon as possible.'

'That's what I hoped you'd say,' he sounded relieved. 'Will you come here or shall I come to you?'

'Can I discuss it with Tash and my mam?' he said. 'I'll call you.'

'Of course you can,' he replied. 'I can't tell you what this means to me.'

'We'll speak soon,' Shay guaranteed.

'Bye son,' his voice was so full of emotion.

Shay ended the call, trembling slightly. 'I'm so proud of you,' I whispered, kissing him.

'That was my dad,' he looked a little shell shocked. 'Could you hear what he was saying?'

I nodded. 'How do you feel?' he was my priority.

'Strange,' he admitted.

'Well you talk to Moira and see what she says,' I advised. 'But soon I'm not going to be able to fly.'

'Am I doing the right thing Tash?'

'I think so,' I answered. 'We could got to Quin, you could see where you mom grew up, get a feel for your roots.'

He took my face in his hand. 'I love you, you know? Really love you.'

'I know,' I enclosed my hand over his. 'And I love you too.'

His eyes held mine for what seemed like an age. 'Am I being disloyal to her?'

'If you thought that then you would never have phoned him.'

He looked down at our entwined hands. 'No, I wouldn't. It's going to be okay isn't it sweet?'

'Yes,' I said confidently.

Thirty~One

'Do you really think it's a good idea?' I chaffed, heading to Bev's to pick her and Dale up.

'Of course I do,' Shay replied, he seemed happy since he had spoken to his dad. Moira had been great too and as a result we flew to Quin the following weekend, staying in the pub that Lexi and I had stopped in. Albie had wanted us to stay with him but I thought it was a good idea for Shay to have somewhere to escape to if it all got too much for him. We only needed Jamie on side now and everything would be nearly perfect.

I had my doubts about my son though, it was all very well Dale setting up a night out with Shay and getting Jamie to go along in the hope that he would grab the offer with both hands but he could be an awkward sod at the best of times and to be honest I wouldn't have put money on him playing ball.

'It'll work out trust me,' his voice was soft, he wanted to do this for me.

'But,' I said again, but he stopped me dead.

'Sweetheart, stop worrying. I am going for a drink with your brother and your son, that's all.'

'That's if Jamie turns up,' I pulled a face.

'He will, Dale will make sure of it,' he smiled as I pulled up outside Bev's lovely three bedroom house that Denny was going to sign over to her, without flinching, as part of their divorce settlement. Millie was in the window and I waved and blew a kiss at her, as soon as they saw my car they came out to us.

'Have you chucked your toys out of the pram lately?' Bev asked Shay on seeing him.

'What?' he frowned.

'Making my best friend get all upset and in her condition too,' she chided.

'We're okay now,' I said quickly, she was always protecting me.

'Are you sure you don't mind driving?' she asked me.

'It doesn't bother me,' I replied. 'It's not as if I can have a drink.'

'Friday night without a drink,' she shuddered as Dale clambered in next to her.

'You get used to it,' I waited for Shay to settle back in before driving to Sam's.

We waited as Dale went to fetch Jamie, they were going to walk to the pub around the corner but I wanted to say hello to my son. They came out together and I could see Sam in the window watching us, a grim expression on his face and a glass of something in his hand.

I got out of the car, my stomach growing daily. 'Hi love, are you okay?' I asked settling for ruffling his hair rather than the hug I wanted to give him.

'Hi mom,' he looked away. Why couldn't teenagers look you in the eye?

'You remember Shay?' I put on my happy voice, crossing everything that they would manage to bury the hatchet.

'Yeah,' he nodded.

'Hey Jamie, shall we go and drunk on the old Irish whisky?' he asked jovially.

'He's drinking pop,' I glared at him.

He held up his hands. 'I was just having the craic,' he shook his head, feeling nervous.

'Yeah, chill sis,' Dale gave me a playful nudge. 'Come on let's go to the pub.'

I'll come and pick you up at ten-thirty,' I told them.

'Thanks dahling,' Shay kissed me on the cheek.

'And you,' Bev warned him. 'She loves you so don't be such an idiot.'

'If I was a paranoid fella I'd think I'd done something to upset you,' Shay said hurt.

'Something like that,' she kissed his cheek playfully. 'Behave.'

He saluted as we got back in the car with Sam still watching us from the window.

'Have a good night,' Bev called as I started the car. 'I hope it's a good idea of Dale's to arrange tonight so Shay can tell Jamie about everything.'

'I just hope it goes well,' I said as I drove us back to mine. 'Life would be so much easier if Jamie could be in the same room as Shay.'

'It will,' she assured me. 'Did you see Sam at the window?'

I grimaced nodding. 'He was like the Grim Reaper.'

'As Bev and I went home the lads were just arriving at the pub. 'What do you want Jamie?' Shay asked.

'Coke,' he didn't meet his eye.

'Dale?'

'Lager please Shayster,' he and his nephew grabbed a table as Shay went to the bar and got the drinks.

Taking them to the table, he licked lager off his hand where it had slopped over the glasses. Settling down he cast Dale a nervous glance and Dale nodded. 'Jamie,' he began. 'I know you don't approve of me and your mom.'

Jamie screwed up his face and Dale gave him a frown. Shay tried again. 'Your mom tells me that you like cars.'

'Yeah,' he had a swig of pop.

'Me and your mom have had a chat and for your seventeenth birthday we are going to send for your provisional licence and pay for some driving lessons.'

His head shot up. 'Really?'

'Really,' he was pleased with the reaction. 'I have an old Corsa that can be done up for you. I'll help you and teach you how to fix it.'

Jamie looked at Dale as if he couldn't quite believe what Shay was saying. 'Listen to him,' Dale advised.

Shay continued. 'I've had a word with my boss and if you want to, he's willing to take you on as an apprentice mechanic.'

'Honestly?' he looked doubtful.

'Yes,' Shay confirmed. 'I'll be totally honest with you Jamie. I love your mom and I want her to be happy. You not coming to see her is making her unhappy.'

'He's right,' Dale agreed, taking a mouthful of lager.

'I'd like us to get on,' he continued. 'I don't want any bad feelings between us and so there you are, my cards are on the table. I will say if you agree to this then we try and get on for your mom's sake. If you give her any grief or even look at her in the wrong way then I take it all away.'

'It's a good offer,' Dale looked fondly at his nephew.

'I promise I'll keep my word,' Shay had a drink to quench his dry mouth.

Jamie thought for a moment. 'I'd like that.'

He smiled relieved. 'Ray will want to see you, I'll arrange it for one of the day's next week, after school.'

Jamie nodded, his face full of excitement. He was getting a car! 'Seriously though Jamie, you don't give your mom any trouble,' Dale warned. 'She loves you, don't forget that.'

'I won't,' he was too busy thinking about his car.

'You'll need to use the money you earn at the garage to save up for you insurance,' Shay advised him.

'Maybe your dad will help you out,' Dale cut in.

'He might,' he replied but he didn't sound convinced.

'The parts for the car I'll sort,' Shay knew he was being more than generous but he so wanted Tash to be happy. Getting out his phone he showed Jamie some pictures of the car.

'It looks great,' a sleek black mean machine that had Jamie's eyes sparkling.

'It will be when we've finished with it,' Shay stated.

'And it will be all yours if you behave yourself,' Dale told his nephew. 'Give Shay a chance, he's a good bloke.'

He nodded, the lure of the car and the job ensuring he was compliant. For the next couple of hours they talked about rugby versus football and cars. Shay and Dale promising to give him driving lessons once his provisional came.

'So can I drive your truck?' he asked Shay hopefully.

'We'll see,' Shay answered stiffly, the truck was his pride and joy.

Dale laughed, the sound dying in his throat as he looked towards the door. 'What is your dad doing here Jams?' Jams was his nickname for his nephew when he was happy with him.

Shay groaned quietly, this he did not need.

'I don't know, he never said he was coming,' he shrugged.

'Lads,' Sam greeted them, his words slightly slurred.

'Didn't expect to see you tonight,' Dale kept his voice light.

'I thought I'd drop by, can I get anyone a drink?'

They all declined as he meandered up to the bar. 'He sounds pissed,' Dale had a bad feeling.

'He was drinking Jack Daniels before I came out,' Jamie couldn't understand what his dad was doing their either.

'Brilliant,' Dale breathed as Sam called his son over to the bar.

'What is that wanker doing here?' Shay said quietly.

'Fuck knows,' he replied darkly. 'Just ignore him and he might go away.'

'I doubt that,' Shay had wanted a clear run at Jamie, not have Sam poking his oar in.

'Just don't rise to anything he says.'

'There you go Paddy,' Sam had returned. 'I got you a cider.'

Dale shot Shay a warning look to reign his temper in. 'Thanks,' he said reluctantly, Sam could clearly see that he was drinking lager.

'Dad I can have a job with Shay and he's going to help me do up my own car, a Corsa that he's got for me. He and mom are going to get my provisional and driving lessons for my birthday.' Jamie told him excitedly.

Sam narrowed his eyes as Dale cut in. 'You know that Jamie has always wanted to do something with cars, well Shay can help him. That's good isn't it?'

He stared at Shay who stared back refusing to intimidated, he still had a score to settle with him. 'A Corsa and who's going to pay for that?' he demanded.

'It was going to be scrapped but it's a good car so I brought it for a couple of hundred. I'll help Jamie do it up,' Shay replied as politely as he could.

'And who's going to pay for the parts?' he wanted to know.

'Me,' Shay screwed up his face, did he think he would tell the lad all about the car and then leave him to find the money for the parts?

Sam sucked his teeth. 'So,' he drew out the word. 'You have my wife and now you're trying to buy my son?'

'Ex-wife,' Shay corrected him sharply. 'Meera is *your* wife.'

'Shut up dad,' Jamie didn't want Shay to get it in his head not to let him have the car.

'Well that's nice,' he looked at Jamie. 'My own son telling me to shut up.'

'Sam did you see the match on Wednesday?' Dale tried to change the subject.

He ignored him. 'So twins, two for the price of one,' Sam leant back in his chair staring at Shay.

'Yeah,' he wished he'd just piss off.

He got out his wallet, making sure all of them could see the wad of twenty pound notes he had. 'Dale go and get us another drink.'

'I'll get them,' Shay stood, needing to get away from the table.

'Nonsense,' he waved the offer away. 'You are going to need every penny you can get, babies aren't cheap.'

'I can buy a round of drinks,' his tone was hostile.

Sam smirked, knowing that he was getting to him. 'I've no doubt about that but twins though? No wonder she's so big. I bet that little mole above her bellybutton will just grow and grow. You know the one I mean Paddy, she always squirms when you kiss it.'

'Let's go up the bar,' Dale tried to get Shay away.

'I mean,' Sam continued. 'What was she thinking getting knocked up at her age, she should have known better.'

'Dad!' Jamie cried.

'Come on Shay,' Dale practically dragged him up the bar.

'I am going to fecking kill him!' Shay could feel his temper rising.

'That's what he wants you to do,' Dale ordered the drinks. 'Twenty minutes and Tash will be picking us up, just hold it together.'

Shay leant towards him. 'I've still got words to have with him after what he said to Tash at Lexi's birthday. I mean what the fuck did she ever see in him?' He took out his wallet paying for the round.

'In different circumstances Sam can be very charming,' Dale paused. 'If I'm honest Tash just wanted a better life than our parents had given us. Sam saw her vulnerability and took it to his own advantage. Don't let him get to you.'

'Wouldn't it get to you?' he asked pointedly.

'Course it would, I'd ram his head through the door but you are a better bloke than me,' he picked up the drinks. 'Bite your tongue.'

He growled in reply. 'Sam,' Dale put the drink in front of him.

'Thanks brother-in-law.'

'Don't thank me, Shay got them.'

'Thanks Paddy,' he tilted his glass in Shay's direction.

He bit down on his lip, this was harder than he expected, even Sam calling Dale his brother-in-law narked him.

'I'm just going to the loo,' Dale said hoping he could leave them for five minutes without them killing each other.

'Me too,' Jamie followed his uncle much to his disapproval.

Sam watched them go before turning to Shay. 'So you think you'll enjoy being a dad then? Tash doesn't have high expectations, her own parents were so shit she'll hold onto any semblance of normality. Really you can do anything and she'll always forgive you.'

'She didn't forgive you with Meera,' he retorted, then wished he hadn't.

'She would have done in time,' he sounded so confident.

Shay leant forward. 'You had your chance with Tash and you blew it. Now back off and leave us be.'

'Do you really think she'll be happy with you Paddy?' he challenged.

'Let me see,' he pretended to think. 'A lying deceitful, little maggot who doesn't give a fuck about hurting her or me?'

'You'll be long gone before those kiddies see their first birthday.' Sam predicted.

'You know fucking nothing,' he hissed as Jamie and Dale came back. 'I'm going outside to wait for Tash.'

'Shay,' Dale just knew that Sam was stirring the shit.

'I'm good,' he answered picking up his coat.

'Sam you are such an arsehole,' Dale could have cheerfully throttle him.

Shay stood knowing that he had to get away from Tash's ex before he did something he would regret. He had wanted to bond with Jamie, tell Tash that it was all sorted and she didn't have to fret anymore.

He left the pub, Sam taking the opportunity to follow him. 'Tell me just one thing Paddy.'

Shay stopped, turning in spite of himself.

'Does she still howl when she comes?'

That was it, the line had been crossed. With a roar he launched himself at Sam, grabbing the neck of his jumper and slamming him against the wall.

'Whoa,' Dale cried, they had followed Shay and Sam out of the pub.

'Dad!' Jamie was horrified, he had heard what he had said and although he was being hard on his mom at the moment he still loved her.

Sam began to laugh. 'That's more like it Paddy. You love her don't you? How must it feel knowing that she had me back twice after I shagged other women? She begged me to fuck her, she wanted me that much.'

Shay punched him, feeling a sense of satisfaction as his fist connected with his jaw. A red mist had descended and he was powerless to stop himself.

'Shay!' Dale tried to pull him away but he was past the point of no return. Every punch he managed to land was for Tash and what that bastard had put her through. Sam was fit though, able to land a few good punches of his own but Shay hardly felt them that would be tomorrow.

'Dad!' Jamie yelled and the sound penetrated Shay's brain. Oh God he was beating his dad up when all he wanted was to get on with Jamie, he had blown it.

He stopped turning to Jamie, to say he was sorry, to say anything so the last couple of hours weren't wasted. Sam saw his chance, using all his strength to push Shay causing him to lose his footing, hitting the ground with a thud. Sam seized the opportunity to get two good kicks in the torso, causing Shay to yelp in pain.

'Dad!' Jamie repeated horrified as Dale finally managed to pull Sam away.

'You absolute fucking arsehole!' Dale hissed in his face. 'I hope he's fucking hurt you!' How was he going to explain this to his sister?

Sam grinned, his face blooded and bruised, turning quickly he kicked Shay once more.

Thirty~Two

'So, I said to Dale, why don't we do what Tash and Shay are doing?' Bev chatted as we headed to the pub to pick them up.

'What have a baby?' I nearly crashed the car.

'No,' she laughed, mellowed by the wine she had consumed at mine. 'Live together, it makes so much sense.'

'What did Dale say?' I peered through the windscreen intently, I wasn't keen on driving in the dark.

'He thinks it's a good idea,' she beamed.

'Well I'd highly recommend it,' I grinned back, hoping the night had gone well and when I did pick them up they would all be friends.

'Do you think Jamie will go for it?' she could read my mind.

I chanced a look at her then turned my attention back to the road. 'Driving lessons, job doing what he wants and his own car? Shay says he will, he says I have nothing to worry about now.'

'Should you be bribing him like this though?' Bev thought Jamie deserved a smacked arse for how he'd acted since me and Sam had split, not rewarded for bad behaviour.

'You pick your battles when you have kids,' I replied, indicating to turn right into the pub car park. 'In times of war you use whatever you can to win.'

'I suppose,' she sounded doubtful. 'What the fuck!'

It took a moment for my brain to process what I was seeing then I slammed on my brakes, throwing us both forward. I abandoned it in the middle of the car park with the engine still running.

'Get off him!' I cried, trying to pull Sam away. He pushed against me and I stumbled, Jamie reaching to steady me.

With a roar Shay was on his feet, laying into Sam once more. 'Don't fucking touch her!' he yelled, landing a few good punches.

Bev stood with her hands on her hips. 'Pack the fuck in now the pair of you!' She bawled in her best fish wife's voice.

They did, staring at her as Jamie stood with his arm around me. 'Okay mom?' he asked.

I hugged him to me, kissing the top of his head. 'I'm good,' I fumed, he shouldn't have witnessed it and I was livid. 'What the hell is going on?' I demanded, staring at the battered faces.

'Darling,' Sam took a step towards me and I moved away quickly.

'Don't,' I held up my hand in a stop gesture.

'Tash,' Shay's voice was full of apology.

'Just get in the car!' I ordered angrily, I didn't want to hear it. Turning to Dale I barked. 'How could you let them fight?'

'Me?' he asked wounded. 'Why is this my fault exactly?'

Shay tried to take my arm but I shrugged him off. 'Get in the car,' I growled.

'Natasha,' Sam gave me my fault title, his voice full of syrup. 'You don't need someone like him, he's a complete nutter.'

I turned on him viciously. 'You! You stay away from us! You make my skin crawl! The only contact I want with you now is if it concerns our children, nothing else. You are not welcome in my home or my life anymore.'

'Darling,' he wanted me to let him explain.

'Stop calling me darling!' I exploded as Shay stood there remorsefully.

'Wait,' he took another step in my direction.

I gave him a withering look. 'Go home to your wife and child and stop being an arsehole.' I turned to my son. 'Do you want to come home with me?'

He shook his head. 'I'll make sure dad gets home.'

'Are you sure?' I wanted him with me.

'Someone's got to,' he sounded so grown up. 'I'll be fine mom.'

'Okay,' I kissed his cheek gently and he pulled his dad away, beginning to walk up the street.

'We'll get a taxi sis,' Dale got out his mobile. 'You get home with Shay.' He didn't wasn't to witness the row that we were undoubtedly going to have.

'I'll take you home,' I was getting annoyed that Shay had still not got in the car.

'Don't worry about us,' Bev said softly. 'I'll see you tomorrow.'

I nodded tightly, still angry. 'Get in the car now,' I ordered Shay and he did so sheepishly.

As I drove away he tried to explain. 'Sweet,' he began, turning to face me with a wince.

'All you had to do was to mend bridges with Jamie that was all I wanted!' I exploded. 'Not have a brawl in the middle of the car park with his dad like a couple of kids!'

'You should have heard what that prick was saying about you,' he rushed to defend himself.

'I don't care,' I retorted through gritted teeth. 'You shouldn't have risen to it.'

'But-,' he tried again.

'Shut up!' my tone was blunt. 'Just shut up!' We drove the rest of the way in silence, me trying to keep my temper in. What had Sam gone to the pub for anyway? It was supposed to a good night where problems were solved not created.

Getting out the car I hurried up the path as Shay followed me cautiously. Turning at the door I used my remote to lock the car leaving him to his own devices. He finally caught up with me in the kitchen. 'Sweetheart,' he took a deep breath.

I turned to him angrily. 'I don't want to know,' I just couldn't deal with him, the worst-case scenario had happened and I was absolutely bloody livid. I had lost Jamie for good now, Sam would fill his head so full of poison against us, I was sure of it.

'Please sweet,' he tried again, a tenor of desperation in his voice.

I glared at him, going into the hall and slamming the kitchen door with a satisfying bang and thundering up the stairs. Going into our room I lay on the bed, tears filling my eyes. I had trusted Shay when he had promised to make everything right. That Jamie and I would be friends again and then he had turned around and done the worst thing in the world, he had beaten his dad up.

Don't get me wrong Shay was pretty battered but Sam had looked worse, the uncharitable part of me hoped that Meera would chuck him out, it was what he deserved. I must have lay there for about twenty minutes then Shay worked up enough courage to poke his head around the door.

I had my back to him and he cleared his throat nervously. 'Are you coming down?'

'No,' I snapped. 'I don't want to be in the same room as you.' Inside the twins were moving as if sensing my agitation.

'Please Tash,' he begged.

'No, leave me alone,' I still wouldn't turn to face him.

'I need you dahling,' he said forlornly.

'Tough, fucking shit,' I stared resolutely at the window as he stood there for a few moments then I heard his footsteps as he went downstairs.

Rolling onto my back I batted the tears away angrily. I suppose I would have to go and clean him up, it's what I did. Reluctantly I went into the kitchen, he was leaning against the cupboard and I gasped quietly at his face, it was such a mess. 'You promised me,' I reproached him. 'You promised me you would make it better.'

'I did try and I would have succeeded if that prick hadn't turned up,' he dabbed gingerly at his split lip. 'I didn't go in there guns blazing, you should have heard what he was saying about you. I had no choice.'

'You had every choice, you could have just walked away.' I felt a little sick. He was going to look wonderful to meet his dad next weekend. 'Sit down,' I pulled out a chair, going to the cupboard and taking out the TCP and cotton wool buds.

Shay sat down, watching me with wounded eyes and I wanted to punch him myself. Jamie would never come around now. I poured TCP onto the cotton wool and with no gentleness I began to see to his cuts and bruises.

'Fuck Tash, that really stings,' he complained until I silenced him with a look. He could man up and take it and to be fair he did. Wincing in silence looking extremely sheepish and totally subdued.

'I can't believe you fought with him. Why? Why?'

'I told you, he was being disrespectful to you,' he looked at me watchfully.

'You should have taken no notice,' I cried. 'You promised me.' I hit him in the chest with the back of my hand and he yelped in pain.

I stared at him. 'Take your jumper off,' I ordered.

'I'm grand,' he went to stand but I shoved him back down. Knowing that he wouldn't fight back I pulled the jumper over his head, feeling a sense of satisfaction when I hurt his bruised face. On his chest I could see a pair of angry red boot marks and tears sprang to my eyes and I began to cry.

'Sweet,' he reached for me unsurely. 'Don't cry.'

'He could have killed you,' I sobbed.

A flash of annoyance crossed his face. 'I can take him you know.'

'Stop being so juvenile,' I felt so tired. 'I mean all it would have taken was a lucky punch and then where would I be? Where would your children be without their dad?' I sobbed louder. 'Or you could have killed him and then you would be in prison.'

His own eyes filled with tears. 'I'm sorry sweet, I just saw red. The things he was saying,' his arms went around me.

'I love you so much,' my words were barely coherent. 'What would I do without you? I thought I'd lost you last week and now this week! It would kill me if anything happened to you.'

'I'm so sorry,' his words were choked as he lay his head against my stomach. 'You shouldn't have seen it, it shouldn't have happened. I'm so sorry.'

'Just promise me it won't happen again,' I pleaded. 'The only contact I'm going to have with him is about our children. Poor Meera.'

'Don't you want to know what he said?'

I shook my head. 'I really don't care.'

He looked up at me. 'I love you dahling, believe me.'

'I do,' I whispered, wondering how Sam was going to explain it all to his wife. I sighed picking up the kettle and filing it. 'Do you want anything?'

'Just you not to be angry with me,' he watched me closely.

'I'm not angry with you, I'm disappointed.' I was still tearful, it had been one hell of a fortnight.

'I'm sorry sweet,' he came to me, wincing a little with pain. 'It will never happen again, no matter what he does.'

'Thank you,' I made us both Ovaltine. 'I'm going to bed.'

'Can I come too?' he gave me such a cute smile that my heart melted.

'You can bring the mugs and I'll lock up.' I went round securing the house, I missed Millie being with us but she was having the time of her life at Bev's being spoilt rotten. He went upstairs and I could hear him getting ready for bed as my phone pinged.

It was Dale. 'You ok sis xx.'

I quickly replied. 'I am thanks hun xx.'

Dale asked. 'Is Shay ok?'

I answered. 'Yes, we r just going 2 bed'
I think he was concerned about us. 'Be good.
He was only defending you.'

Defending me? By beating up my ex, but I replied. 'I won't,
nite bruv. Sleep tite xx

'You 2 xx'

I looked at my phone thoughtfully, Dale was turning out to
be a good man thanks to Bev. I hoped he would carry on the good
work, it suited him. Shay was in bed when I went upstairs and I put
my nightie on and after using the bathroom I climbed in beside him.

'Shall we go to mam's Sunday for lunch?' he asked softly.

'Yes, but she'll go mad at you for fighting.' I predicted.

'Not when I tell her how he provoked me,' he stared at the
ceiling.

'I doubt it,' I was getting curious as to what Sam had said but
I didn't want any more quarrels.

'Tash,' he turned on his side.

'Leave it for tonight please, I've said my piece and I have
work in the morning.'

'Okay,' his voice was tender as he placed his hand on my
tum. 'Night babies, night beautiful, I love you loads.'

'Night, I kissed him, careful not to hurt his split lip. Rolling
away I tried to get comfortable.

Sam hurried through the door, closely followed by Jamie.
Without a word he headed straight upstairs just as Meera came into
the hall. 'Hi Jamie,' she said surprised. 'Has your mom dropped
you off?'

'No, I came back with dad,' he replied taking off his coat.

'Your dad?' Sam had told her that he was just popping to the
golf club. 'Why is your dad with you?'

'He turned up at the pub,' Jamie went into the kitchen for a
packet of crisps.

She stared after him for a moment before going to the bottom
of the stairs. 'Sam!' she called shrilly.

'I'm going to bed,' he replied and she could tell that he was in the bathroom.

'Sam get down here now!' Her voice rose, she'd had an uneasy feeling since he had spent the evening drinking Jack Daniels before abruptly going out.

'I said I'm going to bed,' his words were muffled.

'Get down here now Sam, I want to know exactly where you've been and don't you dare lie to me,' she waited for a minute but he showed no sign of coming to her. 'Sam if you don't come down here then I'm coming up.'

He did so reluctantly, head bowed so she couldn't see the full extent of his injuries. 'Oh my God,' she cried. 'What the hell happened to you?'

'It's nothing,' he wouldn't quite meet her eyes.

'Look at the state of you!' She was glad that Sophie was in bed, he had blood on his jumper, on his jeans. 'Where have you been?'

'Nowhere,' he lied as Jamie ventured out of the kitchen.

'Don't you dare bare face lie to me Sam,' she warned. 'Jamie has already told me that you turned up at the pub.'

'Why ask then?' he shrugged, needing a drink. He pushed past his son, going into the kitchen and pouring himself a large measure of Jack Daniels.

'Sam!' Meera marched after him. 'Who have you fought with, tell me!'

'It's him!' He took a mouthful of bourbon. 'That mad Irishman that Tash lives with, he just attacked me.'

Jamie stood in the doorway, munching on his crisps. 'No, he didn't.'

Sam looked at his son annoyed. 'Go to bed Jamie.'

Meera glared at her husband. 'You tell me the truth now or I'm going to see Shay and get it from him.'

'I told you, he just attacked me,' Sam finished his drink.

'Jamie?' she turned to her stepson.

'You kept provoking him dad,' he screwed up his crisp packet, throwing it in the bin.

'I thought I'd told you to go to your room,' he snapped.

'You were saying some shit things to him about my mom,' he continued.

'What were you saying about Tash?' Meera demanded.

He declined to answer, filling up his glass again. 'Sam,' she raised her voice, she knew this would happen, had dreaded it happening in fact.

Jamie told her exactly what had been said to Shay and she listened with mounting horror. 'Thanks son,' Sam spat the words at him.

'Well you shouldn't have done it. I was having a good night and you spoilt it,' he shot back.

'All you care about is yourself. He's trying to buy your friendship and that's what he's done with your mom,' Sam wet some kitchen roll, dabbing at his cuts.

'You're the selfish one Sam,' Meera snapped. 'Jamie love, can you give us some space? I need to talk to your dad. Will you check on Safi for me?'

He nodded, he liked Meera. She waited until he was upstairs before she tuned on Sam. 'You still want her don't you?'

'For God's sake,' he swore getting more kitchen roll.

'It's always been her hasn't it, the ghost between us,' her eyes filled with tears. 'Be honest with me for once, do you still love her?'

'Meera just leave it,' he slumped at the table.

She sat opposite him leaning forwards. 'I need to know,' she tapped her chest. 'If you don't tell me the complete truth you will never see Safi or me again and I will tell my family.'

He took another drink, not answering.

'I will ruin you Sam,' she promised. 'All this will be taken away from you, I swear on our daughter's life.'

'Fine, you know what, you're right. I do still love her, satisfied?' he barked.

She reacted like she had taken a punch in the stomach. She knew it was the truth but to hear her husband say it was something else. Tears sprung into her eyes. 'Then why did you marry me?'

He dry washed his face. 'You were pregnant with Safi.'

'Does Tash want you back?' she didn't want to know the answer but she *had* to ask.

He hesitated for a moment, the answer was no. 'Don't you love me at all?' Meera's voice was small.

He did what he did best, he looked after himself. 'Of course I love you, don't ask stupid questions.' He knew what he had to lose.

'But you love Tash too?' she stared into his eyes, trying to read him.

'I've known Tash since I was twenty-three, we've grown up together as it were,' he chose his words carefully. 'She's the mother of my children so of course I love her still.'

'Why did you say all that to Shay though?' she picked at the scab.

He gave her his most charming smile. 'It's just me having a bit of fun with him. I do love you Meera, but you give all your energy to Safi, there really is none left for me. You have to forgive me if sometimes I want my old life back where I was her world. I'm tired of playing second fiddle to your family, I need you to put me first.' It was exactly the same speech that he had given to Tash all those years ago.

She wanted to believe him, she loved him but she also knew that he had been married to Tash when they had first got together. Tash had thrown him out, he had never wanted to leave. 'It rips my heart in two that you still have feelings for her.'

'It was never going to be straightforward with us, you stole me away from her without any thought to how she was feeling,' he began to relax a little. Meera had gone from angry to being petrified of losing him in a short space of time, just like Tash used to. 'We have a complicated history Tash and I. If she was here though she would be patching me up not giving me the third degree.'

Meera flushed, going to the cupboard and fetching the first aid kit. 'Don't bother,' he was once again in charge.

'Sam,' she hated how he made her feel sometimes.

'I'm going to have my shower and then I'm going to bed,' his swagger had returned. 'I'll clean myself up.'

She watched him go, not trusting a word he said. Tears fell unheeded down her cheeks as she lay her head on her arms and sobbed.

Thirty~Three

I had left Shay asleep when I left for work the next day. Another month or so and I would have to think about a finishing date for my maternity leave, how fast was the time going? His face was more cut than bruised and I prayed he would be healed by the time we went to Ireland.

Bev looked as tired as I felt when I arrived at the salon. 'How's Rocky?' she asked on seeing me.

'Sleeping like a baby when I came out.'

'Did he tell you exactly what Sam had said to him?' she made me a leaded coffee.

I shook my head, feeling spent, this pregnancy was beginning to wear me out. She leant forward on her stool and gave me chapter and verse. 'Jesus,' I gasped. 'No wonder Shay tried to beat the shit out of him.'

'I would have done,' she looked out to the car park.

'I wonder how he explained it to Meera.' I mused.

She got off her stool slowly. 'You can ask her,' she inclined her head towards the door.

I got up also, my stomach rolling as she pushed open the door to the salon. 'Hi Tash,' she said wearily, looking as if she hadn't slept.

'Hey,' I answered softly. 'Are you okay?'

'Not really, can we talk?'

'Go in the back,' Bev gave us both a smile.

I led the way, Meera sitting down on one of the stools at the breakfast bar. 'How's Shay?'

I blushed. 'He's okay, the stupid shit.'

'Jamie told me everything,' tears filled her eyes. 'Sam wants you Tash.'

I took a deep breath. 'Sam has always wanted what he can't have. He doesn't deserve you Meera, you are worth so much more.'

'I love him,' she said simply.

'He doesn't deserve your love,' I said gently. 'I would never want to see a family split up but you could be so much happier without him.'

'Like I say, I love him. You of all people should know how that feels, you had him back twice,' she stated without accusation.

'The first time was for love I grant you but the second time was purely for the kids and it damaged them so I wish I never had. He crushed me Meera, I don't want him to crush you.'

'Too late,' she gulped back the sob that tore up her throat.

'Meera,' I cried going to her and putting an arm around her. 'Don't sweet.'

She took a deep breath. 'I don't think you should cut our hair anymore or come to the house.'

'No,' I agreed. 'Please believe me I haven't done anything to make him think-.'

'I know,' she moved away from me, trying to stem the flow of tears. 'I have Safi to think of, she needs her father,' her agitation was showing.

I shook my head. 'Does she really need a father like him?'

'Don't,' she looked at me with reproof.

I felt winded. 'I love Safi, I still want to see her.'

'You can't,' her voice softened. 'Thank you for everything you have done for us, for her but it's just too complicated. Anything to do with Lexi or Jamie I'll text you, not Sam. I'm really sorry Tash, you've been so good to me but I can't have you near Sam.'

'I don't want him,' I felt I was being punished for something I hadn't done.

She smiled sadly. 'He wants you though. You would only have to crook your finger and he would be with you in an instant. I can't compete with you Tash, I've never been able too. Sam has always said you were the best wife a man could have and that I was a poor second.'

'It's Shay I love, not him,' I felt hopeless.

She nodded. 'I have to go, I am sorry.' She hurried out the salon.

'Is everything okay?' Bev asked as Carling arrived, late as usual. She would have to be on time when I started my maternity leave.

I shook my head. 'She's blaming me.'

'How can she blame you?' she pulled a face.

'Because she loves him,' I was completely gutted at her attitude towards me.

'The stupid cow,' she cried as Carling came into the salon. 'You're late gal, again. Make a drink.'

'Sorry,' she gave us a dazzling smile, going into the back room.

We worked in relative silence until my two o'clock came in. 'Hi Tash,' she greeted me brightly. 'You're looking blooming.'

'Thanks,' I was still rankled by how Meera was near enough putting all the blame squarely on my shoulders. Thinking about it thought hadn't I done exactly the same thing the first time it happened to me and Sam?

She settled in the chair and I began to dry cut her hair. 'I see your ex is up to his old tricks again?'

'Sorry?' I pulled myself into the present.

'Your Sam, well not your Sam now but you know what I mean,' she turned to me in confidence. 'He's only knocking off my next door neighbour. I keep seeing his car parked outside and the noises,' she shuddered. 'It's a semi and the walls are paper thin.'

I exchanged looks with Bev. 'Who is she?'

'I don't think you know her, her name's Kate Bishop,' she kept her voice low. 'She's young, late twenties. Pretty thing, lives by herself. Aren't you glad he's all behind you now?'

I nodded. Why would Sam do what he was doing if he was conducting an affair with someone else? It didn't make any sense.

I said little else until Bev and I had a few quiet moments in the back. 'Why the fuck would Sam cause so much trouble with you if he's shagging someone else?' Bev demanded.

'I don't know,' I was bloody angry.

I stewed until I got home, Shay was sitting on the settee listening to music. 'Okay beautiful?' he asked, the bruises coming out on his face lovely now.

I grunted picking up his empty coffee mug and going into the kitchen. He followed me a troubled look on his face. 'Sure nothing is wrong?' he thought I was still angry at him.

I leant against the sink, my arms folded tightly across my chest. 'I am absolutely fuming!' I exploded. 'Sam is having an affair with the next door neighbour of a lady that comes into the salon.'

He frowned. 'Why are you angry about that?'

The look I gave him was cutting, wasn't it obvious? 'Because of what he did last night.'

'Is that all?' he asked quietly.

'What do you mean is that all?' I demanded and then understanding dawned. 'Oh my God! You think I'm jealous?'

'No,' he said swiftly.

'Yes you do,' I contradicted. 'I can't believe you would even think that! I am absolutely fed up of this. I have had Meera come into the salon telling me to stay away from Sam like it's all my fault, telling me I can't see Safi anymore even though I've treated her like one of my own.'

'Tash, I didn't mean-'

'Yes you did,' I cut him off sharply. Getting out my mobile I found Sam's number and waited impatiently for him to answer.

'Who are you calling?' Shay was looking at me resignedly.

I held up my hand as Sam's voice came on the line. 'You complete and utter fucking bastard!' I yelled.

'Darling, what?' his voice was full of charm.

'Don't you dare darling me, you total wanker,' I spat as Shay looked at me shocked. 'Why do it Sam? Why say all those things to me and turn up to pick a fight with Shay last night when you are SHAGGING SOMEONE ELSE?'

'What? I'm not,' he stammered.

'Don't you dare lie to me,' I was on a roll. 'Her name is Kate.'

'Tash,' he tried to get a word in. 'You're mistaken.'

'Don't treat me like a fool, you've done that once too often,' I snapped. 'I even know her last name's Bishop and she lives in Fane Road. Another young bint you can't keep your hands off.'

'Darling there is no need to be like this, just say the word and I'll dump her. It's you I want.'

I went bright red. 'Oh my God I'm not jealous you fecking eejit.' Now I was channelling Shay. 'I'm livid! I've had *your wife* come into the salon warning me to stay way like it's all my fault.

'Tash,' he tried again.

'I don't want to hear it Sam. I've heard it enough over the years,' I was still shouting as Shay sat at the kitchen table cringing. 'I'm going to do what I should have done five years ago when I chucked you out.'

'Please don't do this darling, think about us,' he begged.

I ignored him. 'This is what's going to happen. You are going to leave me alone, you are going to leave Shay alone. You do not visit, text or even think about us. The kids are old enough now, if anything happens they can tell us themselves. I don't want you Sam and if Meera had any sense she wouldn't want you either.'

I stopped for breath. 'If you were the last man on earth I wouldn't have you back so stop trying to ruin my relationship with Shay because we won't let you. Now fuck off and leave us alone.'

I ended the call, glaring at Shay. How dare he say that I was jealous of Sam's affair? 'Do you want a drink?' he asked timidly.

'No,' my tone was curt. 'I'm going for a lie down, I'm tired.' With that I stormed upstairs, slamming the bedroom door shut.

It wasn't fair, I hadn't done anything to deserve this and even Shay was unjustly accusing me of envying Sam's new bimbo. I lay on my side, facing the window. I thought after last weekend and all the drama of finding Albie I was hoping that this weekend would be peaceful but apparently not.

I screwed up my eyes feeling drained but I couldn't drop off, I felt too wired. I must have lain there for ten minutes when Shay plucked up enough courage to open the door and pop his head around. 'Do you want anything to eat beautiful?' he asked meekly. 'I can make you something.'

'What, so you can give me indigestion?' I was being such a bitch.

'Okay,' his voice was small, he knew I was angry at him for thinking I was jealous of Sam's affair. 'Sweet, I'm sorry.'

'Fuck off!' I retorted rudely.

'Okay,' he repeated, disappearing for a moment. Reluctantly I turned to face the door feeling a little bad at being so horrible to him.

Suddenly the tune to The Stripper filled the air and a jean-clad leg appeared around the door followed by the rest of Shay. My mouth twitched unwillingly. 'You are not going to get round me like that, gobshite,' I informed him cuttingly.

He pouted at me, swivelling his hips and peeling off my yellow washing up gloves slowly in time to the music. Hang on, why was he wearing my rubber gloves? Turning his back to me he leant slightly forward, twerking his bottom beautifully. I could feel my resolve going and I bit down on my bottom lip, trying not to laugh.

With a flourish he faced me once more, slowly peeling off his t-shirt. Moving in time to the music, he began to unbutton his jeans and I have to admit I would have paid to watch him strip, he wasn't half bad. Looking sexy and comical at the same time was mean feat but he managed to pull it off. Holding my gaze he tugged down his jeans provocatively and I couldn't stop my smile.

Realising he still had his boots on he tried to kick them off as The Stripper music started again on a loop. Misjudging the fact that his jeans were now round his knees, he pitched forward, falling to the floor with a thud.

'Shay,' I cried rolling off the bed. 'Have you hurt yourself?' I was trying not to laugh.

'Feck,' he swore winded, hurting his chest where Sam had lain the boot in the previous night.

'Are you alright?' I helped him up the best I could and lay him on the bed. 'It was a very good strip.'

'You liked it?' he raised an eyebrow. I nodded laughing as I freed him from his boots and jeans. 'I'm sorry sweet,' he said softly. 'Deep down I know you don't want Sam, I'm just a jealous fucker.'

'Yes you are,' I agreed, lying next to him.

'It's because I love you so much,' he rolled on his side, grimacing.

'You have to truly believe that I don't want Sam,' I had to be sure.

'How you ripped him a new one just?' he began to unbutton my blouse. 'Remind me never to piss you off.'

I smiled sitting up so he could pull the blouse from my shoulders. Concentrating he freed me from my trousers, kissing me. Then he took off my underwear, kissing a trail from my throat to my breasts, then my stomach.

I was full of anticipation as he turned me on my side, him lying behind me and his fingers dipping into me. I moaned leaning back against him. I could feel him shedding the rest of his clothes and I moaned biting on my bottom lip. Carefully he thrust forward, tangled in each other we took our time until we were spent.

'Tash,' he began softly afterwards as we snuggled against each other.

'Hmm,' I felt so content.

'No more unhappiness from now on, positive thinking all the way.'

'Sounds good to me,' I nodded.

'Tash.'

'Hmm,' I could have gone to sleep and it was only seven o'clock.

'Is my cooking that bad?' he looked at me with his beautiful brown eyes.

I thought about sparing his feelings but decided that honesty was definitely the best policy. 'You're not the best cook in the world.'

'We were going to cook together on a Saturday night,' he reminded me.

I did feel guilty because I had promised him. 'I know but we never seem to have much time.'

'I want to be able to do my share when the twins are here,' he did so want to do his best.

'Come on,' I yawned loudly. 'I'll show you how to cook chicken nuggets and chips, kids love them and they are nice and quick.'

He nodded, it was a start.

Thirty~Four

Everything was now back on a more even keel thankfully. I couldn't cope with any more dramas, oh, no. Jamie had gone to see Ray on the Monday night after school and he was going to start work in four weeks' time, he was so excited.

In fact he told me that Jamie was quite chatty with him and didn't seem to be holding the fact that Shay had beaten the shit out of his dad against him. I was so pleased, all I wanted was for them to rub along nicely.

Now it was Saturday and we were in Ireland, Quin actually, pulling up outside the Monks Well pub. Shay paid the taxi driver and we alighted into the late May sunshine. He looked at his surroundings, the place was his mother was born and brought up. He had seemed quiet on the way to Quin and I was concerned he was having second thoughts about meeting his dad.

'It's a lovely little pub,' I chatted as he wheeled our suitcase to the entrance. 'The foods excellent, well the breakfasts are anyway. We had white pudding can you imagine that? Not black pudding but *white* pudding, amazing.'

He gave me a patient look. 'I've had white pudding before.'

Of course he had, he was Irish. I was just waffling on because I was starting to feel nervous myself. With an encouraging smile, I pushed open the bar door, leading the way to the bar.

'Hello,' the barman cast his eye over me appreciatively and I beamed. I'd still got it, even at six months pregnant.

'Hi,' I trilled. 'My name is.'

'Ms Turner,' he smiled slowly.

'You remembered,' I was chuffed.

'You're written in the book,' he twinkled his eyes at me. 'Although to be fair I never forget a pretty face.'

'Aw, thank you,' I blushed.

'You stayed here a couple of weeks ago with your daughter,' his eyes moved to Shay and he did a double take as if he knew him but wasn't sure where from. He pulled his eyes back to me. 'Can I help you with your case?'

'I can manage thanks,' Shay replied.

'Irish?' he said surprised. 'Are you visiting relatives?'

'Just visiting,' Shay replied not giving anything away.

With a smile I took the key from him. 'Same room as before,' he informed me and I said my thank you before leading the way up the stairs.

'He as totally giving you the glad eye,' Shay pursed his lips.

'He did that the last time I was here too,' I preened a little, okay a lot.

He smiled sweetly shaking his head. 'I'm going to have to keep my eye on you,' he teased.

'What can I say, if you've got it, flaunt it,' I flicked back my hair with a giggle. 'To be honest its nice having someone check you out when you're the size of an elephant.'

'I check you out all the time,' he retorted as I faffed with the key, trying to get the door open.

I gave him a smacker on the lips. 'I know and thank you.' Opening the door I flopped down on one of the beds.

'Twin beds?' he said disappointed.

'It's all they have. There are only three rooms and they all have twin beds. We're fortunate that they do B and B at all.'

'What time did you say we would be at the Cassidy's?' he sat on the other bed.

'Two,' I looked at my watch, it was twelve, two hours to kill. 'And why call them the Cassidy's, why not dads?'

'It's strange now we're actually here,' he got up to the window which gave a perfect view of the village. 'Did you see how the barman was looking at me?'

'Maybe he was checking you out?' I teased. 'I wonder if he was thinking, bloody hell you look exactly like Albie Cassidy.'

He agreed still looking out of the window. 'So this is where my mam was born and raised?'

'Pretty isn't it?' I leant against the headboard.

'Yeah on the surface,' he was quiet for a moment. 'Ugly on the inside though.'

'Ugly?' I frowned slightly.

He turned to me. 'What kind of place makes a woman run away with her unborn baby because of religious prejudices? The inability to think outside the box? She couldn't even come back for her own parent's funerals.'

'Maybe not everyone's like that, give them a chance hun,' I said gently. 'Do you want some lunch?'

'I'm not that hungry,' he came back to the bed.

I nodded, I'd had to threaten him to eat something for breakfast. 'Shall we freshen up and grab a coffee?'

'Can we just stay up here?' he reached for my hand.

'Of course we can. Are you sure you're okay?' I kissed the back of his hand.

'Yeah,' but he sounded unsure. 'I just never I would be meeting my dad that he'd even know I existed.'

'Well you will be today,' I toyed with his curls.

'What am I going to say to him,' he fretted.

'It will come, something will just pop into your head and away you'll go,' I sounded confident but I was unsure. What would I have talked about in the same circumstances?

'You know I think I will freshen up, I need a drink,' he let go of my hand.

'Okay but I don't want you turning up there smelling of alcohol,' I badgered.

'Tash,' he grimaced.

'Never mind Tash,' I smiled. 'They probably wouldn't mind though thinking about it. They were plying Lexi with single malt.'

He forced a smile of his own, going into the tiny bathroom. I followed suit when he had finished, washing the journey away.

We went down to the bar, Shay ordering a lager while I plumped for a mineral water. Not wishing to sound like an alcoholic but I really missed having a drink. I blamed my dad, not only did he give me his good genes but also his drinking gene. I could have done with one, I was nearly as nervous as Shay was pretending not to be.

We sat by the window, him lost in his thoughts and me noticing how many of the customers were looking at Shay with curiosity, he really did look like his dad. The time seemed to race, Shay checking his watch every few minutes, his feature's growing more grave if that was possible.

'What's up?' I finished my water.

'Nothing, why?' he took a mouthful of his own drink.

'Your face,' I wanted him to smile.

'It's just my face,' he did attempt one but it fell a little short. 'Everyone is staring at us.'

'We're strangers in the village,' I reasoned. 'They all wonder who we are and what we're doing here. Shall we take a slow walk to the cemetery, take some flowers to your grandparents' grave?'

'Why not? I mean they really bothered with me,' he stared down at the table.

'Well that's their loss. As I've said you don't stoop to their level.'

'Fine, I'm tired of people staring at us anyway.' We walked into the sunshine and I linked my arm in his.

Going to the local shop where Lexi and I had brought the flowers from last time. The homely looking woman beamed at me as I paid for them. 'How long have you got to go?' she indicated to my bump.

'Three months,' I beamed. 'It's twins.'

'Twins, how wonderful!' she cried. 'Beautiful miracles.'

'They truly are,' I confirmed passing the flowers to Shay.

She frowned at him, going to say something and then changing her mind. 'Have a good day,' she smiled.

'You too hun, thank you,' I took his hand showing him the way to the cemetery.

I stopped by the large statue of the Virgin Mary, genuflecting in front of it. 'What are you doing?' he chuckled.

I ignored him. 'Hi there,' I spoke self-consciously. 'Please let everything go okay today, thank you in advance. Amen.'

'You really aren't right in the head,' he informed me wickedly.

'That is not a nice thing to say to the mother of your children,' I admonished. 'It never hurts to ask for a little divine intervention.'

He gave me an amused look as I took him to his grandparent's grave. He lay the flowers on it staring at the inscription. 'Hi,' he said, his voice low. 'I'm your grandson, the baby you were going to make your daughter put up for adoption. You know what? I'm glad she left here, I'm glad she defied you.

She is the best mother I could have ever asked for and you didn't deserve either of us.'

'Not at all bitter are you love?' I raised an eyebrow.

'Just saying it like it is darling,' he grinned.

'Shall we make tracks? It's nearly two.'

'In a minute,' he was staring at the grave, making no move.

'But we said we'd be there at two and it's nearly that now,' I chaffed, I hated being late.

He didn't answer, still staring at the headstone. 'Shay?' I prompted. 'Don't you want to see him?'

He shrugged, not looking at me.

'We've come all this way,' I reasoned. 'It seems a shame not to go and meet him now.'

'I know,' his voice was barely audible. 'It's such a huge thing. I'm going to meet my dad Tash, my dad. The man I had built up in my head to be this huge presence. What if I'm disappointed? What if he is?

I took his hand. 'You won't know until you meet him. He is going to love you, just like I do.' I promised. 'I'm right here with you, you don't have to do it by yourself.'

He smiled at me. 'I don't, do I? Thank you beautiful. Come on then.'

I kept hold of his hand, tightening the grip as we made our way to Albie's bungalow. Standing outside I faced him, he looked so handsome in his skinny jeans and lightweight black jumper, his hair pushed back from his face but curtaining the back of his neck.

I took his face in my hands, kissing him gently. 'I'm so proud of you,' I whispered.

He touched my cheek. 'It's going to turn out okay isn't it?'

'It is,' I walked up the garden path, the door opening before I had chance to ring the doorbell and Niamh stood there.

'Natasha, how are you?'

'Really good,' I answered, feeling on tenterhooks. This was it. Shay was going to meet his dad. He was going to change everything, I really hoped they would hit it off.

I stood aside and she gasped, a hand flying to her mouth. 'Oh my,' she breathed. 'Come in, come in.'

I walked into the hallway and she pointed us in the direction of the living room. Entering I saw Albie sitting on the edge of his seat, a nervous look on his face. 'Hi Albie,' I smiled giving him a big hug.

'Sweetheart,' he greeted me. 'Look at you.'

'I know, I'm huge,' I grinned as Shay stood behind me.

Albie raised himself to his feet unsteadily, his face clouded with emotion. 'Son,' his voice was barely a whisper.

'Dad,' Shay's voice had equal volume.

Niamh and I looked at each other, identical tears in our eyes. They stared at each other for a moment and then Albie was moving forward, taking his son in his arms. Shay allowed himself to be hugged but his stance was stiff.

'I never dreamed,' Albie floundered, tears falling down his cheeks.

'Albie Cassidy don't be such a big girl's blouse, Shay will be wondering what kind of eejit you are, Niamh scolded good-humouredly.

He steered Shay next to him on the settee, staring at him in amazement. 'You are so like me,' he stammered.

'I am,' Shay was looking at himself in thirty years' time, it was a little un-nerving.

'It's freaky isn't it?' I found my voice. 'You would never be able to deny parentage.'

'I wouldn't want to,' he was staring at his son mesmerized.

'No, of course not,' I flushed. 'Oh Moira has sent you this.' I got the photo album from my bag, she had asked Lexi and Bell to get copies of pictures of Shay for him. 'It's photos of Shay through the years. School pictures, things like that.'

When Albie made no move to take it Niamh held out her hand. 'Thank her, that's very kind of her.'

'She just wanted Albie to have some,' I explained, both he and Shay were looking at me and I realised that I was their buffer. It was up to me to make sure today went well.

'So Albie,' I began unsurely. 'Maybe you could Shay a little about Quin, tell him about where his mom grew up.'

'Of course,' he said hurriedly. 'Ask me anything.'

'I'll make tea,' Niamh fussed. 'Natasha what can I get you?'

'Tea would be wonderful, thank you,' I allowed myself one cup of caffeinated tea or coffee a day and I think I was going to need one now.

She disappeared into the kitchen, Shay waiting until she had gone before saying. 'Did you love her?'

I cringed a little, cut straight to the chase, why don't you?

Albie took a sharp intake of breath. 'I worshipped her,' he answered, a faraway look on his face. 'She was so smart and beautiful.'

He paused and I choked back the tears.

'I loved her with all my heart,' he continued. 'The day she left without a word broke my heart in two.'

Shay was watching his dad, that infuriating unreadable expression on his face.

Albie turned his attention to his son. 'I make no excuse for my actions, the affair. My first wife was a fragile thing, she suffered from depression. She would spend days locked in her own little world,' he took a moment. 'Moira was like a breath of fresh air. She had an opinion on everything.'

'She still has,' Shay cut in with half a smile.

Albie chanced a smile of his own. 'She was warm and caring, a live wire. I shouldn't have been unfaithful to my wife but I couldn't ignore my feelings. I wished I had met your mam first, what a life we would have had.'

'If you felt so strongly about her then why didn't you leave your wife?' There was no accusation in Shay's tone, just curiosity.

'I was brought up a devout Catholic, I still am,' he paused again, trying to keep the tears at bay. 'I had so much guilt about it, about all of it.'

I fished a tissue out of my bag and passed it to him and he took it with a thank you.

'I wish I'd had the courage to do what my heart wanted me to do, to be with Moira, the woman I truly loved. I was a coward though,' he choked out the words. 'When she left Quin I thought it was a sign. My punishment for being a bad Catholic boy. I thought that Moira leaving meant that she didn't love me, didn't feel the same way. I made a decision to be a proper husband to my wife, to never stray again.'

Shay nodded, staring down at the floor, he was struggling a little. How overwhelming must it be to meet you dad after all this time? Thinking about it though I wish someone would tell me that I had a long lost dad somewhere, one who preferably bothered with me.

'I did try and find out where she had gone but no one knew,' he continued.

'Her parents knew,' I contradicted. 'They were the ones that told her she would have to give the baby up for adoption.'

He scowled. 'They bare-faced lied to me.'

'What happened to them?' Shay asked thickly.

'They died a couple of years after Moira left, within six months of each other. I wanted her to come back for the funeral, I wanted to check that she was happy but she never came.'

'It's so sad,' I blew my nose, bloody baby hormones, making me all emotional.

He nodded. 'If I'd have known the real reason why she had left then I would have stepped up to my responsibilities. I would have been such a large part of your life, I promise you that.'

'But you didn't know,' Shay was thawing a little.

'No, I didn't,' he paused as Niamh came back with the drinks. I wondered how she was coping with all of this. Having a son that her husband knew nothing about thrust on her? Plus me and the twins, what a shock.

'Thank you,' I said politely taking the cup and saucer from her, she had got her best china out.

'Thanks,' Shay looked at her. 'And you Niamh?'

'Me?' she looked at him surprised.

'It must be a jolt, me appearing out of the blue,' he said softly. 'It's good of you to meet me.'

She sat down on the other chair. 'Yes it was a shock, I can't deny. When Natasha and Lexi turned up I could hardly believe what she was saying to us.'

'I can imagine,' I sympathised.

'But it means so much to Albie and I love him and want him to be happy,' she smiled at her husband.

Shay nodded.

'So,' Albie wanted to get the conversation on a more sedate level. 'You know that you are the spit of me, you have some of my mannerisms but tell me some more.'

Shay gave him his beautiful smile, the first since he had arrived. 'I've worked as a mechanic since I've left school. Lived in

Cork with my mam and just basically worked, went out and that was it.'

I smiled at him lovingly.

'Ray, who owns the garage where I work, his wife has family in Cork and I knew them. I fancied a change so I asked if there were any jobs at the garage and thankfully there was,' he explained.

'So you moved to England,' Niamh sipped her tea.

His eyes fell to me. 'Yes and I'm glad I did because I met Tash and now we are going to be a family.'

'All thanks to a gammy condom,' I declared.

Three sets of eyes looked at me and I flushed. Why couldn't I have just smiled?

'Sooo,' Albie drew out the word slowly. 'What do you in your spare time Shay?'

'Go to the gym, go to the pub, play pool,' he replied.

I looked at him surprised. 'When do you play pool?'

'When Dale and I go out for a pint,' his smile was for me.

'I never knew that,' I hated not knowing things about him.

'It keeps the magic alive,' he teased.

I smiled shaking my head. 'And you Natasha?' Niamh enquired.

'Me?' I went blank for a moment.

'Beautiful reads the most trashy historical bodice rippers you can imagine,' he replied for me. 'Proper shite and she devours them.'

'Hey,' I protested. 'They may not be classics but they're not that bad.'

'They are terrible and you sit there reading them with a big old grin on your face,' his eyes sparkled, Albie was watching us closely.

'That's mean,' I pouted. 'At least I read, the only things you read are the labels on your lager bottles.'

Niamh tittered, looking at us amused.

'He cries at soppy films too,' I got my oar in. 'And he's untidy, he does my head in.'

'You have OCD and you're a control freak,' he countered.

'You are so messy,' I hit back. 'I am picking up after you all the time.'

Niamh laughed again. 'You truly are you father's son,' she said. 'Albie is just the same.'

I bobbed my tongue out at Shay and we all laughed. 'Tell me more,' Albie was finally beginning to relax.

'Well,' Shay thought for a moment. 'Tash's son Jamie, is nearly seventeen and he's coming to work with me at the garage. For his birthday in a couple of weeks we are getting him his driving lessons and I brought him an old Corsa and we'll do it up together.'

'You're close to him?' Albie wanted to know.

'Jaysus no, he hates me.'

'He does not hate you,' I argued.

'Sweet, he does,' he shook his head bemused.

'You're getting on better now,' I reasoned.

'That's because I'm bribing him,' he clarified. 'So you don't have to worry about anything.'

'Like me with Erin,' Albie confided.

'Don't,' his wife pulled a face.

'Who's Erin?' I asked.

'My daughter,' she answered. 'Erin is,' she paused.

'Hard work?' Albie offered helpfully.

She had to agree. 'To be fair she misses her dad terribly, he died a few years ago.'

I nodded, everyone had their hardships.

'So you have Jamie and Lexi, you must be proud of them?'

I nodded. 'I love them to pieces. I also have a brother, Dale, who Shay plays pool with apparently.'

'Do you have any photos?' Niamh was taking an interest, bless her.

I took out my mobile phone, scrolling through the pictures. Perching on the arm of Niamh's chair and I showed them to her as Albie leaned across. 'That's Lexi and Belle, her,' I hesitated for a long moment. 'Well her girlfriend, Lexi is gay.'

'They are a pair of fantastic girls, both doing really well at university, we couldn't be more proud of them,' Shay cut in, not wanting his Catholic father to disapprove.

'We know,' Niamh read his mind. 'It was such a pleasure to meet Lexi, she is a credit to you Natasha.'

'Thank you,' I beamed. 'That's Jamie.'

'Oh, he's a handsome chappie, he doesn't look like you though does he?'

'No,' I agreed. 'He's like his dad.'

'Well his dad must be a good looking man,' she stated.

I grimaced. 'Only on the outside.'

'He's a maggot,' Shay cut in.

'You don't get on?' Albie smiled.

'Shay has tried,' I rushed in to defend him. 'But Sam is such an idiot.'

'He didn't do?' Albie motioned to the couple of faded bruises on his son's face.

'Like a pair of kids they were,' I admonished. 'In the past now though.'

'I hope you won,' Shay's dad settled back in

'Yeah,' he answered coyly.

Niamh tutted. 'What are you like Albie Cassidy? Anyway the two of you are staying for a bite to eat with us?'

'We don't want to put you out,' I said quickly.

'You're not, I've made my world famous Irish stew with homemade soda bread.'

'Irish stew?' my stomach rumbled loudly.

'World famous?' Shay smiled.

'Famous in Ireland,' Albie twinkled. 'Well okay in Quin.'

I laughed. 'Thank you that's very kind.'

'You're welcome,' she helped me from the arm of the chair with a smile.

Thirty~Five

We had spent a lovely few hour with Albie and Niamh, her Irish stew was to die for and I made sure she gave me the recipe. The best part however was how Albie and Shay hit it off. After the initial expected awkwardness you would have thought they had been the best of friends for years.

We learnt that Albie liked to fix things, that he could play the fiddle and had a decent singing voice. He liked long walks and went to church every Sunday, he was devoted to his religion.

He and Shay were currently on their fifth glass of single malt whisky, it was getting on for nine o'clock and I had hit the wall. The excitement of Shay meeting his dad coupled with my pregnancy was wearing me out, I was truly too old to be having babies.

'Aw will you look at Natasha,' Niamh smiled, her own eyes growing tired.

Shay went to wake me but Albie stopped him. 'Leave her be, she needs her rest.'

He nodded smiling at me lovingly. 'Will you be getting married now you're having the babies?' Albie wanted to know.

'I would marry her tomorrow, I've asked her twice,' Shay admitted. 'But she won't. What her ex did damaged her,' he was mellowed by the whisky. 'But trust me, she will be my wife.'

'Good man,' he paused. 'I can't tell what all this means to me. I used to imagine what it would be like to have a child, a son.'

'And?' Shay gave him a cheeky smile.

'Moira has done such a good job of bringing you up. You are more than I could have hoped for.'

'Thank you dad.'

He bristled with pride at his son calling him dad. 'And me?'

Shay looked at him for a moment. 'Tash told me when she came back from seeing you the first time that you were a lovely man, that she had liked you from the moment she had met you. I have to say that you haven't disappointed me, not one bit.'

'I'm going to be crying in a minute,' Niamh sounded choked. 'We need more whisky I think.'

'We can go on from here, can't we son? I can be part of your life now?' he held his breath.

'Of course,' Shay's reply was soft. 'I'd like that. I've spent thirty-three years wondering who you were.'

'But you weren't happy with Natasha when she first sought me out?' he prised.

'I was concerned about my mam,' he was truthful.

'But she's fine with you coming to visit?'

He nodded. 'She is remarkable.'

'Does she and Natasha get on well?'

'They totally adore each other,' he smiled. 'Tash's parents were shite, her dad died a few weeks ago, she found him in his flat. It shook her up pretty badly, it's what gave her the idea of finding you. She didn't want me to have any regret at not knowing my dad like she had regrets with her dad. I can't understand either her mom or dad, not wanting anything to do with their children or their grandchildren. She has had a really tough life.'

'Natasha has you now though,' Albie stated.

'And she always will. Can you do me a favour though, call her Tash? She's too polite to say anything but she hates being called Natasha, it reminders her of her mother.'

'Duly noted,' he replied as Niamh came back into the room with the drinks.

'One more then I need to get her back to the room,' Shay picked up his glass.

'You'll come tomorrow? I want to take you for pint,' Albie looked hopeful. 'We don't have to tell anyone who you are, we can just say that you are a relation if you want, not my son.'

Shay looked at him, a twinkle in his eye. 'I don't mind people knowing.'

'I wanted you to say that,' he answered relieved. 'Thank you.'

Shay smiled, draining his glass. Coming to me he gave me a gentle nudge. 'Sweet.'

I mumbled in my sleep, moving slightly.

'Beautiful,' he said a little louder. 'Time to go.'

'What?' I shot up with a groan.

'Come on sweet, time to go,' he pulled me up.

'Sorry,' I felt disorientated.

Albie and Niamh stood also. 'We'll have our lunch in the pub, they do good food there,' he said.

'We'll meet you there then,' Shay answered taking my hand.

'You won't be going to church then?' he asked.

'Mam never forced any type of religion on me,' Shay admitted.

'Oh,' his dad tried to hide his disappointment, he had hoped his son was raised in the Catholic religion.

I could see he was saddened so I said. 'I'm so sorry I fell asleep, it had nothing to do with the company.'

'Don't you worry,' Niamh told me. 'I was exactly the same when I was having Erin.'

I smiled, still feeling a little groggy, as I pulled my jacket on. It was now June and the weather was finally turning mild. It was strange to think that this time last year I was a singleton who was yet to meet Shay.

'I'll walk with you to the pub,' Albie was a little unsteady on his feet but he was one very happy man.

Hugging Niamh and thanking her for their hospitality we walked out into the night. The village was pitch black, I counted only two streetlights. Some of the houses had lit windows but it seemed the whole place was fast asleep even though it wasn't very late.

I could every star in the sky as I held onto Shay's arm, Albie walking the other side of me, insisting I take his arm too. The air felt so pure and fresh, it was lovely.

The pub was still quite full, so that was where all the locals were and we stopped at the door. 'Thank you Albie,' I hugged him tightly. 'See you tomorrow.'

'We'll meet at one-thirty if that's okay?' he asked us and then he turned to Shay a huge smile on his face. 'Goodnight son.'

'Night dad,' he replied and they embraced which caused my eyes to fill again with tears.

We waited as he walked back home and then Shay took my hand and we made our way to the room. 'How do you feel?' I asked as the noise of the pub drifted upwards.

'Great, better than I thought I would when we arrived this morning,' he lay on one of the beds. 'I really like him Tash, and Niamh too.'

'We need to call your mom, let her know how we got on.' We would have to use the telephone in the bar, neither of us could get a signal again.

'I'll come down to you in a minute,' he made no sign of moving.

'Well hurry up then lazy, the barman might try and run off with me even in my condition,' I teased leaving him on the bed.

I flashed my eyes at the barman, whose name I found out was Ruairi (pronounced Rory, how weird was that?) and he passed me the phone with a flirty smile. I dialled Moira's number and she answered it just as someone began to sing in the bar. 'Tash,' she cried. 'Is everything going okay?'

'Hi Moira, it's gone great, better than we hoped.' I leant against the wall.

'Is Shay coping? How is he?' she mithered.

'He's fine, he'll be here in a minute if he can stir his arse after consuming half a dozen glasses of single malt,' I laughed. 'How are you doing?' This was all nerve wracking for her too.

'I've been unable to think about anything else all day,' she sounded full of emotion

'You'll always be his mom Moira, that is never going to change,' I soothed. 'He worships the ground you walk on.'

'I just don't want to see him hurt,' she said.

'He won't be,' I assured her. 'And you will always be his number one.'

'I know, I'm being an eejit,' she cried. 'It's just always been me and him, no one else. Our lives are changing so much.'

'I know but just think, I am going to need you so much when the twins are born. They are going to need their gran.' I wanted to say the right thing.

'Really?' she sounded so unsure.

'Really,' she just needed to know that she was wanted. 'Come round for supper Monday when we get back, you and Alan.'

'You need your rest,' she argued.

'We get back early so it's not a problem, plus we want to see you. We have wedding plans to finalise,' I chuckled.

'That's kind of you, we'll be there,' she sounded a little better now.

'Shall we say six?' I stifled a yawn. 'I love you loads you know Moira, thank you for everything you do for me.'

'I love you too sweetheart,' her reply was soft.

'Oh here's Shay,' I saw him coming into the bar. 'See you Monday.'

'See you then,' she replied as I passed him the phone.

'Hey mam,' he greeted her jovially. 'How ya doing me dahling?'

'Worried about you,' she was glad to hear his voice.

'I'm good, really good. He's a nice man.'

'I'm glad,' she paused for a moment. 'And his wife?'

'She's nice too, they are making us feel very welcome,' he winked at me and I smiled. 'We'll see you soon mam and I'll tell you all about it. I love you so very much.'

'Love you too son, take care and safe journey home.'

I gave Ruairi a sexy smile before we went back upstairs, I knew I shouldn't but it did amuse me a little. Shay went back to his position on the bed as I locked the door. 'Do you think she is okay?' he asked not even taking his jacket off.

'Feeling a little insecure I think.'

'Insecure?' he frowned.

'I can understand it,' I took off my own jacket. 'It's been just the two of you for so long, no family, no nothing. Then I came along with my kids and now you've met your dad and whatever will come with that. She's scared she's going to lose you.'

'She'll never lose me,' his frown stayed in place. 'Why didn't she tell me she didn't want me to meet him?'

'Because she does want you to meet him,' I stood at the window. 'I'll let you into a little secret love, women are complicated creatures and you will never know what's in our heads. She just needs you to reassure her. She and Alan are coming for supper Monday night.'

He got off the bed coming to join me at the window. 'That's good of you sweet,' his hands laced around me, his head resting on my shoulder.

'I don't want to anything to upset her, I do love her and I feel partly responsible because I'm the one who found your dad.'

'And she loves you and so do I,' he reached to kiss me.

'Is it strange looking at your dad when he is so like you?' I asked.

'A little, but at least I know I'm still going to be good looking in my sixties,' he smiled.

'You could never be anything else,' I took his hands in mine.

'I was so proud of you today,' his breath was warm in my ear. 'So proud that you are mine.'

'Ditto,' I replied, staring out the window. 'It really is a beautiful, if dull place.'

'Not as beautiful as you,' his hands dropped to my waist, caressing my bump, mouth kissing my neck.

I leant back against him, it had been a wonderful day, a successful day and I was happy.

Hi hands went up my top, feeling the skin. 'We have to make love in Ireland, in my own country,' he whispered.

I smiled turning to go back to the bed but he held me fast, one hand caressing my back, his other hand going to the waist band of the black maternity trousers I lived in now. 'Shay we are at the window,' I gasped.

'No one will see us,' his voice was soft.

'Turn the light off then,' it would make me feel less self-conscious.

He went to the lamp, flicking the switch and plunging the room into darkness before coming back to where I was. 'The amount of whisky you've consumed are you sure you can manage?' I teased.

'I'll show you who can manage,' he pulled down my trousers and I stepped out of them. Then I heard him undo the zip of his jeans, his hands on my boobs, my bum, every part of me.

'Hold onto the window frame,' he whispered, filling me with all of him. I groaned, biting my bottom lip, the walls were paper thin. He held me against him as he pushed forward, careful I didn't hit my bump on the window sill.

'Shay,' I gasped as his movements became more hurried, the village ghostly silent outside the window. I ached for a time when we did not have to be so careful, when we could make wild, rutting love like we did before I got pregnant.

'Shit,' he drew out the word, one hand above mine on the window frame.

'Oh,' I tried not to make too much noise but it was difficult, I still wanted him like crazy.

We came together and I resisted the urge to collapse in heap on the floor. He began to laugh, his whole body trembling. 'I love you so much,' he told me, hot breath tickling my ear.

'That was wonderful,' I too was shaking as I untangled myself, taking off the rest of my clothes and pulling on my dressing gown before lying on one of the beds.

He lay on the other one, staring at me. 'This is it, isn't it Tash?'

'What?' I felt so content, what a lovely ending to the day.

'As good as it gets,' he reached for my hand. 'What we have together, it's practically perfect.'

'I think so,' I confirmed, although that small part of me, the part that could never allow me to be feel truly happy was trying to rise to the surface. I was getting to the same point in my pregnancy that I was with Jamie when Sam had first strayed.

'I don't like having to sleep in separate beds,' he grumbled.

'We are never going to manage in just one,' I smiled. 'It's only for a couple of nights.'

'Dad asked me if we are going to get married,' he rolled on his side.

'Don't spoil things love. We don't need to get married to prove what we have,' I was so scared of making that step, in my experience getting married didn't stop someone from breaking your heart. 'Lots of people get married but it doesn't stop them not being happy and looking elsewhere.'

He turned on his back. 'Okay,' although what he wasn't saying to me was how I hurt him by not wanting to marry him. He hid it well.'

It was my turn to roll on my side so I was facing him. 'We love each other, a piece of paper and a wedding ring isn't going to make what we have more special. We've only known each other a few months anyway.'

'Yet here we are, having twins.'

'Your looks, my brains,' I joked. I didn't really believe that he wanted to get married anyway, I thought he was just saying what he thought people expected him to say.

'They will be lucky babies,' he was lost in thought. 'Tash?'

'Yes,' my eyes were growing heavy again.

'I'm not him you know?'

My eyes snapped open. 'I know you're not Sam,' I replied. 'You are so much better.'

'You think you're going to reach a certain point in your pregnancy and I'm going to cop off with the first woman that gives me the glad eye,' he frowned slightly. 'That history is going to repeat itself.

'Please love, it's been a really nice day.'

'I know,' he cut in taking my hand. 'I just need you to know that I would never do that to you.'

I nodded without reply. 'I need my sleep hun,' I yawned but I felt guilty, he looked a little down. 'The babies are moving.'

He gave me his beautiful smile, coming to sit on the edge of the bed, his hand resting on my stomach. 'Incredible isn't it?' his eyes sought mine.

'It is,' I agreed. 'We still have so much to do and get for them and we only have three month.'

'We'll do it,' he guaranteed me. 'I'll paint the nursery next weekend and we'll go shopping for more things as well.'

'It's all so expensive,' I fretted. 'It would be so much easier if we were only having one.'

'No, two is much better,' he stroked my stomach. 'I'll see if Ray can give me any overtime.'

'I'd rather have you with me.'

'That's so sweet,' he gave me a kiss. 'We'll be okay, I promise.'

'Will you hold me for a while?' I asked.

'Sure,' awkwardly he lay on the bed and we squashed together and that's how we fell asleep, content in each other's arms.

Thirty~Six

When I awoke the following morning though I wished we hadn't fallen asleep like that, my neck was stiff and my back was aching. Shay stirred behind me, stretching. 'What time is it?' he mumbled.

I peered at the clock. 'Eight, breakfast is served until nine-thirty.'

'Plenty of time,' he got up going to the bathroom.

'We don't want to eat too late if we're having a big lunch,' I warned, trying to relieve the aches and pains. I was due at the doctors again on Wednesday, they were certainly looking after me being the age I was plus having twins I was at a higher risk apparently. Luckily though everything was progressing as it should be.

'Half an hour and we'll be ready to go down, he replied.

I pulled a face, you are going to think I'm very strange but I always felt uncomfortable hearing someone else having a wee. It was bad enough in a public toilet in a cubicle next to someone you don't know but when it was someone you knew.

Bev, for example, was murder. When we were out she would follow me to the ladies and talk to me when I was sitting on the loo! I could go in there bosting to go and as soon as she started chatting not a dribble would come out! I made Shay cover his ears much to his amusement.

I think he'd finished. Oh, wait, another little squirt. I should have stood in the corridor. He ran the tap as he washed his hands and then he came back, hair all messy and yesterday's clothes on.

We went to breakfast around nine, both of us ordering a full Irish breakfast despite the fact we were going to have lunch in a couple of hours. At least I had had the excuse that I was eating for three now.

'Is it strange being here, where your mom was born and bred?' I asked as we waited for breakfast.

He thought for a moment. 'Mam has always spoken fondly of Quin. It's funny to think I could have lived here myself in different circumstances, I would have been bored shitless. I think mam's biggest regret was losing touch with her family.'

'I can understand that,' I replied as Ruairi stood behind the bar watching us closely. 'Her parent's missed out on so much.'

'They did,' he pondered it for a moment. 'How could they demand that she got rid of her baby? It would be like my mam telling us we couldn't have the twins.'

'Different way of doing things,' I looked at him cheekily. 'Am I forgiven then for poking my nose in and finding your dad?'

He chuckled. 'You were forgiven last week. There is one thing I've learnt about you beautiful.'

'And what's that?' I poured tea out of one of those stainless steel teapots that dribbled everywhere.

'You have a heart of gold and although you may not always think of the consequences you do things for the right reasons.'

'Hey,' I cut in.

He continued with a smile. 'It's one of the things I love about you.'

'Good,' I beamed.

'My babies are going to be so fortunate to have you as their mother.'

'You might want to get Lexi and Jamie's opinion on that before you say anything,' I laughed. 'They may not agree.'

'Lexi absolutely adores you,' he replied. 'She would have my balls for a pair earrings if I hurt you.'

'Rightly so,' I agreed. 'I'm so proud of her, she's turned out better than I could have ever wished for. She did go through a phase when she hit out at everything, she couldn't cope with what her dad was doing, and she rebelled for a while.'

'Lexi?' he was surprised.

I nodded. 'She doesn't think I know but she had underage sex with a boy in her year at school.'

'I thought she was gay?' he was confused.

'She is,' I grinned. 'She was fifteen and Dale copped them at it. She had taken the keys I had for his flat and let herself in not knowing that he wasn't at work he had booked a day off. It's probably what put her off men for life. I wanted to ground her until she was forty but Dale stopped me even saying anything to her. He understood her need to feel loved.'

'Has Dale always been close to them?'

'He has, he's got a lot of time for them,' I answered. 'When Sam left he helped me with them, especially Jamie. Dale just likes people to think he doesn't care about things.'

'Sam wasn't there for them?' he wanted to know.

'Sam is a good dad, when he's not fooling around,' I couldn't say anything else. 'I confess I didn't always make things easy for him.'

Shay grimaced but I wasn't going to lie, I stopped Sam seeing them at times, well when we first split up. It was only when I could see the effect it was having on them that I swore to not let the divorce affect them.

I rubbed my stomach absently. 'I sometimes wonder how they would be if our marriage had been different.'

'If you were still happily married to him you mean?' Jealously was in his tone.

'No,' I shot him a knowing look. 'I mean if we had just fallen out of love with each other with none of the arguments or recriminations. His affairs affected Lexi and Jamie too. I'm glad he was a shit though because if he wasn't then I wouldn't be with you.'

'Aw sweet,' he looked up as breakfast arrived, smelling divine.

'I put extra bacon on yours, for the baby,' Ruairi gave me his most charming smile.

'Babies,' I corrected him. 'It's twins.'

'Grand, twice the fun,' he turned to Shay. 'I have to ask you, are you related to Albie Cassidy, because you look just like him.'

He hesitated for a mere second before nodding. 'He's my dad.'

I bristled with pride, well done the Shayster, as our Dale would say.

Ruairi looked surprised. 'I didn't realise he had children.'

'Neither did he,' Shay began to eat his breakfast and the barman got the hint that the conversation was over.

'That will get him thinking,' I ate my own breakfast hungrily. 'Albie will be pleased that you don't mind people knowing.'

'I'm doing it for my mam too,' he clarified. 'I'm not hiding away like I'm her dirty little secret. Rightly or wrongly I am the product of two people who loved each other, just like our babies are. That's nothing to be ashamed off.'

'You are amazing,' I praised.

He held me with his smouldering eyes. 'You want me don't you?' he teased. 'You want me to take you now on this table right in front of the barman.'

'His names' Ruairi,' I grinned. 'And you are one randy Irishman.'

'I'm making the most of it before we have the kids, from what everyone tells me it's not the top priority then.'

I felt a flash of panic. 'We have to make time.'

'Sweet,' he said patiently. 'I'm teasing, if we have to bribe my mam with cold hard cash we will have time to ourselves. I fancy you too much not to want to touch you. If you don't stop comparing me to Sam I'm going to slap your arse with my tongue.'

I laughed loudly. 'I'll look forward to that,' my eyes were sparkling.

'So,' he drew out the word. 'After breakfast shall we go back to bed?'

'I guess we could,' I tried to keep my tone casual, I was knackered from the lack of sleep I had last night but I wanted to keep him happy and I did want him.

He cocked an eyebrow. 'Don't sound too keen.'

'No, it's not that,' I said quickly. 'It's just we're running out of positions now. I like to look at you and I'm so big.'

'Sit on top then,' he suggested.

'I'll squash you,' I protested.

'No, you won't,' he argued. 'Come on it'll be fun.'

Or give me serious indigestion, I thought but did not say. 'Well?' he pushed. 'We have a couple of hours to kill.'

'We should really have a look around Quin,' I did want him to take me to bed but I was beginning to feel as sexy as a wet sock.

'We've looked around Quin, it's one street, one church, a cemetery and a big fuck off statue of the Virgin Mary,' he twinkled. 'We've even seen the local shop, job done. If you don't feel like it, it's fine sweet.'

'I do,' I told him hurriedly, deciding to be truthful. 'I just don't feel very sexy at the moment. I mean I want you, God yes but all I can see when I look down is my huge belly.'

'It's a beautiful belly,' he told me. 'You seemed okay last night.'

'It was pitch black and I had my back to you and my top on so I didn't feel so conscious of it. I would die if you thought I looked hideous in broad daylight. I can't even shave my legs properly now, let alone keep my lady garden neat and tidy.'

'Your what?' he spluttered.

I flushed red. 'My lady garden,' I repeated. 'You know what I mean.'

He was laughing so much I thought he was going to choke. 'I have never heard it called that before. Your lady garden.'

'Can you say it a bit louder? I don't think they heard you in Dublin.'

'Sorry,' he chuckled as we finished our breakfast. We sat for ten minutes letting it settle and he had a thoughtful expression on his face.

'Penny for them?' I smiled as Ruairi came to collect the plates, I said our thank you's as I waited for Shay to answer.

'Come on, let's go back upstairs,' he grabbed my hand leading the way to our room. Once inside he lay a towel on the bed.

'What are you doing?' I asked as he disappeared into the bathroom.

He came out armed with his shaving foam and his razor. 'I'm going to tend to your lady garden.'

I began to giggle loudly, taking a step backwards. 'Sod off.'

'I am not having any woman of mine going around with an untidy lady garden, not on my watch.' He stood there, an innocent expression on his face.

'You are not coming near my nether's with that razor,' I held up my hands.

He pulled off his jumper, moving towards me. I squealed moving back but the wall was behind me and I was trapped.

'So,' he stood directly in front of me, one hand on the wall behind me. 'So you think you're not sexy?' I nodded, looking coy. 'You think you have nothing now that would turn me on?'

Again I nodded. Looking at me for a moment, he kissed me long and hard, one hand going to the top of the leggings I wore. 'Lie on the bed,' he instructed, his voice firm but husky.

I did, giggling like a schoolgirl. Carefully he undressed me, his breathing becoming heavier. I bit my lip in anticipation as he squeezed shaving foam onto his palm. With a flourish he began to sort out my *lady garden*.

'Stop shaking,' he scolded but I couldn't, I was giggling too much. 'Tash, I'm going to cut you if you don't keep still.'

'I can't,' I hiccupped, trying to get my laughter under control.

'There,' he declared. 'All done and looking beautiful.'

'Thank you,' I answered shyly.

He shrugged modestly. 'It's looking good even if I do say so myself. Very Irish.'

I looked at him alarmed. 'You haven't shaped it like a shamrock have you?'

He began to laugh. 'A shamrock?'

'Shay,' I warned, trying not to giggle, his laugh was so infectious. 'Tell me,' I demanded.

He tapped the side of his nose. 'It's for me to now, you won't see it anyway,' he caught my hand. 'I like the idea of your lady garden being shaped like a shamrock and I will certainly keep it in mind for future reference.'

'Who say's I'm going to let you do it again?' I teased. 'Gawd knows what I look like.'

'Shall I get madam a mirror?' he offered. 'Then you can admire my handiwork.'

I laughed, squeezing his hand tighter. 'No, I trust you.'

'So you should.'

'Now,' he moved up the bed. 'Let me see you.' He kissed me again, moving down to my breasts, making me squirm. 'Sit on me.'

'I'm too big,' I protested, but I really wanted too.

'Come on, it'll be grand,' he coaxed me. Lying next to me made me move and I did so awkwardly, sitting astride him and while most of Quin were good Catholics and went to church Shay and I bonked each other's brains out.

'Amen,' he declared when we were lying side by side on the bed, well as much as we could. 'Better?'

'Better,' I grinned, trailing my fingers across his hairy chest. We lay like that until it was time to get ready for lunch. I dressed in my leggings and short sleeved tartan tunic teamed with ballet pumps. The day was warm and sunny, not a cloud in the sky.

Shay had his grey skinny jeans and white t-shirt on, he looked casual but absolutely gorgeous. 'It's probably all-round the village by now that you are Albie's son,' I told him as I checked my make-up. 'How do I look?'

'Perfect,' he smiled. 'I should imagine it is, I hope I did the right thing.'

'You did, as I said Albie will be over the moon,' I checked my handbag. 'Ready?'

'Yes,' he let me lead the way down to the bar.

Thirty~Seven

We greeted each other with hugs and settled at the table, a few of the locals filling the bar for their post church drink. 'How did you sleep?' Albie asked.

'Not the best night I've ever had,' I admitted. 'I'm struggling to get comfortable these days.'

'Next time you stay with us,' he stated. 'I should have insisted this time.'

'Not to worry,' Shay stood. 'What are you drinking? Oh and by the way, the barman knows that I am your son.'

'How?' he looked puzzled.

'He asked me if we were related because we look alike and I told him the truth. I hope you don't mind?'

'Not at all,' he looked pleased as Niamh gave his hand a squeeze.

'Now what's everyone having?' Shay asked again.

'Mineral water please,' I replied.

'I'll have a red wine please,' Niamh held a gift bag in her hand.

'I've always thought that if I had a son,' Albie began. 'That we would have a pint of Guinness together. Will you have one with me son?'

Shay hesitated, he was never really struck on the taste of Guinness but it seemed to mean something to his dad. 'Sounds good,' he nodded going to the bar.

'Aw it was a grand day yesterday,' Niamh chatted. 'Albie was like a big kid, he couldn't sleep at all last night.'

'I couldn't,' he confirmed. 'We won't leave it for months before we see you again will we? I want to know the minute those babies are born.'

'We can talk all the time,' I established. 'Lexi showed me how to make a phone call on Snapchat, you can see each other and everything.'

'I know how to do that, Alice, my granddaughter taught me,' Niamh chimed in.

'Excellent,' I beamed. 'Oh Albie,' I moved so I was standing next to him and put his hand on my bump. 'That's twin one,' I waited a moment moving his hand slightly. 'And that's twin two.'

'Let me feel,' Niamh reached over, a big smile on her face. 'I remember feeling Erin moving inside of me, it is so special.'

'I love it,' I admitted. 'Shay lies for hours just waiting for them to move.' I sat back down as he returned with the drinks, many of the locals taking an interest in us.

'Babies moving?' he asked putting the drinks on the table.

'They are, lively little buggers too,' I picked up the menu. Believe it or not I was starving again. 'What's everyone having?'

'The roast is very nice,' Albie recommended.

'I'll have that then,' Shay nodded. 'Niamh and Tash?'

'The same,' we echoed.

Albie got out his wallet but Shay waved him away. 'This is our treat,' he went up to the bar to order four Sunday lunches.'

'That's kind of you,' Niamh said when he returned. 'These are from Albie and me, for the babies.' She gave him the gift bag.

There were an assortment of the booties and mittens plus baby socks and hats all I suspected knitted by Niamh. There were also two emerald green outfits declaring the legend, *50% Irish ~ 100% Gorgeous* on them.

'I love them,' I squealed delighted. 'Where did you get them from?'

'Dublin, we went last weekend and I just had to have them,' she replied.

'They are perfect, thank you so much for everything,' I smiled.

'Yes thank you, they are great,' Shay echoed.

'They will look so cute in them,' I was aware of the stares that we were getting from the other customers.

Albie followed my gaze as I looked around the bar. 'Being the village postman for so many years everyone knows me so they are all curious. I think it's time I made an announcement.'

'Love,' Niamh cautioned, Quin could be a very narrow minded place but he shrugged off her concerns.

Standing he cleared his throat. 'Ladies and gentlemen,' he began and the bar fell silent. 'I can see you are all taking an interest in our guests so I thought I may as well introduce them to you.'

I cringed a little in my seat but Albie's voice was clear and I realised that he was quite a strong person how was going to let anyone show him or us disrespect. He turned to Shay. 'This is my son, Shay. Up until two weeks ago I did not know that he existed but I could not be more proud to say this. The past is of no consequence but the future is everything.'

Shay stood, standing shoulder to shoulder with his father. Albie put an arm around his shoulder. 'I am going to be a granddad too. Shay's beautiful girlfriend Tash, is expecting twins. And yes, I said girlfriend, not wife. So there you have it, now I'll answer no questions, all anybody needs to know is what I've just said.'

He smiled at Shay and sat back down satisfied. 'There, that will give them something to gossip about until Christmas,' he laughed.

'Not everyone's going to like it,' Niamh chaffed.

'That's their problem, not ours,' his reply was short.

'It was very brave,' I applauded him. 'Will you tell them who Shay's mom is?'

He shook his head. 'That is not my place, it is up to Shay or Moira.'

Shay nodded, grateful at his dad's discretion. 'I told Tash that I would not act like my mom's dirty little secret, to be hidden away but it's up to mam I'll go with whatever she says.'

'Some may guess,' Albie cautioned. 'We were discreet but there was still gossip.' He left out the part where it had driven his first wife nearly mad with the rumours around the village, still effecting her for a few years after Moira had left.

We settled down as our lunches arrived. 'I'm just glad it's all out in the open now,' Albie admitted.

'They are still looking at us though,' I glanced around the room.

'They have never seen such a good looking foursome,' Shay seemed perfectly relaxed and I was glad, I didn't have to worry about him now. With a chuckle I tucked into my roast beef.

'After lunch we'll take a walk around the village, I'll show you the house your mam grew up in,' Albie chatted.

'I'd like that,' Shay replied. 'I used to wonder about it. Mam told me things but it would be good to see for myself.'

'I do love this place,' Albie admitted. 'When I was the postman I had a bike, I had to go and deliver in the next village too.'

'Shay has a bike,' I interrupted. 'And he is going to kill himself on it.'

'No, I'm not,' he argued.

'Yes, you are,' I contradicted. 'You go to the pub on it.' I looked at Albie and Niamh. 'Honestly he and Dale are like a pair of big kids.'

'I'd like to meet your brother,' Albie had a smile on his face. 'He sounds good fun.'

'He is,' Shay agreed. 'One of the good guys.'

'Er my Dale?' I pulled a face.

'Yeah, 'he gave me his lovely smile. 'Tash brought him up. She was only ten when he was born but she acted as his mom.'

'Babe,' I warned, they didn't want to hear my sob story.

'No,' he shot me down. 'Everyone should know what an incredible woman you are. You were ten years old Tash and your mother left you to do everything for a new-born baby.'

I shrugged indifferently, noticing how quiet the pub had become. Conversations held in whispers, I cast another glance around the bar, people looking away as they caught my eye.

'You know this pub is called *The Monks Well*,' I speared a carrot with my fork.

They nodded at me.

'Well I don't think the monk *is* well judging by the look on people's faces,' I joked.

Shay smiled at me indulgently. 'It's certainly giving them something to talk about.'

'You know if you'd announced it in a pub in Wolverhampton where we live they would use it as an excuse to throw a party,' I pulled a face.

'Everyone would get hammered,' Shay agreed. 'Jaysus, I'm beginning to get a complex the way everyone is watching us.'

'It's that kind of village,' Niamh said sadly. 'They accused Albie of sneaking over to my house and staying the night when we were courting and he never did.'

It was on the tip of my tongue to say did it matter if he did but then I realised it did matter. Quin was a totally different ball game to where I'd been brought up.

'It was those holier than thou's at church stirring up the rumours,' Albie sounded vexed.

'You find that with religious people, they think they are all saints and everyone else is wrong,' Shay said darkly.

I grimaced, the only blot on the horizon, Shay had no time for religion. His dad looked a little hurt and he quickly recovered it. 'Sorry dad, I know the church is important to you but it's the one thing I can't share with you.'

Albie would have given him the world when he called him dad. 'We'll agree to disagree,' he replied with a soft smile.

'Sounds like a plan,' Shay finished his meal. 'Are we having desert?'

'I couldn't eat another thing,' I declared patting my very full tum.

'We can have another drink though can't we son?' Albie was enjoying himself.

Shay nodded going to stand but his dad stopped him. 'I'll get them.'

He went to the bar, not surprised to see his nearest neighbour, Rod, propping up the counter as he always did after mass. 'Albie,' he greet him. 'That was some announcement you made there.'

He shrugged ordering the drinks. 'It had to be said.'

'He looks in his early thirties,' Rod looked over to Shay. 'He would have been born a few months after Moira Flynn left the village. All those rumours flying around about the pair of you.'

Albie shot him a look. 'You should never listen to gossip. Anyway it was a long time ago.'

'Is she his mom though, Moira?' Rod pushed. 'She just upped and left without a word to anyone.'

Albie turned to him wearily. 'None of that matters. I won't have anyone saying a bad word about Moira. She was, is, a fine woman. Better than the majority of the people in this village.'

'No one would be surprised Albie,' he smiled. 'No one could understand her being alone, she was a beautiful woman.'

'She was,' he agreed. 'Smart too.'

'So are you going to tell me if you've been a naughty boy with the delightful Moira then?'

He picked up the drinks, declining to comment. 'Everything okay?' Niamh asked, her husband looked a little peeved.

'Rod was trying to find out if Moira was Shay's mam,' he pulled a face.

'And how did you answer?' she frowned.

'I didn't,' he shrugged.

Shay glared at Rod, who was still standing by the bar. He was going to let *no one* bad mouth his mother. 'Take no notice,' Albie advised. 'As you said it was no wonder Moira felt she had to leave.'

'You two have your drinks and then we'll go for that walk, I could do with some fresh air,' Niamh recommended.

I did feel sorry for her, she was being so good about everything and she must have felt like she'd had a ton of bricks dumped on her head. 'We will,' Albie replied and then changing the subject he said. 'So what did you two get up to while we were at church?'

Shay and I looked at each other trying not to giggle. 'Oh this and that,' he answered vaguely.

'Niamh and I had a chat and we want to buy you both something for the twins,' he smiled.

'We don't expect you to do that,' I said hurriedly. 'You've brought us enough already.'

'We want to help.' Niamh cut in.

'That's really nice of the two of you,' I was touched.

'We could buy the pram?' Albie sat back in his seat.

'That's kind but mam has already said that she's buying the pram,' Shay explained.

'The cots then,' she suggested. 'It would mean a lot to us.'

'Thank you,' Shay had a feeling that his dad was trying to make up for lost time. 'It's very kind.'

'Excellent,' Albie looked pleased, then he looked around the bar. 'Shall we have that walk? I'm tired of people staring at us.' We nodded and Shay finished his pint, without a backwards glance we walked into the sunny Sunday afternoon.

He walked a little ahead with his dad and Niamh and I followed. 'Are you sure you're okay with all of this?' I asked softly.

She looked at me openly. 'I'm a little worried Tash,' she admitted. 'Moira was the great love of his life, I never thought she would come up again.'

'You can really love someone but know it isn't what you need,' I was thinking about Sam. 'Moira loves Alan, not for one minute do I think they are going to fall into each other's arms like last time. I wouldn't have looked for Albie if I'd thought that.'

'I suppose not,' she replied as Albie halted outside a large white detached house. 'This is where Moira lived with her family.'

Shay stared at it. 'So in different circumstances this is where I'd have lived?'

Albie nodded. 'Moira, her parents and her dad's sister, aunt Sinead.'

'Aunt Sinead?' his mother had never mentioned her and he suddenly realised that he had family he knew nothing about.

His dad grunted. 'She still lives there. She won't speak to me, never has done. If I had to take her a parcel she would receive it without a word. I expect, looking back, she knew Moira was pregnant, it makes sense now.'

'Shall I knock on the door, I'd like to meet her,' Shay was ready to defend his mom, even after all these years.

Albie knew what he was thinking. 'She's in her nineties now, no age to be upsetting her.'

'Like you say she must have known about me. She could have fought my mam's corner, made her parents see sense.'

'She's a devout Catholic son,' he frowned. 'It was just her way.'

He scowled and I took his hand. 'It doesn't matter hun,' I soothed. 'The only thing that matters is what happens now.'

He stared at me for a moment. 'You're right.'

'I usually am,' I grinned reaching to kiss him.

'Let's get back home,' Albie steered us in the direction of the bungalow.

When we got inside I was surprised to see a woman in there with a girl of about ten whose hair was cut in the strangest style. 'Erin,' Niamh had a look of shock on her face.

'Where have you been?' she demanded. 'Alice and I have been waiting ages.'

Niamh looked a little uncomfortable. 'I said that we were going for lunch with Shay and Tash.'

'I thought you would be back earlier,' she complained looking both of us up and down.

Niamh grimaced. 'Anyway we're here now. This is Shay and Tash,' she introduced us. 'This is my daughter Erin and granddaughter Alice.'

'Hello,' I said politely. She had one of those pinched faces that never found joy in anything. She looked like she had a bad smell under her nose, permanently. I could tell straight away that she wasn't going to welcome us with open arms.

'Good to meet you Erin,' Shay put on his best smile, in a roundabout way she was his stepsister, well kind off and he was going to make an effort.

She grimaced a hello as Albie pulled a face behind her back.

'What has Alice done to her hair?' Niamh was looking at her granddaughter who promptly burst into tears.

'I've cut it for her,' Erin's reply was short.

'You can't leave it like that,' she cried alarmed. 'All the children will have her life.'

'Its fine,' she dismissed her mother.

It truly wasn't fine, the sides were uneven, the fringe cut at an angle and there was literally chunks out of it. 'Hmmm,' I hesitated then decided to go for it. 'I could tidy it up for her.'

Erin glared at me. 'It's fine,' she repeated.

'Oh Erin don't be so rude,' Niamh scolded. 'Tash is a qualified hairdresser, let her cut it properly.'

Her granddaughter was looking at me hopefully and I gave her my best smile. 'Would you like me to cut your hair sweetheart?' I asked.

She nodded rapidly. 'See,' Niamh looked pleased. 'Sit on one of the kitchen chairs Alice. What do you need Tash?'

'A sharp pair of scissors and a towel please.'

'I'm perfectly capable of cutting my own daughter's hair,' she snapped.

'But as everyone can see, you are not,' Albie shook his head.

I cast a quick glance at Shay, it wasn't the best of starts but I couldn't let the poor mite go to school looking like she'd had her hair cut by a hedge trimmer. Erin pursed her lips as I draped a towel around Alice's neck.

'You can trust Tash,' Shay tried to smooth the waters. 'She's the best hairdresser I know.'

She actually smiled at him or it could have been wind. So she was one of those woman, had no time for the female of the species but plenty of time for the male. I turned my attention to Alice. 'You've lovely hair sweetheart,' I chatted checking it over, I was going to have to cut it quite short. I looked at Niamh. 'I'm going to have to take a lot off.'

'Do what you have to do,' she was ignoring Erin.

Shay and Albie had settled in the living room on the single malt again as Erin watched me closely. 'So are you and Shay going to get married?'

'No,' I pulled a face, concentrating on the job in hand. What was it to her? 'We're happy as we are.'

'But you are pregnant,' the look she gave me was one of utter disapproval.

'So?' I drew out the word, checking Alice's hair.

'The bible says,' she began.

'No offence Erin,' I jumped in quickly. 'I respect anyone's beliefs but yours are not mine. Shay and I are perfectly fine as we are, more than fine in fact. We don't need a certificate to prove it.' I had a feeling I was being a little rude but hey-ho.

She pursed her lips, turning on her heel and going into the living room. 'Sorry Niamh,' I said. 'I think I've upset her.'

She waved her hand at me, motioning to Alice so I clamped my mouth shut. I didn't need Alice repeating things to her mom. In silence I worked my magic, finishing her hair which I had cut into an elfin style and it really suited her.

'Go and look in the mirror,' her Nan instructed. She did, her face breaking into a big smile as she saw how pretty she looked.

'Thank you Tash,' Niamh touched my arm as Alice went in search of her mom. 'You must let me pay you.'

'No,' I screwed up my face. 'I don't want paying. You're family, I can cut your hair.'

Niamh looked at me delighted. 'Family,' she echoed. 'I like the sound of that.'

'Me too,' I admitted with a grin, they really were a wonderful couple. 'I am sorry if I've upset Erin.'

'It's just different views on life. I have to admit I would love you and Shay to be married with you having the wee one's and I do struggle to understand why you don't want to be but I do respect it.'

'It wouldn't do for us all to be the same,' I smiled going to seek out the others as Niamh swept up the hair. Alice was sitting between Shay and Albie, a big smile on her face. 'How's that sweetheart?' I asked settling in the chair.

'I like it, thank you,' she was such a well-mannered little girl, a real poppet.

'You are very welcome,' I beamed, aware that Erin did not like me one bit. 'Do you mind if I get a glass of water please?' I asked Niamh as she came into the room, I had heartburn again. Oh the joys of being pregnant.

'Go and help yourself,' she replied.

I did, going into the kitchen and finding me a glass, then jumping in surprise at Erin standing directly behind me. 'He hasn't got any money you know,' she informed me bluntly.

I turned on the tap, filling the half the glass. 'Sorry,' I forced my voice to be polite.

'Albie, he has no money if that's what you are after. He was only a postman,' she said the word with disdain.

I turned slowly. 'Nothing wrong with being a postman, we all need mail,' I said through gritted teeth, snobby cow. 'Money hadn't even entered out heads Erin.'

'Hasn't it?' she challenged. 'If you think for one minute that there is some juicy inheritance at the end of all of this then you are sadly mistaken.'

'Oh my God,' I gasped. How dare she! I was tired of always being polite to people, of always keeping the peace. Plus my hormones were all over the place.

'Don't take His name in vain,' she had to a pious tone to her.

I turned on her angrily. 'Shay just wants to know his dad and his dad wants to know him,' I cried squaring up to her. 'You know nothing about us. Money is the last thing on our minds.'

'You come here, not the least bit ashamed that you are having those children out of wedlock.'

I didn't let her get any further, she was not going to bring my morals into the equation. 'Stop right there Erin,' I spat out the words. 'Leave us be or you'll regret it.'

'You jezebel,' she wasn't about to back down. 'Parading yourself about with a much younger man, do you have no decency?'

'Enough,' I warned. 'You may think you have the moral high ground with your direct line to God but it doesn't make you a better person than me. Take your archaic opinions and stick 'em where the sun don't shine.' I pushed past her using my shoulder with a little more force than I strictly needed to.

I was fed up, what was it with people? Fallon had taken an instant dislike to me when she had started dating my brother and now Erin. I must have one of those faces. I didn't get it though, I was a really nice person who would do anything for anyone. It just wasn't fair.

I set my face in a smile as I went back into the living room, acting if nothing had gone on. They need never know about our little exchange unless Erin opened her gob.

So we spent the next couple of hours awkwardly with Erin jumping down my throat at every opportunity and laughing like a hyena at Shay's jokes. She was a clever woman, she couldn't be rude to Shay because that would upset Albie and for some reason she didn't want to do that at all but I was a different matter. Like I said she was a cow. I was glad when she announced it was time to take Alice home.

When we were alone Niamh turned to me. 'Sorry about that,' she looked mortified.

'You are not to worry,' I said charitable. 'Everyone's entitled to their opinion.'

'She is just like her father,' she said darkly. 'He could be a righteous fecker too.'

Shay guffawed, relaxing back in his seat. 'Alice is a little sweetheart though.'

'She is,' she agreed, brightening. 'Anyway, tea and cake anyone?'

We all said yes and we spent another agreeable evening in their company. By the time we retired to our lodgings I was exhausted. 'It was another good day,' Shay threw off his coat. 'Pity Erin had to turn up though. Fancy cutting her daughter's hair like that, good job you could put it right. I don't think Erin appreciated your intervention though.'

'Erin is a fucking cow,' I swore.

He looked at me immediately alert. 'What happened?'

'Nothing,' I replied making a big deal of putting my nightclothes on.

'Tash,' he warned.

I sat on the bed wincing. 'She thinks that we are after Albie's money.'

'She what?' He did not look happy.

'Oh don't worry I soon put her right, the absolute cheek of that bloody woman,' I fumed. 'And she called my morals into question, being pregnant out of wedlock with a younger man. I notice she never said one word to you.'

'That's because she fancied me,' he laughed.

'What?' my head shot up.

He came to sit on my bed, leaning against me. 'She wanted me,' he whispered furtively. 'I could tell. She wanted me to take her there and then in front of the hearth.'

'Delusional is what you are,' I gave him a pitying look.

'Don't you believe me? She wanted me to bang the back out of her,' he used one of Dale's favourite sayings.

'Whatever love,' I tapped his hand.

He gave me a sly look. 'I bet she would marry me if I asked her.'

I dug him painfully in the ribs. 'Stop it,' I warned. 'I'm glad I put her right though, I'm not going to let anyone walk over me anymore.'

He gave me a loving look. 'My feisty little fecker,' he praised. 'No one is going to mess with you now.'

'They are not,' I granted.

He got up going to the bathroom. 'She's not worth it beautiful.'

'No,' I ran my hand over my bump. 'We have more important things to concern ourselves with.'

He popped his head around the door. 'Exactly,' he agreed.

Thirty~Eight

We left Quin early the next morning, going to say our goodbyes to Albie and Niamh with promises to keep them updated on my pregnancy and inviting them to visit us. I think Niamh was nervous about coming over to England, a little worried at the thought of Albie possibly seeing Moira again, which I could understand.

I felt quite sad leaving them, as I said, I liked them a lot. Shay too seemed content as if meeting his dad was the final piece of his jigsaw. I was pleased for everyone. Moira and Alan came for a bite to eat as arranged and although there was a slight uneasiness on Moira's part I'm positive that between Shay and myself we aligned her fears.

Shay loved his mom with such devotion, she truly had nothing to fear. She laughed when he told her what a horror Erin was. 'At least I have a wonderful daughter-in-law,' she twinkled at me and I was chuffed, she always called me that.

I wasn't at work on the Tuesday either, I was using the last of my holidays before I went on maternity leave, which was approaching at an alarming rate. Before we blinked the twins would be leaving school.

For a change we decided to go shopping in Stafford, the Queens Shopping Centre to be precise. Shay was getting fed up of going into Wolverhampton. To be honest the weekend had really tired me out but I was determined not to let the pregnancy rule me.

'Okay?' he asked for the tenth time since we had arrived.

I smiled taking his hand. 'I would be if you'd stop asking me if I was alright,' I replied lightly.

'Noted,' he gave me his beautiful smile as we wandered around the shops buying more things for the babies.

I had a couple of new bras too, although they looked more like surgical contraptions then sexy lingerie. Unfortunately though needs must. 'Shall we get you some new clothes as well?' he asked knowing that fitting into anything I had was beginning to be a struggle.

'I don't want to spend money on new stuff that I'm only going to wear for a few weeks.'

'You need new things,' he argued. 'Unless you're planning on walking round naked for the last few weeks of your pregnancy.'

I admitted defeat and went into Matalan where I picked up the first jogging bottoms and oversized t-shirts I could find. I really had no interest.

'Don't you want something pretty?' he frowned.

'What's the point?' I pulled a face. 'I don't feel pretty.'

'You look gorgeous to me,' he contradicted.

I gave him an indulgent look. 'You have to say that. I'll buy something pretty after I've given birth.'

'Sexy underwear?' he asked hopefully, a cheeky grin on his face.

'Love,' I began softly. 'Do you really think that when you have watched me giving birth to twins you are still going to find me sexy?'

'Yes,' he answered hurt. 'You've never quite got that part have you?' He leant into me. 'I fancy you rotten.'

I smiled in spite of myself. 'Sexy underwear it is then.'

'Excellent,' he kissed my hand before veering off in another direction.

'What's caught your eye?' I followed him.

'Just browsing,' he looked through the shelves in the baby section holding up a cute outfit of shorts and a long sleeved top for a boy. 'Aw look.'

'How do you know we're having a boy?' I enquired. 'We could have two girls.'

He put his arm around my shoulder. 'My great, great, great, great grandmother was a wise woman who lived in the woods just outside of Quin. They say she had second sight and I have it too.'

'You do talk a load of blarney,' I shook my head laughing.

'It's true,' he cried. 'Gypsy Rose Flynn, biggest hooped earrings you have ever seen. I'm just like her and I predict we will have a boy and a girl.'

'Or we could have two boys,' I pointed out.

'Let's have a wager. I say a boy and a girl.'

'What, we're having bets?' I watched him closely, he was so lovely.

'If I'm right you have to do a slow striptease for me.'

'And if I'm right?'

'Then I'll do one for you,' his eyes twinkled.

'What again?' I pulled his leg. 'Okay deal, I say two girls.

He spat on his hand holding it out. 'Shake on it then.'

I did laughing, the sound dying in my throat. 'Sweet?' he was looking at me puzzled.

I frowned slightly. 'I'm sure I've just seen Sam with a young woman.'

He looked around the store. 'I can't see him.'

'I'm sure it was,' it was not any of my business but to be fair I was naturally nosey or curious as I liked to say.

'Perhaps it's that girl he's having an affair with?' he suggested.

'Could be,' I agreed as we placed more baby clothes in the basket, all in neutral colours just to be on the safe side. 'Can we stop for a coffee?' I needed my caffeine fix.

'I don't like you drinking coffee.'

'One a day isn't going to hurt,' he was such an old woman. I paid for it after though, the twins got their caffeine shot and it felt like they were having a disco in my tummy.

'Let's pay for these then and I'll take you to Costa's.'

'You are so good to me.'

'And don't you forget it sweetheart,' he put on an American accent.

I grinned as we joined the queue to pay. 'Dad gave me a cheque to buy the cots,' he chatted.

I shot him a look of mock alarm. 'See Erin was right, you are after him for his money.'

He ignored me. 'Shall we pop into Mothercare after our coffee?'

'We can do,' I leant against him.

'Do we get one big cot or two?'

'Two, you can buy them so they turn into beds when they are old enough,' I replied. 'I think the bedroom will be ample big enough. I can't believe we are going to be parents even though I'm the one carrying them.'

'Do you think they'll look alike?' he mused.

'Hard to tell when they are non-identical, I hope so though.'
We paid for our purchases and retired to Costa's, my feet singing.

'I'll finish the nursery this weekend,' he promised as we
settled at the table.

'Thank you,' it was good to take the weight off my feet. 'Do
you think if I wasn't pregnant we'd still be together?'

'Tash,' he warned.

'I'm curious,' I beamed.

'Of course we would. I've told you before when you asked
me to move in that once I did I would never leave. It's you that I
love, who I want to be with, the twins are a wonderful bonus.'

'That is a lovely thing to say,' my eyes filled with tears.

'I am lovely,' he grinned. 'So once we get the pram and the
cots I think we are done,' he was mentally crossing things off his
list.

'We are,' I confirmed. Moira's spare room, Shay's old
bedroom was full to bursting. I was being very superstitious not
wanting much at our place in case we jinxed it. The twins had so
many booties, hats and jackets thanks to Moira's knitting it was
unbelievable. I think it kept her from being nervous about the
wedding. All you could hear when you went round was the click-
clack of the knitting needles.

I was at the doctors again the following day and I had to
admit I was getting a tad nervous. At my age they had to monitor
me so closely it was a little stifling. They were talking about giving
me a caesarean section but I really didn't want one but I had to be
guided by them.

'Have you decided on an outfit for mam's wedding?' Shay
poured brown sugar into his coffee.

I shook my head, at the size I was growing I would need a
tent. 'I haven't the heart to look yet.'

'You have to have something nice for the wedding.'

'Don't worry I will, I won't turn up in my jogging bottoms
and t-shirt,' I was slightly put out. 'I won't let you down.'

'I didn't mean it like that. What is it?'

I was sitting upright in my seat like a Meerket. 'Sam,' I
hissed.

'Where?' he scowled, he couldn't see what I could, he had
his back to the room.

'He's just walked in with her, so I did see him earlier.' I knew I hadn't seen things. 'It must be that Kate Bishop who lives by my customer.'

'Really?' He swivelled around in his chair. 'Bloody hell, he's taking a chance isn't he?'

'He wouldn't dream for one moment that anyone he knew would be shopping in Stafford on a Tuesday afternoon.'

Shay was watching him openly. 'Will you look at the brass neck of him, has he no shame?'

I was looking at him, he was sitting next to her, all touchy-feely. 'The absolute balls of your man,' he muttered.

'He's not my man,' I retorted, hurrying to finish my coffee. 'He'll crawl up his own arse if he sees us.' I was getting an idea.

'What are you up to beautiful?' Shay was starting to know me so well.

I smiled in reply, sorting out my bags. 'Have you drunk your coffee?'

'Tash,' he warned good-humouredly, but he drained his cup. 'Leave it.'

I began to walk to Sam so Shay had no option but to follow. The look on my ex-husbands face was absolutely priceless as I stopped by his table. 'Hi Sam,' I greeted him pleasantly.

'Tash,' he went pale. 'What are you doing here?' he asked as his friend looked at us with curiosity.

'Shopping for the babies,' I indicated to the bag. 'How about you?'

He looked a little sheepish. 'Just having a coffee.'

'Nice,' I murmured. 'And how is your lovely wife and gorgeous daughter?'

He shot me a look of pure venom as I carried on. 'Sorry, I haven't introduced myself,' I gave his companion a smile. 'I'm Tash, Sam's ex-wife, mother of his two eldest children. He kept cheating on me though so we got divorced. Never could keep it in your trousers could you sweetheart?'

She had gone ashen and he looked livid. 'You live by one of my customers,' I tilted my head to one side. 'You're Kate Bishop aren't you?'

She nodded mutely.

'Tash,' Shay tugged at my arm. 'Time to go.' If Sam started anything he *would* fight him again.

'Coming,' I gave him a brilliant smile. 'See you Sam, love to Meera and Safi, although I might see them first so I'll pass on that I've seen you.' With that I swanned out of the coffee bar.

'You enjoyed that didn't you?' Shay laughed.

'Every second,' I admitted. 'Let him stew a little thinking I might tell Meera.' I wouldn't though, she would think I was trying to cause trouble. Let Sam wrestle with him own conscience.

'He is going to be shitting himself,' Shay predicted.

'Good,' I retorted with a snort. 'He shouldn't have kept provoking you when all we did was get together and you tried to build a relationship with Jamie.'

'Aw sweet, I'm touched that you were doing it on my account,' he grinned as we walked to the car. 'Jamie and I are getting on better. This time next year we'll be the best of buddies.'

'I hope so,' it was Jamie's birthday on Thursday and he was having his first driving lesson on Saturday.

'Trust me,' he tone was confident as he put the shopping in the truck.

Thursday arrived, a damp summer's day, it had rained when I was in labour with Jamie, that really long labour that was seared into my brain and making me nervous about what was to come.

I sat thinking about it at work as I waited for my first customer. I had called Jamie, he was still in bed but he did answer begrudgingly. At least he was excited about starting his apprenticeship soon.

'Hey babe,' Bev bustled into the salon with Carling and Millie.

'You're both late,' I rebuked.

'Sorry miss,' Bev was in a good mood. 'Carling make a brew.'

'Okay, do you want one Tash?' she asked.

'Please hun,' I stifled a yawn, I was shattered.

'How did it go at the docs?' I made Bev yawn too.

'Great, everything as it should be,' I replied thankful.

'Dale and I are going to move in together,' she cried, clapping her hands together.

'Yay!' I applauded her as Millie decided to give me a love, she really missed me – not. 'When?'

'In a couple of weeks,' she giggled like a schoolgirl.

'That's brilliant, I'm really pleased for the both of you.' And I was, Bev had loved Dale for years although I never approved of the fact that they were carrying on behind her husband's back.

'I feel positively dizzy,' she laughed as Carling came in with the teas.

'And how about you Carling?' Bev did look so happy. 'How's your fella, Aaron?'

'Just perfect,' she answered dreamily. 'I'm so lucky.'

'He's lucky,' I corrected her with a smile, we were getting on really well at the moment.

'Aw thanks hun,' she rubbed my tummy, she did it every time she saw me, she said it brought her luck.

'Now,' Bev tapped a pen against her mug. 'Before the hoards descend on us I want to call a staff meeting.'

'About what?' I was immediately curious.

'You go on maternity leave in three weeks Tash.'

'Correct,' I knew that.

'When you do come back after nearly a year away you are just going to do Thursday's, Friday's and Saturday's.'

'Correct,' I repeated, there was no way I could come back full time. The cost of childcare was horrendous. As it was Moira had insisted on having them Thursday's and Friday's with Shay picking up the reigns on a Saturday's if he wasn't needed at the garage, it was a nightmare.

'We're getting quite busy now, word of mouth is a wonderful thing,' she continued. 'We won't manage with just Carling and myself.'

'So what's your solution?' I enquired.

'Do you remember Kim Roberts?'

'The mobile hairdresser from Bloxwich?' I did vaguely. She was a nice enough woman but a bit high maintenance.

'Well she is going to come and help while you're on maternity leave full time and when you come back to work she will come in part time unless we really need her,' Bev looked pleased with herself. 'Oh and now Carling is fully qualified I'm bringing in a new junior.'

A little of my insecurities kicked in, the silly part of me felt pushed out.

'Tash?' A look of perplexity crossed her face.

I rallied a little. 'It's a good idea but Kim comes under Carling, she's earnt her stripes.'

'Of course, it's only to help me out,' she frowned slightly.

'Thanks Tash,' Carling whispered a huge grin on her face before going to the loo.

'Everything okay?' Bev asked me concerned.

'Yeah, it's just me being daft,' I blushed a little.

'I still need you babe,' she could read me like a book. 'I'm not going to replace you, you're a better hairdresser than me and the customers adore you.'

'I know I'm being daft,' I tapped her hand.

'What are you like? Do you think Shay will help Dale move, get those two gypo's he knows to move some of his stuff in their truck?'

'I should think so, I'll ask him. He and Shay are helping Moira move too. Everything's changing.'

'Dale said he was helping, its August isn't it?'

I nodded. 'Moira wanted to move in before the wedding but not too early so people wouldn't gossip.'

'I don't think they would,' she pulled a face.

'No, people aren't that small minded around here but it bothers her.'

'Oh bless,' we were all fond of Shay's mom. 'Like you said though, everything is changing. I never thought Dale and I would live together.'

'I never thought I'd be a mom of twins at forty-three,' I mused.

'And I never thought that I would be head stylist,' Carling joined us, beaming.

'Don't push it,' Bev retorted grimly.

Thirty~Nine

Meanwhile over at Ray's garage Alison was on reception trying desperately not to yawn, her husband had kept her awake all night snoring. She could remember a time when they stopped awake all night for something else but not anymore.

She clicked more keys on her keyboard, she had worked for Ray for nearly twelve years and she loved it, the boys were a good bunch and the boss wasn't too bad either. The door opened and in walked a woman in her early thirties, long blonde hair, done up to the nine's and head to foot in designer clothes.

'Can I help you?' Alison asked politely.

'I brought my car in yesterday and I just wanted to thank the mechanic who fixed it,' she held aloft a bottle of expensive wine.

Alison narrowed her eyes, who brought a mechanic a bottle of wine when they were just doing their job and been paid for the pleasure. She could guess which mechanic she had come to sniff around – Shay.

'What car was it?' she asked curtly.

'BMW Z4,' she replied with a smile that said she *always* got what she wanted.

Alison checked on the computer, pursing her lips before opening the door that connected the office area to the garage. 'Shay!' she bawled. 'Customer to see you.

He came through, wiping his hands on an oily rag as Alison made herself scarce.

'Hi Shay,' the blonde trilled. 'I just wanted to thank you for doing such a good job on my car.'

He frowned slightly, alarm bells ringing. 'You don't have to do that, it's what I get paid for.'

'I love your accent,' she gave a false coy smile. 'My name's Amelia and I was wondering if you would like to go for a drink sometime. Tonight maybe?'

'Thank you but no,' he answered quickly.

Her smile slipped. 'Sorry?'

'It's kind of you to ask but I can't,' he was wishing Alison would come back.

'Tomorrow night?' She tapped a manicured nail on the desk.

'I have a girlfriend,' he frowned again.

'So?' she raised an eyebrow. 'It would just be a drink,' she looked him up and down liking what she saw. 'And possibly anything else we can think off.'

He'd had enough of women like this to last him a lifetime, he much preferred Tash with her bashful ways. 'I'm very happy with my girlfriend,' he said, relieved when Nick came into the office.

'Alright?' he winked at Shay, Alison had told them all of his visitor.

Shay seized his chance. 'If you want to share a bottle of wine with a mechanic then I'm sure Nick would oblige.' With that he nipped back into the garage.

'What are women like today?' Alison tutted. 'She looked like she wanted to eat you all up.'

'I've left Nick with her,' he shuddered. 'Why would she come onto me like that when I only fixed her car?'

'Because you are gorgeous with a sexy accent,' Rob told him. He was the straightest gay man that Shay had ever met.

'So Tash tells me,' he shook his head.

Nick joined them, rubbing his shaved head. 'She moves quickly that one when you offer to give her one.'

'You've got Rachel,' Alison clipped him around the ear.

'I'm joking,' he rubbed it tenderly. 'Here Shay, she left the wine, she forget to take it with her in her haste to get out. Take it for you and Tash.'

'Tash can't drink at the moment,' he replied so glad his dating days were over, he would never cope now.

'Keep it for after she's dropped the sprogs,' he thrust the bottle at Shay. 'It's good stuff.'

He took it reluctantly as Ray came to stand by him. 'I'd have given her one,' he dodged out of the way of Alison's hand.

He pulled a face. 'I'm more than happy with Tash thank you.'

'Never thought I'd see the day when you were settled. Talking of your beloved go and get your surprise for her then,' Ray was extremely fond of the Irishman.

He nodded his thanks, heading for the truck.

I was just sorting out my hospital case when he came in, I was being a little premature but I did so like to be prepared. 'Beautiful,' he cried waltzing me around the kitchen. 'Come outside.'

'Why?' I asked as he took my hand and I followed him up the path frowning. 'Where's your truck?'

'Ta-da!' He threw open his arms.

'What?' I looked around confused.

He clicked his tongue impatiently. 'The car,' he pointed to the big silver thing next to him.

I frowned, still not understanding.

'It's our family car,' he cried. 'It's perfect. Vauxhall Astra estate, only two years old, just the thing for when the twins are here. We'll get all their stuff in it.'

'Where's your truck?' I repeated, hoping he hadn't done what I thought he had done.

'I part exchanged it for this,' he so pleased with himself.

'But you love that truck,' I protested but I was touched.

'I love you more,' he cut in. 'I want you to be safe, I want you to be able to get all the things we need for the twins in there. You have the Astra and I'll go to work in your old Clio. In the summer I can ride my bike to work, it'll keep me fit.'

My eyes filled with tears. 'Thank you,' I whispered. When I had fallen pregnant with Lexi I had to beg Sam on my knees to give up his two-seater sports car for something more suitable and here was Shay doing it without me even having to mention it. They truly were polar opposites.

'Do you like it?' he opened the door. 'It has all the kit on, air con, heated seats, CD player, USB port, hands free,' he paused looking at me.

I kissed him deeply before climbing into the driver's seat. It did feel nice with its leather upholstery, perfect for cleaning with babies and that lovely new car smell.

'It's just the job isn't it?' he said unsurely.

'I love it, you really are good to me aren't you?' I smiled softly.

'I want to be,' he caressed my cheek.

'Nice car mom,' Jamie appeared from behind Shay.

I scrambled out of the car. 'Love, happy birthday,' he allowed me to hug him. 'Hello Abbie.'

'Hello Mrs Turner,' she said shyly.

'Tash please,' I smiled, I wanted her to feel welcome.

'Where's your truck?' Jamie asked Shay.

'Part ex'd it for this baby,' he replied. 'So your mam isn't struggling when she takes the babies out.'

Jamie looked disappointed, he'd really wanted a driving lesson in the truck. 'Come inside,' I fussed as Shay locked the car.

They followed me into the house, sitting at the kitchen table. 'Have you eaten?' Shay asked them and they both shook their heads in unison. 'Shall we have a takeaway for you birthday, my treat.'

'That's a good idea,' I loved Shay for trying his hardest with Jamie. 'What shall we have? Let the birthday boy decide,' I was pleased he had chosen to drop in on his birthday.

'KFC?' he asked hopefully.

'KFC it is,' Shay picked up the car keys. 'Family feast?'

'Yeah,' I liked the sound of that, I so wanted us to be a family again.

'Tash, we've brought you something for the twins,' Abbie passed me the carrier bag she was holding.

I peered inside, taking out two identical teddy bears dressed in tops that read *My First Teddy Bear* on each one. 'Oh, thank you, they are lovely.' I gave her a hug, Jamie side-stepping me, he'd already allowed me one today.

'They're great,' Shay agreed. 'Thank you both, that's really kind.'

'Would you like me to help you fetch the KFC?' Abbie shot a look at me and then at Jamie.

Shay nodded, figuring out that Jamie needed some time alone with his mom. 'I'd love some company, we'll test drive the new car.'

'Do you need money?' This was better than I could have hoped for, seeing Jamie on his birthday and us all sitting down for a meal.

'I'm good,' he tapped his back pocket leading Abbie to the car.

I waited until they had gone before turning to Jamie. 'Abbie's a lovely girl.'

He nodded embarrassed. 'Yeah.'

'I hope you're being careful though.' I couldn't cope with being a new mom and a grandmother at the same time.

'Mom,' he grimaced.

'Never mind mom,' I cut in. 'Is she on the pill or are you using condoms?' I didn't want to think about it but we'd all done it at their age. It didn't seem five minutes since the only thing he was interested in was his Xbox.'

'We're using condoms,' he looked mortified.

'Just don't buy them from the pound shop like I did,' I pointed to my stomach. 'We don't want another accident.'

He began to giggle and we eyed each other amused and then I was joining in. I hugged him to me and he didn't resist. 'I love you baby boy,' I planted a smacker on his cheek. 'I'll always love you.'

'Mom,' he wiped it away.

I grew serious. 'You know you can come home anytime you want, your room will always be here.'

'I'm okay, I'm nearer Abbie at dads,' he stopped, frowning.

'What's up?' I asked.

'I think dad is up to his old tricks,' he confided.

'Why?' My stomach dropped, Jamie should not have to go through this again.

'He and Meera keep arguing, she thinks he's got someone else.'

I knew he had but I kept schtum, the complete and utter bastard. 'Please Jamie, come home.'

'I want to make sure Safi's okay,' he replied. 'I know she's only a kid but she can tell that something is wrong.'

'You're a good brother, I hope you feel the same about the twins when they are here,' he didn't answer and I didn't push it. 'I mean it love, you can always come back here if it gets too much.'

He cast me a sideways glance. 'Shay wouldn't like that.'

'He really wouldn't mind, he likes you,' I countered. 'He would love for you both to get on and so would I.'

'He's alright,' he conceded. 'And you are happy aren't you mom? Dad never really made you happy did he?'

I was surprised at his insight. 'I was too scared that he would have another affair,' I wasn't going to pretend otherwise any longer.

He nodded staring at the top of the table. 'Lexi and I have been talking.'

Good old Lexi, whatever she had to him and with Abbie's influence little Jams, as Dale called him, was finally growing up.

'I can remember some of it,' he continued and I let him. 'Mostly the rows you had.'

'I'm sorry angel that I put you both through it,' and I was, I should have thrown Sam out when he had his first affair, not his third.

He looked at me frankly. 'It wasn't you though was it? You never went off with anyone else.'

'No,' I admitted. 'I just wanted us to be a family, that's all.'

'Abbie and me are going to Moira's wedding. Abbie said it's important that we go.'

'She's right. Moira will be over the moon,' I was happy too. 'She thinks you're wonderful.'

He smiled pleased. 'She is nice. Lexi say's that Shay's dad is nice too.'

'Albie is lovely,' I agreed. 'You'll meet him when he comes to visit.'

'I just wanted you and dad to get back together.'

'I know love, but I couldn't, not after all he had done.'

'Dad got really drunk the other night and told me what he had done to you. He still loves you mom.'

'It's not proper love,' I pulled a face. 'It's more like wanting to own something.'

He nodded understanding. 'We're not going to Thailand now, dad said that none of us deserve to go.'

I cringed. If I saw Sam again I would throttle him, he was like a spoilt child.

'I'm not really bothered though, they would spend the two weeks arguing and Safi would be upset. He's a bastard isn't he mom?'

'He's your dad,' I stated softly.

'Sometimes I don't like him very much,' he confessed.

'That's fine as long as you still love him,' I ruffled his hair.

'Meera always says that you are too nice, that no one can be as good as you.'

'And what do you think?' I frowned.

'I think that you are,' he gave me a lovely smile. 'I know you can be that nice.'

'That's sweet,' I took his hand as Shay and Abbie returned with the KFC.

'So,' Shay came into the kitchen giving me the food to sort and joining Jamie at the table. 'Your first driving lesson on Saturday then?'

He nodded, so very excited.

'Why don't you meet me at the garage at five on Friday and I'll give you a go in the Clio?'

'Will it be safe?' I fretted.

'There's a huge forecourt, I'll get him driving round, doing the gears and steering,' he assured me going to the fridge to get them all a bottle of lager and ignoring my disapproving look. 'Doesn't Lexi want to learn to drive?'

'She's never been fussed, I hope she changes her mind though,' I replied.

'She will,' he sounded confident.

'I can't wait,' Jamie drank his lager eagerly.

'Right,' Shay sat back at the table raising his bottle. 'Happy birthday Jams.'

'Happy birthday,' we echoed, tucking into our feast.

Forty

On the twenty-eighth of August, a month before I was due to give birth to the twins I was going to turn forty-three, how shit was that? I was heading for my mid-forties whilst Shay was only in his mid-thirties. It would be better if he was going to give birth, after all he had youth on his side.

Kim, the mobile hairdresser, had come into the salon this week to find her feet and get in the routine. She was a nice enough woman but she was a few years younger than me and still enjoyed going clubbing and having meaningless flings here, there and everywhere so I had little in common with her.

Carling on the other hand seemed to get on famously with her and Bev too seemed pleased with her choice, it was just me being a little jealous. It was now the last Saturday in July and also, coincidently, my last day at work. I could put it off no longer, I was starting my maternity leave.

I had to admit I was freaking out a tad about giving birth. I hadn't said anything to Shay, he was on cloud nine and nothing could bring him down. He had put up the cots, (thank you Albie and Niamh) and test driving all the prams, (thank you Moira and Alan) and basically not giving it a thought to how I'd got to push these two little miracles out of my fluff. He'd done the easy bit, he was there at the conception.

My own mom? I hadn't seen her since that day in the salon after dad had died. She hadn't got in touch and I hadn't the heart or the energy to go and see her.

I had finished at the salon at two o'clock all week, it was now impossible to be on my feet all day. My back ached and as the twins got bigger I found myself short of breath not to mention needing the loo every five minutes, or so it seemed. Plus my ankles and feet were swollen so I was living in my flip flops.

I could just about manage to do my customers hair, my bump kept getting in the way. I was becoming more of a hindrance than a help so it really was time to finish. On the plus side Jamie and Shay were finally getting on well. Shay had taken him out on a few driving lessons and although he always came back needing a large glass of whisky, he assured me that my son was making good progress.

Lexi and Belle had taken themselves off to Cornwall for a couple of weeks having a well-earned break before their last year at university, I hoped they both got their degrees, they had worked so hard.

'Ready?' Shay stood in the bedroom doorway, dressed casually in jeans and a black t-shirt, his lush curls scrapped into a man bun and a beard on his gorgeous face. A beard, that he had informed me, would not be shaved off until his mom's wedding.

'I'm ready,' I replied. He was taking me to work as I was finding driving uncomfortable. I had on my favoured black leggings and a maternity tunic that one of the old dears at the salon had given me, she had worn it herself when she was pregnant over forty years ago. I loved it, it was funky and vintage at the same time.

I heaved myself up and he smiled lovingly at me, he was being so attentive but last night –

Well last night I'd had a bath, while I could still manage it and afterwards I lay on the bed naked trying to cool down, we were having a run of really warm weather. Anyway, I digress, Shay had come into the bedroom to do his usual job of keeping my lady garden neat. It was something he had took on himself to do since we had gone to Ireland, I couldn't see to do it myself properly.

So last night he had tidied me up, declared it a work of art and then promptly gone back downstairs to watch television. I had lain there shocked. Never had he seen me naked on the bed before without at least having a ferk, but nothing.

I couldn't blame him, who'd want to shag a beached whale? It did unsettle me thought, I'd gotten it in my head that he was going off me, just like Sam had done.

'Last one in the car stinks,' he called childishly, knowing full well that I couldn't move very fast. By the time I'd levered myself into the car he was watching me with a big grin on his face. 'You stink,' he told me gleefully.

'Juvenile,' I muttered under my breath, trying to do up my seatbelt.

He grinned again, pulling away from the house. I was quiet on the journey to the salon, thinking about things. The nursery was all done, Dale had moved in with Bev and they seemed really happy. Moira was moving in with Alan in a couple of weeks and all the preparations for their wedding were done.

I'd even gotten myself an outfit, a stretchy maxi dress in a delicate shade of coffee that I could pretty up with accessories. All was rosy in the garden, or so it seemed.

'I'll pick you back up at two,' he parked in front of the salon.

'Do you still love me?' I asked softly.

He looked a little surprised. 'Of course I do?'

'Sure,' I was being silly.

He tilted towards me, his face tanned by the sun, he did look so gorgeous. 'To the moon and back,' he replied solemnly kissing me.

My heart lifted, then jumped as someone banged on my window. 'Get a room!' Carling and Kim were pulling funny faces at us.

Shay laughed as I opened the door and Kim helped me out. She was one of those people who acted like they had been your best friend for years even though she had only known you five minutes. Not that there was anything wrong with that, it was better than being a miserable cow.

We waved goodbye to Shay and he left the carpark tooting his horn. 'He is so gorgeous,' Kim told me. 'And so are you. Those babies are going to be a right pair of lookers.'

'Thank you,' it was a nice compliment.

I wondered if they had something nice planned for my last day? Maybe a banner or two wishing me luck or something like that but when I walked into the salon a big fat resounding nothing.

'Morning girls,' Bev made us a brew.

'Morning,' I mumbled, trying to hide my disappointment.

It was just business as usual and that was how the day went, no one mentioning the fact that it was my last day for months.

Shay arrived on the dot of two and I got my bag, going to standing by the reception desk. 'Well, bye then.'

'All the best Tash,' Kim called looking up from the perm she was doing.

'Yeah good luck babe,' Carling called brightly.

'I'll see you tomorrow,' Bev smiled, she and Dale were coming for lunch.

My face fell. 'Yeah, see you tomorrow.' I walked out to the car, trying not to get too upset.

'Good day beautiful?' he asked as I got in the car.

I shook my head. 'I'd thought they'd do something.'

'Who?' he frowned.

I pointed at the salon. 'Them lot. Sixteen years I've worked for Bev and all she said was see you tomorrow,' I was beyond disappointed. 'I'm good enough to cook bloody lunch though.'

'Never mind,' he gave me a sympathetic smile. 'I have to pop to Lidl before we go home, is that okay?'

'Fine,' I sulked. I sat in the car while he went inside, he seemed to take forever and I was getting more and more fed up. Then he was coming back, putting his mobile phone back into his jeans pocket.

'What have you been doing, buying up the whole shop?' I whinged.

'I've brought the girls some cakes as a thank you,' he put the bags in the boot.

'A thank you for what?' I scowled.

'Sweet,' he said patiently. 'Don't be in a mood. We'll drop them off at the salon and then I'll give you a nice foot rub when we get home.'

'Take me home first,' I didn't want to go back.

'It'll take five minutes,' he ignored the look I gave him as we headed back to my work.

'I'll stop in the car then,' I pouted when we arrived.

'You'll come in with me,' his voice was firm.

Reluctantly I followed him inside, grumbling under my breath as he pushed open the door.

'Surprise!' They all shouted and I jumped startled. Every inch of the salon was decorated with baby shower paraphernalia and all my regular customers were there, even Moira. They must have worked flat out after I had left.

I promptly burst into tears. 'Hey,' Bev put her arms around me. 'You're supposed to like it.'

'It's lovely,' I hiccupped. 'You load of bitches making me think you didn't care.'

'Of course we care,' she laughed. 'We wanted it to be a surprise and if you knew about it then it wouldn't be, would it?'

'I'll be back later to take you and mam home,' Shay grinned.

'Did you know?' I demanded.

He nodded his smile widening.

'You're not going are you?' Kim asked him. 'We thought you'd do us a turn as the stripper?'

His laugh was loud. 'I wouldn't want to put your husbands to shame,' he joked. 'See you soon,' he left to a cacophony of wolf whistles.

Moira too was laughing as she steered me to my chair. The badge she pinned on me said *MOM TO BE* and the sash that she had difficulty getting over my stomach read **WIDE *LOAD***. Plus they made me put on a headdress of dummies that Carling had fashioned.

I felt like a princess as platters of sandwiches and goodies magically appeared from the back room, along with numerous bottles of wine and one solitary carton of orange juice.

Once everyone had a glass of vino Bev called for order. 'Ladies, thank you so much for coming. We are here to give Tash the best send-off possible as she prepares to become a mother for the third, oh and fourth time, the crazy woman.'

Everyone laughed and I sat in my chair wishing that I could have a glass of wine and really let my hair down. 'I've known Tash for sixteen years when I first opened the salon in fact. She came for her interview with her then one year old son as she couldn't get anyone to babysit him and I nearly told her to sling her hook there and then.'

She paused feeling choked. 'But she won me over, the way she does everyone. By the end of the interview I was rocking Jamie to sleep on my lap.' Absently she wiped away a tear. 'That was the day I got the best friend that anyone could ask for. We've been through some shit ay we gal?'

I nodded my agreement. 'But many good times too and I have to say that I have never known Tash as contented as she is now and we have a gorgeous Irishman with twinkling eyes to blame for that, our Shay. Thank you Moira for giving birth to a wonderful man who has made my friend's life so happy.'

Moira tittered loudly and I smiled lovingly at her.

'Tash, as you may or may not know is a born mother, Jamie and Lexi, her two older children, are testament to that. Although

I've never quite forgiven Jamie for mixing all the hair dyes up when he was ten.'

'That woman's hair turned green,' I remembered pulling a comical face.

'I know you were unsure at first when you found out that you were pregnant babe but you and Shay are going to make fantastic parents. So I ask everyone to raise their glasses to Tash and Shay. God help them, they are going to need it.'

'Tash and Shay,' they all chorused.

'Can I say something?' Moira blushed getting to her feet.

'Of course,' Bev inclined her head graciously.

She cleared her throat a little nervously. 'The girls at the salon are just so nice, they took me under their wings when I first came in. You are all wonderful.'

'Yay!' Carling cheered.

'I knew that Tash was something special to Shay as soon as he met her, he never stopped fecking talking about her.'

The room went *Ah*.

'No seriously, he bored the fecking knickers off me about her,' she teased.

We all laughed. 'Tash was worried at first about the age gap but she is so perfect for my son. The pair of you are giving me one of the most precious things in the world, grandchildren,' she was making me tearful. 'And I just want to add that I am available for babysitting at a very reasonable hourly rate but only because you're family,' she finished.

'Nice one Shay's mom,' Kim cried.

She laughed softly. 'The pair of you are going to be such fantastic parents,' she raised her glass. 'To Tash, Shay and the two babies. I can't wait to meet you.'

'Tash, Shay and the two babies,' they echoed dutifully.

Carling and Kim disappeared into the back room as Moira hugged me tightly. 'You okay sweetheart?'

I nodded, wiping away my tears. 'What you said was just lovely.'

'I meant it,' she touched my cheek.

'Anyway,' Bev had the floor again. 'Despite the fact that you are always bloody here we have managed to have a collection for you and all the regulars have chipped in.' she stopped as Carling and Kim came back with two large boxes. 'Just a few things to let you know how much we all love you loads.'

I was crying again. 'For me?'

She nodded as I delved into the first box, it was rammed with everything the babies would need. Practical things like wipes, lotions, nappies etc. The second box was filled with a variety of baby clothes, plus things for mommy and daddy like alcohol, chocolates, pampering toiletries and for some unfathomable reason chocolate body paint.

Kim scooped it up giving me a wicked smile. 'I know I would if I had him at home,' she whispered making me laugh.

'Also,' Carling passed me a white envelope. 'A voucher for a three course meal at that posh restaurant in Trysell, it's valid for twelve months.'

'I'll babysit,' Moira called.

I got to my feet unsteadily. 'Thank you all so much, I'm a little overwhelmed. I don't deserve any of this.'

'Yes you do,' Bev cut in. 'And more.'

'You all make working here so much fun,' I caught my breath. 'You aren't just my customers, you're my friends as well. To us.'

We drank more wine, well I didn't, I was on the orange juice.

'Anyway enough of this,' Carling pushed the boxes to one side of the room. 'Time for the party games to begin.'

'Party games?' I repeated with a sinking feeling.

She nodded, making me sit at my station where on the mirror was a large cut out of a baby. 'We are going to play pin the dummy on the baby. You go first Tash.'

I groaned as they blindfolded me. 'I be that's not the first time is it Tash?' Kim teased. 'I bet Shay blindfolds you every night and re-enacts *Fifty Shades of Grey*.'

I blushed as Carling put the dummy in my hand and I stumbled about until I thought I had hit the mark. 'Bloody hell Moira,' Lin, (my basecoat and foils) said. 'Don't leave Tash alone with those poor babies.'

I pulled off the blindfold tittering, I had pinned the dummy to its bottom. The others took their turns, some doing better than others, as Bev put some music on and poured more wine. 'Are you having a good time?' she asked topping up my juice.

'I am,' I caught her hand. 'Thank you.'

She smiled playing the hostess to perfection, when everyone had tried their luck Carling announced it was time for the next game.

'What is it?' I asked intrigued.

'We need to divide into teams,' she produced numerous rolls of toilet paper. 'The team to put the best nappy on one of their members, using these, wins. Tash you are the judge and your decision is final.'

With much joviality I watched as they all tried to be the winning team, it was very entertaining. 'I should have worn me Tena ladies,' Babs, (cut and blow dry every four weeks), cried.

'Me too,' Bev was howling with laughter.

I announced the winner and the team was given extra glasses of wine. We played a few more games, I enjoyed that one with the sticky notes. You know the one I mean, you had to guess who was on it when it was stuck on your forehead.

We were all sitting around the room in high spirits, when Carling said leaning towards me with her eyes sparkling. 'We are going to have a little Q & A.'

'What?' I wished I wasn't the only sober one.

'You have to truthfully answer the questions we are going to ask you,' she explained.

'No,' I protested. 'I could imagine what kind of vein they would be in.

She gave me a stern look. 'You have to.'

'Right,' Kim got out a large piece of card. 'If you answer truthfully we can all have more wine.'

'Play nice Tash,' Lin heckled.

'Now,' she peered at the card. 'Did you fantasize about shagging Shay the first time you saw him?'

'Er his mom,' I pointed to Moira.

'Don't mind me,' she patted my hand. 'I'm as curious as everyone else.'

I blushed prettily. 'Answer the question Natasha,' Carling beamed.

I took a deep breath, my face burning. 'Yes,' I admitted.

'You owe me a fiver,' Carling said to Bev.

'You are never like that where blokes are concerned, you're much too sensible,' she thought it would be a sure bet.

I shrugged, grinning. 'Okay, second question,' Kim looked at the card. 'On a scale of one to ten how good is Shay in bed?'

'Er,' Bev interrupted. 'Are these questions for Tash or for your benefit?'

Kim laughed loudly. 'I'm sorry Tash and Moira but I so would. He is absolutely gorgeous.'

'So would I,' Carling admitted. 'Well not now he's with Tash obviously but when he first came into the salon. That night in Wolverhampton, remember Tash the first time we all went out with Dale and Shay. I don't know how you poured yourself into that dress but all the blokes were looking at you, you didn't look too bad for an old un. Shay kept sitting by you having a perv.'

'So how did you and Shay actually get together?' Babs wanted to know.

'Pissed on Irish whisky weren't you love?' Moira twinkled her eyes at me and I blushed redder. Did Shay tell his mom everything?

'She won't be the first to let alcohol rule her legs,' Tracy, (light trim), laughed.

'Oi,' I giggled. 'You make it sound so sordid.'

'Wasn't it?' she beamed.

I hesitated for a moment. 'At times,' I replied to whoops of delight from everyone.

'When did you realise you loved him though?' Moira was intrigued.

'The day after Dale's birthday,' I answered promptly on much safer ground. 'He came to mine hungover with a bunch of wilted flowers he had brought from the garage and I just realised that I was in love with him.'

Everyone sighed so I turned it round so they had to tell me how they fell in love with their other halves.

'So Bev, when did you fall in love with Dale?' Kim asked.

She looked at me unsurely and I gave her a brilliant smile. 'I've loved Dale forever,' she whispered. 'He's everything to me.'

'How sweet,' Carling sighed.

'He loves you too,' I told her.

She hugged me tightly and then we continued having our fun. By the time Shay came to pick me up we were all tiddly and I hadn't even had a drink! 'Look what everyone's brought us,' I showed him our gifts, his pupils dilating at the chocolate body paint.

'Aw thank you ladies, that is so kind,' he said and bless him he went to give each and every one of them a hug and a kiss.

Kim gave him a proper snog full on the lips and he came up for air alarmed. 'Sorry Tash, I couldn't resist.'

I smiled tightly, I'd make sure he washed that kiss off before he came near me. Moira and I piled in the car and as Shay drove us home Moira began to sing an Irish folk song in a low soothing voice.

'Are you hammered mam?' he looked in the rear-view mirror.

'Merry,' she retorted as we pulled up outside her house and she struggled to get out of the car.

'Can you manage?' I asked giggling still in my sash and headdress, I had never seen Moira drunk before.

'Yes. Shall I pop over Monday for coffee?' she swayed a little.

'Yes please,' I replied as she leant in to kiss my cheek.

Doing the same to her son she weaved up the path, Alan opening the door. They both waved their goodbyes and Shay pulled away from the kerb tooting his horn.

'Have you had a good time beautiful?' he asked.

'I've had a fantastic time,' I confirmed stroking my tummy, contented.

Forty-one

I was bored, absolutely bored shitless. I had finished work six weeks ago and I had caught up with my boxsets, blitzed the house every couple of days and shopped until I was fed up to the back teeth of Wolverhampton. I was bored!

So today I had baked that many cakes that I could open my own bakery. Shay loved my muffins and cupcakes so I would take him and all his workmates some to have with their afternoon cuppa.

The day after tomorrow Moira would be married and I was looking forward to it, even though I looked like a sumo wrestler, I had to enjoy myself. Now to catch the bus. I waddled down to the bus stop cursing the fact that I could no longer get behind the steering wheel of the car.

When the bus finally arrived the September sun was beating through the window as I sat on it making me feel hot and even more uncomfortable if that was possible, I hated public transport. It took thirty minutes to get to the garage and by the time I did I wished I hadn't gotten in my head to bring the cakes in the first place.

'Tash love, how are you?' Ray greeted me, wiping his hands on a piece of rag. 'You look bigger every time I see you.'

'I know,' I grimaced. 'I've baked some cakes for you all, muffins and cupcakes,' I held aloft the bag.

'Brilliant,' he rubbed his hands together, he had tasted my baking before and had grown rather partial to it. 'Go and see him then,' he took the bag from me. 'He's under the red Mercedes,' he beamed at me and I smiled back, he was a lovely man.

Going into the garage the smell of oil and car fumes hit me and I felt a little nauseous. I spied the Mercedes with a pair of legs sticking out from underneath and used my foot to gently rub the top of his thigh. He moved quickly, rolling out from under the car and I went bright red. It was Nick, not Shay under the car and I could hear Ray peeing himself laughing behind me.

'Thanks for the offer Tash,' Nick said with a grin. 'But I think someone got there before me.' He pointed to my baby bump.

I blushed harder, my sense of humour seemed to have deserted me. I was full of baby hormones and I couldn't wait to give birth, I felt like I would never be the same again. I was at the doctors again on Monday, they wanted to discuss inducing me which I had been against all through the pregnancy but at that precise moment I would have agreed to anything,

'Ray said you were Shay,' I mumbled.

'Classic,' Ray guffawed as Shay emerged from the toilet.

'Your missus has just made a pass at me,' Nick told him gleefully.

'I thought he was you,' I defended myself.

'Natasha I can't leave you alone for one minute,' Shay scolded playfully.

'I've made cakes for everyone, I gave them to Ray,' I pouted.

'Thanks dahling, we all love your cakes,' he smiled. 'How are you?'

I pulled a face as the others carried on working. 'I'm bored. It took me half an hour to get here on the bus, it was really hot on there. I feel so big and uncomfortable.'

'You look glowing,' he assured me.

When did it go from beautiful, which he usually called me, to glowing? I felt so huge and unsexy, I was lucky to get a peck on the cheek from him the last couple of weeks. He seemed to be treading around me wearily and I had lots of time to think all manner of things. Same old Tash.

'Jesus, Mary and Joseph, Shay Flynn!' a voice cried behind me and I turned round. The woman was stunning, gorgeous. Tall and willowy with long dark poker straight hair, bright blue eyes and perfect skin.

She launched herself at Shay and he caught her deftly, a huge smile on his face. 'How ya doing Ava?' he said. 'It's been an age since I saw you.'

'It's been too long,' she kissed his cheek.

I stood there watching them closely. Who was she? Why were they so friendly? He saw the look on my face and took a step back from her.

'You found him then?' Ray asked, sauntering over.

'I did and he's still as gorgeous as ever,' her accent was Irish and lilting, did Shay know her from Ireland?

'Not my type love,' Ray joked.

I felt sick, I knew there had to be something in his past. Had he gone out with her? Loved her? Was serious about her? My active imagination was working overtime and my face must have looked full of my insecurities.

Shay knew what I would be thinking. 'Ava,' he said. 'This is Tash, my girlfriend,' he introduced me.

Her blue eyes took me in and I shifted uncomfortably. I was dressed like Ray in unflattering tracksuit bottoms and an oversized t-shirt that was shapeless. 'Hey,' she smiled. 'Uncle Ray said Shay was going to be a daddy but I didn't believe it, not the Shay I know.'

I forced a smile. 'Twins, actually,' I managed to say without clawing her eyes out.

She clapped her hands together. 'Oh my, no wonder you look so huge,' she cried. 'When do you have them?'

'Three weeks,' my smile was faltering.

'Going to name them both after me aren't you Tash,' Ray laughed jovially.

'I still can't believe that you are going to be a daddy,' she hugged Shay's arm in an overfriendly manner.

I'd seen enough. Immediately I thought about what Sam had done across me and I felt the same kind of dread. Shay and I had not made love for what seemed like weeks. Partly it was me, I was tired all the time but on his part he never even tried now. Sam had cheated on me because I was pregnant, I didn't want history repeating itself.

'I'll leave you to it,' I tried to keep my smile in place.

'You don't mind if I take Shay for a drink when he finishes work, just for old time's sake?' she gave me a mischievous smile.

What could I say? If I said I did mind then I would look like a jealous cow and if I said I didn't mind then I was pushing them together. 'No, of course not,' I forced another smile.

'Aw thank you,' her laugh tinkled. 'What do you say Shay?'

He looked at me awkwardly. 'Sure?'

'Yes, enjoy. I'll see you back at home,' I kept my voice bright even though it was killing me.

'Do you want a lift home Tash?' Ray asked. 'I'm just heading off on a breakdown.'

'No thank you, I'll be fine catching the bus.'

'Let Ray take you home, you look knackered.'

I gave Shay an annoyed glare, I didn't need the fact that I was dead on my feet pointing out, Ava was already making me feel old. 'No, the bus will be fine. Nice to meet you Ava.'

'You too Tash and good luck with the babies,' she replied.

I smiled my thank you as Shay walked me outside. 'Who is she?' I rounded on him as soon as we were out of earshot.

'She's Rita's niece from Ireland,' he answered.

'You seem very friendly with her,' I couldn't keep the accusation from my tone.

'I know her from Cork, we all used to hang out together.'

'Is that all?' the sun was beating down and I felt hot and sweaty. My hair was scrapped back into a ponytail and I had no makeup on. I felt old and ugly.

'Does it matter Tash?' he asked pained.

'Yes,' my eyes filled with tears, I was so hormonal. 'It matters to me. Did you go out with her?'

He sighed. 'It's in the past. I've got to get back to work, I won't be late tonight. It's just a catch up drink, that's all.'

'Fine, I'll see you later.' I wanted to stride away with my head held high but all I could manage was a waddle.

I could sense that he was watching me but I couldn't look back. I headed for home having the luxury of the next several hours to imagine that they were getting up to all sorts. So Ava was Rita's niece, Ray's niece by marriage. I knew Rita had family in Cork, that was how Shay had got the job at the garage but why was he being so evasive?

I went and lay on the bed, so exhausted. It was stifling with the sun shining even with the window open so I couldn't sleep and that gave me plenty of time to think. Lying on my side I stared at the window, my stomach like a manmade mountain. With both Lexi and Jamie I had neat little bumps, you couldn't tell that I was pregnant from the back and I moved around gracefully in stylish maternity clothes.

With these two though, I was colossal, every item of clothing I had stretched to its limits to accommodate me, no wonder Shay didn't want to touch me. I groaned trying to get comfortable. I wanted to give birth now, to get these babies out of me. I couldn't shake the feeling that something bad was going to happen.

Eventually I must have dozed off, waking as Shay sat on the edge of the bed. Glancing at the clock it read just after eight, I had managed a couple of hours sleep. 'You're back early,' my voice sounded croaky.

'I said it was just a quick catch up drink, she's here for mam's wedding.'

So Moira knew her too, why hadn't she told me? I couldn't remember seeing her name on the guest list but saying that I had only skimmed it. Moira and Alan was sorting that, I'd just done everything else.

'Who is she?' I asked again, picking at it like a scab.

'I told you Rita's niece,' he pushed my hair away from my hot forehead.

'No, I mean who is she to you? Why has Moira invited her to the wedding?'

He fought to keep his voice patient. 'I've already told you, we hung out together in Cork, mam knows her from then.'

'Have you slept with her?' my voice was blunt.

'What tonight or in Cork?' his own tone was light.

'Don't,' I warned, flippancy I could do without.

He sighed, thinking for a moment. 'We used to sleep together, occasionally,' he finally admitted.

A lead weight appeared in my stomach. 'Do you love her?'

'What? No!' He got up going to the window. 'It was never liked that, it was just a casual thing. We would go out in a group and sometimes we would end up in bed together.'

My eyes filled with tears. 'How long for?' I demanded.

'Tash,' he sounded tired.

'Tell me!' I pushed.

'For a few years off and on,' I could tell he didn't want to say.

Icy water filled my veins. 'When was the last time?'

'I'm not answering,' he stared out the window.

I struggled into a sitting position. 'Tell me,' I sounded close to hysteria.

He turned reluctantly. 'A couple of months before we got together, I went home for a visit and I saw her then.'

I looked away tears rolling down my face. I knew people said one thing but meant another, had known it all my life. 'So you thought you'd have a quickie tonight for old times' sake because your girlfriend is the size of a house?'

'For God's sake Tash!' he shouted making me jump. 'This is why I didn't want to tell you. Do you honestly believe that I would cheat on you? I am not that kind of man.'

I gritted my teeth. 'I know all about men cheating on their wives when they are pregnant.' Okay technically I wasn't his wife but it came down to the same thing.

'Oh my sweet baby Jesus,' he ran his hand through his hair. 'Why do it Tash?'

I stared at him defiantly.

'Why keep torturing yourself that I'm going to do the dirty on you? What the hell is the point of all this if you are so sure I will?' he was angry. When I didn't reply he continued. 'I should be able to tell you about Ava without this. She was before I even knew you, give me a break.' His accent became more pronounced as it always did when he was angry or drunk.

Both twins kicked at the same time as if they were also telling me to behave myself. I winced, my hand going to my stomach. 'Tash?' he was by my side concerned.

'It's nothing,' I was still crying as I rubbed my tummy trying to soothe them.

'You are so damaged,' his voice became soft. 'By your parents, by your ex-husband.' I couldn't argue, he wasn't wrong.

'What do I have to do sweet? Tell me and I'll do it. This should be a happy time, in three weeks we are going to be parents, we should be looking forward, not back,' he frowned slightly. 'Tell me what I have to do please?'

The babies kicked again causing my stomach to jerk and Shay watched it mesmerised.

'You won't even touch me now,' I said sadly. 'And Ava is very beautiful.'

He struggled to keep his patience. 'Oh God, we can't keep doing this.'

'She's beautiful and young.' Why couldn't I just shut up?

He sighed. 'I thought we'd got past all our insecurities on both parts. I thought we knew that we could trust each other?' He took my hand. 'I didn't fall in love with Ava, I did you. I have never wanted her in the way I want you. I could have walked away that day at the police station and never see you again but I couldn't keep away from you. I didn't want to keep away from you. I want to be with you and only you.'

Fresh tears fell down my face.

'Look at you though sweetheart,' his voice became gentler. 'You are exhausted, you haven't slept properly in weeks. You're uncomfortable, you're huge. What kind of man would I be if I pushed myself on you? I'm worried about hurting you, hurting the babies. Plus I'm tired too, I feel you moving about at night.'

I groaned softly, I was such an idiot, I really didn't deserve him. 'I'm sorry,' I whispered.

He stood, walking to his side of the bed and we both lay down so he could spoon behind me, holding me as tightly as was possible. 'Please dahling,' he begged softly. 'Let's just concentrate on us.'

I nodded. 'I just feel so unattractive,' I admitted. Of course Shay had a life before me, same as I had before him.

'You are always beautiful to me,' he kissed the back of my neck.

I caught his hand, resting it on my tum, the babies were playing a game of football or so it seemed. 'Marry me Tash,' he whispered. 'Let me show you how much you mean to me.' 'I don't want to get married, it doesn't prove anything,' I sighed.

'I want you to be my wife,' he persisted. 'I want to cement what we have. Marry me.'

I turned awkwardly. 'You really mean it don't you?'

'Yes,' he kissed me.

'Why?' I frowned.

'Why what?' he kissed me again.

'Why do you want to marry me?' my emotions were all over the place.

He raised himself on one elbow. 'Because of the babies, I want us all to have the same surname but most importantly simply because I love you and I want you to be my wife.'

I turned on my back, even though it gave me heartburn. 'Okay.'

He gave me his beautiful smile, the first since he had arrived home. 'Seriously?'

'Yes,' and I wanted to, I really did.

'Thank you,' he kissed me again. 'When?'

'Well,' I said vaguely. 'Lexi has got to finish university and we have the twins to pay for.'

'Oh no. You are not saying yes and then keep putting it off. I'm going to phone my dad, he'll be made up,' he grew serious. 'You can't keep being insecure though beautiful. It's you and only you that I want, end of.'

'I know,' I burped loudly, it was lying on my back.

He laughed nuzzling my neck. 'I don't know why though, cos you're no fecking lady.'

Forty~Two

'Sideways view!' I cried, holding the phone so Albie and Niamh could see how big I was now. I'd called them on WhatsApp so we could see each other. It was nice having them to call now I was mainly confined to barracks.

'You look so blooming,' Albie chuckled. 'Tell Shay that I'll speak to him Sunday and give Moira and Alan all our best wishes for tomorrow.'

'I will, speak soon,' I ended the call waiting for Shay to return with his mom. She was staying the night with us, I couldn't see her sped the eve of her wedding alone.

She would take Jamie's bed and Lexi and Belle would camp out in the living room. I was going to put a bit of a spread on as a kind of hen party so I busied myself putting quiches, chicken drumsticks and a selection of other delectable nibbles in the oven. I truly was a feeder but I so wanted Moira to have a good night.

'Tash I am so fecking nervous,' Moira burst into the kitchen, Shay following with her case and wedding outfit draped over her arm.

'I would be too,' I smiled. 'Shay will you hang the dress in Jamie's room please?'

He saluted going upstairs as Moira held my hand. 'How are you love?' she asked softly.

'Massive,' I grinned as he came back into the kitchen, he and Dale were meeting up with Alan and various family members for a drink.

'You look wonderful,' she placed her hand on my stomach. 'Hello my two beautiful grandchildren, I can't wait to meet you.'

I smiled again turning to Shay. 'I've spoken to Albie, he said he'll call you Sunday.' Then to Moira I said. 'He and Niamh have asked me to pass on their best wishes for tomorrow.'

'That's kind of them,' she smiled.

'Enjoy your evening,' I said to Shay. 'None of you too drunk please.'

'We won't be late,' he promised, kissing me softly, one hand rubbing my tum. 'See you soon my babies.' 'Bye daddy, don't get pissed,' I answered for them as Dale pulled up outside, he was on driving duty tonight much to his disgust. We waved at him through the window as Bev tottered up the garden path.

'I have wine! I have nibbles!' She declared holding aloft two shopping bags.

'When I've had these two I am going to get absolutely plastered,' I told them. 'Might even have some Irish whisky.'

'You don't have to do that now for Shay to sleep with you,' Bev teased as his mom tittered.

I smiled primly, looking at Moira, who was currently taking charge of the cooking! In my kitchen! Good job I loved her.

'We'll have a good time tonight,' Bev predicted as Lexi and Bell came up the path, a little later then they said they'd be.

'Ah, here are my two girls,' Moira hugged them once they were inside. She enjoyed spending time with them and they in turn adored her. Lexi classed her as her Nan and I had my suspicions that Belle did too.

'Hello,' Lexi returned the hug before pinching a handful of crisps.

'Will you help me carry everything into the living room please?' I asked and they did leaving just me and Moira in the kitchen.

'I've asked Rita and Ava to pop round for a drink, I hope that's okay?' she asked checking the rest of the food.

I tried to hide my disdain and failed. 'Yes, that's fine,' I replied tightly.

'Sweetheart,' she began softly. 'Shay said that you met Ava yesterday.'

I nodded, shoving scotch eggs onto a plate.

'And you know all about him and her?' she leant against the cupboard.

'He eventually told me,' I pulled a face.

'You don't have to be jealous love,' she folded the tea towel.

'I'm not, we had a good talk.'

'Are you sure?' she gave me a knowing look. 'I could never understand the pair of them. I mean either you're going out with someone or you're not. It was all so casual.'

'So he told me,' I had gotten over my strop but that didn't mean I wanted to talk about Ava, let alone have her in my house. 'Anyway, it's just baby hormones making me paranoid.'

She touched my cheek. 'I think you were insecure before you got pregnant because of that fecker you were married too.'

I remained silent, tears filling my eyes, I couldn't disagree.

'He loves you sweetheart, like he's never loved anyone else,' she continued. 'Don't push him away, enjoy what you have and look forward to those two precious gifts that God has given you both.'

'We are, we're okay now,' a single tear slid down my cheek, Moira knew me so well, what I was like.

'What's wrong mom?' Lexi asked concerned.

We both turned, not realising that she had come into the room. 'Full of baby hormones,' I smiled brightly at her. 'Moira go and sit with the girls and I'll bring you a glass of wine.'

'You shouldn't be waiting on me,' she scolded.

'I need to keep moving, if I sit too long I seize up,' I shooed her, along with Lexi, back into the other room.

They crossed paths with Bev as she came to me demanding. 'More wine!' Whilst giving me a hug. 'How are you hun?'

'Okay,' I sighed, getting everyone a drink. 'I'll be glad when I've given birth to the pair of blighters.'

'Not long now,' she smiled.

'No, not long,' I paused for a moment. 'I was introduced to a woman yesterday that Shay used to sleep with when he lived in Cork.'

'Sleep with as in the biblical sense?' she was a little shocked.

'No they just used to have a really good night's sleep together.'

'Less of the sarcasm,' she told me off. 'Is that how he introduced her?'

'No,' I scowled. 'I made him tell me.'

'Oh Tash,' she knew how unconfident I could be. 'Who is she?'

'You know Ray who owns the garage?' I asked and she nodded. 'Well she's his wife's niece.'

'Blooming hell,' she took a large mouthful of wine.

'We had words,' I admitted. 'I mean I know he loves me. I believe him when he says it so why do I always feel so insecure?'

'It's conditioned into you after Sam. You think if you allow yourself to be happy then someone will come along and take it away from you,' she paused. 'So you feel safer being miserable.'

'I thought you were my friend?' I was a tad hurt.

'I am, that's why I tell you the truth,' she smiled. 'So what's she like?'

'You can see for yourself in a while. Moira has invited her and Rita to have a drink with us.'

'It's a bit bad not asking you first. So was it serious between Shay and this Ava?' Bev wanted to know.

'Apparently not, they just used to occasionally have sex.'

'Shag buddies like me and Dale used to be,' she nodded as if she was agreeing with herself.

'And now you two live together,' I cocked my head to one side, wishing that she would stop talking.

'Shut up Tash,' she reprimanded as the doorbell rang.

I waddled to the door, it was Rita and Ava. 'Tash you look like you're going to explode,' Rita greeted me, I hadn't seen her for a few weeks.

'I feel like I'm going to. Three weeks and it will all be over,' I forced a smile. 'Ava, hello again.'

'Hi Tash, thanks for inviting me,' her tone was overconfident.

'Not a problem, please, go through.' I wanted to say I didn't invite you, you gypo bint, Moira did but instead I played nice and settled them with the others. I did the introductions and then went into the kitchen to get them wine.

Bev emerged to help me. 'Aw she's a pretty thing, lovely figure.'

I gave her the evils. 'Thanks Bev, just what I want to hear.'

'I'm just saying,' she tittered. 'You're much prettier and your figure,' she cast an eye over me. 'Is definitely more voluptuous.'

'Bitch,' I grinned, then I grew serious. 'I do really love him Bev, I don't know what I'd do if he left me.'

'He's not going to leave you.'

'I look at him sometimes and he literally takes my breath away.'

'That would be the smell of his feet,' she wasn't going to let me feel sorry for myself.'

'Bev,' I pulled a face. 'I know I shouldn't worry that his head might be turned but Ava is stunning. You'd probably be the same if it was Dale.'

'I suppose,' she conceded.

'Come on or they'll wonder what we are up to,' I took a deep breath, the babies were moving like billy-oh again.

She took the wine from me. 'Babies are kicking again,' she told everyone.

'Let me feel my grandchildren,' Moira demanded.

'Look,' I lifted up my top and you could clearly see elbows and feet poking through my skin. Ava blanched and I smiled smugly, she had no idea how wonderful it was to feel your own babies moving inside of you.

'My beautiful babies,' Moira cooed, her hand warm on my skin. 'I'm your nanny.'

'I read somewhere that you should sing to them while they are in the womb,' Bev sipped her wine.

'Don't let mom sing to them or they'll never want to come out,' Lexi laughed.

'Oi cheeky,' I looked at her lovingly.

'But accurate,' Belle chimed in. 'Singing isn't your strong point.'

'Will you breast feed Tash?' Rita was making herself comfortable.

'I'll give it a go I think, I'm not sure,' I did sound indecisive. 'I breastfeed Lexi and Jamie but two at the same time may be a whole different ballgame.'

Bev pulled a face. 'I wouldn't let anyone suck my tits who wasn't old enough to drive.'

'Bev!' Moira literally spat out her wine and we all laughed.

'Sorry,' she said sheepishly.

'Thanks for letting me kidnap Shay last night.' Ava was bored of the conversation.

I looked at her sharply. 'No worries, he wasn't out that long,' my smile was sweet but forced and I think she knew it.

'It was good to catch up,' she emphasised the words, staring at me like a cat.

'So Ava,' Moira butted in seeing what she was up too. 'Are you still working at the coffee shop?'

She reluctantly moved her attention away from me. 'Yeah it's okay.'

'I am so excited about tomorrow,' Moira had finally took her hand from my stomach and sat back down.

'Me too,' Lexi had never been a bridesmaid before. When her father married Meera they had the same kind of wedding Sam and I had, basic.

'You're going to be such a help,' she said.

'That's what I'm here for,' Lexi was such a good girl.

We chatted some more about the wedding and the babies. Heaving myself up I went into the kitchen to get more food. By now it was nine o'clock and I was hoping, uncharitably, that it wouldn't be a late night. It was true what they said about being an older mother, it was exhausting.

Shay and Dale came back a few minutes later, singing at the top of their voices, "I'm getting married in the morning" to Moira. I smiled as I poured more crisps and nuts into bowls and put out the cheeseboard. I did hope that Moira was enjoying her night.

I heard Shay say. 'Where's the mother of my children? I hope you're not letting her wait on the lot of you hand and foot?'

I smiled wider as Lexi replied. 'You know what mom's like.'

'I do,' he answered and the next moment he was in the kitchen. 'Hey beautiful.'

'Hey,' I kissed him. 'Have you enjoyed yourselves?'

'It's been good,' he helped himself to the nuts. 'Have you?'

'I have and I think your mom's enjoying herself too. Will you help me carry these in?' I motioned to the bowls.

'Sure,' he followed me into the living room.

'Oh, I've forgotten the nuts,' I said going out the room as Shay sat on the settee and Dale fussed around Moira, telling her how she was going to make a beautiful bride. Our Dale could charm the birds from the trees when he wanted to. I'd also clocked him checking out Ava and I wondered if Shay had told him the full story?

Anyway it wasn't important, I just had to keep telling myself that. It was going to be a wonderful wedding and we were all going to enjoy it and I could blank Ava, not a problem. Going back to them I stopped dead. Ava had moved from the chair and was now sitting next to Shay. He was watching me with an apologetic expression on his face and I gave him a soft smile. I had put Erin in her place in Quin and if need be I'd put Ava in her bloody place as well.

'Son, you and Dale don't have a drink,' Moira fretted.

'Driving Mrs F soon to be Mrs C,' Dale replied. 'I'll have a coke though please the Shayster.'

He nodded getting up and disappearing to the kitchen. Ava watched him go and then said. 'Can I use your toilet Tash?'

'Top of the stairs,' I told her as Moira gave me a discreet shake of her head.

Shay was sorting out the drinks when she joined him in the kitchen. 'This is a very cosy domestic arrangement you have here,' she said standing close to him, her voice low.

He cast a glance in her direction. 'I like it.'

'Oh come on lover,' her laugh was soft. 'You and domestic bliss? It really doesn't suit you at all.'

He tried to keep his voice pleasant. 'You don't know me at all then, do you?'

'Tell me the truth,' she touched his arm. 'You're only with her because she's pregnant aren't you?'

He let his annoyance show through. 'Like I said, you don't know me at all.'

She walked her fingers along his arm. 'You know I'm always here for you,' her voice was lilting. 'We had some good times in Cork.'

Shay looked down at her hand, his eyes narrowing. 'I am no longer that person Ava, things have changed.'

'Your knocked up older woman? Yeah, she's just what you need,' her voice was full of sarcasm. 'You forget I know exactly what you like, what you need, I always have done.'

Shay put down his bottle of lager, turning to face her fully. 'No, you don't know what I need. It's being with Tash what has made me realise what we did in Cork never actually meant anything. I have never felt about anyone the way I feel about her. I'm *in* love with *her*,' he leant forward wanting her to get the message loud and clear. 'I love the very bones of her and even if she wasn't pregnant right here is where I want to be.'

She blinked rapidly, taking a step back.

'Don't try and cause trouble Ava, I'm not going to allow it. If you upset Tash or do anything to spoil my mam's wedding,' he left the rest of the sentence unspoken. 'Now I'm going back to the others.' He picked up the drinks, re-joining us in the living room.

I gave him a troubled smile and he winked at me, sitting on the arm of my chair as he gave Dale his coke.

'Is Alan okay?' Moira was happy to have us all around her.

'He's like an excited kid,' Dale answered with a grin. 'I told him though, don't expect Mrs F to turn up tomorrow, cos I'm going to elope with her tonight.'

'Oh you,' she flushed delighted, as Ava came back in the room, her expression not quite hiding how pissed off she felt.

'Don't break my heart Mrs F, say you'll dump Alan and marry me,' he teased.

'I don't want you as a fecking stepdaddy,' Shay shook his head, his arm around my shoulder. 'Anyway I want to make an announcement.'

'Blimey mom, you're not really having triplets are you?' Lexi joked and everyone laughed, well Ava sort of grimaced.

'No,' I replied wondering what he was going to say. 'Don't wish that on us.'

Shay took my hand, looking at me adoringly. 'This beautiful woman has made me the happiest man alive and as you can probably see she is carrying very precious cargo,' he kissed my hand as everyone laughed. He took a deep breath before carrying on. 'I never thought this would happen to me, she is an incredible woman.'

'Get on with it son,' Moira heckled as I flushed at the unexpected speech he was doing, it was lovely.

He laughed, holding my hand tighter. 'Last night I asked Tash to be my wife and she said yes.'

'Yay!' Lexi cried punching the air, then launching herself at us. Shay caught her in his arms hugging her tightly.

'We weren't' going to say anything until the wedding,' I couldn't keep the smile from my face but I didn't want Moira to think that we were stealing her thunder.

'Its wonderful news,' she was tearful as she congratulated us both.

'Sorry mam, I don't want to overshadow your day but I just couldn't wait to tell the world,' he apologised.

She waved it away. 'I never thought I could be happier, me marrying Alan tomorrow, having the grandchildren to look forward to but this is the icing on the cake.' She said. 'I'm so happy for both of you.'

I looked at my brother. 'Dale?' I queried.

He stood, one hand on his chest. 'Made up for you both,' he sounded choked.

'Are you crying?' Bev asked suspiciously.

'No,' he answered quickly. 'My eyes are just sweating.'

'Uncle Dale, you big tit,' Lexi chuckled.

'When will you do it?' Bev wanted to know.

'Quickly,' Shay replied for both of us. 'I want her to be Natasha Flynn as soon as possible.'

'It's lovely,' Rita declared and I did wonder if she thought anything about Shay and her niece being shag buddies in Cork. To be fair she was always nice to me so it couldn't have bothered her really. 'I love a bit of good news.'

Ava though had stayed mute, the look on her face saying it all. Did she really think, despite already knowing, that Shay had a pregnant girlfriend that she could come over here and carry on where they had left off? Had she no shame? If she wasn't careful she'd feel the back of my hand and I didn't care if I was pregnant.

I held Shay's hand to lever myself up off the chair. 'I need the loo, the babies are doing a happy dance on my bladder.'

He stood with me. 'Okay beautiful?' he asked.

'I am,' I replied and I was. Shay choosing to make our announcement in front of Ava just cemented how we felt about each other. We *were* going to have our happily ever after.

I toddled off to the toilet, which always took me twice as long lately and then came downstairs, Shay calling me from the kitchen.

'What's up?' I asked reaching for the light switch, he was standing in the dark.

He stopped me flicking the switch, his mouth finding mine. 'I've realised something,' he said softly.

'And what's that?' I enquired, wishing we hadn't got guests.

'It's exactly a year today since we first slept together,' he whispered. 'God bless Jameson whisky.'

I laughed, flattered that he had remembered. 'So much has happened since then.'

'It has,' he agreed, as his lips sought mine again.'

I pushed back his curls. 'Have I ever told you how much I love you?'

He thought for a moment. 'I think you may have mentioned it once or twice,' he chuckled and then increased the pressure of his kisses. 'Shall we start kicking them out soon? Doctor Flynn thinks you need bedrest.'

'Shay Flynn are you trying to have your wicked way with me?' I raised an eyebrow, it was the first time in weeks that I even remotely felt like making love.

He held me as close as he could. 'If you feel like it.'

'But we have guests,' I said thinking about Moira and the girls staying.

'Well don't howl as loud as you usually do,' he ran his hand down my back.

I cupped his groin. 'It's not me that makes all the noise,' I joshed him.

'Shit,' his breathing became more rapid, then Lexi came into the kitchen, making us jump apart as she switched on the light.

'What are you two lovebirds doing in the dark?' she inquired starchily.

'Nothing that will get her pregnant,' he grinned cheekily.

Lexi giggled. 'Everyone's going now, Moira said she needs to rest.'

'Cheers,' he got everyone's coats and we went into the living room.

'Oh I've had a lovely night,' his mom seemed a little tipsy.

'We'll see you tomorrow,' Rita hugged Moira. 'Thank you Tash, you've been the perfect hostess,' she rubbed my stomach. People always did that when you were pregnant, it was a little annoying.

We all walked to the front door and I noticed that Ava and Shay hadn't exchanged one word and of course my mind began to wonder if something had gone on between them. Dale and Bev were dropping them off back home and we said our goodbyes and watched until we could see Dale's car no longer.

'Can I grab the bathroom first?' Moira asked. 'I'm dead on my feet but I doubt whether I'll sleep a wink tonight.'

Lexi gave her a cuddle. 'I don't think you will.'

'Ah princess, for sure,' she agreed, tottering upstairs.

'Come on Lex, let's finish tidying up while your mom and Shay have a minute,' Belle pushed up her glasses.

'Thanks girls,' he flumped down on the settee and I sat next to him.

'Have you and Ava had words?' I asked taking his hand. Tomorrow was going to be such a long day, I only hoped I had the energy for it.

He looked satisfied. 'She knows exactly how it is, you don't have to worry about anything, soon to be Mrs Flynn.'

I smiled softly. 'Excellent. Are you looking forward to tomorrow?'

'I am,' he confessed. 'Mam deserves her special day.'

'She is going to look such a beautiful bride,' I predicted.

He leant into me. 'Are you going to be up for doing everyone's hair tomorrow, it's a big job?'

'Bev's going to help me, to be fair it shouldn't take that long with us both doing it.'

'Well,' he whispered in my ear. 'Do you want to save some of that energy for tonight?'

My nethers twitched. 'How can you want to do it with me, the state I'm in?' I asked mystified.

'You look beautiful,' he nibbled my ear. 'You are carrying my children, how can that not be amazing?'

I went to reply but Lexi and Belle chose that moment to come in the room. 'We're going to have to kick you upstairs in a minute, we need our beauty sleep,' my daughter informed us.

'Not a problem,' I answered as Shay heaved me from my seat. We followed them upstairs, waiting until they had finished in the bathroom before sorting ourselves out.

'Night everyone!' I called from the landing then joined Shay in the bedroom.

'Now,' he said lying on the bed. 'Do you want it spooning or doggy?'

'Shay Albie Flynn, shush or your mother will hear you,' his voice wasn't exactly quiet.

He pulled me to him. 'She won't hear a thing if she's lying on her good ear, we could howl all night.'

I began to giggle, clamping my hand over my mouth, he reached for me, hands kneading my boobs. 'I feel like a naughty schoolgirl creeping into my boyfriend's bedroom for a bit of slap and tickle and it's my house.' I confessed making him laugh.

'Get your clothes off,' his voice was seductive. 'I want to see you naked.'

I looked at him coyly. 'I want to play hard to get.'

He was looking at me with a comical expression on his face. 'I think that ships well and truly sailed,' his answer was dubious causing us both to start tittering again.

I lay beside him trying to ignore the heartburn as he lazily undressed me, trailing kisses over my swollen stomach and plump breasts. 'Beautiful,' he whispered, making the breath catch in my throat. 'Do you have any idea how much I love you?'

My breathing became more laboured as he helped me on my side, then onto all fours, using the pillows to support my stomach. His fingers softly caressed the skin on my back as he got behind me, hesitating for only a second before gently pushing forward.

I groaned using the pillows to steady me as he fingers sought my clitoris, toying with the delicate bud. It was too much and I had to bite the pillow to stop myself screaming out in pleasure.

He paused pulling back before easing forward again, the movements measured. 'Shay!' I gasped, mindful of our guests.

'Shush,' he warned, building up the rhythm while his fingers still did wonderful things.

I could feel myself beginning to lose control, Shay doing the same. I bit heavily on my lip as I came to a shuddering climax, him following suit seconds later.

He took his weight on his arms, laying his head on my back. 'Shit Tash, wow.'

'Wow indeed,' I whispered, every nerve in my body on high alert. 'That was.'

'Wonderful?' he suggested helpfully, moving slightly.

I lay on my side, trying to control my breathing and hoping that our guest hadn't heard.

'I can't wait to marry you,' he stroked my face. 'Show everyone that we are for keeps.'

'Especially Sam?' I asked slyly. Jamie had told me that things were still really bad between his dad and Meera. Sam had been quizzing him nonstop about me and Shay, if he was still around, if we were happy.

'Do you have to mention his fecking name?'

'Sorry,' I grinned. 'What a pair we are, I go off on one about Ava.'

'Even though you have nothing to worry about,' he cut in.

'Hey,' I thumped his arm. 'I'm allowed to be insecure a bit, you are an exceptionally handsome man, of course I'm going to be worried about you having your head turned by a beautiful, *young* woman.'

He laughed softly. 'But don't you see that's how I feel sometimes? You don't half do yourself a disservice. You are a beautiful woman, inside and out, you just can't see it, it's what I love about you. When we go out I see men admiring you and I'm so proud that you're mine. Besides,' he cast me a crafty glance. 'Sam is also a handsome, charming man who has made it quite plain that he wants to get back into your knickers.'

'Shut up,' I retorted, taking his hand. 'Go to sleep, busy day tomorrow.'

He laughed again as we snuggled down. 'Night dahling, night baby Flynn's.'

'Night daddy,' I replied feeling content.

Forty~Three

My bladder woke me at six, Shay was lying on top of the bed, naked as the day he was born. I took a moment to enjoy the view, I was going to marry this man, I was going to be Mrs Natasha Eileen Flynn. I went into the bathroom, wincing at the ache in my back, pregnancy was literally a pain sometimes.

'Tash,' Shay's voice was fuddled as I went back into the room.

'Don't worry, it's early. Go back to sleep,' I got back in bed.

He grunted snuggling into me, I could hear movement downstairs and the sound of muffled voices. 'Sounds like someone's up,' he yawned loudly.

'It does,' I grimaced, twinges again. I couldn't be under the weather today, I had too much to do.

'What's wrong?' he asked, rubbing my back gently.

'Oh the usual,' my answer was vague, he would only fuss.

'I wish I could have them for you,' he whispered.

'I bet you do,' I retorted cynically, men always said that, they knew there was no chance.

His kiss was soft. 'I would,' he argued.

'Go back to sleep,' I said. 'I'm getting up, I feel really uncomfortable.'

'Okay,' he shut his eyes tightly.

I stared at him for a moment before getting out of bed and pulling on my dressing gown. Moira was making tea in the kitchen, Lexi and Belle slumped at the table. 'Hi mom,' Lexi was having trouble keeping her eyes open, not used to being up so early.

'Hi sweet,' I kissed the top of her head.

'Did we wake you Tash?' Moira fretted.

'No, the babies did,' I replied joining them at the table.

'Everything okay?' she asked concerned.

'Yeah, I didn't sleep very well, that's all.' I yawned loudly.

Lexi got up making us all a cup of tea. 'Do you think baby daddy will want one?'

'Yes, but I'll take it up to him.'

'Mom, I can walk up the stairs, I learnt at a very early age,' she said cheekily.

I narrowed my eyes. 'Fine but when I left him he was lying stark naked on the bed.'

'Shag-,' she began but I silenced her with a look. She was going to call him shaggable Shay and in front of his mom too! Giving me another cheeky smile she told me. 'I'll announce myself before I go in.'

'Be sure you do,' I warned, how embarrassing would that be?

She disappeared upstairs, followed by Moira, who had an attack of nervous peeing. I sat at the table wincing.

'You okay Tash?' Belle asked.

'Braxton Hicks,' I informed her.

'What are they?' she asked a mixture of interest and concern on her face.

'False contractions,' I explained. 'It's like your body is practicing for the real thing.'

'Does it hurt?'

'It can do, like now,' I sipped my tea.

'If there is anything I can do let me know,' she rubbed her eyes sleepily.

'Just don't tell the others, they'll only be fussing around me and I'm fine.' I had to be, it was Moira's big day.

'Ay Shay got a hairy chest?' Lexi came back with a big grin on her face.

'You didn't just walk in there without knocking first?' I spluttered alarmed.

'Chill mom, he had the duvet over him,' she rolled her eyes. 'I just caught a glimpse of his chest, it must be like shagging a gorilla.'

'Oi,' I warned her, she was getting mouthy just lately, her confidence seemed to be soaring.

She pulled a face as I finished my tea, trying to ignore the pain in my back. 'Do you want breakfast?' Belle asked. She and Lexi had already demolished two rounds of toast each.

'I'll have a couple of slices please,' I replied hoping it would settle me as Moira returned from the bathroom.

'How can you eat?' she demanded.

'Because I'm not the one getting married,' I answered.

'You will be soon,' she predicted. 'My son won't want to wait.'

I pulled a face. 'We need to save up for it first.'

'Will you have a proper wedding dress this time?' Lexi asked.

'What do you mean a proper wedding dress?' Moira wanted to know.

'Poor mom had a really shit wedding when she married dad, just a registry office and a pub meal. No dress or anything.'

'It wasn't that bad.' I frowned, the day itself hadn't been, Sam and I were in love then.

'You didn't even have a bouquet! Dad was that tight he didn't even buy you an engagement ring,' she rolled her eyes.

'You had a wedding ring though?' Moira was horrified.

Lexi held up her right hand, showing off the plain thin yellow gold band on her finger, I had given it to her when we divorced. 'Cheap crap from the Argos,' she informed her.

'You could always give it me back,' I growled.

'Poor Tash,' Moira patted my hand as Shay wondered into the kitchen looking like he'd come through a hedge backwards.

'You lot are noisy,' he moaned, slumping at the table.

'And you are hungover,' his mom gave him a disapproving look.

'I'm not,' he denied. 'It there any toast for me?'

Belle nodded putting bread in the toaster. Bev and Dale were due at eight, with the bridesmaid coming half an hour later. The time was flying by already.

'Are you going to shave that fecking beard off?' Moira asked her son.

'Yeah, when I have my shower.'

'How long have you had it for?' Lexi asked.

He shrugged. 'Couple of months, why?'

'Because your face is tanned and if you shave it off that area of skin will be white. You'll look like a right knobhead.'

'You had to grow a beard didn't you?' Moira rebuked.

'We'll get the beard trimmer on it, it'll be fine. Neat, stubbly,' I guaranteed her.

'Will you cut my hair?' he asked me. 'I fancy something different.'

'No,' my answer was short. 'I like it as it is,' and I did. It was all tousled and sexy.

'I'll ask Bev then,' he began to eat his toast.

I shot him a look, it was going to be a long day. By nine-thirty all the bridesmaids' hair had been styled and into pretty pinned up curls, diamantes here and there. I used that much hairspray that I thought little Elise was going to have an asthma attack. They had spent all their time running around the house, shrieking with excitement. I was glad when the little cherubs went home to put their dresses on, we were all meet back up at Moseley Old Hall.

The car was picking Moira and Shay up at ten-fifty and at ten-forty-five we were all assembled in the kitchen waiting. Lexi looked beautiful in her dove grey bridesmaid dress with cowl neck and cap sleeves. The satin hugged her curves and a delicate teardrop diamante necklace lay against her neck. I wished she wore dresses more often.

While I was getting ready Bev had cut Shay's hair, taking off a couple of inches, using product she had enhanced every curl and it shone, his beard neatly trimmed. He stood by the sink in his navy blue suit and dove grey waistcoat looking absolutely scrummy.

'Will I do?' he asked me softly.

'Yes,' I whispered. 'You'll more than do.' I wished I looked half as good as he did. I had decided on a hat to complete my outfit, a really large hat. I thought it would distract from how big my stomach was but unfortunately all it succeeded in doing was making me look like a gigantic bump with a hat on top.

It was Moira who stole the show though in her delicate pink lace outfit. To put it simply she looked stunning and I hoped that I would age as well as she had. 'Time to go,' Shay said as the car pulled up outside. A vintage Rolls Royce curtesy of someone he knew. Jamie and Abbie arrived at the same time too, talk about cutting it fine.

'Son,' Moira grabbed Shay's hand, trembling with nerves.

'It'll be grand,' he kissed her cheek and she took his arm.

So Moira, Shay and Lexi were going in the Rolls and the rest of us were going in a minibus that had also just arrived. 'See you there beautiful,' Shay winked at me.

I nodded, filling up. Weddings always made me cry. Dale directed us to the minibus, the driver taking one look at me and blanching. 'You're not going to drop it on the way are you?' he asked alarmed at the size of me.

'Oh you funny man,' I muttered as Belle and Jamie hauled me in.

'I'm being serious,' he retorted, getting us to the venue in double quick time in case I did indeed give birth on his shitty plastic upholstery.

We went inside first, having a chat with Alan's family, it was nice to see them and the atmosphere was lovely in the room. I had pride of place on the first row so Shay could sit by me, along with the bridesmaids and the pageboys. Dale, Bev, Belle, Jamie and Abbie on the row behind.

'Mom, I can't see with your stupid big hat on,' Jamie complained in my ear.

'Shut up,' I hissed feeling extremely uncomfortable in my seat. I hoped the ceremony didn't last too long, all I wanted to do was go back to bed and I needed the toilet again.

The bridal march started and we stood, watching as Shay walked his mom down the aisle, looking as proud as punch. Alan, on the other hand, looked a bag of nerves.

I would love to tell you about the ceremony, what was said, how the bride and groom took their vows but unfortunately my thoughts were elsewhere. Discreetly l looked at my watch, trying to control the feeling of panic that was swamping me.

Somehow I got through the service. I even managed to sit through the meal and the speeches at Longford House but by the time the disco was going full throttle it became clear that I could not hold on much longer.

I was on my way to the loo when Jemma stopped me, (remember Sam's second affair?). 'You look amazing,' she said.

I stood, platting my legs. 'Thanks.'

'It's been a fab day hasn't it?' She continued and I nodded. 'I'm so glad that dad's found happiness again after losing mom. Just like you with Shay.'

'Yes, it's lovely,' my smile was genuine. 'Can we catch up in a bit? I really need to pee.'

She nodded. 'Sorry Tash, you know me I can talk for England.'

'I'll come and find you,' I promised, diving into the ladies.

Sitting in the cubicle I took a deep breath. Shit, this was really going to happen. The main door opened and I heard the unmistakable sound of Lexi and Belle talking. Awkwardly I came out. 'Mom,' she cried on seeing me. 'Have a word with your beloved, he's on the whisky and nicely pissed already.'

I shut my eyes, taking another deep breath. Tonight of all nights I needed my Irishman sober. 'Is everything okay Tash?' Belle was staring at me.

'Girls,' I tried to keep my voice steady. 'Will you go and fetch Shay for me?'

'Mom?' Lexi was immediately on the alert.

'Honey just go and get Shay, don't let anyone else know, I just need him.'

'Mom,' she repeated, panic on her face.

'My waters have broken,' I admitted. 'That's why I need you to get him but do it,' they were frozen and then they flew out the door. 'Quietly,' I finished to the empty room.

Shay was talking to Alan and Dale, nicely mellowed by the whisky. 'Do I call you dad now or Uncle Alan?' he asked with a cheeky drunken smile on his face.

'I don't mind either,' he replied with a chuckle as Bev and Moira joined them.

'Where's Tash gone?' Bev asked, glass of wine clasped firmly in one hand.

Shay thought for a moment. 'I'm not sure, I think she was mingling.'

'You are hopeless,' she chided as Lexi and Belle came bowling over to them.

'Ah, here they are, my two princesses,' he smiled.

'Shay mom needs you.'

'Where is she?' he looked around the room.

'In the ladies, come on. Hurry,' Lexi tugged at his arm.

'Dahling,' he put his arm around her. 'Where's the fire?'

'Shay!' She wanted to slap him. 'Her waters have broken.'

He was motionless for a moment, then he was running to the ladies, the others close on his heels. 'Tash! Tash!' He slammed onto the room as I held onto the sink trying to steady my breathing.

'It's fine. My waters have broken and we need to go to the hospital, no biggie,' I explained.

'Shit!' He rubbed his face as the others crammed into the room.

'Did you not understand "just tell Shay and no one else"?' I demanded and then another contraction hit and I doubled up.

Lexi looked at me sheepishly as Shay took my hand. 'Sweet?'

'Are you okay love?' Moira was full of concern.

I let out a long breath. 'Shay and I really need to go now,' already I was getting the urge to push.

'How long have you had these contractions?' Bev was looking at me suspiciously.

I looked away. 'Since I woke up this morning.'

'Why didn't you say anything?' Moira was aghast.

'I didn't want to spoil the day.'

'You told me they were Braxton Hicks,' Belle said crossly.

'I thought they were at first,' I retorted, aware that Shay as in my face panting loudly. 'What are you doing?' I demanded.

'Helping you with your breathing like they showed me at the classes,' he looked like a helpful puppy dog and I could have slapped him.

'Well stop it! It's really annoying,' I gave him the evils.

'Right,' Alan decided someone had to take charge, bless him. Everyone else was just gawping at me like I was going to a magic trick, (maybe they thought that instead of a baby I'd produce a bunch of flowers out of my fluff).

'Bev go and call for an ambulance,' he continued. 'Or a taxi.'

I shook my head. 'I'm not going to be able to wait for either.'

'Right,' he thought again. 'Troy! Troy is in his car, he'll take you,' he hurried out the ladies.

'What can I do mom?' Lexi hovered by me.

I pushed my handbag at her. 'Take some money from my purse, you and Belle get a taxi home and get my hospital bag, it's under my bed. Bring it to the hospital please,' I instructed as another contraction hit, succeeding in me nearly breaking Shay's fingers.

She nodded grabbing Belle's hand. 'How close are the contractions?' Moira asked, what a present for a bride on her wedding day.

'Every five minutes,' I blushed. 'I'm so sorry, I've spoilt your day.'

She touched my cheek. 'That is the last thing you've done,' she whispered, kissing my forehead.

I nodded as Bev came behind me, wrapping her shawl around my waist. 'Your dress is a bit of a mess babe, must have happened when your waters broke.'

'Oh,' I gulped, I was going to have to walk through the room with everyone looking at me, how embarrassing.

'Troy is going to take you to the hospital,' Alan reappeared. 'He said he's sorry he hasn't got a siren but I said we'd get Shay to hang his head out of the window and make the noise.'

'Everyone's a comedian,' I muttered. Shay didn't even raise a smile, I think reality was kicking in.

Alan gave me a cheeky smile, holding out his arm, Shay on the other side as we went back into the main room. Everybody gave me a round of applause and I went bright red. They all shouted their best wishes just as I heard Ava say to Rita. 'Well that's well and truly trapped him now.'

I glared at her, in two minds whether to march over there and give her what for but Shay steered me in the direction of the exit. Troy was waiting for us, a huge grin on his handsome face. 'Come on, let's get you to the hospital.'

I nodded, another contraction sweeping over me. 'Oh,' I spluttered leaning against Shay.

I didn't realise that Ava and Rita had followed us. 'Tash, Shay take care,' Rita called. 'Let us know when there is any news.'

Shay nodded as Ava whispered. 'And he had the nerve to warn me about ruining the wedding.'

He propelled me towards the door shaking his head. 'Gypo bitch,' I hissed.

'Tash!' Troy gave me a look of surprise and I shrugged, I knew it wasn't very politically correct but frankly I didn't care.

'You're not going to ruin my upholstery are you?' he joked, he had a lovely red BMW X6.

'I'll try not to,' I promised but just to be on the safe side he lay a tartan picnic blanket across the seat.

'Breath sweet, breath,' Shay fussed around me and I was grateful that he wasn't as drunk as Lexi had made out. He was a bit annoying though.

'Would you like to swap places with me?' I asked as Troy manoeuvred me onto the back seat.

'I would if I could,' he looked hurt as he got in next to me but I ignored him, concentrating on my contractions.

Bev had phoned ahead to tell the hospital that we were on our way and when we arrived I let Shay help me out the car. 'We need a wheelchair,' he looked around the grounds, a little in shock that he was nearly a father.

'I don't need a wheelchair,' I jumped in.

They ignored me. 'You go that way and I'll go this and we'll try and find one. You wait here Tash,' Troy shot me his megawatt smile. 'Won't be a tick.'

I watched in amazement as they shot off in different directions like headless chickens. Sighing I put my handbag on my shoulder, going inside.

'Are you by yourself?' the nurse asked.

'No, but part of me wishes I was. They've gone to find me a wheelchair.'

She looked at me puzzled and I shrugged, she was lovely and by the time Shay found me I was in the delivery room, putting on a hospital gown. 'I got you a wheelchair,' he came into the room looking a little sulky.

'I didn't need one,' I retorted as he took off his suit jacket, he did look a stylish dad to be.

'Hello Natasha,' the midwife bustled into the room. 'I'm Ruby, one of the two midwives who will be looking after you today.'

'Hi,' I gasped, that was a strong one. 'The contractions are every three minutes and I really want to push.' I was stooping, my top half on the bed and my feet on the floor, it was easing the pain a little. Shay was behind me rubbing my back.

'Hop onto the bed then and we'll take a look at you,' she smiled as a blonde haired lady joined us, the other midwife. 'Jacqui this is Natasha and Shay.'

'Hi,' she said brightly, seeing to the equipment.

Shay helped me onto the bed and she examined me. 'You are ten centimetres dilated,' she informed us with a smile. 'These babies are impatient to be born.'

'Oh,' I gasped, tears filling my eyes and Shay looked pretty choked up to. Jacqui attached two monitors to my stomach, one for each baby.

Shay sat on the chair beside me, looking like he was going to faint, he was certainly sobering up quickly. I howled out, the contractions were really powerful now and lasting longer. Shay rubbed my arm feeling helpless as I took a large gulp of gas and air. I had forgotten how bloody painful giving birth was.

'Okay then Natasha,' Ruby said. 'The first baby is travelling down the birth canal.'

Shay was staring at her intently, taking it all in. 'Do you want to hear the two heartbeats?' she let him listen and his eyes grew wide.

I cried out as another contraction hit. 'Sweet,' he gripped my hand.

Ruby gave me a knowing look as she put the cannula in my hand in case I needed a drip later. 'Can I push?' I cried. She nodded so I did.

'Aargh!' I cried, using every ounce of strength I could muster.

'Excellent,' she praised. 'Shall we go again?'

I nodded, screwing up my face and pushing before falling back against the pillows. Shay was still rubbing my arm, panting along with me.

'I haven't seen a labour this quick for years,' Ruby said as Jacqui kept an eye on the monitors.

'Do I get a prize?' I joked weakly, it was hurting a lot now.

'She's been in labour since this morning but she never told anyone,' Shay said and I glared at him. He was telling me off and I was delivering *his* babies.

'I didn't want to spoil your mom's wedding,' I snapped.

'Oh I love a good wedding,' Jacqui beamed. 'Was it a nice day?'

'It was lovely,' Shay turned to her. 'Mam looked gorgeous.'

'Church wedding?' she queried.

'Moseley Old Hall,' he replied. 'It's a nice place.'

I cleared my throat nosily, don't mind me I was just giving birth. He gave me a sheepish look. 'It's your fault anyway,' I snapped. 'You poked them out of me last night.'

'You weren't complaining then,' he retorted.

Jacqui giggled. 'Let's get back to business.'

I moved on the bed, going onto all fours, it felt more comfortable. 'I've just had a flashback to last night,' he whispered grinning.

I growled in reply. 'Rub her back Shay,' Ruby instructed. 'How are we doing?'

'I need to push again,' I panted as Jacqui gave me more gas and air.

'Okay now,' she watched as I bore down again. 'That's really good Natasha,' she praised.

I wasn't comfortable though and with Shay's help I got into a sitting position, legs up in the air. 'Again!' I cried putting my head down and pushing.

Shay leant into me just as I brought my head back up and we clashed with a thud. 'Feck Tash,' he cried. 'That really hurt.' Then he was aware of the three of us staring at him and he fell silent.

'Did it hurt love? Did it?' My tone was full of sarcasm. 'Well now you know how it bloody feels.'

I gasped, pushing with all my might. 'Stop now Natasha,' Ruby instructed. 'The baby's crowning, come and see Shay.'

He went to the *business end,* peering closely. 'Beautiful, it has hair! Lots of dark hair!' I really hoped he wasn't confusing it with my lady garden. 'Dark curly hair,' he repeated amazed.

'Excuse me,' Jacqui moved him slightly, easing the head out. Next came the shoulders and the rest of the body. She picked it up deftly and I peered over my bump.

'Is it okay?' I asked concerned.

'Perfect,' she replied. 'A little boy. Shay? Shay?'

He was looking at his son, all covered in blood, gunge and a white waxy substance and felt a little green around the gills, apparently he was a little tickled stomach. 'Yay,' he swallowed heavily.

'Don't you dare faint on me,' I warned him.

'I'm not,' he tried to redeem himself.

'Do you want to cut the placenta?' Ruby asked.

He rallied a little, nodding. Shaking slightly he did, then Jacqui clamped it, lying the baby on my chest. 'Hey little man,' I cooed, falling immediately in love. 'Hello. Hello. I'm your mommy.'

Shay was desperately trying not to part company with everything he had eaten that day. It truly was a miracle but he never realised how messy it would be. I tilted the baby towards him. 'And this is your daddy.' He leant forward to kiss his head and then immediately pinched the gas and air. 'Your big brave daddy,' I sighed.

'How are you Natasha?' Jacqui asked, checking me. 'Are you ready for baby number two?'

I groaned, I was shattered. 'I don't think I can,' the urge to push was coming again but I hadn't the strength.

Shay put his face inches from mine. 'You can do this beautiful, I'm so proud of you.'

I looked at him, holding our son tightly. 'I'm here, I'll always be here,' his voice was soothing me. 'I love you.'

I nodded, twin number two was just as impatient to be born. 'I love you too.'

Ruby took our son as I conjured up all I had, holding Shay's hand and bearing down, bless him, if I hurt him he didn't let on. It took another twenty minutes to deliver our second child and we both cried a little when Ruby announced it was a girl. How perfect was that? One of each.

I would go into minute detail of how I delivered the placenta also but you might be eating so I won't. They cleaned us all up and I sat propped up in bed, my hair plastered to my head with the exertion of the labour and I felt like I had been hit by a truck.

Swaddling the twins in nice soft blankets they brought them to us. Shay was perched on the bed beside me, kissing the top of my head. 'You were amazing,' he praised, his eyes filled with tears. 'I told you we'd have one of each. You owe me a striptease, a really slow one.'

'Hold one of your children, smut bucket,' I smiled but I would honour the bet.

He nervously took one of the twins. 'Which do I have?' he asked me.

I peeked under the blanket. 'Boy,' I replied.

He nodded. 'They are beautiful,' a single tear slid down his cheek. 'Just perfect.'

'They are,' I agreed, feeling pretty emotional myself. 'Just wait until we tell everyone.' We chuckled as a nurse came in.

'I bet you would love a nice cup of tea?' she smiled and we both nodded. From my waters breaking at the restaurant to delivering two healthy, perfect twins it had taken roughly three and a half hours, I couldn't believe it. 'Oh by the way your families are still in the visiting room in all their wedding finery.'

'They are all here?' I was astounded, feeling exhausted but euphoric at the same time.

Ruby was thoughtful for a moment, looking at Jacqui who nodded. 'We shouldn't really do this but if you're up to it Natasha they can all come in for five minutes but no longer.'

I nodded eagerly. I wanted to show the twins off, to share the moment with the people I loved most in the world. Shay passed me baby boy and on slightly shaking legs he walked out into the corridor and followed the nurse to the visitor's room.

Seven pairs of eyes looked at him expectantly. 'Son?' Moira asked when it looked like he wasn't going to speak.

A big grin broke out on his face. 'A boy born at eight thirty-seven, five pounds two ounces and a girl born at eight fifty-seven, four pounds twelve ounces.'

'Get in!' Dale yelled, pumping the air with his fist.

'And they are okay, Tash is okay?' Moira held her breath.

'They are just perfect,' he hugged his mom tightly. 'She was amazing, they are so gorgeous. Tash has given me everything.' The tears were falling down both their faces.

'You big tit,' Dale teased.

Bev slapped his arm. 'Leave him alone, it's lovely.'

He took a step back, not caring if he was a big tit. 'Come with me, the midwife said you can see them for five minutes but that's all. Tash is exhausted.'

Eagerly they followed him back to the delivery room, mindful to keep the noise down. I looked up as they came into the room, a shattered but happy smile on my face. 'Hey,' I whispered.

'You look rough sis, what have you been up too?' Dale asked jovially.

I shrugged, a twin in each arm, snuggled against me. 'Oh nothing much.'

'Everyone,' Shay began. 'I'd like you all to meet,' he pointed to the first twin and I mouthed boy. 'Albie Shay Flynn.' We had gone with the names we'd chosen a few weeks ago but had kept it quiet.

'And Molly Moira Flynn,' I finished.

'Oh,' Moira promptly burst into tears. 'That is lovely, thank you.'

'Well done sis,' Dale was blinking his eyes rapidly. He had cried when Lexi and Jamie were born too.

'Yes well done mom,' Lexi beamed still in her bridesmaid dress.

'I can't believe how much hair they have,' Belle said in amazement. 'Just like their daddy.'

'Daddy,' Shay repeated, savouring the word.

I looked at Jamie, glad that he had come to the hospital. 'They're really cute mom,' he said with a shy smile.

My heart soared, that meant the world to me and I gave him a special smile. 'Thanks Jams.'

'Photo opp,' Lexi declared taking out her mobile.

'No,' I protested, I looked a complete state.

'Just you, Shay and the twins,' she said. 'Only one. We'll take the others when you've done your hair and got a bit of slap on.'

I rolled my eyes but let her take the photograph, our smiles tired but very happy.

Ruby came bustling into the room. 'Come on now, let mommy and daddy sort themselves out, you can come back tomorrow.'

Everyone did as she said, saying their goodbyes and heading off home. Shay and I sat in the silence for a while, savouring it all. 'Thank you, I love you,' he whispered, his lips gentle on mine.

'I love you too,' I replied and I did, so much.

Forty~Four

I was dozing lovely when Shay arrived the next day, it was early and he looked more knackered than I did. The twins were asleep in their cots next to my bed. 'Morning beautiful,' he kissed me and then kissed each baby in turn. 'I still can't tell which ones which,' he admitted.

'You will, Molly is slightly smaller. You look like you didn't sleep very well.'

'I didn't, I was too buzzed.' He replied. 'How did you sleep?'

'Better than I thought I would,' I answered. 'I'm sore though.'

'I can imagine,' his tone was sympathetic. 'It's like me trying to push a satsuma through my mickey.'

'Exactly,' I agreed, trying to get comfortable. I was in my own room and it was wonderful. 'Did you call your dad?'

He nodded, sitting on the chair. 'I sent him the picture Lexi took, he sends all the love in the world.'

'Oh bless,' I yawned loudly. 'We'll call him later.'

'I expected you a little earlier than this,' I thought he would have arrived at first light how excited he was.

'The girls and I went shopping.'

'Shopping?' I frowned, I thought there was plenty of food in.

'Yes, I want to do this properly,' with that he went down on one knee.

'Shay,' I felt my eyes fill with tears.

He silenced me, taking a ring box from his jacket pocket. 'Tash you are everything to me, you are my world. Will you marry me?'

He opened the box and I stared inside. The ring was lovely, shaped like a solitaire but made up of diamond chips, all set in a white gold mount. 'Is this what you brought?' I asked amazed.

'Will you answer the fecking question?' he smiled amused.

I laughed softly. 'Yes, I'll marry you, my gorgeous Irishman.'

He jumped up, kissing me tenderly, then taking the ring from the box he placed it on my finger. 'It fits,' I said surprised.

'That's why I asked Lexi to come with me, she wears your old wedding ring. Plus, she knows your taste in things'

'Clever,' I caressed his cheek as the twins began to cry hungrily.

'They make a lot of noise for such tiny things,' he got to his feet going to them.

'This is only the beginning my fiancé, you wait till they are teething,' I glanced at my left hand. 'My ring is beautiful, thank you.'

'You're beautiful,' he told me.

I smiled again. 'Right daddy, time for your first lesson on feeding Albie and Molly.'

The nurse brought the bottles in and I showed Shay what to do. I had changed my mind about breastfeeding them and yes, I know it gave them the best start in life but, well you do it then.

'Now lay her against your shoulder,' I instructed, when they had finished their feed. 'And gently rub her back to bring her wind up.'

'I'm worried about hurting her,' he was all fingers and thumbs, bless him.

'You won't, they are more resilient than you think.'

'Hello,' Moira popped her head around the door. 'Can we come in?'

'Of course,' I was pleased to see her. 'You've just missed feeding time.'

'Look at you son,' she was becoming tearful, as she sat down, Alan following.

'I'm getting Molly's wind up,' he beamed.

'You've given them good Irish names,' she approved.

'He is going to be a natural dad,' I praised, he was already pretty hands on.

'Can I?' she held her hands out to me.

'Of course,' I passed her Albie and Alan took some pictures, then she held Molly and then both of them. Then Alan had a turn and I took the photographs, it was all very exhausting.

When he had finished he asked if we wanted a hot drink from the vending machine. 'Good idea,' Shay said. 'I'll give you a hand.'

'Moira,' I began as she sat with a twin in each arm, cooing over them. 'I hope you don't mind him being called Albie. We wanted it because it's Shay's middle name and his dad's name and well, we just really liked it.' I was blushing a little.

She had a knowing smile on her face. 'It's fine, don't worry. Besides Molly has my name so all is well,' her eyes widened. 'What is that on your finger?'

I beamed. 'Shay proposed properly this morning, he and Lexi went shopping for it earlier.' I showed it off.

'Alan, will you look at this stunner?' she cried as they came back with the tea.

'Congratulations,' he hugged me and shook Shay's hand.

'Oh, I don't want to go on honeymoon tomorrow,' her face fell. They were due to fly to Cape Verde, her first proper holiday.

'I promise to send you an update every day,' I crossed my heart.

'But it's a whole ten days!'

'It will whiz by,' Shay assured her as Lexi and Belle arrived.

'Hi everyone,' Lexi burst in with balloons and things, going to Moira and kissing the babies.

'Should all of us be in here?' she fretted.

'They'll soon tell us to sling it if not,' Alan sat on the other content, he had his wife and she was happy.

'They are so gorgeous,' Belle pushed her glasses up. 'Can we take them home with us?'

'I'd say no but ask me again when they are crying the house down at two o'clock in the morning,' I joked.

'Did the doctor say when you can go home?' Lexi was taking loads of photographs.

'Wednesday at the latest. He was really pleased with us, said the whole labour had been text book,' I was more than happy at the thought of going home.

'And I've spoken to Ray as from tomorrow I have two weeks paternity leave followed by a week's holiday. They all send their best.'

'Even Ava?' I asked slyly.

'Natasha,' Moira scolded, letting Lexi and Belle take a twin each.

Shay ignored me, perching himself on the edge of the bed and putting his arm around me. 'Have you met my fiancée?'

They all laughed and we sat chatting for the next forty minutes, then Alan suggested that he and Moira take the girls out for their Sunday lunch, like Moira he too enjoyed their company.

Amid hugs and kisses Moir collared me. 'You will message me every day and send me pictures.'

'I promise,' I hugged her. 'You have a fantastic honeymoon.'

'We will,' Alan kissed my cheek. 'You've done us proud my dear.'

'You'll have more grandchildren than you'll know what to do with Gramps,' I teased.

'I like that, Gramps,' he beamed.

'Mom, we'll see you soon.' They said their goodbyes.

After they had left Shay turned to me. 'This visiting lark is a bit exhausting.'

'Wait till we get home and we have a houseful,' I smiled ruefully. 'Shall we call your dad?'

He nodded and I dialled the number, Albie answering straight away as if he had been waiting for the call. 'Tash,' he greeted. 'You look really well.'

'Make up and sheer willpower,' I smiled.

'Hi dad,' I moved the screen so he could see Shay too as Niamh stood behind her husband.

'So, do we have names?' she asked.

'I wanted to tell them when we were together,' Shay explained.

I passed him my phone, I didn't want to move from the bed. He went to the cots, training the camera on them. 'Molly Moira Flynn,' he introduced proudly.

'Oh, that's lovely for your mam,' Niamh said.

'And Albie Shay Flynn,' he smiled.

There was silence for a moment and then his dad spoke. 'You're calling him Albie?'

'Yeah, we like the name and it's something that you and Shay share,' I answered as Shay came back to the bed.

'I wish they were awake,' Albie said wistfully.

'We'll call you when they are,' I still felt like I had gotten felled by an elephant.

'I can't believe the dark curly hair,' Niamh shook her head. 'Your mouth and nose Tash though, Shay's eyes and colouring.'

'Everyone says that,' I agreed.

'Dad, Niamh,' Shay took my hand, holding the phone in his other. 'We have more news.'

'What?' on the small screen they were both smiling.

He held my hand up. 'We're getting married.'

They cried out with delight. 'Erin will be so pleased,' Niamh joked.

We all tittered. 'We'll can you when the twins are awake, so you can see them.' Shay said. 'And we'll have a good chat.'

'Speak soon, take care,' Albie blew kisses at the screen.

'There is no way he is going to wait until the beginning of October to come and see them.'

'I know,' he agreed. 'Would that be a problem?'

'They'd have to take us as they find us.'

'They would,' he said. 'So, you wouldn't mind?' He really did want to show off his children to his dad.

'If they gave us a week to settle down it wouldn't be a problem.'

'That's great,' he looked pleased as Dale and Bev arrived just as I was going to show him how to change a nappy.

'What is that smell?' Dale held his hand over his nose. I pointed at Molly. 'There is no way something that tiny could conjure up that smell,' he gasped.

Bev tittered, sitting down. 'It smells like one of yours,' she teased him.

'I'd be proud to put my name to that. How you doing Shayster?'

'Grand,' he smiled contented. 'Just grand.'

Dale nodded satisfied and I looked at him annoyed. 'Er, I'm okay too, after all I've only given birth to twins.'

'I know *you're* okay,' he twinkled his eyes at me.

Bev shot him a look, shaking her head. 'I have to admit they are a pair of beauties,' she wasn't one for cooing over babies. 'Do they usually have that much hair?'

'Lexi and Jamie were both bald.'

'That's right,' Dale remembered. 'Right pair of mini skinheads.'

'Oh, bless them,' Bev handed me a big bar of chocolate.

'Have you let mom know?' Dale asked quietly.

I shook my head. 'Do you want me to tell her?' Bev inquired.

'No,' I replied. 'I don't think so, oh I don't know.'

'She hasn't bothered with you sis,' my brother pointed out.

'Let her do the running,' Shay advised. 'You've got no call to bend over for her.'

'I suppose,' I admitted, not wanting to spoil how lovely everything was.

'You know he's right,' Dale said as Jamie arrived with Abbie.

'Jams!' I cried, over the moon that he had come to visit, I never expected him to. 'Hi Abbie, lovely to see you.'

'Hi Tash,' she gave me the bottle of champagne that she held in her arms. 'From my mom and dad, they asked me to pass on their congratulations.

'That's really kind of them, please tell them thank you.'

'Yeah, we'll certainly enjoy it,' Shay grinned.

'Tell them to pop round to see the twins, we can all have a celebratory drink.' Shay shot me a discreet look that said stop inviting people over or we'll never have anytime to ourselves.

Jamie was bending over the cots, holding each twins hand with just one finger. I smiled, he really did like babies and he had actually turned up, result! Abbie joined him and they fussed around Albie and Molly, I hoped they weren't getting any ideas.

'How's the job going Jams?' Dale asked him.

He cast a sly glance at Shay. 'Good, yeah.'

'He's doing really well,' Shay praised quickly. 'Picking up things as if he's done them for years.'

'And the driving lessons?' Bev broke off a piece of my chocolate.

'I thought that was for me?' I asked in disgust.

'I'm only having a bit,' she protested.

'Yeah, they are going good. Clive said it won't be long before I can put in for my test,' he replied politely. 'I've got my theory on Monday.'

'I wouldn't want to pass my test again,' she shuddered. 'Are you learning to drive Abbie?'

'Yes, my parents have brought me a Fiat 500 for my birthday,' she replied, so taken with the twins.

'Our stylist has one of those,' she pinched another piece of chocolate so I moved it away from her.

She bobbed her tongue out at me as she popped it in her mouth. They all stayed for another hour and then it was feeding time again and they left us to it. I stood unsteadily, I still felt a little wobbly, to hug my son. 'Thank you for coming Jamie, it means the world to me. I love you so much.'

He hesitated for a moment before kissing my cheek and mumbling. 'Love you.'

I could have burst into tears there and then, it completed my happiness as sentimental as that sounds. 'See you soon,' Abbie gave us her best smile and taking Jamie's hand they left.

Bev looked at me approvingly. 'He seems a different kid.'

'I just hope it lasts,' I fretted, Abbie was such a positive influence on him.

'It will,' Dale sounded confident. 'You know sis you still look about eight month pregnant.'

I cuffed him round the ear. 'You stretch your stomach muscles with twins for eight months and we'll see how quickly yours spring back.'

'Take no notice of him,' Bev pushed him out of the way to hug me. 'Do you need anything?'

'No, thank you.' Then I leant in to whisper. 'New lady bits wouldn't go amiss though.'

'Sore?' she commiserated.

I nodded. 'Very. I can't see me having sex again until the kids are at least five years old,' I joked.

'Poor you,' she hugged me again, then she noticed my hand. 'Oh my God, he's got you an engagement ring!'

'I know,' I really was over the moon.

'We did say we were getting married,' Shay gave her a bemused look.

'I know but when did you buy it?' she examined it closely, nodding her approval.

'Lexi and Belle came with me this morning,' he picked up Albie, who was starting to get a little niggly.

'Did you do it properly?' she let go of my hand.

'On one knee and everything,' he confirmed.

'Oh,' she gasped, whispering to me. 'I want one.'

'You never know,' I replied although Dale was pretending he hadn't heard.

'You so deserve all of this' she sighed. 'Come on stud, you can buy me lunch as Tash is refusing to cook.'

He laughed and so did we. 'If I must,' he rolled his eyes, shaking Shay's hand. 'Well done the Shayster, making an honest woman of her.'

'That'll be the next thing, organising the wedding,' Bev stated, her eyes sparkling with excitement.

I shooed them out, I planned on us having a long engagement, we had to save our pennies and it wasn't going to be easy with everything we were paying out. They left laughing as Shay stood by the window, holding Albie carefully. 'Should you tell the nurse if you're that sore?' he asked concerned.

I smiled softly. 'I'm sore because I've just given birth to two babies. I'll be fine soon.'

'You know I won't pressure you,' he looked so solemn.

'About what?' I picked up Molly who was awake also.

'Making love,' his eyes sought mine.

'It's only been a day,' I chuckled. 'I haven't the energy for it, sorry babe.'

He flushed a little. 'I don't mean now, I mean in a few weeks. I'll wait for you to let me know.'

'So I'm going to have to beg you for a bit of nookie?' I said tickled.

He broke into a smile. 'No, we could have a code,' he thought for a moment. 'When you put on your pink sexy nightie, the one you brought for Lytham, then I know you want to.'

I shook my head amused. He was only trying to do the right thing, bless him. 'Pink nightie it is then,' I agreed.

'Excellent,' he grinned.

Forty~Five

The hospital let us come home on Wednesday morning and I nearly ran to the car. I couldn't wait to get home and start living our new life. Carefully we strapped the twins in the back of the Astra, Shay driving so slowly that for a moment I was convinced that we were going backwards.

Looking out the window I thought about how much my life had changed in the last twelve months. Before I had seemed to live in a state of perpetual dread. Dread that my parents didn't love me, didn't want me, (they didn't). Then Sam had come along and a few years of relative calm, although, looking back, I think I had known all along that he had a wondering eye, I just choose to ignore it. I had a fantasy that I could change him, that I would be enough for him.

I desperately needed someone to love me, to put me first and to be fair Sam did, on the surface anyway. He did make me feel wanted but it was a ploy, a way to make me rely on him, to believe that I was nothing without him and for a long time I did. When I realised what he was up to it broke my heart, it truly did. I loved him and I had the two children, I never thought that I would get over him but in time I did.

I was more than happy by myself, I enjoyed being alone, pleasing no one but Lexi and Jamie. I didn't have to worry about having my heart broken again, all I had to do was bring up my two children the best way I knew how.

Then along came Shay and he was so gorgeous that my resolve completely vanished. I just wanted him and the more I got to know him the more I craved him. I glanced at the engagement ring he had surprised me with, it glinted in the September sunshine. It was lovely, just perfect, I turned to smile at him and he returned it.

'Okay?' he asked looking back at the road.

'I am,' I replied, he was going to be such a good father and husband. If you had asked me thirteen months ago if I would have fallen in love with a man a decade younger than me, had twins with him and agreed to marry him I would have laughed in your face. It's the truest saying ever, you never knew what was round the corner.

Pulling up outside our house I got out gingerly, leaning in the back of the car carefully to bring our children to the place they would always be loved best.

'Everything went well then?' Joe our neighbour, had nipped out of his house with his wife Diane.

'Yes, thank you,' I replied, as I said earlier I had lived next door to them for years.

'Oh, look at the pair of them,' Diane gasped. 'They are so gorgeous.'

'Aren't they just?' Shay beamed proudly.

'Just a little something,' Joe gave me the gift bag he held in his hand. 'Lexi came to tell us the good news.'

'Oh thank you,' they had been such good neighbours. I remember the first time I had chucked Sam out, he had turned up drunk, upsetting me, distressing the kids. Joe had stepped in, getting him out of the house and making sure he didn't come back, well that night anyway.

Then they had put up with the noise from the kids, my rows with Jamie, they must have heard everything. Oh gawd, do you think they could hear me and Shay having sex?!

I blushed at my thoughts. 'When we're settled you'll both have to come round for a cuppa.'

'That would be lovely,' Diane smiled. 'If you need anything you know where we are.'

'Aw thanks,' everyone was being so kind.

'Let's get them inside,' Shay dug out the house keys.

'See you soon,' Diane blew kisses at Albie and Molly.

We said our goodbyes and went inside, the house was spotless, in the living room Lexi and Belle had draped a banner over the fireplace. ***WELCOME HOME THE TWINS FLYNN.*** Balloons on either side.

'Oh bless them.' They were back in Birmingham but would be coming the weekend.

'They cleaned up too,' Shay carefully put the baby seat on the floor before taking Molly from me and putting her beside Albie just as my mobile pinged. 'Mam?' he asked.

I nodded, since they had gone on honeymoon Monday she had texted me three or four times a day.

'Sorry,' his smile was apologetic.

'It's nice that she cares. I can't moan about that,' 1 took a picture of the sleeping twins and sent it to her with an update on everything.

'You're good with her,' he knew some women would have found it stifling.

'She's very good to me,' I smiled looking at the pile of cards on the coffee table. 'Where are all these from?'

'People who care about us,' he smiled. 'Cup of tea?'

'I'd love one,' I sat down, I wasn't as sore as I had been thank goodness. I'd had a very fortunate to have a labour that had been so straight forward without any complications, especially at my age. Lucky too that the babies had come out so perfect.

'Mam has filled the freezer with so much food,' he chatted. 'She must have spent the first day of her married life cooking.'

'Oh bless her,' Moira was a very good cook.

He nodded, making the tea. We sat side by side on the settee just wanting our babies sleeping, our hands entwined. 'By the way I spoke to dad this morning,' he stifled a yawn.

'Are they well?' Him yawning was setting me off too.

'They're grand, he hesitated for a moment. 'He's asked if they can visit earlier then they planned. He really wants to see Albie and Molly.'

'I thought he would,' I smiled knowingly.

'Well?' he raised an eyebrow.

'I don't mind. They can have our room and I'll lend Bev's double air bed and we can camp in the nursery.'

'He said they would stay in a hotel.'

'Rubbish,' I retorted picking up my mobile and finding his number. 'Hi Albie, how are you?' I asked when he answered.

'Grand and yourself?'

'Back at home with our babies,' I grinned. 'Shay said you want to bring your visit forward?'

'If that isn't going to disrupt you. We'll stay in a hotel,' he added quickly.

'No you won't,' I replied. 'You'll stay with us, I insist.'

'We couldn't put you out,' he countered.

'You aren't putting us out,' I chuckled. 'You're family and family stays with us.'

'That's kind of you,' he was chuffed that I had called them family.

'When were you thinking of?' I could get things organised then.

'Would it be okay if we came next Thursday, we would only stay a few days.'

'Yes, that's fine,' I was looking forward to seeing them. 'Will you fly or take the ferry?'

'Fly probably, why not?' he laughed lightly.

'I don't blame you,' I paused for a moment. 'That's settled then. You arrive next Thursday and come and meet your grandchildren.'

'I can't wait,' he enthused. 'I'll let you know the flight times.'

'Speak soon Albie, love to Niamh.' I ended the call.

'That's really good of you sweet,' Shay gave me a gentle kiss. 'Isn't it going to be a bit much for you though?'

'I've given birth not had open heart surgery,' I scolded lightly. 'All the running about will do me good anyway, get rid of this baby belly.'

'You look stunning,' he praised.

'You are biased,' I was quiet for a moment. 'What do you think Moira will do? She'll be back when they arrive. What if they bump into each other?'

'There's every chance beautiful,' he sighed. 'Especially with him staying here.'

'When is your mom due back?' I bit my lip, worrying.

'Wednesday,' he was thoughtful. 'We'll just have to explain the situation to her.'

'Let them enjoy their honeymoon first,' I advised. 'I hope she isn't too upset that we are putting them up.'

'Maybe we can keep them separate. Mam will be good whichever we do.'

'I hope so,' I smiled suddenly. 'Make the mother of your children another cup of tea please.'

He smiled at my cheek. 'Coming up, soon to be Mrs Flynn.'

I leant back on my seat contented, waiting for Albie and Molly to wake up for their feed.

Forty~Six

We settled down to a routine, it helped that Shay was off work, he was absolutely golden. By Saturday though I was going a little stir crazy, I needed fresh air. 'Should we be taking them out yet?' he fretted as I swaddled them in blankets.

'They'll be fine,' I dismissed his fears, he was such a worry wort at times. 'We'll pop to the Asda and then go to the salon, see what everyone's up to.'

He looked at me doubtfully, he knew I wanted to see how they were getting on without me, which was partly true but I also wanted to show the twins off. Walking around the supermarket I picked up something tasty for supper. We had lived off Moira's cooking since I had got home but now I wanted to cook for my man.

I had the small trolley whilst Shay pushed the double pram. It was amazing how many people stopped us to admire the twins, they were little superstars. We were by the cakes, I was going to take some to work when a voice cried. 'Aunty Tash!'

I turned just as Safi launched herself at me. 'Aunty Tash, I've missed you.'

'Hello princess,' I gave her a big hug. 'I've missed you too.'

Meera was walking towards us and I took an intake of breath, she looked how I had all those years ago. She had lost weight, dark shadows ringing her eyes. Her once glossy hair looked dull and brittle.

'It's none of our business,' Shay's tone had a warning in it. 'What happens between her and Sam we shouldn't interfere in.' He kept his voice low.

'I know,' I pulled Safi to me. 'I'm not interested.'

'Tash, Shay,' Meera greeted us. 'Congratulations on the twins.'

'Thank you' I stepped aside so she could have a good look at them.

'Oh my goodness,' she took her daughters hand. 'They are gorgeous, your mouth and nose Tash but everything else pure Shay. Jamie said they were adorable.' She was just relieved they did not look like Sam, part of her had wondered.

Shay's smile faded as he saw the aforementioned Sam baring down on us. 'Hi,' my ex nodded curtly.

'Hey,' I really did not want to talk to him.

Shay kind of grunted at him and I just wanted to get away, I no longer wanted him tainting my life. 'Hmm, congratulations.' He said but it looked like he was swallowing razor blades.

'Aren't they beautiful?' Meera's voice was over bright as she looked at her husband. 'Albie and Molly.'

He stared at them, a long, cold hard stare. 'Yeah,' his eyes sought mine and they were so full of venom that I recoiled a little.

I held onto the trolley, a flush creeping up my face. 'Can I come and see you aunty Tash?' Safi clung on my arm.

I hesitated looking at Meera but she was giving nothing away. 'Of course you can,' my voice was unsteady. I knew just by looking at Meera that she thought Sam still wanted me and I groaned inside.

'We have to go,' Sam said impatiently.

'In a minute,' her tone was rattled.

'Now,' he barked. 'We can't be late for your precious family.'

God, how awkward was this? 'I'm coming,' her eyes held mine, tears forming in them. 'Sorry.'

'It's okay,' I touched Safi's cheek lovingly. I did miss seeing her. Meera was worrying me a little though, she looked like she could do with a friend but Shay wasn't wrong. It was none of our business.

'Well,' I kept my tone light. 'If you're passing pop in, we'll catch up. Take care.'

'Thank you, you too,' she replied turning to leave.

Shay stood next to me, his body half in front of mine, a lion guarding his pride. Sam glared at us before striding off, Meera and Safi running to catch up. He gave me a comical look. 'Did you get the impression that your man wasn't very happy with us?'

'He's not "my man",' I tutted. 'Poor Safi and Meera.'

'Poor Safi, Meera is old enough to tell Sam to piss off,' he corrected me.

'Do you think that Sam is still fooling around?' I asked checking on the twins.

He nodded. 'Judging by the state of Meera I would say so.'

'Does he never learn? I thought after we saw him in Stafford he would behave himself. I can't understand him, he has a lovely wife and daughter.' I could have cried for them.

'You probably know him better than anyone, the bloke is a maggot.'

'He is,' I had to agree, I felt like banging his balls between a couple of house bricks.

We carried on with the rest of the shopping, I hated to say it but seeing Sam had left a bad taste in my mouth. I wanted to scream at Meera to dump him, to build a new life with her daughter, to not leave it as long as I had and waste so many precious years on him.

'You okay beautiful?' Shay was looking at me.

I pushed the trolley along the crisps and snacks aisle. 'I am, I have you.'

'Always,' he confirmed. 'Let's go and pay then take the cakes to the girls.'

So that's what we did. I knew we wouldn't have a cat in hells chance of getting the double pram through the salon door so we carried them in their car seats. The place was full as we went inside, so many familiar faces. 'Hello,' Bev greeted us delighted. 'What are you doing out and about?'

'We've come to see everyone and to bring cakes,' I smiled balancing the car seats on the nail counter.

Bev and Carling crowded around us. 'Oh Tash they are adorable,' Carling said, a hand against her heart. 'They are so tiny.'

'They were a good weight for twins,' I told her.

Lin you may remember, my foils and base colour lady, got out of her chair to come and see them. 'You look really well Tash,' she beamed at the sleeping babies.

'And how's baby daddy?' Kim had also abandoned her customer to come and see us.

'I'm good thanks,' he gave her his most striking smile.

'Can I hold one?' Lin asked as they both began to stir.

I nodded, like I said I wanted to show them off, the little beauties.

'Can I too?' Carling jigged up and down a little.

'Carry on,' I inclined my head as Shay unbuckled the straps.

'So Shay I bet your right hand is seeing a lot of action now Tash is incapacitated?' Kim gave him a cheeky look.

He smiled bemused, not sure how to answer.

'Do you have time for a coffee?' Bev led the way into the back room. 'So how are things?' she asked as she put the kettle on.

'Good,' I replied. 'No, better than good. Fabulous in fact.'

'You certainly look happy,' she stated busying herself with our drinks.

I watched Shay through the open doorway, he was playing the proud father to the hilt. Kim was clucking around him, flirting outrageously.

'He's loving being a dad isn't he?' Bev was beside me.

'He was born to it,' I agreed.

'Look at him,' she chuckled.

He was chatting away to all the ladies, even the new junior, Carmen, seemed really taken with him and the twins. They were all looking at him adoringly, he had them eating out of his hand, especially when he handed out the cupcakes he had brought.

'Tash!' Kim called.

'Yep?' I picked up Shay's mug of coffee to take to him.

'You know I like you, well I am offering to service Shay why you can't.'

I put his mug on the reception desk giving him a huge smile. 'There you go my gorgeous Irishman, it's the best offer you're going to get at the moment.'

He grinned at me. 'If I sleep with Kim it would just spoil it for all that came after me. You know how good I am Tash, it just wouldn't be fair on her.'

'True,' I conceded, pushing a wayward curl from his eyes.

She looked at us solemnly. 'I am willing to take the risk.'

He laughed, pulling me to him. 'Show them your stunning ring.'

'What ring?' Kim pricked up her ears.

I flashed my hand in front of them. 'Oh my God,' she cried. 'It's a true fairy-tale romance. Shay you have put my faith back in men. There are some Prince Charming's out there after all.'

I shook my head going back to Bev. 'How's big dog?' I did still miss Millie, especially now I wasn't at work.

'She is great, such a good dog. She's at home with Dale.'

'And how are you and my brother getting on now you're shacked up together?'

'Better than I could have hoped for,' she looked quite shy.

That made me happy, everything seemed to be coming together. 'We popped in the Asda before we came here, saw Sam with Meera and Safi.'

'Still together then?' I had told her about seeing them in Stafford. 'Did they speak?'

'They had to, Safi came running over to us.'

'And?' she prompted.

'Sam looked really pissed off,' I confided. 'As if he didn't really believe that I would have the twins even though he knew I was pregnant.'

'Just watch him,' she cautioned.

'I don't think he's finished with us yet,' I got the impression he still would cause ructions between me and Shay if he could, even though we knew about his fancy bit.

'He'll never leave you alone Tash, he still thinks you'll take him back,' she told me wisely.

'I've told him to fuck off and I'll keep telling him,' I pulled a face. 'Albie and Niamh are coming to visit, I'm a little worried about how Moira will take it.'

'Will she be back from honeymoon?'

I nodded. 'I don't want her upset but they will be stopping with us for a few days and you know Moira won't want to keep away.'

'It might be better if they do see each other,' she was thoughtful.

'How do you work that out?' I frowned helping myself to one of the cupcakes Bev had secreted away from everyone else. I still thought I was eating for three, it had to stop.

'For the last thirty-odd years they have put each other on a pedestal. It didn't end properly. She just upped and left,' Bev explained. 'Denny and I came to our natural conclusion, we dotted the I's and crossed the T's.'

I frowned. 'I don't get what you mean, Moira and Albie weren't married.'

'Oi baby brain,' she rolled her eyes. 'Closure, that's what they need. Moira was by herself for so long maintaining that Albie was the only man she had ever loved. So perhaps by seeing him again she will realise that he is just a man, not this idol that she has built up in her mind.'

'What if they run off together?' That was the thing that worried me most.

'It's not an episode of some shitty soap opera,' she smiled. 'They won't but I do think it will do them good to meet.'

'Will you and Dale come over, take some of the pressure off us?'

'Course we will. You should have asked them to stay in a hotel.'

'It's Shay's dad, I couldn't do that.'

'You're too soft, you've just had twins. When are they coming?'

'Thursday,' I ate my cake. 'We'll tell Moira when she's back from honeymoon.'

She smiled softly, then her face grew serious. 'Sue knows about the twins.'

'Mom? She hasn't got in touch, how do you know?' That old feeling of hurt wrapped itself around me.

'I saw her in the pub, well Dale and I did and we told her. Sorry babe.'

I blinked back the tears, mom wasn't going to ruin my happy mood. 'I bet she was *so* interested.'

Bev shrugged. 'You don't need her, you have us.'

'I can't understand her, I could never understand her. If Lexi had a child I'd be up the front, Moira is.'

'They are two very different women,' she tried to resist having a cake then gave in and picked up one with pink frosted icing.

'I suppose,' I agreed as Shay came in with Albie.

'Can I change him in here, he stinks.'

'You change nappies too? I am impressed,' Bev and I got out of the way and I fetched him what he needed from the changing bag.

'Jesus,' Bev gasped at the smell. 'What are you feeding him?'

'He's a chip off the old block,' I commented drily pointing to my beloved.

He grinned. 'Nothing wrong with healthy bowels.'

'Talking of shit my mom knows about the twins.'

He pursed his lips. 'And as we can see she just can't keep away. Take no notice beautiful,' he sympathised, but he knew it would hurt me. 'Her, we don't need.'

'That's what Bev said,' my voice was quiet.

'You know I never knew nappy changing was such a spectator sport but I am impressed with you technique,' Bev neatly changed the subject.

'Piece of cake,' he grinned doing up Albie's all in one.

'Such gorgeous, cute babies,' she sighed. 'You know I'll babysit when they are older. I couldn't do it now, the heads loll too much. Babies scare me a little, I always think I'm going to break them.'

'Thanks hun,' I smiled once more.

'Are you looking forward to your dad visiting?' she asked Shay.

He looked at her, Albie in his arms as I got rid of the dirty nappy. 'I am,' he confirmed. 'It'll be great.'

'It will,' I echoed, hoping that Moira would be fine with it all.

Forty~Seven

Moira and Alan returned from honeymoon Wednesday afternoon coming to straight from the airport to our house looking nice and tanned. 'Where are my babies?' she demanded when I let them in, I pointed her to the living room where Shay and the twins were.

'Hey mam,' he greeted her as she swooped down on a sleeping Albie and Molly. 'Good honeymoon.'

'It was wonderful,' she stood over the twins as Alan followed me in. 'How have they been?'

'As good as gold,' Shay stood. 'They seem to be asleep most of the time.'

'Really?' she looked surprised. 'You were a little shite who continually bawled the house down.'

'Wait till they start teething,' Alan warned drolly.

I nodded my agreement. 'It's not fun.'

'I'll put the kettle on or would you like something stronger?' Shay asked with a smile.

'Tea would be great,' Alan was also admiring the babies. 'They are lovely.'

'I'll have a whisky,' Moira patted her son's cheek. 'I feel like I'm still on my honeymoon.'

He nodded, disappearing into the kitchen, Moira looking at Alan and then at me. 'When Albie and Niamh come over I want to meet them.'

'What?' I was thrown for a moment.

'I want to meet them,' she repeated.

'Oh,' I didn't expect her to be so forthright.

'Well, what do you think?' she peered at me.

I was flustered for a moment. 'I don't know,' I admitted. Was it a good idea, I mean really? What if the old feelings were still there between them?

'Here you go,' Shay brought in the drinks, tea for Alan and me, whisky for him and his mom. 'What's up?' he looked at my face.

'Natasha doesn't like the idea of me seeing Albie when he comes to visit,' Moira explained. I don't think she was happy with me, she had used my full name.

His face didn't hide his disapproval. 'Why would you want to do that? Why would you want to see him?'

She shook her head. 'Not want to see him, *need* to see him.'

'Why?' he screwed up his face.

She tutted loudly. 'Look at the pair of you,' she chided. 'We have met before you know.'

Shay chanced a look at Alan. 'I don't know mam,' his answer was cagey.

'Don't look like that Shay Albie Flynn!' She cried. 'I am a grown woman.'

'I know you are,' he necked his whisky. 'I thought things would be better if they were kept separate.'

'Separate?' she raised her voice a little, immediately lowering it again when she remembered the twins were asleep. 'What do you mean?'

He shifted uncomfortably in his seat. 'I just think it would be better.'

'And why do you think that?' she challenged. 'Do I embarrass you? Are you ashamed of me?' She flung the questions at her son.

'Moira,' I cut in softly, I didn't want her thinking that.

'I am asking my son,' she snapped, two high points of colour on her face. I recoiled, I had never seen her like this before.

'So?' She pushed. 'Are you ashamed of me? Am I someone to be kept hidden away like he had to hide me from his wife? I brought you up, me! And now you are ashamed of your own mother, aren't you?'

Shay tried to answer but she ploughed on. 'Pushing me away after I walked every step of your life with you. Me, no one else! You answer me!'

'I'm trying to fecking answer if you give me a chance,' he was beginning to riled.

'Don't swear at your mom,' I told him off, a little panicked at how fast things had escalated into an argument.

He glared at me. 'I'm trying to explain that I'm not pushing her away.'

'This is getting you both nowhere,' Alan said calmly.

'I was thinking of you,' Shay looked at his mom.

'Me? How is this thinking of me?' she cried. 'Oh it's all nice and shiny and new with your dad now but he hasn't had to go through all the shite I had to. He just gets the perfect son, with the lovely girlfriend and adorable grandchildren.'

'What's that supposed to mean?' he snapped.

'Can you keep your voices down please?' I asked pointedly, I didn't want them waking the twins waking up.

He wouldn't look at me, fixing his intense expression on his mom. 'Well?' he pressed.

'It's all very well waltzing in here enjoying all the good bits,' she twisted her wedding ring around her finger agitated.

'Love,' Alan put his hand on her arm but she shrugged him off.

'He wasn't there when we were struggling to make ends meet. When I missed meals so you could have a full belly,' she gasped for breath. 'He didn't pick you up when you hurt yourself or comfort you when you had a bad dream.'

'He couldn't, you never told him that I existed.' Shay retorted making Alan and I cringe in unison.

She looked like she'd had a slap in the face. 'You ungrateful little maggot,' she spat. 'You absolute gobshite.'

'If it was such a problem for you me seeing my father then why did you give me your blessing?' he snapped back.

The twins woke, crying loudly. 'Thanks a lot,' I snarled at both of them. 'Thanks a bloody lot, I'd just got them settled.'

Shay moved towards them but I stopped him. 'You and your mom got in the kitchen and sort it bloody out.'

'Tash is right,' Alan picked up Albie. 'You need to stop this arguing, it's doing you no good.'

They stared at us chastised as I rocked Molly in my arms, Alan doing the same with Albie. Moira had tears in her eyes and I for one was shocked. I had never seen them argue like that before but boy was I pissed off that they had woken my babies up.

'Tash, I'm sorry, I didn't mean to wake them,' she apologised.

I held Molly tighter. 'I wish to God I had never got it in my head go to bloody Quin and look for Albie,' I swore. 'Look at the pair of you,' I could feel tears in my own eyes. 'I didn't want this.'

'Beautiful,' Shay looked at me concerned as I lay Molly back down.

'No,' I kept my voice low. 'The last thing I wanted as it to cause ructions between you and your mom.'

'It hasn't,' he said. 'Honestly.'

'No, it hasn't,' she agreed as Alan looked at her doubtfully.

'I just don't understand why you want to meet him after everything,' Shay had calmed down a little.

Moira flopped back in her seat. 'Both of us are going to be in your life, Tash's life, the babies lives.'

'And?' he drained his glass.

'Jaysus, no wonder people think the Irish are thick,' she groaned and I tried to hide my smile. 'We need to get on,' she shrugged. 'I don't want future family events where one of us feels we can't be there because the other one is. Like your wedding.'

Shay rubbed his face wearily, Albie and Molly settled once more. I could understand what Moira was saying, look at how hard I had tried to keep things smooth with Sam for the sake of our kids.

Moira looked to Alan. 'Plus I need to lay the ghost to rest.'

'What ghost?' I frowned sitting on the arm of Shay's chair.

She leant forward. 'I have put Albie on a big pedestal all these years, no one could touch him, and then I met Alan.'

Shay looked at me uneasily. The argument with him mom had left a bad taste in his mouth. I shook my head discreetly, what could we say?

'I need to know that I am well and truly over him,' she continued. 'For Alan's sake, for my sake.'

'How do you feel about this?' Shay asked Alan.

He shrugged picking up his now lukewarm tea. 'Moira needs to do what she feels she should.'

'Shit,' Shay drew out the word. 'I don't know what to say. They'll be here tomorrow.'

'Tomorrow,' she wobbled a little. 'So soon? Which hotel are they staying in?'

I glared at Shay, this was going to start the argument again. 'They're staying here,' I faltered.

Moira stood quickly. 'So they will be here all the time?'

'Yes,' I replied hoping she wouldn't start shouting. 'I'm sorry Moira.'

'You hardly know him,' she whispered.

'Mam, I need to get to know him, especially now I'm a dad myself,' he sounded jaded.

'So if you got your way and kept things separate,' she said the word like it was dirty. 'Then I wouldn't be allowed to visit, wouldn't be allowed to see my grandchildren until they went home?'

'It's not like that,' Shay dry washed his face.

'Isn't it?' she asked tearfully.

'No,' I said quickly as Alan steered her gently back down.

'He wasn't there for you all those years and I know that is my doing but it feels like you're putting him first.'

'I'm not mam,' he replied dismayed. 'You will always be one of the most important people in the world to me, please believe that. I wouldn't hurt you for anything.'

She sniffed loudly and I felt awful. This was all my doing, no getting away from it.

'Tell me what you want me to do,' he continued going to kneel in front of her. 'I love you, you are my mam.'

She caressed his face. 'I don't want to lose you.'

'You're not going to lose me,' he soothed her. 'Never.'

She began to cry softly and he gathered her in his arm. 'Mam, please don't,' his voice was pained.

She tried to push him away but he held her fast. 'I just need to do this but he will never mean as much to me as you do.'

I looked at Alan, my own eyes bright with tears, he gave me a worried smile and I looked away. 'Oh will you look at the state of me?' she batted away her tears. 'What am I like?'

Shay smiled softly, kissing her cheek. 'Will you stay for something to eat?'

'Tash?' she was making sure I wanted them to.

'Please stay,' I replied getting to my feet and going into the kitchen. Moira followed me as I bustled about.

'I'm sorry for my outburst,' she caught my hand and I turned to face her.

'No, I'm the one who's sorry. I'm the one who's stirred all this up. Shay loves you so much Moira, he's never going to push you away. You mean too much to him for that to happen.'

'I know, deep down,' she looked contrite.

'I love you too,' I felt myself blush. 'I need you and so do Albie and Molly.'

'Oh sweetheart,' she hugged me tightly. 'It's just with my boy we have fought every battle alone, celebrated every victory just the two of us. I understand that he wants to know his father I truly do.'

'Not at the expense of hurting you thought,' I interrupted.

She shushed me. 'Albie is a wonderful charming man but I don't want Shay to get hurt.'

I frowned. 'I don't think Albie will hurt him. He seems as keen to know Shay as Shay is to know him. He just wants to fill in the blanks.'

'You must think I'm an eejit,' she sniffed.

'Not at all. I hate the thought of my kids loving Sam more than they love me which is a bit childish really,' I admitted.

'You have no fear of that with Lexi and I think Jamie is finally wising up to what his dad's like.'

'I don't want them to hate him,' I said quickly in case that was how it sounded. 'I keep on to Lexi to visit but she's grown woman with her own mind. Good job she doesn't know he's up to his old tricks or she'd rip his balls off.'

'You haven't told her then?'

'No, it's none of my business,' I shuddered. 'I won't influence her one way or another.'

'She's a fine young woman though, a credit to how you've brought her up. My grandchildren are in good hands.'

'Thank you,' I smiled shyly.

'So she doesn't go and see her dad then?'

'She goes to the house usually when Sam isn't there, she seems to time it to perfection so she can say she does visit but he's never home. She loves Safi and she's close to Meera but has little time for her dad.'

'Sam has made a rod for his own back, all because he can't keep his own rod in his trousers.'

We began to giggle, the upset over. 'That's true enough,' I smiled. 'Will you help me with supper?'

She nodded, busying herself. We sat down an hour later, Shay and his mom back to normal and Alan helping to keep the conversation flowing. When they had left for home and everything was tidied away I found shay in the living room, a thoughtful expression on his face and a glass of whisky in front of him. 'Hey beautiful,' he greeted me.

'That was horrible,' I sat on his lap. 'I didn't like you and your mom arguing.'

He wrapped his arms around me. 'It didn't thrill me either.'

'Was Alan really okay?' I fretted.

'He seemed to be. He knows why mam has to see my da and he supports her. He's a good man one of the best.'

'We have to make sure he doesn't feel pushed out either,' I played with his curls.

'My Tash, always worried about everyone else,' he kissed my hand. 'I didn't think mam would be so intense about it all.'

'She's scared she's going to lose you,' I told him. 'That's all.'

'Never,' his tone was firm.

'I know,' I kissed him lovingly.

His fingers walked up my thigh, a twinkle in his eyes. 'What, no pink nightie?'

'Easy tiger,' I grinned. 'It's just a comforting hug.'

'Oh,' he sighed.

'You'll just have to amuse yourself,' I ruffled his hair.

'What do you mean?' he was mystified.

'Think what God gave you your right hand for,' my smile was huge.

'Sweet,' he slapped my arm playfully. 'I'll wait patiently thank you.'

'Just make sure your mom feels loved and wanted,' I kissed him again.

'I already do but I'll try harder,' he promised.

Forty~Eight

I was on tenterhooks the next day waiting for Albie and Niamh to arrive. I was looking forward to them coming but since Moira had announced that she wanted to see Albie I was really nervous. Shay had left earlier to pick them up from the airport and my nerves were increasing. I just wanted everything to be wonderful, everyone to be happy but life rarely turned out like that.

I heard Shay's key in the front door and I went into the hallway to greet them. The house was spotless and I had cooked a large lasagne for their first night. Albie and Molly were fed, changed and currently flat out and smelling of baby talc. 'Tash,' Albie spilled through the door, enveloping me in his arms. 'How are you dahling?'

'I'm great,' I ushered them inside. 'Niamh, come in and I'll put the kettle on.'

She hugged me as Shay came in with their cases. 'Where are they?' Albie looked at me.

I motioned them to follow me. 'They've just gone down but they'll be awake again soon enough,' I kept my voice low. 'Niamh, Albie this is Molly and little Albie.'

Niamh gasped. 'They are so perfect. Look at their hair! Albie will you look at the pair of them.'

'I am looking,' he sounded choked. 'They are,' he paused, unable to find the words, tears in his eyes.

'They are,' I agreed, telling them to take the weight off their feet. Shay had taken their cases into our room. 'I'll make the tea or would you prefer coffee?'

'Tea would be grand,' Albie smiled. Niamh perched on the edge of the settee nervously as I went to make the drinks.

'Okay beautiful?' Shay asked coming into the kitchen.

'Yes, do you want tea?'

'Please,' he leant against the sink. 'How do they like the twins?'

'Cooing over them as we speak, Niamh seems a little nervous.'

'It's a big thing, coming over here,' he picked up their mugs, leading the way.

'Oh Shay they are adorable,' she smiled. 'They have your eyes and colouring and of course your hair.'

'I was pleased they had his hair,' I sat on the chair glancing at the clock, it was just after three.'

'I bet is was so special seeing them born,' Albie said pensively.

'He nearly passed out,' I teased. 'He had to have some of my gas and air.'

'I did not,' he leapt to defend himself.

'Yeah, you did. I swear to God you were green at one point,' I laughed.

'I can't help being a little tickled stomached,' he smiled.

'Bless,' I looked at him lovingly.

'I still can't get over their hair,' Niamh shook her head.

'It's proper Cassidy hair,' Albie said proudly. 'They'll be growing a beard by the time they are twelve.'

'And that will just be Molly,' Shay joshed. 'I've put your cases in our room.'

'We can't take your bed,' Niamh said quickly.

'It's no bother,' I smiled.

'But where will you sleep?' she fretted.

'I've got Bev's double airbed, we've put it in the nursery.'

'You can't sleep on an airbed, you gave birth to twins less than two weeks ago,' she cried.

'Tash will be fine,' Shay grinned. 'She's made of sturdy stuff.'

'Thanks,' I wasn't sure if it was a compliment or not.

He did his infectious laugh. 'Beautiful.'

Albie and Niamh were also laughing, then she asked. 'How's your mam?' To Shay.

'She's really good thanks,' he replied. 'They got back from their honeymoon yesterday, they had a great time.'

'I do love a nice wedding,' her eyes went to the framed photograph on the wall. I called it my journey wall, it was filled with pictures of family members, friends, all spanning the years. Albie and Niamh were also on there.

The picture of Moira and Alan's wedding took pride of place, a group shot of the bride and groom, Shay and me, Lexi and Belle, Dale and Bev, even Jamie and Abbie, I loved it. You would never guess by looking at it that I was actually in labour when it was taken.

'Your mam looked very happy,' she said quietly.

'It was a good day, a bit fraught towards the end because someone was having contractions and not telling anyone,' Shay scolded me lightly.

'It turned out well in the end though,' I bobbed my tongue out.

'Soon it will be you two tying the knot,' Niamh was enjoying her tea and Albie hadn't taken his eyes off the twins.

'Well we need to save up first,' I ignored Shay's look, weddings were expensive.

'It will be soon,' he said firmly, he really didn't want to wait but we had to be practical. I wanted a proper wedding, not a make do.

'Will you do it in church?' Albie looked at us hopefully.

'I don't think so, neither of us are religious,' my tone was apologetic.

'Oh,' he looked a tad disappointed.

'So,' Niamh cut in. 'Will we be seeing Lexi and her friend Belle?'

I nodded. 'They'll be here over the weekend, my brother and his partner will pop in too. Dale can't wait to meet you and tell tales on Shay.'

'His partner is Bev isn't it? The lady you work for?' Albie remembered.

'That's right,' I picked up my tea. 'I am going to apologise in advance for my brother.'

'Dale's great, I'm going to ask him to be my best man.'

'I was going to have him give me away,' I moaned. 'He can't do both.'

'He's my best mate,' Shay argued.

'And he's my brother,' I retorted, I'm sure that top-trumped him.

'We'll discuss it another time,' he smiled tenderly at me.

'Fine,' I turned my attention back to Albie and Niamh. 'Anyway we have a few things planned.

'We don't want to put you to any bother,' Albie said swiftly.

'It's no trouble,' Shay smiled as Molly began to stir.

'Would you like to hold her?' I asked Albie.

'I would love to,' his voice was thick with emotion.

I picked her up, she was such a perfect little thing and placed her in his arms. 'Molly this is your grandad,' I said softly.

He held her gently, staring down at her. 'She is beautiful, just like her mom,' he glanced at me with a smile. Little Albie, as if sensing his sister was awake, roused also. 'Niamh, do you want him?' Shay asked.

'Can I?' she sat back on the settee, holding out her arms.

When they were settled and we had taken some pictures I drank my tea enjoying the cosy domestic scene. 'Oh will you look at the pair of them?' Niamh said adoringly. 'It does bring back happy memories.'

'So we thought a family dinner tonight to settle you in and then tomorrow we'll go somewhere,' Shay chatted. 'Well in walking distance anyway, they say the weather will be fine.'

'Like we said we don't want to put you out, you have enough on your plate,' Albie said to his son.

'Its fine,' I smiled. 'We're glad you're both here.'

'Thank you,' he looked at Niamh, taking a deep breath. 'Do you think your mam will meet me?'

I looked to Shay. 'Moira wants to see you too,' I answered.

'She does?' he looked surprised.

Niamh looked at her husband a little unsure. 'Why?' she asked.

We both hesitated, not sure how to word it then Shay spoke. 'Probably the same reason as you do.'

'I expect,' he looked thoughtful. 'So we will meet then?'

Shay nodded. 'I don't know why either of you want to though.'

'Why shouldn't we meet?' Albie frowned slightly. 'We have you in common.' I chanced a look at Shay as he continued. 'Niamh's okay with it too.'

'I just don't want any upset,' he admitted.

'Son, Moira and I were acquainted all those years ago, before you were born. We enjoyed each other's company, why wouldn't we want to catch up?'

'Fine,' he did seem unwilling for the two of them to mix.

'Good,' he looked satisfied but only I saw the uneasiness in Niamh's eyes.

We ate at six, then Niamh helped me bathe the twins as Shay chatted to his dad, drinking single malt whisky. I didn't mind, I couldn't imagine what it was like to have a dad that didn't know I existed. I'd just had a dad who pretended I didn't exist. They were both trying so hard to fill in the blanks, to build that father, son relationship. He could have all the time in the world as far as I was concerned, as long as he was happy.

We came from upstairs, the baby monitor in my hand. 'Are they asleep?' Shay asked.

'Yes,' I smiled, flopping down on the chair. I truly didn't have the energy now as I had when Jamie and Lexi were born.

'Can I get you a whisky or a glass of wine Niamh?' Shay asked.

'Whisky would be just grand,' she replied.

'And I'll have a cup of tea,' I butted in.

'You'll look like a cup of fecking tea,' he grumbled.

'One of us has to stay sober,' I retorted hotly.

He made my tea and brought Niamh her whisky as we sat and talked, I mean really talked. We spoke of our lives, our dreams. I told them about my marriage to Sam, about Lexi and Jamie.

Shay told them a little of his life in Ireland before he moved to England. How he met and fell in love with me. The whisky was mellowing them as I did the late feed on my own. I was knackered and ready for bed but they showed no sign of making a move. 'Listen, I'm going to bed, I'm shattered,' I announced when I went back to the living room.

Albie looked immediately guilty. 'Sorry dahling, we're keeping you up.'

'Don't worry. I just want to catch up on a little sleep before the night feed. You stay where you are,' I kissed Shay. 'See you in the morning.'

'Night,' they chorused as I went upstairs, making myself comfortable on the air bed, within seconds I was fast asleep.

They all slept late the next day, Shay hadn't even stirred when the twins had woken for their night feed. He was the first of the three to stir though, coming into the kitchen and kissing his babies.

'Hey beautiful,' he said. 'How ya doing?'

'Better than you by the look of it,' I teased. 'Did you enjoy your whisky last night?'

'Jaysus, they can put it away,' he groaned rubbing his face. 'I thought your Dale could drink. Sorry sweet, I've left everything to you.'

'That's okay, as long as you're happy,' and I meant it, this was important to him.

'I am,' he put his arms around me, giving me my morning kiss.

'Have you brushed your teeth?' I pulled a face.

He looked sheepish. 'Not yet.'

'Then please do,' I pinched his bum as Albie and Moira joined us.

'Morning,' they too looked a little hungover.

'Morning,' I smiled. 'Did you sleep okay?'

'We did,' Niamh came to stand by me. 'Shall I make coffee?'

'If you don't mind,' I replied. 'Does everyone fancy a full English?'

'Sounds good,' Shay began to help, or rather I made him lay the table, open the baked beans, nothing that involved cooking. I waved away Niamh's offer of help.

I was a little over protective of my kitchen, it was my domain. The two things I was really good at was hairdressing and cooking. We ate hungrily before wrapping the twins up warmly and going out into the September sunshine. We walked for miles showing them around. As Shay rightly pointed out it was nowhere near as pretty as Quin but it was home.

Shay's text alert went off as we returned home, it was Moira saying that they would be at ours at four. He pulled me to one side to tell me.

'Shit,' I panicked. 'Should we put them off?'

'No,' he shook his head. 'Let's get this over with.'

'Okay,' I picked up my own phone texting Bev. We had made up a code name as a joke so she knew that I needed her and

Dale to buffer a potentially awkward situation, so I texted her *"Operation Paddy"*.

She answered straight away. 'Will be there ASAP.'

I breathed a sigh of relief, Bev and Dale would bring a bit of light relief to the proceedings if it all got a little heavy. I started to prepare the food, I would do a pasta bake with garlic flatbread and salad. Bev was bringing a pot of her special chilli.

'What are you doing?' Shay had left his dad and Niamh looking after the twins in the other room.

'I'm cooking, we can all sit around the table and eating and being civil.'

'We'll get a takeaway,' he insisted. 'Come and sit down, you haven't stopped since they got here.'

'I can't, my stomach's rolling,' I pulled a face. 'I'm dreading this.'

'It'll be fine,' he tried to sound positive but I think he was a little concerned also.

We were all in the living room when the doorbell rang, I jumped up rushing to answer it. 'Hello sweetheart,' Moira hugged me. 'You look knackered.'

'I feel it,' I admitted. 'How are you?'

'I'm grand, why shouldn't I be?' she had made an effort, looking elegant in a mint green dress. I could totally relate to that. Who wanted to meet their ex looking like a bag of rags. She waited as Alan followed her and I shut the door.

On impulse I hugged him. 'Are you okay?' I whispered.

'I am,' he gave me a smile. This had to be hard for him. I had hated Ava turning up and she had only been Shay's shag buddy, this was so much more than that.

Going into the living room I said in an overly bright voice. 'Your mom's here Shay.'

Albie jumped up looking nervous as they came into the room. 'Albie and Niamh, this is Moira and Alan,' I did the introductions and then immediately realised what an idiot I was.

'And I'm Shay,' my other half said amused.

I grimaced, glaring at him.

'Moira,' Albie said gently. 'It is good to see you again.'

She took his hands. 'You too. You're looking really well.'

'So are you,' they held each other's gaze and I could see a little chemistry between them even after all these years.

Moira recovered first. 'This is my husband Alan,' she said proudly.

'Pleased to meet you both,' he shook their hands.

'Same,' Niamh was looking at Moira with naked curiosity.

'Tash is cooking for us,' Shay was nervous now they were all together. They settled down and he fetched a couple of kitchen chairs for him and me to sit on.

'Oh love, don't trouble yourself,' Moira adjusted her dress.

'It's no problem,' I flushed. 'Dale and Bev are popping over later.'

She gave me a knowing look, then turned her attention to the sleeping babies. 'Ah will you look at those two.'

'They are due a feed soon,' I said. 'They'll be screaming the house down.'

'Just like their da used to,' her tone was reflective.

'I still do if Tash doesn't feed me on time,' he joked and then an awkward silence descended on the room.

'So,' Alan drew out the word. 'Did you have a good journey over from Ireland?'

'Yes, good thanks,' Albie answered. 'Not too bad at all.'

Again silence filled the room and I looked at Shay uneasily. 'And the wedding went well?' It was Niamh's turn to try.

'It was a lovely day,' Moira replied. 'We had the best wedding present in the world.' Her eyes went back to the sleeping twins who were dressed in their *50% IRISH, 100% GORGEOUS* outfits.

'I bet,' she agreed.

'Your wan here,' she pointed to me. 'Having contractions all day and not saying a word to anyone. I thought Shay was going to pass out.'

'I was not that bad,' he was a tad fed up of everyone thinking he was a wimp.

'Like a headless chicken by all accounts,' she teased.

'Yep, he was,' I confirmed. 'Him and Troy running around trying to find me a wheelchair at the hospital so I had to go in by myself. I'd nearly had them by the time he found me.'

'Hey,' he pushed me playfully.

I laughed, then realised I hadn't offered them anything to drink. 'Tea or coffee anyone?' I jumped up.

They all requested tea so I hurried to the kitchen, Shay on my heels. 'Get back in there,' I ordered.

'I'm helping you,' he protested.

'Don't leave them by themselves, the atmosphere is so strained,' I kept my voice low.

'I don't know what to say, what to talk about.' He admitted.

'Talk about anything,' I dug out my old teapot with matching milk jug and sugar bowl.

'Like what?' he frowned.

'You'll think of something,' I pushed him towards the living room.

When the tea as made and I carried it to them I could feel that the atmosphere was still heavy. 'Shall I be mother?' Moira took over, pouring us all a cup. 'Got your best china out sweetheart?' she twinkled her eyes at me.

'Yeah, well,' I shrugged.

We must have sat without saying a word for what seemed like an age when the doorbell rang. 'Thank God,' I exclaimed. 'I mean I'll get it.'

I practically ran to the front door. 'Hello, come in.' I was so relieved to see Dale and Bev.

'I've left Kim and Carling to it,' Bev kissed my cheek. 'How's it going?'

I grimaced. 'Like we've all taken a vow of silence.'

'We'll see about that,' Dale grinned barging on ahead. He went into the living room, took one look at Albie and declared. 'Fucking hell you are the absolute spit of each other.'

'Dale,' I cried horrified. 'Don't swear.'

'No one's taking any notice,' he grinned sitting in my chair.

'Albie, Niamh, this is my brother Dale and his better half Bev,' I told them.

'Hello,' they said cautiously.

'Mr C, Mrs C,' he nodded his head before turning to Moira and Alan. 'And you're Mr C and Mrs C too. This could get confusing.'

'Not if you call them by their first names babe,' Bev stated drlly.

He laughed peering over at his niece and nephew. 'And the Rugrats Flynn.'

'Don't wake them,' I threatened, feeling a little better now they were here.

'I wouldn't dare,' he lay his arm over the back of the other chair. 'What are you drinking tea for? This is a celebration.'

'Is it?' I raised an eyebrow, it didn't feel like one.

'Yes,' his smile was full on. 'Love, crack open the champagne.'

'Did you bring any?' Bev asked sweetly.

'No,' his face fell.

'Can't crack it then can I?' she retorted.

'Shall we go to the offie?' he suggested to Shay.

'Bev and me will go,' I jumped up quickly. 'We won't be long.'

'Good idea Tash,' she agreed and we hurriedly got our coats and went to her car.

'Phew,' I breathed a sigh of relief, doing up my seatbelt. 'Am I glad to be out of there for five minutes.'

'That bad,' she pulled away from the kerb.

'No one's speaking,' I had so wanted it to be okay.

'It will be, it's got to be strange. Doesn't Albie look so much like Shay?'

'Told you he did,' we went to the off licence by All Tressed Up, Bev insisting on paying.

'Are you having a drink Tash?' she asked as she put an assortment on the counter, wine, whisky and beer.

I shook my head. 'I need a clear mind with the babies.'

'One won't hurt, 'she cocked her head to one side.

'Truthfully if I have one, I'll want more. I've got some flavoured water in the fridge, I'll drink that.'

'But you haven't had a drink in months,' she protested.

'Honestly I'm okay,' I always worried that if I did have a drink when I was with people I wanted to impress that I would come out with something stupid.

'You've got more willpower than me gal,' she pulled a face.

'Everyone's got more willpower than you,' I teased as we got our purchases and went back to mine.

'Listen,' Bev said as we stood in the hallway.

I did and all I could hear was Dale holding court. 'Bless him,' I smiled. 'See it does help that he's a gobby little shit at times.'

'At times,' she retorted drily, taking the alcohol into the kitchen before popping her head around the door and taking the drink orders.

'Have they killed each other yet?' I fretted a little.

'They seem to be okay, it's hard to tell with Dale not letting anyone get a word in edgeways,' she ginned. 'Oh Tash, I do love him.'

'Someone has too,' I ribbed as we sorted out the drinks.

'Tash,' Moira said when we took the drinks to them. 'I changed Molly, she was a little stinker.'

'Thank you,' I smiled as Dale got up from his chair as did Shay so Bev and I could sit down.

'I was just telling Albie and Niamh how I wasn't happy when you and Shay first started seeing each other,' Dale perched himself on the arm of Moira's chair.

'No, you weren't,' I agreed as Shay gave me his gorgeous smile, sitting on the floor by my feet.

'But if anyone is going to poke you then I for one, am glad it's the Shayster,' he declared.

'Dale!' He could be so bloody embarrassing at times and he hadn't even touched his drink yet.

'What?' he gave me his most boyish smile. 'Listen Tash you ay no Virgin Mary. They know you've had sex, you've got four kids.'

'Pack in,' Bev warned.

He ignored her. 'Do you want to know how I see it?' he continued, holding onto his bottle of lager.

'How do you see it?' Shay asked amused.

'It's all to do with how we feel we should be acting, not how we want too.'

'What?' Bev screwed up her face.

'Okay, I'll explain,' he slipped his arm around Moira's shoulders.

'Please do,' his better half folded her arms.

'Moira and Albie used to get jiggy with each other years ago.'

'Dale!' I was absolutely mortified, what was he doing?
He held up one hand. 'And that led to the Shayster.'
I could have throttled him, the absolute prat.
'Moira's married to Alan, Albie to Niamh and now we're all
sitting here wondering how we should handle them all being
together,' he was warming to his subject. 'Are the old feelings still
going to be there? Will they ride off into the sunset together?'
'That is enough Dale! I exploded.
'Yes, that is enough,' Bev glared at him.
'What I'm saying is this, you shouldn't be worried,' he
swigged his lager. 'Moira and Albie should be thinking, look at
what we made together. An absolute top bloke, everything a son
should be.'
'My man,' Shay held up his hand in a high five gesture.
'So we ay got to worry about anybody running off with
anyone,' he declared. 'We just have to focus on Shay, a better man
than I'll ever be.'
'Shush,' Moira pushed him playfully and blushing
beautifully. She did so adore my little brother.
'Seriously Mrs C, I'm a shit person, well I used to be. Bev
will tell you.'
'Dale,' Bev was glowering at him as Alan, Albie and Niamh
watched him fascinated and quite frankly all lost for words.
'No, I was,' he paused. 'I was a shit to my sister who only
did her best for me. I played around, never gave a thought for
anyone else. I had this wonderful woman here,' he looked lovingly
at Bev. 'She'd do anything for me and I treated her like dirt.'
'Has he been drinking before he got here?' I whispered to
Bev.
She shook her head wanting to suffocate him.
'What I'm trying to say is this,' he necked his lager.
'Dale stop it,' I raised my voice a little.
'I am trying to make a point,' he looked hurt.
'Enough, no one wants to hear your point,' I could have
cheerfully swung for him.
'It's awkward I know,' his mouth kept moving without a tact
button. 'But you all need to know each other, not worry about any
wife swapping.'
'Dale!' I blasted. 'I am going to send you home in a minute.'

'Leave him alone,' Shay was finding it all highly amusing.

'Thank you, you little Irish superstar,' he grinned at his friend. 'So we all get to know each other and enjoy what we have.'

'He's right,' Niamh found her voice, colour rising in her cheeks.

'He is?' I said surprised.

'I was so worried about coming here,' she admitted. 'You have always been there Moira, like a shadow. I didn't think I would even like you but I do. You seem a really nice woman.'

'Thank you,' she smiled softly. 'I think the same about you too.'

'See,' Dale looked pleased with himself.

'I hate the thought that you all know Shay better than I do,' Albie said and with all of us sitting in a near enough circle we looked like we were at self-help group taking confession. 'He's my son and I know so little about him.'

'Of course you feel like that,' I think Dale was channelling his inner Jeremy Kyle. 'You've missed out on a stack of things but now you have the chance to catch up.'

'Yes, I do,' he agreed.

'Because we all know Shay we can help. Tell you all his dark and dirty secrets.'

'Little angel me,' Shay drank his lager leaning up my leg.

'Yeah, you are, aren't you? You are such a boring bastard,' he laughed.

'I think you've said enough now Dale,' I didn't want him upsetting their Catholic sensibilities with his potty mouth any longer.

'My best mate,' Shay raised his bottle.

'My soon to be brother in law,' he mirrored the action.

'Oh God, I think I'm going to cry,' Bev's tone was loaded with sarcasm.

'Love,' he looked at her solemnly. 'Shay has the chance to know his dad.'

'No shit Sherlock,' she gave me an amused eye roll.

'What Tash and I would have done to have parents who cared. Do you know mom hasn't even bothered to come and see the twins or even get in touch?' he continued.

'That woman is a waste of space!' Moira spat. 'And she calls herself a mother '

'Actually not if she can help it,' my tone was heavy.

'You know both our parents were shit? Even if dad was still alive he would be exactly the same?' He hugged Moira to him. 'When Tash took Shay to tell mom she was pregnant she made a pass at him.'

'Please stop,' I begged, ashamed at my own mother.

'No,' he held up a hand in my direction. 'You are a wonderful woman sis. She should be proud that you are her daughter.'

'She is a cow,' Bev agreed with him.

'You raised me Tash, gave me all the love in the world. So I say this Moira, Alan, Albie and Niamh. Take what's on offer, get to know each other. Love your grandchildren and children. Cherish it all but most of all, enjoy it.'

'Did any of that make sense to you?' I asked Bev quietly.

'None at all,' she confirmed.

'Good, I thought it was me being thick.'

'What are you two whispering about?' Dale demanded.

'I'm trying to work out if I was adopted, anything so I don't have to admit being related to you.' I shook my head.

'You wouldn't want anyone else as your brother,' he said confidently.

'Oh, at this precise moment in time I would.' I said firmly.

'Come on hun, let's sort the food out.' Bev stood and I followed suit, waving away the offers of help from the others.

'They must wonder what they've walked into,' I groaned, warming up the food.

'Alan hasn't said a word, I feel for him. Newly married and then the ex appears on the scene and not just any old ex. The love of his wife's life,' she shuddered.

'Stop it, I feel so responsible,' and I did. Everything that happened now was solely my doing.

'It is,' she ribbed. 'Shay seems happy though.'

He does, doesn't he?' I smiled. 'And that's the main thing.' I heard the twins stirring and Moira calling. 'Don't worry sweetheart, we'll see to them.'

'Thank you,' I called back.

'I wonder if she still fancies him.' Bev kept her voice low. 'I wonder if she looks at him and thinks "I'd still give him one"?'

'Bev!' I blanched, what a thought.

'I'm just curious,' she smirked.

'Well don't bloody ask her,' I warned.

'As if I would consider doing such a thing,' she began to prepare the salad. 'As I said, just curious.'

'I don't even want to think about it,' I fetched the dishes from the cupboard.

'He's a good looking man, at least you know that Shay is going to age well.'

'I guess,' I replied, hoping we were still together when he was Albie's age.

The food was ready fifteen minutes later and everyone piled into the kitchen. 'I have to say Moira your dress is beautiful,' Niamh complimented her.

'Thank you,' she accepted gracefully. 'I had it from Birmingham when I met Lexi and Belle for lunch, there is absolutely nothing in town.

'I'm the same, Albie and I have to go into Dublin for anything decent.'

'I'll take you to Birmingham on Monday if you want, we could meet up with Lexi and Belle,' Moira held out the hand of friendship.

Niamh smiled, accepting it. 'That would be lovely, it will give Albie and Shay some alone time.'

'Sorted then,' she looked pleased.

'Well if you're going to do that than tomorrow night what say me and Shay take Albie and Alan to the pub, we could have a game of pool?' Dale suggested.

'Don't forget we're all out for lunch tomorrow,' I reminded hm.

'We can do both,' he gave me his cheeky grin.

'Sounds good,' Alan agreed. 'Although I'm not getting as drunk as I did last time I went out with the pair of you.'

'Drunk wasn't the word,' Moira tutted.

'You were merry,' Shay joined in. 'We were all a little merry, good night though.'

'It was,' Alan agreed.

'I'm looking forward to it,' Albie piled rice and chilli into his bowl. 'I'd like to see my son play pool.'

'He's a shark,' Dale grinned. 'Don't let him hustle you.'

Albie smiled fondly at his son and my heart swelled, everything was turning out just fine.

Forty~Nine

We arrived at Berry Brook Farm around one, Lexi coming in our car, sitting between the twins in their car seats. Belle, Jamie and Abbie hitched a lift with Bev and Dale. As arranged the day before Albie and Niamh travelled with Moira and Alan.

'Do you think they're alright just the four of them?' I fretted.

'They seem fine,' Lexi waited patiently for me to get Albie out of his seat so she could scuttle over and get out. 'Next thing you know they'll be going on holiday together.'

'It's nice,' Shay looked relieved as he got Molly. 'Will you grab the changing bag please Lexi when I've got the twins in the pram?'

'Sure, will uncle Shay,' she beamed at him.

He gave her an amused look as he passed Molly to her and then sorted out the pram. 'Thank you dahling.'

We waited for the others to join us, Moira and Niamh chatting ten to the dozen, not really taking notice of anyone else.

'Look at them,' he whispered. 'They look like they've been friends for years.'

I nodded, watching as Albie and Alan brought up the rear. It had worked out so well, better than I could have ever hoped for.

'Can I push?' Lexi took the pram from Shay.

'Course,' he put the change bag over his shoulder. She and Belle walked ahead as I kept pace with my son and his girlfriend.

'I'm so glad you came Jams.' I told him.

'No problem,' he answered quietly.

'Seriously, it means a lot to us,' I smiled at Abbie. 'I'm glad you're here too.'

'Thank you for asking me,' she said politely.

'The more the merrier,' Shay hung the bag over my shoulder then walked to his mom and dad, leading the way inside.

'Don't worry, I'll carry the bag,' I called after him, pulling a face.

Bev laughed, linking arms with me as Dale went ahead with Jamie and Abbie. 'Happy babe?' She asked.

'I am,' I confirmed.

'Well you look absolutely knackered,' her smile was sweet.

'It hasn't been easy having the twins and then two weeks later having house guests,' I admitted.

'You should have let them stay in a hotel,' Bev leant into me.

'It's important to Shay,' I replied. 'I don't mind, anyway I'm used to just getting on with things. Anyway, at the moment all is well with Tash's world.'

'It's about time too.' We walked into the pub, the friendly young girl showing us the long table with the reserved sign on it.

'Oh, I wish we could all sit next to each other,' Moira sighed. 'Whoever sits on the ends will seem miles away.'

'Bev and I will take one end,' Dale offered.

'And me and Belle the other,' Lexi steered the pram to the end of the table.

'I need to sit there, the pram won't fit anywhere else and I have to see to my babies,' I put my coat on the back of the chair.

'Come and sit by us,' Dale looked at his niece fondly. 'Let your mom sit by the rugrats and I'll sit with the rug munchers.'

'What's a rug muncher?' Niamh asked puzzled.

'Dale!' I chided, hoping he wasn't going to start again like last night.

'It's just a nickname Niamh,' he said soberly.

'Oh,' she still looked a little confused.

'I thought rug muncher was a les...' Moira began.

'Mam,' Shay cut in quickly. 'Where would you like to sit?'

'Put me next to Niamh and Alan and Albie can sit opposite. Albie next to Shay, Niamh next to Tash,' she organised us.

We sat nicely, the same young waitress taking our drinks orders that had showed us to the table. 'Oh, they are so beautiful,' she cooed over the twins. 'Look at their hair. How old are they?'

'Just over two weeks,' I replied proudly.

'They are gorgeous,' she sighed, going to fetch our drinks.

'Just like their mammy,' Shay smiled at me.

'Like their dad,' I returned the smile.

'Shaggable Shay,' Lexi fussed over Albie and Molly.

Niamh looked at us alarmed and I sighed 'Lexi,' I scolded. 'Don't.'

She zipped her mouth, going to sit by Dale. 'What did she just call me?' Shay questioned.

I blushed. 'It's what she used to call you when you first hung round with our Dale. She doesn't mean it in a sexual way though.'

'Of course not, she's a lesbian.'

'She used to say it to wind Dale up,' I explained. 'Dull Dale and Shaggable Shay.'

He laughed quietly, passing me the menu. I took it reading the tempting food on offer. Our cheery waitress brought the drinks and we sat around chatting and trying to decide what to eat. I glanced up, noticing Jamie and Dale taking an interest in something by the bar.

Shay caught me staring. 'What's up?'

'Not sure,' I replied, my eyes going to where they were looking, causing my stomach to flip.

Jamie had come to us, a stricken look on his face. 'Mom,' he was worried he'd get the blame and Shay would take the car from him.

'Did you know he was coming?' I asked.

'No, what the hell is he doing here?'

'I don't know,' my smile was false as I looked at my ex standing by the bar, pint in front of him and a cocky expression on his face.

Shay's face changed, his features growing hard, he went to stand but I put a restraining hand on his arm. 'Leave it,' I tried to sound unconcerned but I was worried.

'He is not spoiling our lunch,' his voice was livid.

'Please don't,' I didn't want a scene in front of everyone.

He set his mouth in a firm line, folding his arm. The others were looking at us wondering what was going on.

I bit my tongue, my own temper rising. No, it was no good, *I* wasn't going to put up with it either. I got up from my seat.

'You are not going over to him,' Shay forbade me.

I ignored him, striding over to Sam. He had a smug grin on his face and I could have punched him. 'What are you doing here?' I cut straight to the chase.

He motioned to his drink. 'I'm just having a quiet pint.'

'No, you're not,' I contradicted him. 'So, stop trying to cause trouble.'

'Me?' His face had taken on an innocence look. 'I'm not doing anything.'

'Just go Sam,' I was angry. 'This isn't your local. I meant what I said, I *will* tell Meera if you don't stop being a prat.'

He shrugged infuriatingly. 'Tell her, I don't care. It's only you I care about.'

'Not this again,' I could feel my face burning. 'Just go please.'

'Dad,' Lexi was beside me. 'Just sod off, you're and embarrassment.'

He looked her up and down. 'Oh, so you do remember I'm your dad, now you've got your new family.'

'Leave mom and Shay alone,' she stood in front of him.

'It looks well when you think more of your mom's fancy man than you do your own father.'

'Shay and mom are happy, so grow up!' Lexi turned on her heel, striding back to the others.

'Do you want to lose your daughter?' I demanded.

'She'll come running back to me when it all goes sour with your toyboy.'

'It's not going to go sour,' I retorted. 'We're getting married!' Oh shit, did that just come out of my mouth? I didn't really want him to know but he had annoyed me.

He looked shocked. 'Married?' he repeated.

'Yes, married,' I crossed my arms defensively.

'You're a bloody idiot,' his features grew rigid. 'Marriage doesn't mean anything.'

'Don't I fucking know it being married to you!' I retorted. 'That's your mantra, not his.'

'Paddy boy won't be any different. First whiff of skirt and he'll be off and you'll be stuck with those brats you've given birth too.'

I clenched my fists, I couldn't cause a scene, not here.

'You are a fucking fool Tash. I warn you this though. You will never be free of me, ever, I will be a thorn in your side for as long as you live.'

Shay was watching from his seat, he couldn't just sit there and do a thing. He didn't want Sam thinking he was leaving me to it, that he had no balls.

'Son?' Albie leant towards him as Jamie looked on mortified. 'Who is that Tash is talking to?'

'Something I have to deal with,' he got up, coming to us and catching the last bit of what Sam was saying to me, unfortunately.

'A thorn in her side?' He snarled. 'I'll show you a thorn in your fucking side.'

'Hey, Paddy,' Sam took a mouthful of beer. 'You're always about, aren't you?'

Shay squared up to him. 'Fuck off or I'll do you for harassment.'

'Whoa, I'm scared. The big bad Irish boy is threatening me with a court order.'

'Shay,' I held his arm feeling a little sick.

The muscles twitched in his face. 'Well let me put it like this you arrogant little prick, if you do not leave Tash alone then I will finish what we started that night at the pub and this time no one will stop me.'

I stood in front of Shay, facing him. 'Leave it please,' I begged.

His eyes went to mine. 'If he wants to play then we'll play.'

'Please hun,' I said softly. 'He really isn't worth it.'

Shay stared at me, his brown eyes even darker with his anger, then he turned his attention back to Sam. 'You've lost everything here, you sad bastard. Admit defeat and fuck off out of our lives once and for all.'

He looked unsure for a moment, something in Shay's demeanour said that he really meant it.

'Let's go back to the table,' I urged Shay. 'Please.'

'Run along now Paddy,' he couldn't resist one last dig.

'Fuck off Sam!' I snapped.

'Do as Tash says or I'll take you outside,' Shay's tone was deadly.

He hesitated for a moment, then stalked out of the bar, I sighed, this we did not need. Silently we made our way back to the others. 'You okay son?' Albie looked at us concerned.

'How the fuck did he know we were here?' Shay exploded. 'The absolute fucking prick!'

'Hey!' Moira wagged her finger at him. 'Remember what company you're in.'

I filled up, I had wanted it to be a nice day. 'He knew from me,' Jamie looked worried. 'I just said I was coming here to have lunch with you all.'

'It's okay love,' I said softly. 'It's not your fault.'

Shay let out a breath. 'No, it's not your fault Jamie,' he agreed. 'Don't worry,' he turned to me, seeing the tears in my eyes, reaching for my hand and holding tightly. 'It's okay dahling, really.'

I nodded, hating Sam with all my heart. 'Come on,' he jollied me up. 'He won't bother us again,' he sounded confident as little Albie began to stir and I picked him up.

'I hope not,' I brought Albie to my face, breathing in his baby scent. What a gorgeous smell.

'Hey,' Shay caught my face with his hand. 'He *will* leave is alone, okay?'

I nodded, I needed to believe this man by my side, the man I loved. He kissed me gently, oblivious to everyone and I loved him for it.

'Get a room,' Lexi heckled. 'Pair of you should know better, look where it got you the last time.'

Belle giggled and I gave my daughter an indulgent look. 'Behave yourself,' I scolded. 'You're turning into your uncle Dale.'

'Mother,' she looked horrified. 'That is possibly the most hurtful thing you have ever said to me.'

'Hey,' Dale cried. 'That's not nice rug muncher.'

'I still don't know what that means,' Niamh frowned.

'I'll tell you when you're old enough,' Dale teased, he stood leaving us, he had a hunch.

He was right, Sam was still in the car park, puffing furiously on a cigarette. 'Sammy boy,' he called. 'Still here?'

Sam turned reluctantly. 'I'm waiting for my taxi.'

'Sam,' Dale said patiently. 'We've had this conversation before and I am getting a little pissed off that I'm having to repeat myself.'

'What conversation?' He chose to act dumb.

Dale sighed, drawing level with his ex-brother-in-law. 'Leave them alone or Shay will beat the shit out of you and I won't try to stop him this time.'

'Can you honestly say he's the best thing for your sister?' He threw his cigarette on the floor, immediately lighting another.

'Yes, I can. He's the best thing that's ever happened to her, apart from having the kids,' Dale put his hands in his pockets.

'Not you too?' He spat. 'What is it with Paddy that everyone thinks the sun shines out of his arse?'

'He's a good bloke,' Dale tried to keep his voice even. 'Do you really want Meera knowing what you are up to?'

'She wouldn't want to upset Meera and Safi, she's too nice.' Sam's tone was confident.

'Tash wouldn't, she really is too good. Me though, I'm not so nice. Where Tash would indeed worry about Meera and Safi I wouldn't,' he answered softly. 'You forget there is still a bit of a bastard in me, I can't help it. I would tell Meera and not really give it a second thought. Twenty odd years we've known each other Sam, a long time and have I ever been any different?'

Sam looked at him unsurely.

'To be blunt mate my concern is purely for my sister. If she's unhappy then so am I.'

'She's going to marry him,' Sam had banked on Dale being an ally.

'Yep and I am so pleased for them. She deserves this after all the shit you've put her through. She's finally found someone who will give her what she needs.'

'Him!' Sam just couldn't see it.

'Yes him,' he ay gonna hurt her or play the games you did,' he paused. 'You took a vulnerable girl, whose parents couldn't give a fuck about her and you screwed her over. This is nothing to do with you loving her, this is to do with controlling her.'

'That's the longest speech I've ever heard you make Dale,' he laughed bitterly. 'Seriously, you'll be running for prime minister soon.'

Dale shrugged modestly.

'She's turning my daughter against me,' he pouted.

'No,' Dale interrupted. 'You've managed that all by yourself. I'm serious Sam, if she tells me you've been bothering her again then I will be having a word with Meera.'

'I thought we were mates?' Sam looked hurt.

'Mates?' Dale frowned. 'Not since I grew up and realised what you had done to her. As I've said to you before, don't play a player. Now I'm going back to my family.' He left Sam standing in the middle of the car park.

'Dale?' I questioned on seeing him.

'Just had a whizz,' he grinned sitting by Bev.

I knew he hadn't gone to the gents but I hadn't the heart to question him more. He shot me a charming smile. 'I'm starving, shall we order?'

I tried to put Sam out of my mind but he kept sneaking back in and I worried it, like a dog with a bone.

Shay wouldn't put up with his nonsense and I couldn't blame him. This was such a happy time for us. Even Moira and Albie were getting on better than we could have ever hoped for.

We ordered the food and I tried to have a good time. Why did Sam think he had a right to do what he did? I had never encouraged him in any way, shape or form, he was just an idiot.

I could sense Shay watching me and I struggled to act normal.

He brought his chair next to mine saying in his soft Irish accent. 'Do you want to go to him?'

'What?' I stuttered. 'No, of course not.'

He put his hand on my back. 'Don't let him spoil this dahling,' he whispered. 'You and me, the A-team, I love you. I can't let him get away with what he's doing though. Even if we weren't together you deserve so much more,'

'Why can't he leave us alone?' I asked miserably.

'Because I have what he wants but you are much too smart to fall for his shite now,' he cast a glance around the others.

I held his hand, pushing away a stray curl. 'I love you,' I said quietly, blinking away the tears, I was still bloody hormonal.

'Of course you do,' his eyes twinkled.

'You were very macho,' I teased.

'What did he call me? A big bad Irish boy, too right,' he puffed out his chest making me laugh. 'That's better, I hate to see you so low.'

'Are you two okay?' Albie came to us as we waited for our meals.'

'Yes,' Shay replied. 'He's just trying to cause trouble.'

'Lexi and Jamie are so embarrassed, poor kids. Jamie thinks it's his fault.'

I looked down the far end of the table. 'Jamie,' I called.

He got up reluctantly. 'What?' There was still a little of the sulky teenager in him, bless.

'Have you told Albie and Niamh about the car you and Shay are doing up?' I asked.

He shook his head.

'It's going to be a beast, just don't tell his mom.' Shay's hand flew to his mouth. 'Oh, didn't see you there,' he said to me making us all laugh.

'Idiot,' Jamie said and I'm sure I could detect a hint of fondness in his tone, I hoped so.

'He's taking me shopping when he passes his test,' Moira leant towards us. 'And I'm taking him to the bingo so he can meet my girls, I want to show off my handsome boy.'

He went bright red, mumbling something under his breath. Moira had really taken to him.

'What do you think about that Abbie?' Shay called. 'My mom is trying to muscle in on your boyfriend.'

She came over to us, a huge smile on her face, she was such a stunning girl. 'He loves all the fuss,' she stated.

'And you Abbie?' Albie asked. 'What do you want to do for a living?'

'A vet, I'm at Sixth Form College now. It's going to be hard work but I love animals and it will be interesting.'

'Yeah, you'd have to love animals to be attracted to our Jams,' Dale cut in taking the drink orders.

'I wanted to be a vet,' Niamh confided. 'But it wasn't really encouraged in my house for you to make anything of yourself.'

'You're allergic to cats,' Albie pointed out.

'There was that as well,' she smiled bashfully.

'I always wanted to be gigolo,' Dale joked.

'Which you succeeded in only you forgot to charge them any money,' Bev joined in.

'Never been the sharpest knife in the drawer have you bruv?' I pulled his leg.

'Hey!' He cried. 'Anyway, all this,' he pointed to his crotch looking at Bev. 'Is solely for your pleasure now and no one else.'

'I think I'm going to cry with the romance of it all,' Alan too liked my brother, everyone did, in fact he was like a magnet to people and finally he was using his gift for good not evil. (Although I had seen him check out every girl in the pub when he came in but now he was only window shopping, not buying)

'What do you do Alan?' Albie enquired.

'I'm a manager at Haughton Manufacturing. Started on the factory floor and worked my way up. I'm currently counting down the weeks until I can retire.'

'I took early retirement,' Albie said. 'Early mornings and cold weather are not so much fun when you get older.'

'Postman, weren't you?' It was nice to see them chatting. 'I envy you all that fresh air and not having anyone looking over your shoulder.'

'It was a pretty place to be a postman in, he conceded.

'Quin always was picturesque, has it changed much?' Moira asked.

'Not at all,' Niamh replied. 'We've just all got older.'

'And my aunt?' She asked timidly.

'Still a cantankerous old dame,' Albie confirmed. 'Still doesn't talk to me.'

'She was horrible when she was young,' Moira pulled a face. 'Is that big ugly statue of the Virgin Mary still by the church?'

'Tash and Lexi enjoyed talking to it when they visited,' Niamh teased.

I blushed. 'I just needed a little divine intervention,' I defended myself.

'Well it worked,' Albie smiled at me fondly as the waitress brought out our food.

It turned out to be a good day, Shay and I managing to push Sam firmly to the back of our minds. I got to know Abbie a little better too, she was really lovely, perfect for Jamie.

Dale told me that Jamie was pleased we'd asked her along, he thought it was quite serious between them which was a little bit of a worry.

I wanted Jamie to be settled but he was only seventeen, he had to live a little also. As Dale pointed out though we was no different to us at that age. We had both craved love and attention because of our parent's divorce and he was only doing the same.

All in all, it was a success, after lunch the ladies had gone back to mine and the men had gone for a game of pool, returning a few hours later nicely merry and all bonded, thank you very much.

Afterwards as Shay and I tried to get comfortable on the airbed in the nursery I felt a glow of contentment coupled with complete exhaustion.

'It's been a good day,' Shay moved so I could snuggle into the crook of his arm.

'It has,' I murmured, I couldn't wait to be back in my own bed. 'I shall miss them when they go.'

'Everyone got on so well,' he stifled a yawn. 'Jamie seems so much happier now he's with Abbie.'

'Dale thinks it's quite serious between them. I hope they don't get it in their heads to get engaged or, God forbid, married.'

'Would it be such a bad thing?' He yawned again.

I looked at him. 'Of course it would. Jamie needs to qualify as a mechanic, Abbie as a vet before they even think about living together. What if she gets pregnant? They've only known each other five minutes.'

'Sweet, people could say the same thing about us.'

'We're older,' I disagreed. 'Totally different.'

'They won't do anything stupid, Abbie is a sensible girl. Anyway, how are you?'

'Me?' I stroked his chest lazily.

'Yes. You've run around after us the last few days, I bet you're shattered.'

'I am,' I had to admit.

'Maybe they should have stayed in a hotel,' he fretted. 'It was too much to ask you to do.'

'Everyone's helped,' I kissed his neck.

'Everyone hasn't just given birth to two beautiful babies,' he contradicted. 'I shouldn't have put it on you,'

'As long as I've got you, I can do anything,' I told him.

'You are something else, you know that?' His tone held a smile.

'Is that good or bad?' I wanted to know.

'Good,' he moved so we were facing each other. 'Thank you.'

'For what?' I caressed his face.

'For everything,' he thought for a moment. 'For you, for our babies. For finding my da. I didn't realise how much I needed to meet him until I did.'

'I would do anything for you,' I whispered in case we woke the twins.

'And I you,' he pushed my hair from my face. 'Meeting my da was pretty special. My mam and da getting on was all sorts of special but Albie and Molly.'

'What?' I smiled, the nightlight casting shadows across our faces.

His face grew serious, 'I can't describe it, I look at them and my heart swells. When I think they are ours,' he looked tearful.

'You soppy git,' I teased.

'I get you more now with Lexi and Jamie, how you feel about them. How you would do the best for them and never want to see them hurt.'

'Do you?' It was good to know.

'I would lay down my life for our children and for you too,' he confirmed.

'Thank you,' we kissed long and hard, his hand stealing to my thigh. He stopped abruptly pulling away. 'Not now I know but soon,' he stated, fingers tracing my lips.

'Yes, soon,' I echoed snuggling against him.

Fifty

The twins were now eight weeks old, where had all the time gone, it was flying by. Albie and Niamh's visit had been a runaway success and since they had returned to Ireland we spoke in one form or another almost daily. Shay had reluctantly returned to work and I filled my days by looking after Albie and Molly, soon I would be going back to the salon part time and I was dreading it.

They were gorgeous our babies, with their dark curly hair, a perfect mixture of Shay and me. The older they got the more I could tell that they had my nose and mouth but definitely Shay's eyes and colouring.

I was just staring dreamily at them when Moira arrived just after lunch on the Saturday. She popped in most days and at first I found it quite stifling but as Belle pointed out it was because I wasn't used to the maternal help but how I appreciated it now

I still hadn't heard from my own mother despite Dale and Bev telling her about the twins. I tried not to dwell on it, as everyone kept telling me she really wasn't worth it. Sam had thankfully kept a low profile too.

'Right you two,' Moira ordered, holding one of her tasty stews in her hands. 'Bed.'

'What?' I asked a tad confused.

'Both of you are knackered, go to bed and I'll keep an eye on the twins.'

'I couldn't,' I was still worried about leaving them, as Shay always quite rightly pointed out, I was a control freak.

'Bed, the pair of you!' She shooed us up the stairs.

'Shay,' I turned to him as we reached the landing. 'It's only one o'clock, I can't go to bed in the middle of the day.'

'Well I'm not going to argue, I'm going to say thank you and catch up on some sleep.' He pulled off his clothes, looking fit standing there in just his undies.

I tutted going into the bathroom and changing into my nightclothes. I had lost some of the baby weight but not all of it and I still felt a little self-conscious. 'I'm not going to be able to drop off,' I complained climbing in next to him but I was wrong. Within minutes I was sound asleep as was Shay.

We slept for five solid hours, much needed sleep. When I awoke I felt so much better, Shay was still pounding the z's so I was careful not to disturb him as I threw on my scruffs and went downstairs.

'Fed, changed and asleep,' Moira informed me as I went into the living room. 'Did you manage some sleep?' she asked, putting down her knitting.

'I did thank you, I went out like a light,' I beamed, looking at my babies. 'Shay's still flat out.'

'Good. I have enjoyed looking after them, they've been as good as gold. Now the stew just needs warming through,' she smiled at me. 'How are you sweetheart? We don't seem to have time to sit and chat anymore.'

'I know, it's just so busy at the moment. It'll soon be time to put the Christmas tree up,' it was fast baring down on us.

'Are you content?' she asked softly.

'Very,' I confirmed, my smile widening. 'Everything is just great.'

She touched my cheek. 'Just don't lose sight of each other. I know the babies take up so much of your time but remember why you want to be together.'

'Has Shay said something?' My smile was replaced by a frown.

'Only how happy he is,' she reassured me. 'I'm here so use me. Go out and enjoy yourselves once in a while. I would love to babysit anytime.'

'Thank you,' she was right, we didn't want to take each other for granted.

'Right, I'll go for the bus. Alan has taken Jakob for his first pair of football boots so we're having a late supper,' she explained.

'You won't catch the bus, I'll drive you. I'll just go and wake Shay.'

'I'm catching the bus. You have a couple of hours before they'll need feeding again. Enjoy the peace.'

'Thank you,' I was grateful. 'Text me when you get home please.'

'I will,' she walked to the door. 'Tell Shay I said goodnight and we'll see you tomorrow.' She was cooking us lunch.

'Thanks so much Moira,' we hugged and I watched as she walked down the street and disappeared around the corner.

She was right about us not forgetting that we were a couple as well as parents. Shay had said to me when I was pregnant that he loved me and wanted to be with me, that the twins were a wonderful bonus. Picking up the baby monitor I hurried up the stairs, the twins would be safe in the living room and if they did stir I would hear them on the monitor. The room was warm and they liked the sound of the television on low.

Freshening up I put on my sexy pint Lytham nightie. How long ago did that seem? Look how much had happened, where we are now to where we were then. Spritzing perfume behind my ears and along my neck I stared at myself in the mirror.

Shay had told me that when I was ready to resume our love life to wear this particular nightie to let him know. Well now I was ready. My body had healed and I craved his touch.

Going into the bedroom I heard his stir and he switched on the bedside lamp. 'What time is it?' he asked disorientated.

'Just after six,' I replied. 'Your mom's just gone, she said she'll see you tomorrow.'

He rubbed sleep from his eyes. 'I was dead to the world,' he declared, then he saw what I was wearing and his eyes darkened with longing.

I walked round to my side of the bed and lay down feeling like a born again virgin, I hadn't felt this nervous when Shay and I had first started sleeping together. 'Albie and Molly are fast asleep, they won't need feeding for a couple of hours at least,' my voice was croaky.

He turned on his side facing me, one finger running down my arm. With that serious expression his lips sought mine and I returned them, growing in intensity, my body responding.

Moving he lay above me, his hand caressing the silky material of my nightie, then he paused. 'Are you sure?' he asked apprehensively.

'Yes,' I breathed, reaching to kiss him again.

He smiled, lying between my legs, lips kissing every inch of my neck. He pushed up my nightie but I stopped him and he seemed to understand without me saying that I wasn't quite body confident yet.

His lips returned to mine as he pushed forward gently, filling me. 'Okay?' he looked into my eyes, still concerned that he was going to damage me in some way.

'Yes,' it felt wonderful, it truly did. I had missed him these last few weeks.

'Sure?'

'Yes,' I repeated, moving my hips slowly against him.

He smiled again, pushing forward and then slowly pulling back. Being so gentle with me like I was bone china that would shatter. I raked my fingers down his back. 'Harder,' I whispered in his ear. He had been gentle with me for the last six months, I needed it to be more now.

Looking a little unsure he sped up. I growled with pleasure, scratching his back. He began to lose control, after all we hadn't make love in weeks. Grunting he increased his thrusts, letting out a guttural groan as he came to a shuddering climax.

With a sigh he lay on me. 'Shit Tash, I'm sorry.'

'For what?' I played with his curls.

He looked at me sheepishly. 'I didn't last very long,' he replied ruefully. 'I just wanted you.'

'Its fine,' I kissed him softly. 'It was still good. Glass of wine?'

'You have a glass of wine?' I hadn't touched a drop since finding out I was pregnant.

'I just fancy one,' I shrugged.

'I'm glad, you seem to be chilling more,' his tone was full of approval.

'I think I am,' I confirmed.

'I'll get us both a glass,' he smiled getting out of bed and pulling on his robe. 'I'll check Albie and Molly.'

'Thanks,' I lay on my back relishing our love making.

'They are both still asleep,' he came back with the promised wine. 'Aw they are so cute sweet. How did we make such gorgeous babies?'

'They are adorable,' I agreed taking my glass from him as he climbed back into bed. Cautiously I took a sip. 'That tastes divine,'

I gasped, it was nearly eight months since alcohol had passed my lips.

'Well tonight you have a drink and I'll be the responsible parent,' he stated.

'Are you sure?' my tone was hopeful.

'You, my sexy dahling, can have anything you want,' he began to kiss me again.

'Thank you,' I rolled so I was lying on him.

'Hey beautiful,' he pulled me against him and I could feel him stirring again.

'What's this?' I teased, my hand going inside his robe and holding him.

He grinned. 'It's your fault, you shouldn't be so fecking sexy.'

I giggled, sitting astride him. 'Now try to last a little longer this time please.'

'Hey,' he rebuked, hands on my hips. I began to rock back and forth, slowly at first and then my tempo increasing.

We came together, collapsing against each other. 'Marry me tomorrow,' he whispered, peppering my face with tiny kisses.

'We will soon.' I did kind of cross my fingers though. I did want to marry him, I truly did but financially it just wasn't viable at the moment.

'Good,' he stroked my back. 'I never thought I would love anyone like I love you, never want to be anyone like I want to be with you.'

'Thank you,' I smiled sweetly.

'Did you say that mam had brought a stew?'

I nodded. 'It just needs warming up, are you hungry?'

'Starving,' his smile was cheeky. 'Good sex always makes me ravenous.'

'Good?' I raised an eyebrow. 'It was bloody excellent. Come on then stud, let's have a shower and sort out food.'

Back in the kitchen I heated up the stew as Shay lay the table, he even put out some candles bless him. 'It looks lovely,' I praised as I cut up the crusty bread.

He stood watching me. 'What?' I asked shyly.

'You, this, everything,' he whispered.

'Are you being all soppy?' I teased bringing the bread to the table.

'Do you mind?' his voice was soft. 'Can't I be happy with what I've got?'

'Of course you can,' I put my arms around him. 'I love you.'

'I love you too,' he rocked me gently. 'Shall we have our supper and then chill out in front of the television?'

'Sounds like a plan,' I smiled just as Albie and Molly decided to make their presence known.

'The joys of parenthood,' I told him wisely. 'You grab Albie and I'll take Molly.'

He nodded and together we went to our babies.

The End

37958179R00256

Printed in Poland
by Amazon Fulfillment
Poland Sp. z o.o., Wrocław